The DREAM

Other Books by Gilbert Morris
Charade
Jacob's Way
Edge of Honor
Jordan's Star
God's Handmaiden
The Spider Catcher

The Singing River Series
The Homeplace

GILBERT MORRIS

The DREAM

The Singing River Series

Book II

ZONDERVAN®

GRAND RAPIDS, MICHIGAN 49530 USA

ZONDERVAN.COM/
AUTHORTRACKER

ZONDERVAN®

The Dream
Copyright © 2006 by Gilbert Morris

Requests for information should be addressed to:

Zondervan, *Grand Rapids, Michigan 49530*

ISBN: 978-0-7394-7410-5

Published in association with the literary agency of Alive Communications, Inc., 7680 Goddard Street, Suite 200, Colorado Springs, CO 80920.

All Scripture quotations, unless otherwise indicated, are taken from the King James Version.

Interior design by Michelle Espinoza

Printed in the United States of America

To Dan and Jan Meeks
Thanks for the memories—and the fine years of fellowship
and love you've brought into our lives.

PART ONE

The Worries

The dream came to Lanie Belle Freeman softly, so gently that the scene enveloped her like a warm, soft blanket. She lay still, caught in that zone somewhere between deep sleep and awareness. As always when the dream came, Lanie was vaguely aware that she was in a world that did not exist, yet at the same time the dream was so wonderfully *real* that she always resisted the pull of the world. The world was filled with cold practicality and hard decisions and heartaches. But the dream—ah, the dream! It was warm and lovely and filled with a joy that the real world could never give!

The dream always began the same, never even the slightest variation. Lanie had endured so many painful changes in the past few years that the most comforting thing about the recurring dream was its reliable sameness.

It began with the sound of Lanie's mother singing "The Old Rugged Cross." Elizabeth's voice was clear as a bell, sweet and pure and true. The words seemed to Lanie to flow like the clear waters of Singing River:

> On a hill far away, stood an old rugged cross,
> The emblem of suffering and shame
> And I love that old cross where the dearest and best
> For a world of lost sinners was slain ...

And then in the dream Lanie felt herself held securely by strong arms, and when she looked up the face of her mother would appear. The firm but gentle mouth, the clear gray-green eyes filled with love!

Then the scene would change, and Lanie would be clinging to her father's hand, and Forrest Freeman would scoop her up, smiling and saying, "Well, now, Muff, how about a song, eh? Just you and me?"

Then Lanie would join her father singing the old hymn "Life Is Like a Mountain Railroad." The voices of the two would blend, then Elizabeth would join in, and finally Lanie's brothers and sisters would add their voices to the song.

The dream went on, sometimes for what seemed like hours, sometimes only briefly, but always the joyous sound of the Freeman family would fill Lanie's world.

When the dream lasted a long time, Lanie would run with her father through the woods while the trees blazed with fall colors, and then she would be digging in the loamy garden soil with her mother, putting seed in the warm earth of spring. At times the dream would take Lanie and her family to the Singing River, where Cody and Davis shouted as they pulled thumping sunfish out of the sparkling waters, and Lanie and Maeva splashed in the shallows while their mother smiled on.

But then dark shadows would begin to gather, clouding the dream with somber darkness. Lanie always tried to fight the shadows, but they covered her with relentless power, pulling her out of the wonders of the dream into the world of pain and disappointment ...

"No!" Lanie cried aloud, as the dream ended abruptly and she found herself sitting upright in her feather bed. For one moment she tried desperately to ignore the world of reality, to return to the warmth and color and joy of her dream—but she knew it was useless. Once the dream was over, there was no going back.

With a quick, angry gesture, Lanie rolled out of the bed and stood on the cool pine floor, disoriented. She blinked a couple times and finally got her bearings. "I can't believe I fell asleep!" she muttered. "I still have more pies to make!" Then she shrugged and turned to face the world of Lanie Belle Freeman of Fairhope, Arkansas, July 1931.

Moving to a small mirror, she paused, thinking with anguish of her life as it had once been. The dream was a longing for her mother, now in her grave, and for her father, who was serving a term at Cummings Prison Farm for manslaughter. The loss of her parents was a grief so poignant that whenever Lanie Belle thought of them, a lump formed in her throat and tears burned her eyes.

Lanie forced the dream from her mind, yawned, and raised her arms over her head in a broad stretch. As she threw her head back, she heard a loud ripping sound, felt the seams give way, and immediately knew what had happened.

"Oh, fuzz!" she uttered with disgust. Reaching to her side, she felt the open seam and shook her head. "I'm going to have to make another dress. I'm getting fat as Jezebel." The comparison was not exactly accurate since Jezebel was the Freemans' four-hundred-pound sow. Lanie, at the age of seventeen, had emerged from adolescence into blossoming young womanhood. Her figure had swelled, and as she looked down at herself, she calculated what she could do to make a new dress.

Turning quickly, she walked across the room, opened a red cedar chest, and rummaged through it until she came up with a group of flour sacks carefully washed and folded. They were white with a delicate green flower that perfectly complemented the shade of Lanie's eyes. Quickly she counted the sacks and then nodded with satisfaction. "I've got enough here to make me a dress. I'll start on it after the celebration tomorrow."

For a moment Lanie Freeman held the material against her cheek and imagined how it would be to go into a store and buy material off a roll. She'd had this experience on a few occasions before her mother died. Since then times had been hard, especially with the Depression that had come two years earlier. But she never liked to spend a great deal of time in regret, so she began to think of the McCall's pattern that she had bought at the general store. She had the kind of imagination that could take the picture of a pattern, along with the color and shape and feel of the material, and envision the finished product.

Suddenly the giggle of a girl's voice came floating in from the outside window. At once Lanie straightened up and glanced over at the clock. "Eleven o'clock!" she exclaimed. "Everyone's supposed to be in bed." She knew the giggle belonged to her sixteen-year-old sister, Maeva. Putting the flour sacks back in the chest, she went out the back door. The silvery moonlight illuminated the yard, and as she walked alongside the house, the voices became louder. Rounding the corner she saw Maeva being kissed by a tall young man. Darrell Watkins had a bad reputation with young girls, and the anger that swelled in Lanie suddenly reached the boiling point. "Maeva, what in the world are you doing out here?"

Maeva Freeman reacted exactly as Lanie expected. As she turned, the moonlight reflected on her red hair and her blue eyes were snapping. "What does it look like I'm doing, Lanie? I'm kissing Darrell Watkins."

If Maeva Freeman was ever afraid of anything—or ashamed of anything—no one ever found out about it. She had the same curves of young womanhood as her older sister and stood there with an impudent grin on her face. "You'll have to wait if you want to get your turn with Darrell, Lanie."

"How did you get out of the house?"

Maeva laughed and pointed upward. "I climbed out that window. Climbed down the walnut tree. If you want to keep me in, you're gonna have to chop down that tree."

"You ought to be ashamed of yourself."

"Well, I ain't," Maeva said defiantly. "Are you ashamed, Darrell?"

Lanie stood there oppressed by a sense of helplessness. Her father would have been able to handle this, but he was in prison, and at the age of seventeen she was now, for all practical purposes, the head of the Freeman family. She had no trouble with her brothers Davis and Cody, and, of course, Corliss Jeanne, at the age of three, was a treasure.

But Maeva Elizabeth Freeman was a rebel to the bone. She had often heard her father say, "I think Maeva gets her contrariness from her mama's side. Couldn't have got it from the Freemans."

Unable to think up a reply that would bring any sort of remorse to Maeva, Lanie turned and snapped, "Darrell Watkins, you get out of here!"

"You don't have to go," Maeva said. She reached out and held the young man by the arm.

Darrell was amused. "Maybe I'd better. Since you got no ma or pa, I guess Lanie there has to be both."

"You ain't afraid of Lanie, are you, a big fellow like you?"

"Well, I always try to be nice to the mamas and papas of my lady friends."

"She's not my mama. I don't have to mind her and you don't have to go."

Darrell was laughing and Maeva was grinning saucily when suddenly a voice came from heaven—or seemed to.

"You big ox, get on your way or I'll shoot your stupid ears off!"

Darrell Watkins whirled and looked up, startled by the voice. He saw an old woman with silver hair framed in one of the upper windows. He was acquainted with Aunt Kezia, but he had never seen her holding a .38, much less one that was trained right on him!

"Hey, now, Miss Aunt Kezia, be keerful! That thing might go off."

"It shore will go off if you don't light a shuck. Now git!"

Darrell was a flamboyant young man and hated to give in to anyone. "Now shucks, Miss Aunt Kezia, you wouldn't shoot me. We go to the same church."

The words were no sooner out of Darrell's mouth when the .38 exploded, sounding like a cannon in the silence of the night. Dirt flew up about two inches from Darrell's right foot, and he jumped up in the air. "Hey!" he yelled. "Be careful with that thing!"

"I'd jist as soon shoot your ears off as spit! Now you git or I'll fumigate you!" She lifted the pistol and Darrell whirled and ran.

Maeva hollered after him, "Don't bother to come back here, you big dummy! Anybody that's afraid of an old woman ain't man enough for me!" She turned around and grinned up at her Aunt Kezia. "Well, are you gonna shoot me?" she demanded.

"Wouldn't be a bad idea, but I ain't decided yet. Now you git back in the house."

"I don't have to," Maeva snorted with disgust.

"That's the way, Aunt Kezia," another voice suddenly broke out. "Show her how the cow ate the cabbage."

Maeva whirled to see her fourteen-year-old brother Cody framed in the doorway, laughing. She flew at him at once, hitting him straight on and almost flooring him. Cody was laughing and at the same time trying to defend himself from Maeva's blows. "Watch out or Aunt Kezia will shoot you," he yelled.

"I'll kill you, Cody Freeman!" Maeva shrieked. She was getting the best of Cody when suddenly Davis, who was eleven months younger than Maeva, appeared. At the age of fifteen he was already six feet tall, lean and strong. He reached out, separated the two, and held Maeva so that she was helpless. "You settle down, Maeva. You've made enough of a fool out of yourself for one night, I guess. Now, you git in the house and go to bed. Tomorrow I'll nail that window down where you won't be pullin' any more stunts like this."

Lanie watched as Maeva went into the house, loudly threatening to run away and join a circus.

Lanie waited until all three were inside, then discovered that she was trembling. These encounters with Maeva always drained her, and she felt like she had failed her parents by not being able to handle Maeva. Davis had once told her, "Shoot, Lanie, Pa couldn't handle her his own self. You know that. She's gonna do what she wants to do."

When she went into the house, she went at once to Corliss's room. The toddler was standing in the bed looking at her with enormous blue eyes. Her blond hair caught the silver moonbeams and she appeared unperturbed. "What was Maeva doing?"

Lanie was always mildly shocked when the child spoke in full sentences. Corliss had not spoken until she was two and a half years old. Then, almost overnight, she suddenly started making sentences.

"Oh, she was just getting into trouble. Now you lie down and go to sleep."

"Did you whip her?"

"No, I didn't whip her. It's late, honey, and tomorrow's your birthday. You'll be three years old."

"Will I feel any different?"

"Oh, you might. Three is a mighty nice age." Lanie laid the child down, kissed her, and said, "Close your eyes now. Think up a story and go to sleep."

"All right, Lanie." Corliss was agreeable, although she was wide awake.

The contrast between Corliss's sweetness and Maeva's meanness was never clearer to her than at that moment. She could still hear Maeva yelling upstairs while Corliss smiled at her with an angelic look. Her heart warmed, and she soothed the child's hair. "Come on, sweetheart, I'll let you have a fresh fried pie because you're such a good girl. Maybe it'll help you get back to sleep." Carrying Corliss, she went back into the kitchen, sat her down on the table, and cut a pie in half. "Half for me and half for you." She handed the pie to Corliss, who took a bite of it eagerly. "Good!" she said.

"It's apple. Got cinnamon in it."

Corliss laughed and then looked serious. "Do I need a fork?"

"No."

"We usually eat pie with a fork," Corliss said seriously.

"Not fried pies. They're supposed to be eaten with the fingers."

Corliss nibbled neatly at her pie and glanced up toward where Maeva's voice could be heard. "Why is Maeva mad?"

"Oh, you know Maeva, Corliss. She didn't get her own way. Hey, in just one hour you'll be three years old. Won't that be nice?"

"Yes." Corliss finished her pie and submitted to the process of Lanie cleaning her face. "When's Daddy coming home, Lanie?"

Lanie never knew how to answer this question. Her father had been arrested and sent to prison for killing a man. It was an accidental shooting, but the judge was strict. Now a big part of Lanie's life was spent going to Cummings Prison Farm as often as she could to visit their father. She was constantly weary from trying to be father and mother to her two sisters and two brothers, but she could not give in to it.

She did not have to answer Corliss's question, for suddenly Aunt Kezia appeared. She was wearing a thin cotton nightgown and sniffed the air as she came in. "I'd shore like to have one of them pies." Aunt Kezia was a small lean woman with silver hair and snapping black eyes. She was in her nineties, but her mind was as sharp as ever.

"I made some of your favorite, Aunt Kezia. Take one of those apricot."

Aunt Kezia picked up an apricot pie and bit into it. "That's plum good. I couldn't have did no better myself."

"Did you ever make fried pies?"

"Sure did. Made 'em for my second husband, Mr. Butterworth. He loved fried pies. When he was a town lawman down in Texas, I made them for him three times a week." Aunt Kezia looked Lanie over and said, "You're wore to a frazzle, child. Go to bed."

"I can't. I need to make some more pies."

"I think it's foolishness."

"Why, Aunt Kezia, we're making pies to raise money for the Lottie Moon Missionary Offering. All the women at church are baking something."

"You can't save the world with pies, Lanie."

Their massive cinnamon-colored dog, Beau, came over and lay his big head on Aunt Kezia's lap. She grinned, reached out, and grabbed him by the ears. "You handsome devil! Get away from me. You just want some more pie dough."

"Woof!"

Aunt Kezia laughed and grabbed some of the spare dough. She fed it to him a little bit at a time, and finally she said, "That's all." He glared at her reproachfully, then walked over toward the wall. When he got there, he suddenly collapsed as if he'd been shot.

"I never seen a dog lay down like that. Why can't he lay down like a normal dog?"

Lanie laughed. "I don't think we have anybody normal in this house."

"Well, *I* am. I'm the most normal person I ever seen."

"Reckon I'll clean up. Maybe we do have enough pies."

"I'll help you." Aunt Kezia glanced at Lanie, noticing the fatigue etched on her smooth face. The girl had struggled heroically after her mother died giving birth to Corliss. It was a tragedy for Lanie to quit school to take care of the house and the other children, and Aunt Kezia admired her tremendously.

Suddenly Lanie turned and said, "I didn't handle Maeva right."

"Yes, you did. That girl can't be handled!" Aunt Kezia sniffed. "I know because I was just like her. She's gonna have to get a few bumps—but she'll be fine."

Lanie came over and stood before the small elderly woman. "Aunt Kezia, sometimes I get to thinkin' about how Daddy's in prison, and Davis can't learn to read, and Maeva's always in trouble—"

"Honey, the good Lord knows about every problem you got. Now, you're a Christian girl, and you know God's able to do anything. You just go on to bed. I'll finish cleanin' up and get the pies ready to go to the celebration. You go on now."

Lanie hugged her aunt, kissed her on the cheek, and then left the room, Corliss tagging along behind. Aunt Kezia watched them go, then began to pray. She always prayed with her eyes wide open, which shocked Cody, who admonished her, "You're supposed to close your eyes."

"Who told you that?" Aunt Kezia always said.

Now the old woman stood there for a moment collecting her thoughts and composing the prayer, and when it was firmly in her mind, she said loudly, "Lord, things around here are right messy, so I'm askin' you to rare back and work a bodacious, humongous miracle that covers everything this family needs. See to it now!"

CHAPTER 2

The Dream came but quickly faded as a light pressure on Lanie's right eye brought her out of a fitful sleep. Lanie tried to ignore it, but the slight tapping of something soft against her eyelid was persistent. Finally she opened her left eye and saw Cap'n Brown, her rangy Manx tomcat, sitting beside her touching her right eye gently with his paw. It had been his way of waking her up ever since he had come out of the woods to become a part of the Freeman family.

Sitting up, Lanie picked Cap'n Brown up and perched him on her lap. "Why do you always have to interrupt my dreams, Cap'n Brown?" she scolded. She stroked his thick fur and was amused as always at the fact that he had no tail, just a stub. He did have enormously long hind legs in the manner of a true Manx, and she reached out and gave him a hug, which he received with a loud meow.

It was still dark outside, but she could see the beginnings of gray light forming in the east. She sat there holding the cat and looking around the room. As she did, it seemed slightly unfamiliar to her despite the fact that she had slept in it almost every night of her seventeen years. What was missing was the furniture. She had grown up surrounded by massive antiques, but they were all gone now, replaced by inexpensive new pieces. She felt a sudden desire to see her old furniture again, but shook her head and scolded herself softly. *Don't be foolish, girl. If we hadn't sold all that furniture, we would have lost this place.*

It was indeed a miracle that the homeplace had been saved. The bank was ready to foreclose, but Elspeth Patton, the owner and publisher of the *Sentinel*, had come to their rescue. She had brought an antique dealer out who made them an offer on the antique furniture that enabled them to pay off the note at the bank and have a little left over. A warm feeling came as Lanie thought of how pleased her father had been that they had not lost the homeplace. She had hugged him when she had visited him at Cummings Farm and said excitedly, "Daddy, now when you get out, you'll have your own place to come to."

The rooster, Franklin, crowed, and Lanie shoved Cap'n Brown aside and grinned. "Franklin thinks the sun comes up because he crows. He's a mighty foolish rooster. It's a good thing he's too skinny for us to eat."

Leaving the room, she walked down the hall to the bathroom. She washed her face with a thin sliver of Lifebuoy soap. "I hate Lifebuoy soap," she muttered. "It stinks. I'm going to get Ivory soap next time. That smells almost as good as perfume."

She began to brush her hair and studied her reflection. She had an oval face with a wealth of auburn hair and gray-green eyes, which she inherited from her mother. Her mouth was wide, too wide, she thought, and she muttered, "I wish I were as pretty as Maeva." No sooner were the words out than she was disgusted with herself. "Nobody's pretty as Maeva, and besides, I ought to be happy I look as good as I do."

Going back to her room, she removed her nightgown and quickly dressed. She would be going to the Stone County Fourth of July County Fair later in the day, but there was work to be done, so she wore the dress with the split seam. It didn't matter much if she was pooching out of it. Nobody would see.

When she was dressed, she moved over to the rocker and turned on the lamp. Sitting down, she opened the worn black Bible that lay on the table. It had belonged to her mother, and she delighted in the notes that her mother had made years ago. There were so many of them, notes of promises that her mother had claimed and then later put down a date when they were fulfilled. The Bible had a great deal to do with Lanie's faith, and as she turned to where the marker indicated her reading, she thought of her mother, and a lump formed in her throat. She still missed her desperately, and it was a constant struggle to overcome her feelings.

She was reading the Bible through from Genesis to Revelation. It was her second time, and she had reached the eleventh chapter of Leviticus. She began reading and was puzzled. It consisted of a list of animals that the children of Israel were permitted to eat along with a list of those that were not permitted. She got down to verse nine and read aloud, "These shall ye eat of all that are in the waters: whatsoever hath fins and scales in the waters, in the seas, and in the rivers, them shall ye eat. And all that have not fins and scales in the seas, and in the rivers, of all that move in the waters, and of any living thing which is in the waters, they shall be an abomination unto you."

Lanie's brow furrowed, and she shook her head. "I just plain don't understand that," she muttered. "Nothin's better than good fried catfish—and yet the Bible says they are an abomination. I'm going to ask the preacher how come it says we can't eat catfish. I know he eats it himself, so it must be all right." She continued reading until finally she got to verse twenty-two, which said, "Even these of them ye may eat; the locust after his kind, and the bald locust after his kind, and the beetle after his kind, and the grasshopper after his kind."

"Who in the world," Lanie exclaimed, "would want to eat a grasshopper or a locust!" She shivered and continued reading down through the chapters, and finally she said, "Well, Lord, I read it, and I don't have any idea what it's all about. If you don't want me to eat catfish, you're going to have to say it plain, because everybody I know eats catfish. But I will promise never to eat any grasshoppers or any locusts." Closing the Bible, she prayed for her family and for the members of her church who were ill and closed by saying, "Lord, I can't do a thing with Maeva. You'll have to do something because she's beyond me."

After closing the Bible, she rose and walked over to the chest of drawers. It was new and not extravagant but well made, and opening the bottom drawer she pulled out two notebooks and took them back over to her chair. Sitting down, she held one with a green cover and smiled. "My first diary," she said. "I couldn't have been more than six when I started it." She opened it and read the first entry. "Dady took us all to see a pitcher show. It was good. I like Mickey Moose best. After the show he bought us all a red soda pop and a moonpie. We hav the best dady in the hole worrld and I will rite a pome about him."

My Dady
My dady has big rough hands,
But when I cry, he understands.
My dady has laffing eyes
And holds me when I cry.
My dady doesn't have much monney,
But I like it when he calls me Honny.

A smile turned the corners of Lanie's lips upward, and she ran the tips of her fingers over the writing. "I wonder where that little girl is who wrote this." It was something she often thought of. *When we grow up, we leave behind that which we are. Aunt Kezia once had been a mere baby, and now she was old and wrinkled and fragile. Where was the child she had been?*

Lanie Freeman frequently had thoughts like this, and she always loved to put her notions into poems and journals. She never showed them to anyone, although she had filled many notebooks. As she sat there musing over the poem about her dad, she thought of a poem she might someday write about her mother. She made a few notes, then for a time let memories of her mother flow over her. She had been unable to do this for a long time following her mother's death, for she always ended up weeping. But time had healed her to some extent, and though the ache would never evaporate, now she could occasionally think of her mother with fond pleasure.

Laying the green notebook down, Lanie picked up the blue one and opened it to a poem that she was working on. For several months Lanie had been working on a series of poems about Jesus of Nazareth. All of them were written from the point of view of someone in Scripture. Her teacher had told her that these were called dramatic monologues. She had written a poem about Mary, about the innkeeper who turned them away, about the shepherds who were told by the angels that the Savior had been born. For some time she had been trying to write a poem about the wedding feast where Jesus turned the water into wine. She liked to make each poem different and was tired of poems that always rhymed and had the same length of line. She thumbed over several pages of failed attempts, and finally got to the one she was happiest with. She wrote a verse of Scripture at the top: "The governor of the feast called the bridegroom, and saith unto him, Every man at the beginning doth set forth good wine; and when men have well drunk, then that which is worse: but thou hast kept the good wine until now" (John 2:9–10).

She read the poem aloud softly:

First Miracle

O child
Of my virginity,
This water felt your touch
And blushed to wine!
See how red it is,
Like Sharon's morning rose,
Yet clear as Hebron's streams
It sparkles in my cup.
O son of strangeness born,
Would that I could know your hidden heart
As clearly as I see this clear wine!
I think your days will be
A bitter draught of pain
(which I too must taste)

A bitter drink and not sweet wine
For Mary's son.
Alone that man must walk
Who touches water into wine — but then
You always were alone,
Not least in humming crowd, and yet
Your silence was companioned by
Unspoken truths.
These have drunk your red, red wine;
But men were never satisfied
By timely tastes.
O son of sorrow,
When these vessels emptied are,
What wine must you pour
From deep within
To quench our thirst?
O son of man, what wine
At last will you pour out
For us?

A good feeling came to Lanie as she read the poem over. She bowed her head and said, "Thank you, Lord Jesus, for helping me write this poem, and may my poems always honor you." She always wrote her poems to please Jesus and felt this was part of her worship of the Savior. For a time she sat there thinking about the next poem she would write. Then, hearing voices from the first floor, she got up with a start. She quickly put the notebooks back under the clothing in the bottom drawer and hurried out of the room to begin her day.

Getting Cody and Maeva out of bed was always a chore that Lanie was glad to leave to Davis. They had learned that if they didn't get up when he first called them, he would dump them out on the floor or pour cold water over them. They were all up now, and Lanie got the breakfast going as they milked the cows, gathered the eggs, fed the chickens, and fed Jezebel the sow along with the goats.

They all came rushing in at about the same time demanding to be fed, and after Maeva set the table they sat down. Lanie stood behind her chair, and they all bowed their heads. Maeva gave a malevolent glance that Lanie ignored.

"Lord, we thank you that we are all alive and healthy. We thank you for this food. We pray that you will be with Daddy and give him a good day. Be with us at the fair, and may we raise a lot of money for the Lottie Moon Missionary Offering. In Jesus' name, amen."

Davis picked up the big pan of scrambled eggs and went around dumping a portion onto each plate.

"Not much for me," Aunt Kezia said. "You know I eat like a bird." Aunt Kezia talked constantly about what a finicky eater she was when actually she ate like a field hand. She also complained about sleeping poorly when actually she slept as if she were dead.

"You gave Maeva more than you gave me, Davis," Cody protested.

"I'm older than you are and bigger," Maeva said. "You're always complaining."

"I don't never complain!" Cody said indignantly. He did, of course, but always immediately forgot.

The breakfast consisted of scrambled eggs, fried ham, grits, and red-eye gravy along with freshly baked biscuits and jars of blackberry jam, red plum jam, and honey.

As they ate, they talked about what they were going to do at the county fair. Maeva was not happy. "What's the use of going to a fair when we ain't got any money?"

Davis bit off half of a biscuit and chewed it with his mouth full. His voice was muffled as he said, "There's lots to see. It doesn't take any money to look."

Cody reached over and punched Davis in the arm. "You better win that ball game today, Davis. I bet Max Jinks my best slingshot against three of his best marbles including his best shooter."

"It's wrong to bet, Cody," Lanie said. "Isn't it, Aunt Kezia?"

"Not always."

Maeva was interested. "You think it is all right to bet, Aunt Kezia?"

"If conditions are right. I made a bet once. I won it too."

"What'd you bet on, Aunt Kezia?" Davis said, his eyes sparkling. He was a fine-looking boy, tall and lean and rangy like his father with the same auburn hair and light blue eyes. He was the best athlete in Fairhope High School even though he was only fifteen. His dad had taught him to pitch, and he was good at almost any sport.

"Well, I made a bet once when we lived in Kansas. Mr. Butterworth was the marshal there. It was a rough place. I never knowed when Mr. Butterworth would come in all shot up."

"Why'd you call him *mister*?" Maeva demanded.

"Because in those days women knew how to respect their husbands."

Maeva laughed aloud. She licked away a smear of blackberry jelly on her upper lip. "You didn't respect your last husband."

"I shore didn't," Aunt Kezia snapped. "He was a boring man. You can't respect a boring man."

"I guess then I'd better marry a man who ain't boring." Maeva winked roguishly.

"You'd better! Anyway, I was on the main street going to the general store when this feller named Buck Slade stopped me. I knowed him, for he fancied himself a bad man. He'd had trouble with my husband, Mr. Butterworth, and wanted to aggravate me just to get at him. He said some rude things to me."

"What rude things did he say?" Cody demanded, leaning forward.

"Never you mind that. They was rude. All that worthless trash that hung out with him laughed at him."

"What'd you do?" Maeva asked.

"I took the .38 my husband give me out of my reticule and told him to git. He just laughed and told me I couldn't hit nothin'." Aunt Kezia's eyes sparkled. She nodded with satisfaction at the memory. "I asked him if he was a bettin' man, and he said he was. I said, 'I bet I could outshoot you.'"

"What'd he say?" Lanie asked, fascinated as she always was at her aunt's stories.

"He took a dollar out of his pocket, held it up, and said, 'I bet you can't hit this dollar while I hold it.' I told him, 'I bet you a dollar I can.' He backed off about ten feet. All them fools that followed around with him was laughin', and I shot at it."

"Did you hit it?" Maeva demanded.

"Well, I come pretty close. I shot him in the hand right through the palm."

Everyone began laughing, and Davis said, "What did he do?"

"Oh, he started cussin' and a comin' to get me, but about that time Mr. Butterworth, he came along. He arrested them all for disturbin' the peace."

Maeva was staring at her aunt with admiration. "Did you mean to shoot him, Aunt Kezia?"

"Ain't sayin', but Buck Slade never bothered me no more."

"What happened to him?" Cody asked.

"Well, he didn't live long after that. The fool tried to hold up a bank in broad open daylight, and Mr. Butterworth and his deputy, who had the foolish name of Hippy, shot him so full of lead he wouldn't even float in the creek."

All the youngsters were leaning forward, and Corliss, who had been silent through all this, said, "Tell another story, Aunt Kezia."

"No," Lanie interjected. "That's enough stories for now. I got a surprise for you, Corliss." She got up, went to the stove, and pulled a small cake out of the warming compartment at the top. It had three candles on it, and she lit them with a kitchen match. Bringing it in, she put it down in front of Corliss. "Blow them out, honey."

Corliss took a deep breath and blew, and as the candles went out, they sang "Happy Birthday" to her.

"Now we've got some presents for you," Lanie said.

Everyone, indeed, had gotten a present for the child. They were all simple things, small toys or candy, and Corliss crowed over each one.

"Well, I've got a surprise for the rest of you," Aunt Kezia said.

She got up and left the room, and Cody said, "What do you reckon it is?"

"I have no idea." Lanie smiled. "You never know what Aunt Kezia's going to do."

Aunt Kezia came back in with a purse, and she reached into it and said, "Looky here. Got one of these for each of you." She gave each one of them a silver dollar, including Corliss.

"Hot ziggity!" Cody said. "I'm gonna ride that Ferris wheel with part of this."

"You'll probably fall off of it," Davis said. "I'm gonna get some of that cotton candy and one of them candy apples they had last year."

The youngsters all talked excitedly about what they were going to do with the money, and Aunt Kezia looked on them with a fond regard. "You're all pretty worthless young 'uns," she said finally, "but I'll reckon you'll do in a pinch."

ᴥ Chapter 3 ᴥ

Lanie pulled the ancient Ford pickup into the line of cars, but even before she stopped she saw in the rearview mirror the occupants of the bed were piling out. Turning to Aunt Kezia, she laughed, "It's a wonder they didn't jump out on the way here."

"I reckon it is, but every time we leave in this contraption I never expect to get to where we're goin' in one piece."

Lanie reached over and hugged Corliss. "Come on. We're going to take our pies over to the sales tables, then we're going to the carnival."

After they delivered the pies, they went at once to the carnival grounds. She could hear the sound of calliope music filling the air, and the crowd that had gathered for the fair added their voices. It was a time of laughter and release, and Lanie noted the expressions on the faces of her brothers and sisters. *They're worn out with working hard and having no money*, she thought. *This will be good for them.*

The fairground was roughly divided into two segments—one contained the buildings where the exhibits were shown, and the other was the carnival. As they joined the crowd that was milling around, Lanie spoke to many of her friends. She felt the excitement in her own breast, and she thought what a contrast all this light and happiness was to the daily struggle for existence. Here people were eating exotic foods like cotton candy and taffy apples. They were riding death-defying rides such as the octopus and the Ferris wheel. The barkers outside of the shows, the freaks, and the menagerie were all so different from the monotony of their regular lives.

"Come on, I'm wanting to go ride the octopus!" Cody yelped shrilly.

"Me too. I want to ride the neck snapper," Aunt Kezia said, nodding toward a ride that slung the occupants around in small cars while spinning them in a huge circle.

Maeva and Cody darted off, and Davis grinned. "You're mighty brave letting those two loose on the fairgrounds."

"I know it, but I can't keep them tied up all the time."

"Don't you worry. I'll keep up with 'em," Aunt Kezia snapped. She headed off in their direction, her small frame upright. She was wearing the same dress she wore to church every Sunday, which amused Davis. "Don't you think it's kind of odd Aunt Kezia wearing her Sunday clothes to a carnival? That Aunt Kezia, she's a caution now."

"I don't know what we'd do without her. Come on, let's take this girl for a ride on the merry-go-round." The three advanced, and Corliss squealed with pleasure as she rode the horses up and down, Davis holding her onto the seat. She insisted on riding twice, and finally they persuaded her that there were other things to do.

"Why don't you go find the kids, and I'll take Corliss over and we'll see if the pies are selling," Lanie said.

"All right." Davis grinned. "I may fall in love with one of those dancers at the side show."

"You stay away from them, Davis Freeman!"

"Okay, Sis." Davis winked and made his way through the crowd.

Holding tightly to Corliss's hand, Lanie wove her way over to the section where several tables were filled with food that was to be sold. As she approached the Baptist table, she suddenly heard a loud voice booming out, "Well, praise the Lord! Glory to God and the Lamb forever!"

Sister Myrtle Poindexter had a voice that, according to many, could make the hair fall out if you stood too close to her. She and her husband, Charlie, operated the Dew Drop Inn, but her main calling in life was as female pastor of the Fire Baptized Pentecostal Church. She was standing in front of the table but turned and smiled broadly as Lanie and Corliss approached. "Give an old woman a hug, Corliss," she shouted as she leaned over, picked up Corliss, and spun her around. Putting her on the ground, she said, "It's good to see you, Sister Lanie."

"I thought you would be opposed to carnivals." Lanie smiled, winking at Charlie Poindexter. "It's pretty worldly stuff."

"I'm not going into the devil's playground," Sister Myrtle said, firmly nodding toward the Ferris wheel and the carnival rides. "But there ain't no sin in goin' in and lookin' at good beef and fine vegetables." She turned and said to William Prince, the pastor of the First Baptist Church, "Reverend, just give me another one of them fried pies."

William Prince was a tall, lanky man of thirty-six. He resembled the pictures of Abraham Lincoln, being rather homely and craggy. He grinned and handed Sister Myrtle one of the pies Lanie had made. "Here you are, Sister Myrtle. That'll be ten cents, please. You know, it's a pleasure to take money for food from you, since usually you take it from me."

Ellen Prince, the pastor's wife, was a small blonde with sky-blue eyes and a winning smile. "You leave her alone now, William. Don't pay any attention to him, Sister Myrtle."

Charlie Poindexter was a lean man without an ounce of fat on him. He had a trace of mischief in him, and as Sister Myrtle bit into her pie, he said, "Why, Wife, I thought you were fasting this week."

Sister Myrtle was well padded, a big woman who wore no jewelry and kept her hair in a bun so tight it seemed to pull her eyes back in a slant. "You tend to your own taters, Charlie Poindexter. I'm takin' this day off from my fast, and I'll start in again tomorrow." She took an enormous bite of the pie and then nodded. "Ooh, Sister Lanie, you are the world's best fried pie cooker!"

"Why, thank you, Sister Myrtle. Anybody can make fried pies."

"Not as good as these." Sister Myrtle finished off the pie, licked her fingers, and turned to William Prince. "Pastor," she said, "we're beginning our annual revival next week. I'm expectin' you to be there and bring all the sinners you can rope in with you."

William Prince grinned. "I'll surely be there, my sister."

"I'm hopin' that things get plum out of control. Out of man's control, that is," Sister Myrtle amended. "I'd like to see the Spirit of God take this town, turn it upside down, and shake it—get sinners under the blood."

Lanie listened and smiled at the pastor's wife. Both of them knew that Sister Myrtle could launch into a sermon just as easily at the fairgrounds as she could in her own pulpit.

Finally Sister Myrtle ceased and said, "What about that brother of yours? Is he playin' in the ball game?"

"Yes, he is." Lanie nodded. The Fairhope Mountaineers were pitted in their annual battle against the Fort Smith Lions. Both of them were semipro teams, and each team sent several players to the big league every year. Although Davis was only fifteen, he was such a talented player that the Mountaineers used him often, usually as a pinch hitter or a pinch runner. He was also a good pitcher, and he regularly played that position as well.

"Well, I don't think God gives a hoot who wins the ball games," Sister Myrtle said loudly. "But I'm gonna pray for your brother anyhow." She raised her voice, lifted both hands, and her volume simply drowned out all sound in a fifty-foot radius. "Lord, give them Lions blind eyes to Davis's fastball. Tangle their feet up so they trip, and give them butterfingers so they drop every fly that comes their way. Strike their hearts with fear when Davis steps on the mound, and let that coach's wife who runs around in public wearing forked pants get a dose of religion that puts her back in her house cookin' and washin' and havin' babies like she ourt to be doin' ..."

The prayer went on for some time, and finally Charlie lifted his head and cleared his throat. "While my beloved wife is finishing up her prayer," he said, "I'll reckon I'll have another pie. Sister Lanie, I'd like to have apricot if you've got it."

Reverend Prince laughed. "I admire your enthusiasm in prayer, sister."

"Well, you can't make a prayer too hot or too long. I like to make 'em sizzle!"

Ellen Prince stood quietly listening as her husband and Sister Myrtle began a long involved discussion on the nature of the second coming. They had carried on a minor debate over this subject ever since the Princes had come to pastor the First Baptist Church. She leaned close and said, "Lanie, why don't you go along and enjoy the fair. I'll look after Corliss for you."

"Oh, I don't mind staying and helping."

"No, I'll be here to take care of all that. We do appreciate the pies." She reached over and gave the girl a hug, for she was genuinely fond of her. "Why don't you go ride the Ferris wheel."

Lanie shivered. "I'm not sure I can, Sister Prince."

"Whyever not?" Ellen lifted Corliss to her hip.

"It's just that, well—last time I rode the Ferris wheel was the day I found out Mama died."

Ellen Prince gazed at Lanie compassionately, sharing the young woman's sorrow. She had always been impressed by Lanie Freeman's courage in raising her family after the loss of both parents. "Well, I don't think your mama would want to feel like she spoiled one of the joys in life."

Lanie was embarrassed. "I guess you're right, Mrs. Prince. Maybe I'll try it again. I always used to love it."

Ellen Prince smiled. "That's the spirit. Now I'll take care of Corliss, and you go along and ride your Ferris wheel. It won't be so bad. I know you can do it."

"All right, Sister Prince. Thank you."

Lanie made sure Corliss was happy in Ellen's care, then left the table, and she could hear the voice of Sister Myrtle until she was within range of the sounds of the crowd and the music. Slowly she came to the Ferris wheel and finally stood under it, watching as it spun around and around. Four times it stopped, and each time she wanted to move forward and buy a ticket, but somehow she just couldn't make herself do it.

"You going to ride this thing or not, Lanie?"

Lanie whirled quickly and saw Doctor Owen Merritt watching her with a smile. Owen was six feet tall and weighed a lean one hundred and eighty pounds. His crisp brown hair was moving slightly with the breeze, and she noticed again his widow's peak, the little triangle of hair that grew right down on his forehead. He had warm brown eyes, a wide mouth, a short English nose, and a very determined jaw. As always, Lanie was a little intimidated by him. When he had first come to town, he had taken the Freeman children under his wing. Over the last three years Lanie had grown into young womanhood and become very much aware that he was the most attractive man she had ever seen. She confided this attraction to her diary and spoke of it to no one, but Maeva had been sharp enough to figure it out. She often said, "You can catch that doctor, Lanie. All you have to do is smile at him and lean against him a little bit and get you some good perfume."

Catching the doctor was not possible, Lanie knew, for he was engaged to Louise Langley, the daughter of the richest man in Fairhope. This shut the door as far as Lanie was concerned, but she could not forget the one time, in a moment of weakness, when Doctor Owen Merritt had kissed her. It started out to be a friendly peck on the cheek but instead his lips fell on hers, and both of them were somewhat shaken by the encounter. Since that time Doctor Merritt was as careful as ever to see to the medical needs of the Freemans, but he walked warily around Lanie.

"Come on. You're not afraid, are you?"

"I don't think so." Lanie immediately covered up her feelings. "Where's Louise?" she said to change the subject.

"Well, she doesn't like carnivals," Owen said. He shook his head ruefully. "We were supposed to meet here, but she didn't show up." He looked at the Ferris wheel going around at full speed and then turned his eyes back on Lanie. "You know, some people are afraid of things like this."

"I can see why," Lanie said. "I'm a little scared myself."

Owen shook his head at once and said firmly, "You are the most courageous young woman I know. Come on now. We're gonna ride this thing. If it falls down" — he winked at her and grinned — "we'll fall down together."

Lanie tried to protest, but he took her arm and led her over to the small booth, where he obtained two tickets. "Come along. Here we go," he said, and the two got into the seat. As Lanie felt the oak bar fasten in front of them, she reached out and grabbed it.

"Look, your knuckles are white. Don't do that." Owen smiled. "It's just a carnival ride. Let's ride it with no hands." He tried to pull her hands away from the bar, but she shook her head.

"No. I want to hold on."

Suddenly the wheel started with a jerk. Lanie moaned slightly and shut her eyes as the seat rocked to and fro. She held on as if she were holding the whole Ferris wheel together. Finally she felt the movement as they went up, and Owen chided her, "Come on. Open your eyes. Part of the fun is looking out."

Lanie opened her eyes as the car crested the top. All thoughts of her mother disappeared. "Look! You can see our truck over in the parking lot. And there's the railroad crossing over there."

Owen leaned back and listened as the young woman breathlessly described the sights. He was glad to see the enthusiasm on her face, for he knew she got little excitement in her life. As Lanie held tightly to the bar and the Ferris wheel stopped to let someone on, Owen said, "How's your dad?"

"I'm going to the prison to visit him next week. I'm really looking forward to it."

Owen listened as she described what all she was going to take to her father, and the love for him was plain in her face. Owen had been present when Forrest Freeman had been sentenced to prison for manslaughter, and now he said quietly, "You miss your dad a great deal, don't you, Lanie?"

"I think about him constantly."

"We'll just have to pray that Orrin Pierce will work a miracle. We need to get him out of that place." Pierce was the lawyer who represented Forrest Freeman, and was now trying to locate a mystery witness who had been present during the shooting and whose testimony could vindicate Mr. Freeman. The witness, however, had disappeared and was apparently in California. Pierce was working with Owen's brother to locate her and felt sure he would soon have enough evidence to ask for a retrial.

Suddenly the Ferris wheel jerked again and started spinning around. It made three circles, and as the ride came closer to the end, thoughts of Lanie's mother returned. When the wheel jolted to a stop with their seat at the very top, Lanie felt herself breathing very rapidly as she remembered that awful day three years ago.

"Here. You're hyperventilating," Owen said quickly. He moved closer to her, put his arm around her, and said, "Now, just take some deep breaths. It's all right. We'll get off this thing, but you need to breathe slowly."

Lanie was so overwhelmed with emotion she did not know what she was doing. His arm around her was comforting, and suddenly she closed her eyes and buried her face against his chest. She held on to him as if she were a child, and finally the wheel began to move. Owen shouted at the man who was operating it, "Stop this thing!" Then he said, "Here. We can get off now, Lanie."

Lanie opened her eyes and then pulled away from Owen with some embarrassment. She hated to show weakness and could not meet his eyes. "I'm such a baby." She immediately saw Louise Langley standing with her father, Otis Langley, and her face turned red. Her relationship with the Langleys was not good, and now she saw disapproval on their faces. Owen stepped out of the car and gave her his hand, and then when she stepped out, he turned to Louise, cleared his throat, and said, "Hello, Louise. I gave up on you."

"So I see," Louise said sharply. She was an attractive young woman with fair hair and blue eyes and wore far more expensive clothes than any other young woman in Fairhope. Her eyes were cold now, and she listened as Owen explained, "Lanie is a little bit nervous around a Ferris wheel, so I thought I'd give her a little encouragement."

"I think we can go now," Louise said tersely.

Otis Langley, Louise's father, was a big man of fifty, fine looking with brown hair and brown eyes. He was powerful in the politics of Fairhope and in Stone County, and had exerted considerable effort to get his hands on the Freeman homeplace, which he knew one day would be very valuable. He had been thwarted in this, and now his lips were turned down as he said, "I suppose we're ready to go if you are, Owen."

"All ready," Owen said. He turned and grinned crookedly at Lanie. "Next time we'll get on the merry-go-round."

"Thank you, Doctor Merritt."

Lanie stood there and watched as the three left, then she suddenly felt weak. *What a fool I was! Louise is so jealous anyway. I know she'll give Owen a hard time.* As she made her way back toward the food table, she felt depressed, and the joy of the carnival was erased. When she reached the table, she picked up Corliss and gave her a big hug, somehow comforted by her little sister. Ellen Prince took one look at her face and said, "What's the matter? Did you ride that Ferris wheel?"

"Yes, I did."

Ellen was a sensitive woman and could sense Lanie's distress. "It wasn't much fun, I take it."

"No," Lanie said, and sadness touched her voice. "It wasn't any fun at all."

~=~ CHAPTER 4 ~=~

About two o'clock in the afternoon the carnival was almost deserted. The music still blared on, but only a few isolated spectators moved amongst the rides. The exhibit halls were nearly vacant, with only a few farmers waiting expectantly for their entries to be judged in the three o'clock cattle show.

The crowd had moved over to the field where the annual baseball game between the Fairhope Mountaineers and the Fort Smith Lions was to be held. The stands, such as they were, were filled, but Lanie and the rest of the Freemans had come early so that they had seats right behind home plate. They were all crowded together, and Cody elbowed Maeva, saying, "Don't crowd me, Maeva. You're just about sittin' on my lap."

"Who wants to sit on your old lap!" Maeva snapped. She started to rebuke him, but at that moment Roger Langley, Louise Langley's brother, came toward them. He was the catcher for the Mountaineers. "Come to see us clean up on the Lions?" He winked at Lanie.

Roger Langley was the object of many a young woman's eye in Fairhope and, indeed, in Stone County. His father had money, and Roger himself was a fine-looking young man. He was over six feet with fair hair and blue eyes, but he seemed unconscious of his good looks. He had known Lanie all of her life, but only in the last year had he become interested in her. When his father had tried to foreclose on the Freeman place, Roger had stood up for the Freemans. The quarrel between him and his father had led to Roger's determination not to depend on the Langley money to make a living. He had taken a job working for a surveyor and was now saving money to go to college.

"You got the day off from work." Lanie smiled up at him. She liked Roger very much indeed, and they had gone out on several dates. He had kissed her once, and she had been excited by his touch, although she tried not to show it. "How do you like surveying?"

Roger tossed the ball up in the air, caught it, and grinned. "Just like a paid vacation," he said. "Lots of fresh air and sunshine and good exercise, and I get to stay here in Fairhope and be close to my best girl."

Maeva, who was taking all this in, grinned and said, "Your old man won't like it. He doesn't care for us Freemans."

"I'm not asking his permission!" Roger shrugged, then added, "Louise told me about you and the doctor smooching on the Ferris wheel."

"We were doing no such thing!" Lanie exclaimed. Several of the spectators were listening and loud laughter went up.

"Well, that's a good thing. He's too old for you anyhow. Now me, I'm just right. How about we go to a movie tomorrow night? The Marx Brothers have got a new one. It's called *Monkey Business*."

Although Lanie was embarrassed by his referring to the escapade with Owen on the Ferris wheel, she enjoyed being with Roger, and it was always refreshing to get out for an evening with him. "All right, Roger." She glanced at the players on the field and warned, "You be careful. Don't get hurt."

"Hurt from those Lions? Not a chance!"

The Lions were warming up on the field and shouting to each other loudly, and Lanie saw they were all much older than Davis. "They look pretty tough, Roger. I'm worried about Davis. He's too young to play against that bunch."

"Well, he's not going to pitch today. He'll be all right." He heard the coach shout and turned to say, "Well, time to go beat the Lions. I'll come by about six tomorrow. We'll get one of the exquisite meals down at the Dew Drop Inn before the movie."

❦

"I'd just as soon not come to this old ball game," Louise Langley complained. She had reluctantly agreed to come with Owen and frowned as she added, "Who cares who wins between these two hick town teams?"

"Everybody in the county cares," Owen said. He had bought some peanuts and was cracking them and tossing them back into his mouth. "Baseball means a great deal to these people, Louise."

"It's just a game."

"I think it's more than that."

"Why would you say that?" Louise Langley turned to study Owen. She knew the two of them were different in many ways, but she was also aware that he was an up-and-coming physician. Doctor Oscar Givens was in his middle sixties and still would practice for a few more years, but he was obviously grooming Owen to take his place. Owen would have a large practice, and anybody who wanted medical care would come to him. Louise saw herself as the wife of a prominent doctor, and she also knew that doctors were at the top of the social scale in Arkansas small towns. "What do you mean," she said, "that baseball's more than just a game?"

"Well, since the Depression hit, everything in the South has pretty well shut down—in the North too, of course. The men and boys in our area get so frustrated. They can't find work. They stand around the pool halls. They chop cotton for fifty cents a day, a twelve-hour day at that. It's not much of a life. But they can play ball, and they become important." He waved his hand and said, "You know who the heroes of every one of those boys are out there on that field?"

"I have no idea."

"Lefty Grove and the Philadelphia Athletics. They know the Athletics are the heroes and the New York Yankees are the villains." Owen popped another peanut into his mouth and shook his head. "Those young fellows don't have much hope of seeing the Athletics. However, they've all got radios, and when a game is broadcast everything stops."

"I know that. I just don't see why men are so interested."

"Well, these fellows are mostly raw-boned young farmers, most of them uneducated. Their brand of baseball is raw and rowdy. Several of the Mountaineers and the Lions too have gone to the majors. You know, I have hopes that Davis will make a professional ballplayer."

"Isn't he only fifteen?"

"Yes, but he's got all the gifts. His dad was a great ballplayer."

"It didn't help him much. He wound up in the penitentiary."

"Louise, let's not talk about that." The plight of Forrest Freeman was a bone of contention between Owen and Louise. She, as a matter of fact, was jealous of all the Freeman family—especially of Lanie. "You spend too much time worrying about them," she often said, but her words had no effect on Owen Merritt.

Owen had given up trying to talk to Louise about some things, and the Freemans were one of those subjects. "Well, the game's ready to start." He looked down and grinned. "Look. There's Aunt Kezia."

Louise looked down and saw Kezia Pearl Freeman waving her hands in the air and shouting as the Fairhope Mountaineers took the field. "That old woman shouldn't be out here."

"Why, she'll have more fun than anyone. See that purse? She's probably got her .38 in it. She carries it everywhere she goes."

Louise had no love for Aunt Kezia. It was the old woman's arrival that had saved the Freeman children from losing the homeplace. Lanie had been sixteen, and Louise's father had pulled strings to get the State to declare that the children would have to be put into foster homes since there was no adult supervision. But Lanie had discovered her father's second aunt lived just over the border in Oklahoma. She and Doctor Merritt had made a trip and persuaded the old woman to come and take up residence in their home. That had given them leverage enough so that they had been able to stay, claiming Aunt Kezia as their guardian.

Louise moved restlessly as the Mountaineers began to throw the ball around, and finally she said, "I don't want to be critical, Owen, but it didn't look good your being on that Ferris wheel with Lanie."

"Well, I waited for you, but you never showed up."

Louise turned to him, her lips in a pout. "It just doesn't look good," she repeated. "There you were hugging her."

"She was hyperventilating and scared to death. Poor kid."

"She is *not* a kid!" Louise said, her eyes flashing. "She's a grown woman. Seventeen years old is no kid."

Owen shrugged his shoulders. He was tired of arguing about Lanie with Louise. "I admire her, Louise. I've tried to make that clear to you. She's got character, and not one young woman in a thousand would have kept her family together the way Lanie did. Now, let's watch the ball game."

Louise started to speak, but she saw the certain set of Owen Merritt's jaw that always meant he was determined. She glanced down at Lanie sitting with her family and made a resolution. *I'm going to have to keep those two apart. She's pretty enough to attract a man, and it would be just like Owen to get trapped. He doesn't know women very well.* She then turned her attention to the ball game that was just beginning, and wished heartily that it was over.

The game was like a minor war between the two sides. Both teams were composed of strong raw-boned boys, most of them rather rowdy and several who'd been in trouble with the law. They were not at all like the church league teams, but more like the strong double-A teams that many of the players would eventually enter.

The game was tight, and by the end of the fourth inning the Lions' pitcher, a big left-hander named Ben Crudden, was dominating. He was a hard-throwing pitcher and already had hit two players and brushed back most of the others. His latest pitch hit Roger Langley, who picked himself up from the dirt and cried out, "You ugly ape! You just wait. You'll get yours."

"What's the matter, baby face?" Crudden laughed. "You didn't get your uniform dirty, did ya?"

The score continued zero-zero until the seventh inning. Thad Little, the Mountaineer pitcher, was throwing a good game. He came up to bat determined to get a hit and win his own ball game when suddenly Crudden threw a hard ball inside. Little turned and twisted, but the ball struck him on his pitching arm. He dropped his bat with a cry, and Aunt Kezia's voice rose up, "Why, you no good, two-bit, sorry hoodlum! You done that on purpose!"

Indeed, the rooters for the Mountaineers were all shouting. Lanie watched as the coach went out at once, and she saw him shake his head.

"That's all for him," Maeva said. "Aunt Kezia, why don't you just shoot that Crudden."

"I may do it before this game's over!"

⸺✦⸺

In the top of the ninth with the score tied, Davis came to the plate with two outs. "All right, baby face," Crudden yelled. "Let's see if you can take the heat."

Davis approached the plate warily. He was a good batter, but the Lions pitcher was the best he had seen all year. Beans had given him instruction. "Don't try to hit. Just take the strikes."

That was fine with Davis. He felt relief, but when Crudden threw the first ball, it headed right toward his head. Davis had exceptionally fast reflexes, and he fell in the dirt at once. He got up, dusting himself off and hearing the Fairhope crowd yelling and booing at the pitcher.

"I missed you that time."

The umpire warned Crudden, but it made no difference. His next ball came in lower and faster and it caught Davis right on the thigh.

Roger yelled and dashed out straight toward Crudden. The rest of the Mountaineers followed him, and the benches emptied in a wild melee. "Would you look at that," Aunt Kezia yelled. She saw the sheriff, Pardue Jessup, watching and said, "Sheriff, you're a lawman, ain't you? Get out there and stop that!"

Jessup grinned. "I'll just do that. Come on, Ed."

Ed Hathcock, the chief of police, joined Pardue, and they charged out on the field. It took both of them to pull the players apart, and there was more than one bloody nose and bruised face by the time they got it stopped.

The umpire was red in the face. He felt embarrassed by losing control of the game, and he said to Davis, "Are you able to play, son?"

"Sure," Davis said.

"Take your base."

Davis trotted out to first base and stood there. He felt good, and Crudden, being a left-hander, was facing him all the time. It was an advantage left-handed pitchers had staring right at first base. They were hard to steal against.

Another player came up to bat. Crudden watched him and went into his windup. Davis somehow knew this was the time. As soon as the windup started, he shot off the base and headed for second. He knew the Lions catcher had a good arm, but with his head down he ran as hard as he'd ever run in his life. In the distance, he heard the ump yell, "Strike!" He threw himself forward, and he felt his fingers touch the bag and instantly heard the thud of the ball into the second baseman's hand.

"Safe!" the umpire yelled, and a glad cry went up from the Fairhope supporters along with yells of rage from the Fort Smith crowd.

Roger came up to bat then, and his eyes were squinted. He took two called strikes then two balls, and then he pointed his bat over straight at the pitcher. "Crudden, I'm going to knock this one in your ear."

Crudden merely laughed. He was pitching a great game and was confident that his team would get him a score sooner or later. He reared back and threw as hard a ball as he had ever thrown, but as soon as he released it he knew that he had thrown it right over the center of the plate. There was nothing a pitcher could do once the ball was out of his hands, and when he heard the crack of Roger's bat, he began to curse. He did not even look to see the flight of the ball, for he knew the meaning of that sound.

"A home run," he said in disgust. "These hicks have beat us with that good-for-nothing pitcher."

Davis came in and was greeted by the entire team as soon as he touched the plate. Roger came in right behind him, and the two were the heroes of the hour.

Lanie ran out on the field. The game was over, but she had trouble getting to Davis. Finally, when she pressed her way through, she threw her arms around Davis and whispered, "Davis, Daddy will be so proud!"

Davis's eyes were misted over. "I hope he will be, Sis."

Roger said, "What about me? I hit the home run. Don't I get a hug?" He picked Lanie up, swung her around, and then kissed her right on the cheek. The crowd was wild, and pandemonium reigned. The hated Lions had bit the dust!

Aunt Kezia waited and walked over to where the disgusted Lions were beginning to pull their equipment together. She walked up to Ben Crudden, the pitcher, and said, "I got half a mind to shoot you."

Crudden was in a bad humor. "Get out of here, old lady." He suddenly stopped and yelled, "Hey, put that thing away!" for Aunt Kezia had pulled a pistol out of her purse.

"Wouldn't do no good to shoot you in the head. You ain't got nothin' there. Maybe I ought to just shoot you in the foot."

"Somebody get her out of here!" Crudden yelled.

Pardue Jessup had witnessed this and came over smiling. "Are you gonna shoot him, Aunt Kezia?"

"I reckon not. Why don't you just arrest him."

"On what charge?" Pardue laughed.

"Being stupid."

"I don't think that's against the law. If it was," Pardue said, "the whole team would be in jail. Come on, Aunt Kezia, don't shoot him. He's humiliated enough as it is."

⤙ CHAPTER 5 ⤚

A s Lanie poured the skillet full of popcorn into small bowls for individual servings, she was thinking about the two weeks that had passed since the county fair. It was now the end of July, and she should have forgotten all about the Ferris wheel episode, as she had come to think of it, but she had not. Louise Langley and her parents had given her nothing but hard looks since then. Roger had laughed it off saying that they would get over it, but Lanie was not at all sure.

She had always had a difficult time with the Langleys. Roger and Louise's younger sister, Helen, was Lanie's age, so they had grown up in the same circles. Helen always treated the Freemans like they were from the wrong side of the tracks and never bothered to hide her disdain. It didn't help that Helen was a terrible student and Lanie had constantly made A's—it just gave Helen one more thing to dislike about the Freemans. *Thank goodness Helen's away at school for a year*, Lanie thought. She was glad she didn't have to deal with Helen's unpleasantness on top of everything else.

Putting the bowls of popcorn onto trays, she went into the living room, where the entire family was sitting around listening to *Amos and Andy*. The radio program was taking the country by storm, and Davis suddenly laughed and shook his head. "That Kingfish is some character. He's always trying to do in Andy some way or another."

"Hey, here's the popcorn!" Cody yelped. He was lying flat on his stomach reading the newspaper and listening to the radio at the same time. Now he jumped up and grabbed one of the bowls and immediately began stuffing it into his mouth.

"Don't eat so fast," Lanie admonished him as she passed out the rest of the bowls. She sat down and gave a sigh of relief. The fatigue seemed to weigh her down into the rocking chair. "What are you reading, Cody?" she asked during one of the commercials for Rinso soap.

"Reading about the tallest building in the world," Cody said. "It says here the Empire State Building is one thousand four hundred and fifty-four feet high. Boy, how'd you like to fall off of that, Davis? Look what it says here." He shoved the paper over to Davis, who was sitting cross-legged eating his popcorn. Davis glanced down, but as Lanie expected, he only said, "Yeah, I see it."

Davis's reading problem was a very real crisis to Lanie. He was behind in school and no one could figure out why he couldn't read. He made straight A's in math where no reading was required and in other subjects that required very little. She had had his eyes examined, and Doctor Bell, the optometrist, had said, "He's got twenty-twenty vision, and there's nothing wrong with his eyes at all."

Corliss had climbed up into Lanie's lap and was eating the popcorn delicately. She looked up and smiled sweetly. Lanie gave her a squeeze and said, "You're a sweet punkin'."

"So are you, Lanie," Corliss piped up. "Can I play the piano?"

Corliss loved the piano. It was a matter of wonder to everyone that even at the age of three she was able, with her stubby fingers, to pick out tunes. Cody had announced that she was going to be a famous concert pianist one day.

Maeva, who was lying on the couch, was fishing in her bowl for popcorn. "Look at this. There's nothing in here but old maids."

Everyone turned to stare at Maeva, and Davis demanded, "What do you mean, old maids?"

"Why, that's what you call popcorn that don't pop," Maeva said. She was in her pajamas. Looking with disgust down at the bowl, she then held it out. "Look at them. Half of 'em didn't even pop."

"I don't know why you call them old maids," Davis said.

"Why, because. Popcorn that won't pop is like a woman that's never had a romance."

Aunt Kezia was sitting in her chair dozing. She complained constantly about her lack of sleep, but actually she slept all the time. Now she woke up and cackled. "Old maids, eh? I never heard popcorn called that, but I've known plenty of women that didn't have no romance in their life."

"You ought not to call people old maids, Maeva," Lanie said. "It's not nice to call names."

"I didn't make it up. I read it in a story," Maeva protested.

"When my husband was the peace officer in Abilene, a funny thing happened." Aunt Kezia reached down and picked up a handful of popcorn, stuffed it into her mouth, and then talked around it. "There was this little, two-bit newspaper and what we called in those days a maiden lady, one that never had no husband, died. Her name was Nancy Jones. Well, the fellow that wrote the obituaries was in the hospital. He was a part-time dentist and he got shot by a patient that didn't like the way he fixed his tooth. So the editor had to ask the fellow that wrote the sports news to write her obituary. "

"What'd he write, Aunt Kezia?" Cody asked, a grin spreading across his face.

"Well, he done the best he could. I remember every word of it. It said:

"Here lie the bones of Nancy Jones,
For her, death held no terrors.
She lived an old maid,
She died an old maid.
No hits — no runs — no errors!"

Davis whooped with laughter and cried out, "That's the best obituary I ever heard."

"Well, I don't think it's funny. You shouldn't make fun of people. Not every woman is going around looking for romance," Lanie said stiffly. "You know Miss Effie Johnson runs that bank and she never married. And if it hadn't been for her, we would have been put out on the street."

Indeed, Effie Johnson had helped save their homeplace by refusing to foreclose against the demands of Otis Langley, but Maeva shook her head, saying, "She'd trade all that money in the bank for a husband and kids, Lanie. Besides, she's ruined her sister Cora's life trying to make her just like she is. She's nothin' but a frump."

The argument went on loudly for some time, but soon their favorite program, *Fibber Magee and Molly*, came on, and Lanie was glad to sit back and relax. After it was over she shooed the kids all off to bed. There were the usual protests, but she insisted, "Tomorrow is church day, and we don't want to be late like we were last week."

Lanie washed Corliss, put her in bed, and told her a story. Corliss went to sleep almost at once, so Lanie went back to the kitchen and began, as usual, making preparations for the breakfast the next morning. She liked to have everything all ready, the eggs in one place, the flour in another, all the dishes washed and ready for a meal.

Aunt Kezia wandered in and walked over to the cabinet. She took a brown bottle out and poured an empty jelly glass half full then complained, "I can't sleep no more without my medicine."

Lanie picked up the bottle and sniffed it. "Why, this is pure alcohol!" she exclaimed.

"It ain't neither. It's my sleepin' medicine made right there in Oklahoma by a purebred Cherokee Indian, a medicine man in his tribe."

Lanie watched with apprehension as the old woman swallowed the mixture, smacked her lips, and put the cap back on the bottle. "There," she said. "That ought to put me to sleep."

"You shouldn't be taking all those patent medicines. You don't have any idea what's in there."

Aunt Kezia sat down and studied Lanie. "Don't you worry about my patent medicines. What I'm worried about is you. You look plum peaked. Maybe you ought to have some of Doctor Alexander's Liver Potion."

"I don't want any of your old patent medicines. There's nothing wrong with me."

"Well, why do you look so worn out, then? I know you work hard, but it's more than that. Ever since the county fair you been mopin' around like a sick coon."

Lanie suddenly sat down on the chair and cupped her chin in one hand. She really had no one to share her feelings with, and the urge became overwhelming to tell someone what was going on in her life. "I've been having sinful feelings."

"What kind of sin? There's sin and then there's sin. They ain't all the same."

"I know that, Aunt Kezia. It's—well, I have impure thoughts about a fellow who hugged me."

"Who was it—that Langley boy?" Aunt Kezia demanded. She leaned forward, her eyes bright, and added, "I expect it was. I've seen him huggin' on you."

"I'm not telling who it was, but it bothers me. I don't think a woman's supposed to have feelings like I'm having."

"Well, stuff and nonsense!" Aunt Kezia exclaimed. "You just passin' from one stage to another, Lanie girl. I've seen it happening ever since I've been here. When a young girl becomes a woman, things happen to her outwardly. You've seen that when you're bustin' out of your clothes that you wore last year. Your figure's developin'. Well, things are happenin' on the inside too." She grinned suddenly and said, "You'll have to tell me all about it, but right now I'm gettin' sleepy. I'll get up early in the morning and you can tell me everything."

Lanie laughed suddenly, got up, and went over and hugged Aunt Kezia. "I'm not telling you anything. You're terrible."

"I guess I'm a hellion just like I was when I was fourteen years old. Good night, sweetie."

Lanie waited until the old woman left the room, then she looked over at Beau, who was asleep braced against the wall. A smile crossed her lips, and she walked over, picked up his tail, and let it fall with a thump. The big dog did not move. Lanie picked up his head, and it was like picking up a dead weight. She dropped the head and it thumped on the floor, but Beau did not even condescend to open his eyes. "You sleep like a dead dog, Beau, I declare!" Lanie exclaimed.

She turned the light out and went upstairs. She washed her face in the bathroom, brushed her teeth, then came back and put on her nightgown. It was only ten o'clock and she felt wide awake. She sat down in her chair, picked up her Bible, and began to read. She could not concentrate her thoughts, and when Cap'n Brown came over and pawed at her, she let him get on her lap. "Well, Cap'n Brown, you can't sleep either?" She stroked the silky hair of the big Manx cat and leaned forward and kissed his forehead. "I'm going to tell you what I wouldn't tell anybody else. Those impure feelings I had were for Doctor Owen Merritt. Don't you think I'm awful, Cap'n Brown?"

But Cap'n Brown apparently did not think she was so awful. He began to knead his claws into her thighs, something that seemed to give him pleasure. He leaned forward and butted her with his head, and Lanie put up with the discomfort for the sake of baring her soul. Sometimes she shared these thoughts in the journals that she kept, but there was always a chance that somebody would find them. Aunt Kezia was nosy enough to ferret them out! Nevertheless she picked up her journal and began to write, intent on getting her soul on to the page:

I know Roger likes me, but he's young and so am I. That's why I think it's wrong for me to have feelings for Owen. He's almost thirty years old and I'm only seventeen. Of course, some girls marry older men, but he's engaged to Louise. Her family has money and she's educated. I've just got to stop making a fool out of myself.

She grabbed Cap'n Brown's ears and looked into his face. She pulled at them until his eyes were slitted, and he said, "Wow!"

"Wow to you. Now get off my lap." She shoved the big cat off, picked up the Bible, and began to read.

She read for some time, concentrating on Scripture. She was reading the story of the temptation of Jesus, and a thought came to her suddenly. Ideas for poems came like that to Lanie. She didn't know where they came from, but suddenly they just burst, like someone striking a match in a dark room, throwing off light.

"I wonder what the devil thought when Jesus came telling everyone he was the Son of God?" she murmured. Even as she spoke, a poem began arranging itself in her mind. She sat there moving words around, exchanging lines. It was one of the pure pleasures of her life. Her high school English teacher, Eden Marie Dunsmore, had taught her how to write dramatic monologues. She had said, "You've got to put yourself inside the body of the one you're writing the poem about. Have him or her speak out. Pretend you are that person."

Lanie had written many dramatic monologues, but lately she was concentrating on biblical figures. Now she was stumped. "How can I try to put myself in the body of Lucifer? That wouldn't be right."

Still, the idea was fascinating, and finding her writing pad and pencil, she began to write. She worked quickly, writing down what formed in her mind, and as she wrote it changed. Finally, after much scratching, she recopied the poem and looked down at it. "Got to have a title," she said. "I guess I could just call it 'Lucifer.'" She read the poem aloud softly.

Lucifer

"And he was there in the wilderness forty days, tempted of Satan."
(Mark 1:13)

They call him "Carpenter" — but O, ye spheres
I see in him mine ancient enemy
Made flesh! Thus now I race in full career
Defeated by this one from Galilee.
How many dignitaries, prophets, priests
I've lured up to temptation's razor edge,
Then plucked them down to death without release.
Now hear, ye hellish powers, my deadly pledge:
I'll empty hell! With demons fill the earth
Until it cracks! We'll sweep on mighty pinions
Wreaking nature to untimely birth;
We'll have this healer under hell's dominion!
What though he spurned my bread — my power — my glory?
When he lies dead, earth will forget his story!

For some time Lanie studied the poem, taking pleasure in how the words and the rhymes had worked out. She had never understood why writing poetry gave her such pleasure, but for a long time writing had been therapy for her. When life pressed in, she could always go to her poetry and find peace.

Finally she closed the tablet, concealed it under the clothing in the bottom drawer of her chest, then turned the light out and jumped into bed. Cap'n Brown joined her, shoving against her back and purring like a small engine.

"Good night, Cap'n Brown," Lanie said. "You sleep well tonight."

Cap'n Brown answered, "Wow!"

Getting off to church was always a hectic affair for Lanie. If she let Cody alone, he would have gone dirty as a pig. Davis was a little bit easier to get under way, but Maeva argued from the time she got up to the time they left for church. She never liked church and usually offered to stay home and keep Corliss, but Lanie always said, "No. Corliss is going to church just like we all do. Now get yourself ready, Maeva."

The weather was beautiful, the sky was blue, and it looked hard enough to scratch a match on as the ancient pickup rattled along. White clouds drifted lazily across the sky, and Maeva said, "It's going to be hotter than a pistol in that church. I don't see why we have to come every Sunday."

"Because it's God's house and it's God's day, Maeva. Now hush."

Maeva continued to grumble and complain. Finally they arrived at the white church with the steeple pointing up like a finger toward the blue heaven. Lanie got the others established in the Sunday school classes where they belonged, and she herself went to the nursery and kept Corliss along with half a dozen other new babies.

After the Sunday school hour was over, she collected them all, and it was like trying to drive bees across the desert, she thought as she collared Davis and Maeva and got them into their customary seats, front and center, three rows back. They could look right up at the preacher, and Maeva hated it. "I don't see why we have to be a spectacle and sit right down in the front. I think the Bible says you ain't supposed to be in the uppermost seat of the synagogue."

"Where's it say that?" Cody demanded.

"I don't know, but if it don't say it, it ought to. Look over there. There's Minnie Hopkins and that worthless husband of hers. Everybody knows he's runnin' around with that Jezebel from over at Seven Point, but there he sits all sanctified and slicked up. I hate a hypocrite!"

"Be quiet, Maeva," Lanie whispered fiercely, "somebody will hear you."

"I hope they do. They need to."

Once the service started and the younger Freemans were shut down, Lanie turned Corliss over to Davis saying, "You watch out for Corliss now, and don't let Maeva leave."

"Maybe I better tie her down." Davis grinned. He pulled Corliss close and hugged her. "Me and this old girl will be all right. You go on up to that choir."

As always, Lanie joined the choir. She had a pure soprano voice, and she had urged Maeva to join her, for Maeva could sing much better than she herself could. Maeva was adamant about this and solidly refused.

The service began, as usual, with a brief prayer, then three songs out of the Baptist Hymnal: "The Old Rugged Cross," "All Hail the Power of Jesus' Name," and "What a Friend We Have in Jesus." Then the announcements were made, though they were printed in the bulletin, but Lyndal Mayfair loved to read the announcements and then take the offering. He made a plea for cash, and Lanie saw Maeva's face cloud over, for she hated such things. She could only hope that Maeva would keep her mouth shut!

Finally the choir sang their special, an arrangement by Dempsey Wilson, who was the coach at the high school and also taught math and science. He had a beautiful tenor voice and led the choir with great pleasure. The arrangement was a mixture of three songs all woven together. "When I Survey the Wondrous Cross," "Beneath the Cross of Jesus," and "At the Cross." Despite herself Lanie felt pride in the choir, for Dempsey had done a miraculous job of pulling together rather mediocre talent to form a competent and at times inspiring group.

Finally Brother Prince got up, and Lanie, who was seated at the far right of the choir, saw that there was something different about him. He seemed tense and uncomfortable. He stuttered slightly when he announced his text, and as he made his way through the sermon, Lanie could tell that he was disturbed. She glanced at Ellen Prince, the pastor's wife, who was seated next to her, and could tell that she was also tense.

"What's wrong with the pastor?" she whispered. But Ellen shook her head and her lips tightened.

Mystified, Lanie sat there, and after the invitation "Just as I Am" was begun, she was shocked to see the Langleys, who were Presbyterian, coming down the aisle to join the church. Roger was grinning broadly at her, and she wondered why the richest man in town and his family were at the Baptist service. There were rumors that they had been unhappy at the Presbyterian church, that Otis Langley was not able to manipulate the Presbyterian pastor, Alex Digby, and there had been some stormy meetings. The rumors came fairly well documented since Henrietta Green, the telephone operator, made it her business to listen in on conversations and pass the information along. She was also a member of the Presbyterian church, so people tended to trust her information.

Finally, after the pastor had spoken quietly to Otis Langley, he turned to the congregation and said, "We are happy to have Mr. Otis Langley, his wife, Martha, his son, Roger, his daughter Louise, and his daughter Helen who is away at school, requesting membership in our church." Brother Prince hesitated and then said, "Most of you are aware that they have been attending the Presbyterian church, but Mr.

Langley informs me that previously his family were all members in good standing of Calvary Baptist Church in Oklahoma City. They now want to return to their roots and be a part of our fellowship. Do I hear a motion that they be received?"

Deoin Jinks, the neighbor who lived across the street from the Freemans, piped up at once. "I move we accept them into our church." A second came quickly, and Reverend Prince said, "Those in favor of receiving the Langleys please be known by saying aye."

The ayes were rather unenthusiastic, and Lanie wondered in a flash, *What would happen if I voted no?* But when the pastor said, "Those opposed vote by nay," she kept her mouth shut, as did the rest of the congregation.

"I'll ask the Langleys to stand here. After the benediction you'll want to come by and welcome them into our fellowship. But first I have a word to say."

Lanie looked up at Brother Prince. She saw that he was rather pale and knew he was about to say something difficult.

"This may come as a surprise to some of you but not to others. My wife, Ellen, and I have felt for a long time that God was going to call us to a foreign mission field. Well, the call has come, and we have been accepted by the mission board of the Southern Baptist Convention as missionary volunteers to serve in Africa."

A sudden chill went down Lanie's back, and she heard a murmur of dismay going across the congregation. She listened as the pastor continued to speak. He spoke briefly of how he had learned to love this church and how it was wrenching to leave it, but still God must be obeyed.

"We will be leaving sooner than I would like, for we have to be enrolled in the language school in two weeks. Ellen and I are filled with joy over this calling, but we are saddened to leave you, our treasured brothers and sisters in Christ. I ask you to pray for my family as we go to serve God in Africa."

He asked the congregation to rise and invited Ed Hathcock, the chief of police, to pronounce the benediction, ending the service.

Afterward the crowd divided itself. Some of the congregation headed for the door, and others went forward. Lanie came out of the choir loft and hesitated. She knew that the Langleys did not care for her. She had beaten out their son, Roger, for academic honors when she was only a freshman, and Otis Langley had been furious, especially since his daughter Helen, the same age as Lanie, did so poorly in school. He was also angry that he had been unable to manipulate his way into buying their homeplace. But Lanie took a deep breath and went at once to get in the line. Otis Langley was first. He stared at her without speaking, and Lanie said, "Welcome to our church, Brother Langley." He nodded without saying a word. His wife did the same. When Lanie smiled at Louise and said, "I'm glad to see you coming to join us, Louise," Louise nodded and said stiffly, "Thank you."

Roger, however, was grinning from ear to ear. When Lanie put her hand out, he grabbed it with both of his, pulled her forward, and said, "Hey, isn't there something in the Bible about greeting the brother with a holy kiss?"

"Roger!" Lanie whispered in protest. She could not keep the smile from coming to her lips. "I can see you're going to be as bad a Baptist as you were a Presbyterian."

"You'll have to take me under your wing. I feel I'll need spiritual counsel."

"I know the kind of counseling you need. Now turn loose of my hand."

Lanie turned to Brother Prince and could barely speak, for she loved the pastor and his family with all of her heart. She tried to say how happy she was, but the tears came to her eyes. "I'm going to miss you so much, Brother Prince. We all are."

"And I'll miss you too, Lanie. You'll never know how proud I am of you."

❦

It was a warm afternoon, and Aunt Kezia and Lanie were snapping beans out on the back porch. Beau was at their side, and once in a while Lanie would give him a small portion. "The crazy dog likes beans," she said. "I never saw a dog that liked beans." August had come, and the First Baptist Church had activated the machinery for finding a new pastor.

Aunt Kezia changed the subject. "I ain't never liked the way Baptists get their preachers," she announced.

"What do you mean, Aunt Kezia? How else will we get a preacher?"

"All this nonsense about a pulpit committee and sendin' people out huntin' for one like they was huntin' for a possum or a coon or somethin'." She shook her head in disgust. "It ain't fittin' and it ain't pleasin' to the Lord."

"Well, how do you think we ought to find a pastor?"

"Let God send him. Elijah didn't wait for no pulpit committee. He just up and went."

"I don't think it would work that way." Lanie thought for a moment. "I'm going to miss them so much. I don't see how the new pastor could be any better than Brother Prince."

"Well, he's gone to Africa to preach to the heathen. Now God's got to send somebody to preach to the heathen here in Fairhope!"

The Dew Drop Inn was packed for the noon lunch. The ceiling fans were moving the air around, but the heat was still oppressive. Charlie Poindexter was the cook and a fine one too, although he had little enough imagination. The special on Wednesday was always meat loaf, fried potatoes, and greens. You could order anything you wanted to, but that was what you were likely to get.

Sister Myrtle Poindexter served the meals, snatching them out of the pass-through and slamming them down in front of the customers at the counter and the individual tables. She took the orders almost with irritation, and from time to time she would admonish a customer, "You don't need none of them pork chops, Ellie Rysner. They just make you fat up even more."

Sweat was pouring off of Sister Myrtle. She mopped her brow with a red bandanna she kept tucked inside of her apron pocket and paused in front of Henrietta Green. "What's that you say you heard on the telephone about the preacher that's comin'?"

Doctor Oscar Givens looked up from where he was seated across from Orrin Pierce, a lawyer with dark hair and shocking blue eyes. The two ate together frequently, and now Doctor Givens snapped, "Myrtle, this town's bad enough for gossip without you encouraging Henrietta."

Sister Myrtle turned to face Doctor Givens. "People ought to live so they don't have to be ashamed of what they say on the phone, Oscar. Now, you hush. I want to hear what Henrietta says."

Henrietta Green was a tall, thin woman with blond hair and faded blue eyes. She was thirty-five, a widow, and a Presbyterian. Now she looked around, and a look of pride came to her. Everyone in the restaurant was forced to listen when Myrtle spoke, for her voice rattled the windows. "He's comin' Sunday. His name is Reverend Ellis Clifford. He's a good friend of Otis Langley. Mr. Langley talked to him over the phone just yesterday. Told him he was going to do all he could to get him called here as the new pastor."

Phineas Delaughter, the mayor of the town, was a tall lanky man. He had a mouth full of Charlie's meat loaf, but now he swallowed it and said with disgust, "Well, Langley didn't wait long before he started trying to take over the Baptist church. He couldn't do it with the Presbyterians, so now he's trying it with us."

"Hush up, Phineas," Myrtle said. "I want to hear about this fellow. What's he like?"

"Well," Henrietta said, enjoying the attention, "he's fifty-two years old and he's been teachin' in a seminary. The way I understood it, I don't reckon he's ever been a pastor."

Sister Myrtle reached over and got a plate full of meat and vegetables. She slammed it down in front of Mamie Dorr so hard that the blue-eyed blonde jumped and cried out, "Don't be so rough!" Mamie owned the Curl Up and Dye beauty parlor and was a real flapper with short skirts and bobbed hair. She had been married, but word in town was that her husband had committed suicide. The sheriff, Pardue Jessup, had grinned. "She probably gave the pore fellow too much lovin'."

Sister Myrtle stared at Henrietta, then looked around and said in a voice that filled the whole building, "We don't need no school-teacher in the pulpit. We need some hellfire and damnation preacher who's not afraid to preach against sin."

Orrin Pierce grinned and said, "Which sin do you think needs the most preachin' against, Sister Myrtle?"

"Don't you be makin' fun of sin, Orrin Pierce. You need to get right yourself. It's time for the folks in this town to turn or burn!"

❦

The matter of the Reverend Ellis Clifford became the center of the town's attention. Everyone took sides, even those who did not belong to the Baptist church. On the day that Reverend Clifford came to preach, the church was full, not only of Baptists but of Methodists, Presbyterians, and even Pentecostals.

However, after the reverend finished his message, Gerald Pink, who owned the pharmacy and was also chairman of the board of dea-cons, asked everyone but members of the church to leave.

Sister Myrtle, who had managed to get a substitute to preach in her own church, said, "What are you going to do? Jesus never done nothin' in secret."

"I'm sorry, Sister Myrtle, but it's a Baptist custom."

Sister Myrtle got up and sniffed. "Well, I'll give my vote right now even though I ain't got one. But if I had one, it'd be against the feller. He's got more degrees than he's got temperature. That's what I say."

A laugh went around, but after the room was cleared, a business meeting was called, and it set a record for business meetings, at least as far as time was concerned. Otis Langley had summoned everyone over whom he had any influence and encouraged them—which was another way of saying demanded—that they call Reverend Clifford.

But there was strong opposition. Lanie was hoping desperately that the church would not call Reverend Clifford, for he was not her idea of a good preacher at all. He constantly referred to what the Scripture said in the original language, and his greatest fear seemed to be that someone would understand what he was saying.

Finally Effie Johnson, owner of the bank, stood up and said in a clear voice, "We can't vote until after the revival. We're bringing in an experienced evangelist to lead us, and I'm trusting that God will speak to us and bring us all to our knees. Then we can make a wise choice about the pastor."

Langley's face grew red. "What difference is it going to make, a revival? Somebody will come in and stir up a bunch of excitement, then two weeks later it'll be all over." His voice rose, and he cried, "Who is this evangelist anyhow? I never heard of him."

Effie Johnson was cool as she answered Langley. "He's a close friend of Brother Prince. He grew up in Africa, Brother Prince informed me, the son of missionary parents. He came back to the States, and he's been preaching in the poor sections of Chicago doing a great work there."

Langley at once objected. "He's a Yankee. We need a Southern man here."

There was considerable heated discussion, and Lanie was disturbed to see that the church was already divided in such a short time after Brother Prince's departure. She knew in her heart that Langley himself had created this division, and she was relieved when Brother Pink announced firmly, "We won't vote on calling a pastor until after the fall revival. Business meeting adjourned."

PART TWO

—✦— ✦—

The Pastor

⟡ CHAPTER 6 ⟡

The sun was falling rapidly in the west as Lanie parked the pickup in front of Planter's Bank. Hopping out, she grabbed two large grocery sacks and entered the bank. Cora Johnson looked up from her desk and rose at once. "Hello, Lanie." She smiled. "Did you bring something good?" Cora was an attractive woman of thirty-eight with light brown hair and warm brown eyes. She had the most beautiful complexion that Lanie had ever seen and a fine figure, which was not obvious because of the frumpy clothes she managed to wear.

"Yes, I did, Miss Cora."

"Good. Take them in to Effie. I hope you brought some tomatoes. You have the best in the whole world."

"I have a whole sack full here. I know how much you and Miss Effie like them."

"Go right on in. There's nobody with her."

Lanie put one bag down, knocked on the door marked President, and when she heard an invitation, she opened the door, picked up the bag, and stepped inside. She closed the door with her heel and said, "I brought your vegetables, Miss Effie."

Effie Johnson got up at once. At the age of fifty-eight she had a stern look. She was a tall woman with gray hair and sharp brown eyes. It was rumored that she had once been in love with a wastrel who had been after her money. He jilted her, and she swore off men, according to the story.

"Let me see what you have," Effie said. She was a warmhearted woman beneath the stern exterior, and now she began rummaging through the sacks Lanie brought. "Look at this okra!" she exclaimed with pleasure. "Young and tender. I can just taste them now. Nothing like fried okra—and look at these tomatoes." She held a beautiful red tomato in her hand and shook her head. "I could just bite into it right now, but that would be a little bit messy." She continued examining the squash and the mustard greens, and finally she said, "Well, you got a fine garden this year. I don't know what Cora and I would do without your good vegetables. Here, let me pay you for them."

"I wish you'd let me give them to you, Miss Effie. You've done so much for us."

"Nonsense. Business is business." She went over to the desk, picked up her purse, and extracted three bills. "Here. I put a little extra in there because this is quality merchandise."

Lanie took the money and said thank you. Then she said, "Has there been any news about the evangelist?"

"I don't know a thing about it except that Gerald Pink got a phone call from him."

"What did he say?"

"He had mechanical trouble of some kind and won't make it in today, but he'll be here for sure for the service in the morning." She frowned and shook her head. "That's no way for a preacher to behave. He ought to be punctual."

"Well, if he had car trouble, he couldn't help that."

"I suppose not. You know, it's been hard to get the word out. We didn't even have a picture of him to put in the paper. We had to run the story, even though all we know about him is that he spent his youth in Africa and has been doing mission work on the streets of Chicago."

"I'm sure he'll be a good preacher. Brother Prince wouldn't have recommended him if he weren't."

"I suppose you're right, but it makes me nervous. I like for things to be done properly and on time."

"I'll bet we have a full house every night."

"I doubt that," Effie said. "People have lost their hunger for God. They're staying home and listening to radio programs like *Little Orphan Annie* and things like that."

"Don't you like *Little Orphan Annie*?"

"It's for children."

"What about *Amos and Andy*?"

"I can't abide that foolishness."

"Well, I have to admit I think it's funny. Be good for you to laugh a little bit, Miss Effie."

"I've got a bank to run and a sister to take care of and a church to look out for. I don't have time to relax."

"Well, you've had time for us. I can never thank you enough for helping save our place. Daddy mentions it every time I go visit him."

Effie Johnson's face softened. "How is Forrest?"

"Well, he tries to hide it by laughing a lot, but he's real sad. He's always been an outdoor person, and now he's in prison."

"But didn't the warden put him in charge of his dogs and his horse?"

"Oh yes, so it's a lot better. I'll be going to see him right after the revival's over."

"Well, let me know. I'll make up a little package to send him. Razor blades and the things a man needs."

"Thank you, Miss Effie. Don't worry about the revival now. I'm sure God's going to do a great thing."

Effie paused. "You know, Sister Myrtle said something once I've never forgotten. She said she'd like to see things get out of control in church services. I thought that was the most foolish thing I'd ever heard. Bankers, I guess, believe in control. But as I read the Bible, I notice that things do get out of control sometimes, like on the day of Pentecost. Everything was going fine until suddenly things started happening." She grinned unexpectedly and looked almost attractive. "Maybe that's what we need. The sound of a mighty, rushing wind."

"And speaking another tongue?"

"Well, that might be going a little far for Baptists. Be all right for Sister Myrtle, of course. Now you run along, child. Let me know if you need anything. I know you're having a hard time keeping the family together, but we'll always find a way."

Lanie suddenly went over and put her arms around Effie. She had never done such a thing before, but she had learned to love this stiff older woman who hid such a big heart. "We can never thank you enough, Miss Effie," she said. "I feel like, in a way, that God's given you to us to look out for us just like Mama would have done."

Effie Johnson stood stiffly for a moment. She was not a woman given to emotional gestures. But as the young woman held her, she suddenly felt a warmth and a joy that she had been able to play a part in saving this young woman and her family. "There, there," she said, patting her on the shoulder, "it was nothing."

"It wasn't nothing," Lanie insisted. She stepped back, and her lips were trembling. "It was *something*, and God is going to reward you for it."

Effie Johnson said, "I think he already has. Just being a part of your family has meant a lot to me."

"I'll see you at church in the morning."

"You sing real good. I understand you're going to sing a special."

"Yes. Brother Wilson asked me to."

"I'll be looking forward to it."

As Lanie left the bank, she felt a glow of satisfaction. She would never be able to repay Effie Johnson for her help and support during the hard time after her father had left. She could have foreclosed on the homeplace at any time but instead fought a fierce battle against Otis Langley to keep the bank from foreclosing. Now the note was paid off, and they had a place to live, and the stern woman that many people feared had helped them to keep it.

❦

Sunday school was over, and Gerald Pink was beside himself. "What are we going to do?" he moaned to Phineas Delaughter. The two of them were pacing outside because there was no sign of the evangelist.

"We'll just have to do the best we can," Delaughter said. He wore an ill-fitting suit, and his lanky form expressed dissatisfaction. "I can't believe a preacher would miss an appointment."

"But what will we do, Phineas?"

"You go inside and tell Brother Wilson that we're going to have to improvise. We'll have the testimony service. You can lead that, and then we'll have a music service. Nothing but hymns and special music."

"The place is packed—what are people going to think?"

"Well, I know what I think," Phineas said angrily. "I think that whippersnapper needs a lesson in manners! Now go on in and get started."

Delaughter walked back and forth, looking up and down the road. He heard the doxology break out inside, as it always did, and knew the service was started. "Disgraceful!" he exclaimed. Finally he heard the voice of Gerald Pink and shook his head in despair. *We won't have a soul here tomorrow night. All this preparation for a revival meetin' and now no preacher.*

Even as the thought passed his mind, he heard a roar and looked up hoping to see the evangelist, but it was only a man on a motorcycle. He watched as the cyclist came barreling in, apparently at full speed, slammed on his brakes, and brought the machine to a screeching stop. He slammed the kickstand down, stepped off, and lifted the goggles from his eyes. He was wearing a soft cap, blue jeans, a colorful blue and red shirt, and motorcycle boots. He was a tall young man apparently in his midtwenties. "Hello there," he said. "Is this the First Baptist Church?"

"Yes, it is. You come for the meeting?"

"Sure did." The man draped his cloth cap over the motorcycle handlebars and did the same with his goggles. He was a well-built fellow, Delaughter noticed, with a wealth of hair, black as a crow's wing. His electric blue eyes contrasted with his tan face, and when he smiled, his teeth looked very white.

"Come on. I'll find you a seat. Sorry we don't have a preacher this morning. The evangelist couldn't make it."

"Yes, he could. That's me. I'm Colin Ryan."

Delaughter stared at the young man, who looked like he would be much more at home in a pool hall than in a church. "You—you're our evangelist?"

Colin Ryan nodded cheerfully. "Sure am. Sorry to be late. I'll explain to the congregation how it happened. Sounds like they've already started."

"Yes—well, we planned just to have a testimony service and singing."

"Not going to let you cheat me out of a sermon. What's your name, brother?"

"Phineas Delaughter."

Ryan held out his hand, and when Delaughter took it, it was like being gripped by a Stillson wrench. "Glad to meet you, Brother Phineas. Let's get inside there. But before we go, let's you and me pray that God will do a great, miraculous thing this morning."

"Well—that would be good." Phineas bowed his head. Colin Ryan began to pray in a way that Delaughter was not familiar with. It seemed like the young fellow was actually demanding that God do something.

Finally the prayer was over, and the evangelist winked. "You better stand back, Brother Phineas. God's going to do something great this morning!"

Lanie was in the choir, and she was one of the first to see the man who came through the front door. She thought he was a visitor, but he looked strange even for a visitor. She took in the faded jeans, the colorful shirt, and the boots and expected him to take a seat somewhere near the back. The ushers had put out chairs since the pews were all filled, but instead he strolled right down the aisle smiling, and as he came forward, Lanie realized with a shock he was coming to the rostrum. Instead of walking up the two steps that led to the platform, he simply leaped up with a graceful motion, turned around, and joined in the song. The hymn was "When We All Get to Heaven," and when the young man joined in, his tenor voice seemed to fill the room. It was a powerful, clear, ringing voice, but even more striking was the joy with which he sang. When they got to the chorus, he practically drowned out the rest of the choir.

When we all get to heaven
What a day of rejoicing that will be,
When we all see Jesus,
We'll sing and shout the victory.

Dempsey Wilson was waving his arms around, but as the song ended he laughed and said, "Well, I don't know if we got an evangelist or not, but it looks like I'm about to lose my job as choir director."

"Not a bit of it, brother. Not a bit. What's your name?"

"Dempsey Wilson."

"I'm Colin Ryan." He shook Dempsey's hand, then waved at the choir. "Good to hear all that fine singing." He turned to the congregation and said easily, "I'm sorry to be late, but I know you'll understand. Last night I was on my way in and came across a wreck down in Springdale. Three people were badly hurt, and I was the first one there. One of them was dying, and I stayed with him. Went with him to the hospital. He didn't make it in this life, but he gave his heart to Jesus. Amen! Glory to God and the Lamb forever! He's singing with Jesus right now. Isn't that glorious?"

Lanie felt a sudden excitement as she saw that the congregation was stunned. The sheer dramatic intensity of the young evangelist was something new and unexpected. She listened as he introduced himself, briefly touching on his early life in Africa among the Masai and then his work in Chicago among the homeless and the alcoholics who roamed the streets of that great city.

"But God has sent me here, and we're going to see a great harvest. I don't hold much for bulletins, but I do hold with the Holy Spirit, so I feel led right now to preach. If it's all right with you, we'll just get right at it." Reaching into his back pocket, he pulled his New Testament out and said, "I don't need this, for we all know this verse. Someone called it the Bible in a nutshell. It's John 3:16." He held the Bible up and said in a ringing voice with his eyes flashing, "For God so loved the world, that he gave his only begotten Son, that whosoever believeth in him shall not perish but have everlasting life."

The First Baptist Church of Fairhope never forgot that sermon! Those that were there would refer to it often as a point of reference. They would say, "It was when Ryan preached his first sermon," or "It was two months after Colin preached his born-again sermon."

And that was what the sermon was. Over and over again Ryan would cry, "You *must* be born again! There's no other way."

Lanie, being in the choir, saw that the church was mesmerized. Many were fascinated, but others appeared angry, such as Otis Langley and those who followed him. She saw with a shock that the members of her own family were staring at the preacher as if he were from another planet. Maeva, who never listened to a sermon but studied the maps in the Bible or sometimes sneaked in a true romance, was watching with eyes wide open, her lips slightly parted. Cody was stock still. His face was pale, and Lanie could not understand what his problem was.

No one in the First Baptist Church had ever heard a man quote so many Scriptures, giving chapter and verse. He ranged to and fro through the Old Testament and the New Testament, from Genesis to Revelation. And never once did his voice lose power. He was not shouting, but there was an intensity to it such as none of them had ever heard.

Finally he came to his conclusion. "I've told you that Jesus is the way," he said, and his voice grew soft. "He's the only way. Those of you who know him are safe forever. Those of you who do not are condemned. You must be born again. Some of you this morning have been touched by the Spirit of God. I've seen it in your eyes. You long for peace, and you long to have this Jesus I preach as your Savior. We're going to sing an old invitation hymn. We don't even need books for it. Brother Wilson, sing the best invitation in the world, 'Just as I Am.'"

The choir began to sing and the congregation joined in. The sermon had touched Lanie's heart, but still she was shocked to see people beginning to come forward. This was almost unheard of at the beginning of a revival. It usually took at least a week for the first to break down before God, and for sinners to come forth.

And then she saw him—Cody, her brother!

She watched with astonishment as Cody moved out of the seat, stepping on toes, and resolutely came forward. He was met by Colin Ryan, and she could see that Cody's eyes were filled with tears. She watched as Ryan spoke with him, then the two knelt and the evangelist put his arm around the boy's shoulders. Lanie's heart gave a great leap, and she silently cried out, *Oh, God, he wants to be saved! Bring him into the family of God!*

Everyone was watching the evangelist and Cody, and finally Brother Ryan held his hand up in the sign of victory. "Praise God, my young friend here has found Jesus as his Savior."

Cody got to his feet and his face was aglow. He looked up and saw Lanie watching him and he saw the tears in her eyes.

"Don't cry, Lanie, I'm saved! I'm born again!" he shouted.

Ryan laughed. "That's what I like to see, enthusiasm in a new believer."

Five people found Jesus in that service, and the church felt as if it had been shaken.

Finally Brother Ryan said, "Well, God has begun to do something in this church. It's going to be exciting, isn't it, to see who will be saved next and what sinners will come to Jesus. But now, my brother, I'll turn the service over to you."

Gerald Pink was thrilled. "All in favor of receiving these that have come by baptism, let it be known by saying aye."

The ayes were resounding. There were no nays, of course, although some were looking rather sour.

"We'll schedule a baptism after the revival is over."

"No. I want to be baptized now!"

Everyone stared in astonishment at Cody Freeman. He turned to face Brother Pink, and his eyes were wide open. "I don't want to wait two or three weeks. Jesus said to be baptized. I want it right now."

"But, son," Pink said. "You can't just—"

Colin Ryan suddenly laughed. "What's the name of that little river I crossed to get to this town?"

"Singing River is its name," Dempsey Wilson said.

"Well, that's one of the prettiest rivers I've ever seen, with a pretty name to boot. What about we go baptize you right now, Cody?"

"That would be great, Brother Ryan."

"Anybody who wants to come is welcome."

"But he doesn't have a change of clothes," Pink protested.

"He'll dry out. Any of the rest of you folks that want to get baptized right now, you're welcome. Come on, Cody."

Consternation fell, and Effie Johnson suddenly began to laugh. She leaned over and said to Cora, "I know what Sister Myrtle meant now by things getting out of control. We Baptists get so set in our ways that when God moves we sometimes don't know it."

"But is it all right?" Cora asked.

"If Cody wants it and that young man's ready, then it's all right," Effie said. "Come on. Let's get down to the river with the rest of them."

Singing River was one of the most beautiful rivers in the Ozarks. The water was crystal clear and at times it was a quarter mile wide. During the dry period it shrank somewhat, but there were always deep pools. The fish were fat and numerous, and one of the favorite sports was floating the river in inner tubes.

There had been baptisms in Singing River back before there was a baptismal tank built in the First Baptist Church. The Presbyterians, the Methodists, and the Episcopalians sprinkled, of course, but that would not do for good Baptist folk. It had to be by immersion.

Lanie walked beside Cody holding his hand as they made their way to the river. The whole church was walking, for the river was only a quarter of a mile away. She noticed that Otis Langley was talking to the evangelist Colin Ryan. There was a cloud on Langley's face, but Ryan was merely smiling. He shook his head from time to time, and everyone knew that Langley was trying to persuade Ryan to put the baptism off.

Ryan, however, was not to be contained. When they got to the shallow bank of the river, he did not stop. He waded out until he was waist deep and said, "Are you ready, Cody?"

"Yes!" Cody practically ran out into the river. When he came to stand beside the tall form of Ryan, there was something everlasting and sweet about the sight to Lanie. The hair of the evangelist was as black as the darkest thing in nature while Cody's red hair gave off golden tints as the midday sun blazed down upon them.

"The Scripture says he that believeth and is baptized shall be saved, but he that believeth not shall be damned. I rejoice that this young man takes the command of the Lord Jesus, who is now his Lord, seriously. In Africa baptism is a serious thing. They don't pay much attention to what people say. A man may say he's a Christian, but until he's baptized it doesn't mean anything to those people. Jesus himself felt it was so important that he walked for miles to get baptized by a Baptist preacher. John the Baptist didn't want to do it, but Jesus said it's a righteous thing. It behooveth us to fulfill all righteousness."

And then Colin Ryan put his hand on the back of Cody's neck, held the boy's hands in front of him, and said plainly, "Grab your nose, Cody, so you won't drown."

Then Ryan's voice rose. "In obedience to the command of our Lord and Savior Jesus Christ, I baptize you, my brother, in the name of the Father and of the Son and of the Holy Ghost."

Everyone watched avidly as Ryan lowered the boy into the river, deep down under, then brought him up. Lanie began to applaud. She had never done such a thing at a baptism before, but others took it up, and soon most of the crowd were applauding.

Then Sister Myrtle's voice was suddenly heard. The building where the Fire Baptized Pentecostal Church met was only a few hundred yards away. Evidently someone saw the Baptists flooding to the river, and Sister Myrtle brought her entire flock so they could join in. Sister Myrtle began to shout, "Glory to God! Glory to God!" and even some of the Baptists echoed her cries.

Lanie could not see for the tears in her eyes. She came forward and grabbed Cody, paying no attention to the fact that he was sopping wet. He hugged her and swung her around shouting, "I'm saved by the blood of the Lamb! Sister, why didn't you tell me it was like this to be a Christian?"

Lanie was stunned, and she watched as Cody moved around shaking hands and asking some of the visitors, "Have you ever been saved?"

Maeva moved closer to Lanie. Even she was intimidated. "What's wrong with him, Lanie?"

"He's gotten saved."

"Well, he's acting like a Pentecostal. You think he'll always act like that?" Then she answered her own question. "Well, of course not. It's like the flu, Lanie. He's acting holy right now, but he'll get tired of it quick enough. It'll pass away."

But Lanie was watching the face of her brother, and she said, "No. What's happened to Cody won't pass away. As a matter of fact" — she smiled — "I think it may even get worse!"

CHAPTER 7

With quick practiced motions, Lanie ironed Davis's shirt, ignoring the heat of the living room. The windows were open and a faint breeze stirred the curtains, but even though September had come, the weather still had not broken.

"It's really hot today."

Aunt Kezia looked up from where she was cracking walnuts on an old iron. She held the iron upside down in her lap, hammer in her right hand and a pick on the table beside her. She cracked a walnut, pulled out a small portion of the kernel, and popped it in her mouth. "It was hotter than this in El Paso, Texas, when me and Mr. Butterworth got married. I told him it was so hot we ought to wait till fall, but he just laughed at me and married me anyhow."

The radio was playing a peppy song, "I'm Looking Over a Four-leaf Clover," and Aunt Kezia hummed it under her breath. Then she looked up with disgust. "That's a stupid song," she said firmly. "Four-leaf clovers never brought nobody any luck."

"That's right. It's just superstition."

"What brings people luck is the foot of a rabbit. Has to be the right front foot, though. The left front is no good, and the back feet ain't worth a lead nickel."

Lanie laughed. "You don't really believe that hanging a rabbit's foot around your neck or carrying it in your purse will bring you luck."

Aunt Kezia looked up, her eyes as bright as a crow's. "Why, certain I believe it!" she snapped. She got up, walked across the room, and turned the dial of the radio. The station she picked up was playing a song that was popular when the Depression first hit, "Happy Days Are Here Again."

"That song is about as dumb as you can get," Aunt Kezia said. "Days ain't no happier than they ever were."

As Lanie continued to iron, she thought of the revival. "Twenty-one people have been saved in the meeting, Aunt Kezia. Isn't that wonderful?"

"Not bad. That preacher's too good-lookin', but I guess the poor feller can't help that."

"He is handsome, isn't he?"

"A *heap* too handsome! Lots of mamas are sayin' they wouldn't trust their daughters with a preacher that good-lookin'."

"Oh, that's silly! He's a fine man. People just like to gossip."

"I wonder what Eve did."

"What do you mean?"

"She didn't have anybody to gossip about, and nobody to gossip with except Adam."

"You have the wildest ideas, Aunt Kezia. Why would Adam and Eve want to gossip?"

"Why do people in Fairhope gossip? Just the nature of them. Why, I tell you, that preacher is gonna get his foot in a trap. He's been goin' around to some of the worst folks in the community. Of course, I think that's the way it ought to be done, but a lot of people don't like it."

Indeed, Colin Ryan displeased many members of the church, the more stuffy ones. He dredged up the worst elements of the county, drunks and women whose reputation were in tatters, and somehow persuaded them to come to church. Baxter Thompson, who had been the town drunk for as long as Lanie could remember, had been saved and was now bringing in others, mostly his old drinking partners.

"Well, I think it's wonderful what he's doing. I don't care what people say."

"If he wasn't so purty, he'd do better, but I reckon—" Aunt Kezia did not finish, for Maeva suddenly came in wearing the new dress she had been working on. She had saved up to buy the material and had spent hours looking over the McCall's patterns. The dress was made out of a sheer blue organza with white polka dots, and emphasized the bust with gathers underneath. A solid blue slip showed from under the dress, and there was a white Peter Pan collar and short puffy sleeves edged with white cuffs. The dress was slightly flared from the waist to where the hem ended just below the knees, and tiny white buttons ran down the front.

"Isn't it beautiful?"

"Well, I wish to my never!" Aunt Kezia said. "If I'd a knowed you could sew like that, I'd a let you make me a pretty go-to-meetin' dress."

Aunt Kezia and Lanie were admiring the dress when suddenly the front door burst open. Cody came in like a tornado. His hair was tousled and he had a Bible in his right hand. Stopping dead still, he stared at Maeva. "What are you doin' wearin' a dress like that?"

"I made it. I'm gonna wear it to the dance over at Springdale."

"Well, you can't wear it!"

All three of the women stared at Cody. His chin was stuck out in the way he had when he grew stubborn, and now he shook his head in short motions. "Why, you look like the anti-Christ in that thing! You can't wear it."

"You mind your own business, Cody."

"It *is* my business, and I'm telling you—you can't wear it!"

Ever since Cody had been baptized he considered himself the spiritual leader of the Freeman family. At first it had been rather amusing, but now Maeva's face was flushed with anger. "There's nothing wrong with this dress!"

"There is too. It shows too much of you, and the Bible says that's wrong." Cody whirled and said, "Ain't that right, Lanie?"

Lanie did think the dress was a little too revealing, but she didn't want to offend Maeva, who was hard enough to get along with as it was. "Well, I'm not sure I agree with you, Cody."

"You got to agree with me. I'm *right*."

"You're not right. You've lost your mind ever since Colin Ryan came to town." Maeva whirled to face Lanie and Aunt Kezia. "You know what he's doing? He's been tearing pages out of the Bible and giving them to people down on the street."

"That's what I been doin', all right," Cody snorted proudly. "This Bible here."

"You're tearing pages out of it?" Lanie said. "I don't think that's right."

"It's a sin is what it is," Maeva cried. "It's a sin to tear a Bible up."

"It ain't neither. I can't afford no store-bought tracts. And anyway the Bible's better."

Maeva snorted with disgust. "He gave a page out of that Bible to Coy Wilhite, who needs God if anybody does. But it was a page out of the book of Leviticus. It was all about the inside parts of a sheep and how to cut it up. Now didn't that do Coy a lot of good?"

Lanie stifled a smile. "I don't think that that was exactly what Coy needed, Cody."

"It's the Bible, ain't it? Coy Wilhite needs the Bible, and I gave him part of it."

Lanie was trapped between two emotions. One was pride that her brother would be such an outspoken advocate of his new faith. The other was concern that in his freshly born excitement he would do some damage. "I think you might be a little bit more careful about which pages you give out."

Shaking his head stubbornly, Cody said, "It's all the Bible, Sister."

"Where have you been, anyway?" Maeva demanded.

"I been out bearin' witness to harlots."

All three women stared at Cody as if he had said he had just been for a visit to the top of the Himalayas. "What are you talking about!" Lanie exclaimed.

"Well, actually it was just one harlot. I went over with Brother Ryan to where old man Jed Tyler lives. You know what a godless bunch them Tylers are. He makes whiskey, and his daughter Lily's a harlot."

"She is not!" Maeva objected. "She's a little wild, but she's not a prostitute."

"Well, she's gonna be one if she don't get saved."

Aunt Kezia interrupted. "How'd the visit go?"

"Why, it went plum fine after we got in. You know how old man Tyler is. He had his shotgun out when we got on his land. He cussed us out. Said some words I never even heard before."

"What did Reverend Ryan do?" Lanie asked.

"He just stood there and started talkin' quiet like. First thing you know that old sinner asked us in. He kept his shotgun in his hands, and I was kind of scared so I talked to Lily. I gave her a page from the book of Ezekiel. All about some temple, I think it was, with a river runnin' through it. Told her she needed to get born again." Cody shook his head in disbelief. "She never heard of it. Can you imagine?"

"I don't expect any of those Tylers have been to church ever in their lives," Lanie said.

"Well, they're comin' next Sunday. Believe it or not, we stayed nearly an hour. Old man Tyler finally put his shotgun down. It was slicker than goose grease the way Colin worked it!"

"Don't call him Colin."

"It's his name, ain't it?" Cody was surprised. "He calls me by my first name."

"That's different. You need to show more respect to the ministry," Lanie insisted.

"Well, anyhow, old man Tyler got prayed over and promised to bring the whole kit and caboodle to the service tonight. It's the last one. I'm expectin' to see the whole bunch get converted."

"Now that's the kind of preacher we need around here," Aunt Kezia said in a tone of satisfaction. "Shake things up."

Cody was not through with Maeva. "Maeva, I don't want you wearin' that dress. You know what the Bible says. It says, 'Can the rush grow up without mire? can the flag grow without water?'"

"I don't have any idea what you're talking about!" Maeva cried.

"Well, it's the eighth chapter of Job verse 11. I liked it so I memorized it. What it means is you can't wear that dress." He turned around and dashed out of the room, calling for Davis loudly.

"You got to do something with him, Lanie," Maeva said with exasperation. "He's just impossible!"

"Well, maybe he'll get over it," Lanie said.

"I hope he don't," Aunt Kezia said loudly. "I hope he gets worse."

Maeva suddenly laughed. "You may think that, but a lot of people in the church don't. I heard that Otis Langley had a fit about all the riffraff that the preacher's bringing into church."

"You said he's called them riffraff!" Lanie exclaimed. "I can't believe it."

"I can," Aunt Kezia said. "He's just the kind that likes a lot of dead folks in church."

"Dead folks? What do you mean?"

"Well, you know how it is. When people get converted, they're excited about everything. It's like a young girl in love. The whole world's wonderful." She made a face then and shook her head with disgust. "But a lot of women, after a few years of marriage, lose all the romance. Let Cody alone. He's gonna make some mistakes and offend some folks, but he's alive." She cackled, and her eyes sparkled as she said, "I'd a heap rather try to restrain a fanatic than try to resurrect a corpse!"

⌐≖⊱

"Roger, you look so tired. I wish you'd quit that silly job," Martha Langley said.

Roger Langley was sitting across the dining room table from his sister Louise. His parents were at either ends of the table, and there was an empty chair next to him that was usually Helen's. The maid, Elsie, was listening without appearing to, as she always did.

"I like my job, Mother. Lots of fresh air and sunshine."

"You've got a bad sunburn," Louise said. "If you have to have a job, you could get one with a little more dignity."

"You think surveying is not dignified?" Roger challenged his sister. "George Washington was a surveyor, and he was a pretty dignified fellow from what I understand."

"You're making a fool out of yourself is what you're doing," Otis Langley said. He forked a morsel of the meat that was on the fine china plate, and he held it for a moment while he glared at Roger with displeasure. "I don't know what's gotten into you. You lost whatever common sense you had."

Roger was accustomed to this conversation. It went on almost every time his family got together. For a moment he considered saying nothing, and his eyes ran around the room. It was a large room furnished with the finest in furniture and china and silver. He knew that the serving table against the wall cost over a thousand dollars, and with men out of work all over the country it seemed to him very close to a sin. He picked up his spoon and stirred his coffee, then lifted his eyes to his father. "I like what I'm doing, Dad."

"What are you doing? You're missing out on a year of college."

"I'm not sure that's a bad thing. I never had to work for anything. You always handed it to me on a silver platter. I wanted to see if I could do something on my own."

Roger knew that such a thing was incomprehensible to his father, but it was something he had to do. He leaned back in his chair and listened as the family took turns explaining why he was wrong. He had different ideas from the rest of them, and sometimes he almost felt like a different species. His parents and his sisters were very much concerned about their position in society and were caught up with material possessions such as automobiles, furniture, and clothing. Roger cared little for any of these things.

"You don't have to work to pay your tuition," Otis Langley insisted. "I've agreed to do that."

"I appreciate that, Dad, and maybe after a while that's what will happen, but for this first year I'm going to make my own way."

Louise stared at Roger and shook her head with distaste. "I wish you'd stop seeing so much of Lanie Freeman."

"Why would you want me to stop seeing Lanie?"

"She's not our kind," Otis said abruptly. "Your sister is right. You ought to go around with a girl like Dottie McGiven."

"She's a stuck-up snob," Roger said.

"Don't be calling her names!" Roger's mother said at once. The McGivens and the Langleys were close friends, and it was the hope of both families that Roger and Dottie would make a match of it, but Roger wasn't interested.

Louise began to speak critically of Lanie, something that angered Roger. Finally he turned to face her and said, "Maybe you'd better start trying to take care of your own affairs instead of meddling with mine."

"What are you talking about?"

Roger suddenly grinned. "I think you'd better be sure you can hang on to Owen. He likes Lanie a lot. She might take him away from you."

"That's the most ridiculous thing I ever heard in my life! Owen's not interested in that girl."

Otis did not want to hear talk like this, so he changed the subject. "Well, at least that meeting is over after tonight and that high-flying evangelist will be gone." He leaned forward and smiled suddenly. "I've been talking with some of the deacons. I think we can get Reverend Clifford in as pastor. It's all a matter of votes. That's the good thing about a Baptist church. Everybody has a vote. It's one of the few democracies left in the world."

"Well, I don't think Reverend Clifford's the man for the church," Roger said. "He just doesn't fit."

"You've been fooled by that motorcycle rider!" Louise snapped. She was still furious with Roger and added spitefully, "He's just a flashy fly-by-night."

An old memory suddenly touched Roger and he said, "Dad, you told me one time about a preacher you liked when you were a boy. His name was Ed Corwin, and he rode fast horses and preached like Brother Colin. You said you thought he was the greatest preacher in the world."

Otis stared at his son, speechless. He had a vivid memory of how he'd been so taken with Brother Ed that he'd followed him around everywhere he could. "That—that was a long time ago, Roger. I've learned better since then how important it is for people to keep traditions."

"But you told me that's why you liked him, Dad—because he refused to be like other ministers."

Otis Langley remembered clearly how the evangelist had violated several hallowed traditions of the church where he'd grown up. It had thrilled him then, and for one moment he thought how much Brother Ed was like this man who had such an influence on Roger. He snapped, "I was wrong—just as you're wrong now. A pastor needs stability, and this evangelist has none. Now I want to hear no more about it!"

"He would be a terrible pastor," Louise agreed. "He may do very well in the slums of a big city, but he'd never do for our church."

"Your sister's right, Roger. A pastor needs to be older and married and a scholar," Otis said and got to his feet. Tossing his napkin down, he added with satisfaction, "He'll be gone tomorrow, thank God!"

The deacons of First Baptist Church were frantically robbing the Sunday school rooms of folding chairs to put around the aisles. Every pew was packed and the ushers were wondering what they would do with the overflow.

"I never seen a crowd like this except at associational meetings," Phineas Delaughter said with satisfaction.

Francis Butterworth, a tall thin man with brown hair, nodded. "Well, this has been the greatest revival meeting we ever had, I think, except when Gypsy Smith was here, but that was before my time."

"Where we going to put these people, Francis?"

"I guess we can open the windows and listen from the outside." Francis was observing all the people in the pews. "Look. There's Butcher Knife Annie. You don't see her in church very often."

Mayor Delaughter looked and saw a tall, gaunt woman with gray hair sitting in the pew with the Freeman boys, Davis and Cody. She was holding the youngest Freeman, Corliss, in her lap.

"Well, at least she's cleaned up a little bit. She usually looks like she came out of a garbage can."

Indeed, Butcher Knife Annie, whose real name was Beulah Ann Toliver, was careless about her appearance. She lived in an old shack just outside the city limits where she kept innumerable cats. Everyone in the county who had an unwanted cat dumped it onto Annie, and she kept them all. She spent her days pulling a Radio Flyer wagon around behind the shops, loading it up with throwaways. She owned three acres, and most of them were cluttered up so that it appeared to be another city junkyard.

Annie caught a glimpse of the two men watching her and said to Davis, "Them fellers don't think I'm fit to be here."

Cody glanced over and saw Francis Butterworth talking with the mayor. He started to get up. "I'll just go straighten them out. This is the house of God. We don't need any hypocrites in here."

Davis reached out, grabbed Cody by the back of the collar, and jerked him down. "You sit down, bud," he said. "You're getting too big for your britches."

"Well, Jesus cast the money changers out of the temple. It might be time we start throwin' a few out around here."

Annie laughed. "I'd like to see that," she said. "Wouldn't you, sweetie?"

Corliss looked up and smiled at Annie. "I would," she said. "Throw them out, Cody!"

"You see what a bad influence you are, Cody." Davis grinned. "Now you hush and behave yourself."

"I might not be able to contain myself," Cody said. "I get so excited at these meetings I want to shout."

"Well, try to hold it in if you can. Sometime we'll go over to Sister Myrtle's church. All those people shout over there. You wouldn't even be noticed."

❦

As Lanie came out of the choir room, she was surprised to see the evangelist standing with his back against the wall. It always gave her a little shock when she saw him, for he never wore a tie. He was wearing a pair of light gray trousers and a white dress shirt that was open at the neck. His black hair was glistening, and she thought again about what Aunt Kezia had said about good-looking preachers. He surely was one of those!

"I wanted to tell you, Lanie, how much I enjoyed your singing."

"Why, thank you, Brother Ryan, and I have to tell you how much I've enjoyed your sermons."

"Nice to hear that. I always feel like I've made a mess of it."

"Where will you go when you leave here?"

"Back to Chicago workin' the streets, if the Lord doesn't tell me different."

"I've been wanting to ask you something."

"Sure. What is it?"

"I've been worried about Cody. He's acting—different."

Colin Ryan smiled. "He's excited. That's all that's wrong with him. I was just like him when I first got saved. As a matter of fact, I think I'm still that way. I hope when they put me in an old folks home I'll run up and down the halls and organize a bed pan Olympics for all of us old folks."

Lanie suddenly laughed. "What an awful thing to say!"

The young preacher turned serious. "I understand you're going to sing a duet tonight with your sister."

85

"Yes. She sings much better than I do."

"I'll look forward to it."

The choir was filing out now, and Lanie quickly went into the choir loft. The service started, and she sang the duet with Maeva. Maeva had a beautiful voice, but she didn't sing in church too often. "I feel like a hypocrite," she always said. "Lanie's the good one. I'm the bad one." Lanie was always half angry when Maeva said this, although she knew there was some truth to it.

Finally the singing was over, and Colin Ryan got up to preach. He had a Bible in his hand, old and worn and practically falling to pieces. "Some of you folks," he began, "have asked me why I don't get a new Bible. Some of you good people even offered to buy me one. Well, the truth is I started marking the answers to prayer that God gave me when I was first saved. This was my first Bible, and I hope it's my last. I can open almost any page and there I'll see a verse and a date written beside it, and if it's really exciting, I might find a star beside it. Thanks for your offer, but I'll stick with this old one.

"I want to tell you how much I enjoy being with you good people. You've been very hospitable, and I'll be praying that God will send you exactly the man you need. Now then. The sermon tonight is—Jesus is coming." A sudden grin turned up the corners of Colin's mouth, and then he laughed out loud. "I imagine most of you have heard sermons on the second coming many times. This one will be a little bit different. I've heard the same sermons you have and read the same books. I've seen the pictures of the beast that comes crawling up out of the sea with thorns in the crown. It all works out very neatly on paper, but tonight I want to remind you that when Jesus came the first time, men had been looking for the coming of the Messiah for many years. The scholars studied it intensely just as they do today. They thought they had it all figured out, and, as a matter of fact, they did have some of it figured out. But you'll remember when the wise men came and asked, 'Where is the king of the Jews to be born?' the scribes shot back an answer. 'Why, in Bethlehem.' They knew the time, they'd got that figured out, the place, and they knew exactly what the Messiah was going to do. He was going to lead Israel to become a great national power and overthrow the Romans."

A hush fell over the church. Something about Colin Ryan's voice seemed to hypnotize the people. They all waited breathlessly for the next remark, and when it came they were surprised.

"The only thing about all of that is they were *wrong* about the most important part. He was *not* the kind of Messiah they had told everyone was coming. And I think whatever system people devise to guess the coming of the Lord is wrong. I think God is going to surprise us. God does surprise us most of the time. We get our little plan made up, and then God interferes with it and tells us we have to change it. So I have two thoughts on the second coming. First, Jesus is coming back. There's no question about that. He said it many times. The second is, nobody knows when he's coming back. And I might add a third. It's foolish to speculate and set dates. When he comes back, I think we'll all be caught off guard. Now, let's see what the Scripture says …"

Seven people came to be saved during the invitation, six came to join the church, and many came to rededicate their lives.

Gerald Pink, chairman of the board of deacons, was elated. He came to stand on the rostrum, and after the new converts were voted into the church, he said beamingly, "We are all grateful to Brother Ryan for coming to bring the gospel during this meeting. We will schedule a baptism in about two weeks."

Suddenly, to Lanie's dismay, her brother Cody stood up. "Mr. Pink," he said loudly, "why can't we have Brother Colin for a pastor?"

A hum went over the congregation, and Gerald Pink looked helplessly around.

"That would not be the fitting thing to do." Otis Langley stood, a big man, imposing and finely dressed. "Young man, I appreciate your comment, but we have ways of doing things here."

But Cody said, "I heard some of the deacons talking about an interim pastor. They said that man would be pastor until the church gets a new one."

"Well, that's true, Cody. That's what we plan to do," Brother Pink said.

"I get a vote now, and I vote Brother Ryan in as interim pastor."

Cody's remark started what was the most active and lively business meeting in the history of First Baptist Church of Fairhope, Arkansas. They were a slow-moving people. It took almost six months to decide what color to paint the walls of the nursery, and here this young boy was telling them to make a decision that would affect the whole life of the church!

Roger sat back grinning as he saw that the tide was beginning to run against his father. He almost felt sorry when he saw his father having to face the dangers of a Baptist democracy. Many of the church sided with him, but the new converts and the younger members of the church won out. At the end of the battle, the vote was to accept Colin Ryan as interim pastor.

When the vote was announced, Colin stood up and said, "I'm honored that you would ask me to be your pastor, and I accept. I will stay until you get a new pastor. "

Louise Langley whispered to her father, "Dad, don't worry about this. That motorcycle rider won't last long! I'll see to it!"

·—⚬ CHAPTER 8 ⚬—·

Looking up out of the window, Lanie saw Dorsey Pender, the mailman, coming up the steps. Getting up at once, she went out on the front porch to meet him. "Good afternoon, Dorsey. How are you today?"

Pender was a tall, lanky man with a balding head and a pair of inquisitive blue eyes. Except for Henrietta Green, the telephone operator, he was without a doubt the nosiest gossip in Fairhope. He also wrote terrible poetry, which amused Lanie a great deal. She took the letter that he handed her and said, "Have you written any poetry lately, Mr. Pender?"

"Shore have." Pender grinned. "How about this one?

"Teeth are very nice to have,
They fill you with content;
If you do not know it now,
You will when they have went!"

Lanie laughed. "That's a good one. Shakespeare would be jealous."

"That letter's from your pa, Lanie. He's a little bit late with it. The last one come nearly two weeks ago."

"That's right." Lanie nodded, wondering how in the world one head could hold so much trivia. Pender knew everything about everybody in Fairhope and was not hesitant to pass along information.

"I hear that foreigner's causin' lots of trouble."

"What foreigner?" Lanie asked.

"Why, that preacher, Reverend Colin Ryan."

"Why, he's not causing any trouble, Mr. Pender. He's doing a wonderful job at the church."

"That's right, but he also went to visit Mamie Dorr at her house— and after dark too." Mamie Dorr owned the beauty parlor and had a reputation that was not particularly good.

Pender nodded and continued. "You know her husband killed himself because she messed around with other men."

"Oh, that's not true, Mr. Pender. He died of cancer."

"Well, she probably caused the cancer. Anyway, that preacher needs to watch where he goes. And it wasn't only Mamie. He's been hangin' out at the pool hall."

"He goes everywhere to witness to the Lord. He's gotten three of those loafers down there to come to church."

"Well, that's as may be, but you better tell him to watch his step. We Baptists don't like our preachers to misbehave. What's your dad have to say?"

"I don't know. I haven't read the letter yet."

"All right. And you pass the word to the preacher to stay away from Mamie Dorr."

"I'll tell him." Lanie went back into the house shaking her head with disgust over Pender's nosiness. She was always excited to get a letter from her father, and before she shared it with the rest of the family, she sat down in the living room and opened it up. She read it slowly, savoring every bit of news that he had. The last line, however, troubled her. "I've been a little bit under the weather lately, so you might say an extra prayer for me."

Lanie's brow furrowed, for her father never complained. This mere mention of not being well was the equivalent of a scream of agony from someone else. She looked up at the calendar and saw that her next visit was scheduled for two weeks away. "I can't wait that long," she murmured. "I've got to go see how Daddy is."

She went into the kitchen and pulled a coffee can down off the shelf. She opened it up and poured the change and the three bills out. She counted it carefully, then shook her head. "Not enough. I need to stay overnight." Thoughts raced through her head, and she wondered how she could cut corners or if there was anything to sell. But nothing came to her. Finally, as she did so often, she bowed her head and said, "Lord, I need to go see Daddy, and I don't have the money. I know you love him and would have me go visit with him, so I'm praying for his healing and I'm praying that you would provide a way for me to go. I ask this in Jesus' name and I know that you're going to hear me. Amen."

Lanie went at once and picked up her Bible and began to search for a promise. It was her habit to go to the Bible and try to find a promise that would apply to her current need. She always marked the date of the prayer in her Bible and then the date that it was answered. Since her Bible had previously been her mother's, it was almost as worn as that of Colin Ryan. Between Lanie's and Elizabeth's hand-written notes, some pages were so marked up they were difficult to read.

For a time she sat there reading through at random. She was turning the pages of Scripture, and suddenly her eyes fell on a passage that she had marked at some time and underlined in red. There was no date or indication that she had asked for any particular thing, but as she read the passage of the verse aloud, it seemed to bring peace to her heart. It was in the sixty-fifth chapter of Isaiah, and it said, "And it shall come to pass, that before they call, I will answer; and while they are yet speaking, I will hear."

Lanie did not read any further for somehow, in a way that had happened to her a few times in her life, she knew that God heard her prayer. Tears came to her eyes, and she said, "Lord, I don't know how I'm going to get to see Daddy, but I know that you heard me, and I'm going to believe you that somehow you'll open up the door." She closed the Bible and sat there for a time, then rose and started her work for the day.

Lanie decided to walk to town, for there was no money to spare for gas. She walked down Jefferson Avenue headed south toward Main when she looked over to her left and saw that Owen Merritt's car was parked in front of Butcher Knife Annie's place. She hesitated for a moment and then became concerned. Annie was getting on in years.

As Lanie approached the door, she was greeted by dozens of cats of all sizes and shapes. Some of them were little more than kittens, while others were old and grizzled. Carefully she navigated her way between them, and when she came up to the door, she knocked. No one came for a moment, and then suddenly Owen appeared.

"Why, hello, Lanie. Come in."

Lanie stepped inside the screen door and looked down the hall. "Is Annie sick?"

"Well, I'm afraid she is," Owen said. He ran his hand through his crisp brown hair and shook his head with enough doubt to give Lanie some concern. "She's had a little trouble with her heart, you know. I thought I'd better stop by and take a look."

"She won't ever ask for help, but I'll see to it that she has plenty to eat."

"I'll have Nurse Pickens bring her supper tonight. Maybe you can check on her tomorrow."

"I'll do that. Could I see her?"

"Sure. Come on in."

Lanie moved down the hall. The house smelled terrible with so many cats, but she'd learned that it was one of those things that she had to put up with. As she went into Annie's bedroom, she said, "Well, now look at you, Annie, getting sick and not telling anybody."

Annie was wearing an ancient robe and her feet were shoved into some leather men's shoes. At that instant Lanie made the resolution to get her some house slippers. She leaned over and hugged Annie. "Why didn't you get word to me you were feeling bad?"

"Oh, I didn't want to trouble you," Annie said. She had traces of snuff at the edge of her lips, and her hair had not been washed recently. But she took better care of herself now than before she had become friends with the Freemans. Aunt Kezia helped with that. She dropped by fairly often, and the two old ladies enjoyed each other's company.

"I tried to get her to the hospital, but she won't go. She's stubborn as a blue-nosed mule," Owen said.

"I'm all right here where I am. I feel a lot better now."

Lanie stayed for a while and when she left she promised, "I'll come back to check on you later this afternoon. I'll bring Aunt Kezia over too."

"Good. That woman encourages me."

Lanie left the house and Owen came out with her.

"Where are you going, Lanie?"

"I need to go to the hardware store. The sink's stopped up and needs a new part."

"Get in. I'll take you."

Lanie hesitated, and Owen turned to look at her. "What's the matter? You ashamed to be seen with an old man?"

"Well, no, I'm not. You're not old. But you're an engaged man."

"That doesn't mean anything. I'm just offering you a ride, not running off with you to the South Seas."

Lanie could not think of any way to refuse his invitation graciously, so when he opened the door, she got in. Owen got in, started the car, and began describing the condition of Annie as he drove. Lanie felt restrained. She had, indeed, felt uncomfortable around Doctor Owen Merritt since the incident of the Ferris wheel.

"How's all the family getting along, Lanie?"

Lanie shook her head. "All right, I guess."

Owen examined her. His warm brown eyes sharpened, and he said, "You run yourself down taking care of your family. What's going on? You can tell me. I'm the friendly family doctor."

Suddenly it all boiled over. Lanie tried never to complain, but she said now, "I get tired, Owen. Davis can't learn how to read, and I don't know why. He's so smart in every other way. Corliss is already starting to learn her letters, and she's only three and talks like a magpie. Cody's gotten so active since he got saved I can't keep up with him. He thinks he's an apostle or something."

"Don't put him down. That's good," Owen said. "What about Maeva and your father?"

"Well, you know Maeva. She's wild sometimes. I don't know where she gets it. Not from Daddy or Mama."

"She'll be all right. She's got good stuff in her, so don't give up on her now. What about your dad?"

For a moment Lanie hesitated, then she said, "I got a letter from him today. He's been sick, and I need to go see him."

"Yes, you do. When are you leaving?" When Lanie did not answer at once, Owen took his eyes off the road and took a quick glance at her. "What's the matter?"

"Well, it's expensive to go down there. Gas and staying all night at a hotel."

"Look, I've told you I can help you with things like that."

"No. I can't take money from you, Owen."

"Why not? I'd take it from you."

"Because I've already made plans."

"What sort of plans?"

"I asked God to get me to Cummings, and he gave me a promise. The most wonderful promise. It's found in Isaiah. 'And it shall come to pass, that before they call, I will answer; and while they are yet speaking, I will hear.' Isn't that a great promise?"

"It sure is. But maybe I'm the answer to that."

"No, I don't think so. I don't know why. I just know."

They arrived at the hardware store on Main Street, and when Owen stopped the car, Lanie got out. "Thank you for offering, Owen. You're always good to help my family. But God will answer. You'll see."

Owen did not try to persuade Lanie. He had discovered that there was a stubborn streak in the gentle young woman. He never heard her speak a word in anger, but there was a certain point beyond which you could not push her. As he turned the corner and went to his office on Oak Street, he was trying to think of some way he could provide the money without being directly involved.

Getting out of the car, he went inside and found that Bertha Pickens, Doctor Givens's nurse, was irritated with him. "You've had three calls while you were out. Who did you see while you were gone?"

Owen gave her a quick grin and recited his visits. "How's the good Doctor Givens?" he asked.

"This is not one of his good days. I'm worried about him."

"So am I. He ought to retire."

Bertha Pickens sniffed. "You just try and get that man to stop working. He'll be seein' patients until the day he goes to meet Jesus."

"I expect you're right about that. I'll go see these people right now."

⌐══━⌐

Louise Langley had just stepped outside of the pharmacy when she saw Owen drive by with Lanie Freeman in the car beside him. Her eyes narrowed and a touch of anger came to her. *He ought to know better than that. He's foolish about that girl,* she thought. She turned and started toward her car thinking that she would speak to Owen about hauling the Freeman girl around, when suddenly she heard a whistle. She turned involuntarily in front of Smitty's Pool Hall and saw three or four loafers leaning against the wall grinning at her. Her face reddened, and she wanted to bawl them out, but she knew that would only please them.

At that instant Reverend Colin Ryan, who had been standing in the shadows, stepped out, said a word to the young men, and came over to her. "Well, it's good to see you, Miss Langley. How about if I buy you a chocolate soda. I'm almost broke"—he grinned—"but we can get two straws."

"I'm an engaged woman."

"Congratulations," Colin said. "I didn't intend to try to win you away from your fiancé."

"That's good, because you couldn't."

Colin fell into step beside Louise, who was walking as fast as she could. He was an insufferable man, and now he said, "You know, I hear your family has money. If you married me, I wouldn't have to work. Your folks could support us, and I wouldn't have to do anything but tell you how pretty you are."

Louise Langley was astonished. She was accustomed to ministers having a great deal of dignity, and she turned to glare at the interim pastor of the First Baptist Church. "I—I can't believe a minister would say such a thing!"

"I can't believe it either," Colin said, but his eyes were dancing. "It's true enough though. The old Hebrews had a custom that I've always admired. When a young couple got married, the man didn't do any work for a year. All he did was hang around the house telling his bride how pretty she was and how wonderful it was to be married to her."

"It doesn't say that in the Bible."

Colin Ryan did not argue. "Well, I'm always saying the wrong thing. Maybe you should counsel me."

"You need it!"

Colin was looking fresh. His coal-black hair caught the afternoon sunlight, and despite herself, Louise was thinking that he was the best-looking man she had ever seen in her life. He was also intolerable!

"I'll tell you one thing the Bible does say. It's in Galatians chapter six in the first verse. It says, 'If a man be overtaken in a fault, ye which are spiritual, restore such an one.' So I'd appreciate it if you would take me in hand."

"All right, I will!" Louise said. She did not understand at that moment that her anger was at Owen for chauffeuring Lanie around. She didn't like Colin Ryan, and without realizing it she began to pour out all her criticisms. "Your clothes are terrible! I never saw a minister who would dare get behind the pulpit without a suit and a tie. And you hang out with terrible people ..."

Colin listened as she enumerated his faults, and finally when she ran down, he nodded and tried to look serious. "Well, Miss Louise, I don't think clothes matter that much, and Jesus hung out with a rough crowd. He said that was the bunch he had come to save. Remember? I'd like to please you, but I'm really more concerned about pleasing God."

"I can't understand why you think you're pleasing God. You're splitting the church. Half the members want you to leave."

"Well, I'm pretty certain which half you belong to. Look," he said, "I know I'm different. And you may be right. I'll tell you what—why don't you be my advisor?"

"What are you talking about?"

"Give me some pointers. You let me call you Louise, and you can call me Colin. Why don't I come and sit on your porch tonight? You can work on me."

Louise Langley laughed shortly. "My father would furnish the reception. He wouldn't permit it. Neither would my fiancé."

"Well, how about this. I'll go ask their permission."

"You stay away from them and stay away from me! Now leave me alone!" She turned and walked away, furious with the man.

"Good talking with you, Louise," Colin called out and waved. "I'll be looking forward to some more advice from you the next time." He watched the young woman leave, noting that she held her head high. *She's smart and pretty, but boy, is she rigid!* he mused. *Still, she's got potential. Maybe she just needs a proper dose of the real world.* The thought pleased him, and he began to whistle a lively tune as schemes to "develop" Louise Langley danced through his mind.

⌖

Two days had gone by since Lanie had prayed and claimed the Scripture in Isaiah. She expected money to come somehow from an unexpected source, but nothing was happening. As a matter of fact, she spent the little money that was left to buy food. Now she was absolutely broke. Even with all everyone did to bring in funds, it just wasn't enough. Cody sold copies of *Grit* magazine at the newsstand. Maeva went looking for sassafras roots that the general store would want to buy, and Davis delivered newspapers. Later, Lanie would do some more canning. The general store wanted more of her apple butter next week.

She had awakened early this morning, and now the sun was rising. She had fixed breakfast, and the children were all off to do their work for the day. Aunt Kezia was sleeping late along with Corliss. The house was quiet. She always liked the early cobwebby time of the morning, and now she drank another cup of coffee feeling guilty for the expense. She wondered if she had been presumptuous in asking God to provide for her this way. "Maybe God doesn't want me to go see Daddy right now. Maybe it's all my imagination."

The doubts troubled her, and even as she sat there, she heard the sound of a roaring engine in front of the house. She got up and walked to the door. She was surprised to see Reverend Colin Ryan stepping off his motorcycle. He was wearing a helmet and shoved the goggles up, and after leaning the motorcycle on the kickstand, he came up the steps. When she stepped out, he greeted her with a smile. "Hello, Sister Lanie. How are you this morning?"

"I'm fine, Brother Colin. What are you doing up and about so early?"

"Out making calls. You're my first."

"Well, it's good to have you, but there's no one here but me."

"Well, that's fine. You and I can get to know each other."

"Would you care for a cup of coffee?"

"I don't see any harm with it"—he winked at her—"as long as there are no women and children present."

Lanie laughed and took him inside. She sat him at the kitchen table, poured him a cup of coffee, another for herself, then sat down. "I guess your preaching has been a success. It's wonderful seeing so many people get saved."

"Well, I'm expecting a big harvest. We've got to learn to trust God for these things. How's your family? Is there anybody I need to pray for?"

A shadow fell over Lanie's face. "We all need prayer, I guess, but I'm glad you asked. It's Daddy. He's not well."

"He's sick?"

"You know he's in prison."

"Yes, I know. I've heard about that. Is he in Cummings?"

"Yes."

"Why, that's not too far. You need to go at once."

Lanie hesitated, then shrugged. "I don't have the money, Brother Ryan, but I asked God and he gave me a Scripture. It's in Isaiah." She quoted the Scripture and said, "I believe God heard me as soon as I asked him, and the answer's on the way."

Colin Ryan suddenly laughed and slapped his hand on the table. "I am the way," he said. "I'll take you to see your dad."

"But you don't even have a car."

"No, but I've got a bike."

For a moment Lanie didn't understand what he meant. "You mean—get on that motorcycle behind you and ride all the way to Cummings?"

"Well, I wish I had a car, but I don't. The church has been giving me some money, but I've been finding people that need it worse than I do. That bike will make it fine."

Lanie was absolutely stunned. "Why, I can't ride one of those things!"

"Sure you can. God's opened a door here, and you've got to go through it."

At that instant Aunt Kezia came through the door. She was wearing a ratty old bathrobe that she loved and would not have exchanged for a new one. "Hello, Preacher," she said.

"Why, Miss Kezia," Ryan said, "how wonderful to see you. An amazing thing just happened."

"Well, what is it?"

"Lanie here has prayed, God told her he'd answer her prayer, and I'm the answer."

"Answer for what?"

"Daddy hasn't been feeling well, and I need to go see him, Aunt Kezia," Lanie explained, "but I don't have the money."

Colin interjected, "Well, I've got enough money for gas to get us there and back. We'll make good time too."

Lanie laughed helplessly. "He wants me to ride that motorcycle with him all the way to Cummings and back, but I can't do that."

Aunt Kezia's eyes twinkled. "Once when I was a girl growing up, a little bit younger than you, my ma got sick. Somebody had to go for the doctor. We didn't have no horses at that time, we were so poor. All we had was a bull. I rode that bull into town to get that doctor and rode him all the way back. If I can ride a one-eyed red bull, I reckon you can ride one of them two-wheel outfits. Don't be a doubting woman, Lanie Freeman."

"Aunt Kezia's right," Colin agreed. "Let's go, Lanie."

"You mean right now?" Lanie's mind was reeling. "But what about the kids?"

"I reckon they'll all survive. Now git!" Aunt Kezia commanded. "God spoke. Don't ever doubt him."

At that instant Lanie Freeman had one of those moments when she knew that God had absolutely spoken. She suddenly stood up and stared at the two and then said with determination, "All right, I'll do it. I'll be ready to go in ten minutes." She turned and ran out of the kitchen, up the stairs to her room.

Aunt Kezia turned to the preacher and studied him. "You're a good-lookin' scoundrel, you know it?"

"I'm glad you think so, Sister Kezia."

"It'll give the people somethin' to talk about, Lanie ridin' all the way down to Cummings in forked pants with a good-lookin' preacher." She suddenly laughed. "Don't be in a big hurry getting' back, son. This'll give the gossip mill somethin' to work on!"

↠ CHAPTER 9 ↞

Lanie dashed into the bedroom that Davis shared with Cody and after a frantic search found a pair of his old jeans. Davis was now much taller than she was, but these were jeans that he had worn before he had started to shoot up. She grabbed one of his old shirts, ran back to her room, quickly pulled on the shirt, buttoned it, and then slipped into the pants. For a moment she was daunted, for they were too long for her, which didn't matter, but they were also almost skin tight. Davis had always been lean, and the jeans were not made for a curvaceous young woman of seventeen!

For a moment she stood there uncertainly and thought of going back, but these were the only ones she'd found that she could get into. She drew her lips together and said firmly, "They'll have to do. That's all there is to it."

Leaving her room, she went downstairs and found Aunt Kezia chatting in the kitchen with the preacher. She was trying to convince him that he should try some of Major Scooby's Liver Extract but without much success. They both turned when Lanie came in. She saw Aunt Kezia's eyes open wide, and instantly she flushed.

"Well, that's quite an outfit you got on there. Is that what motorcycle riders wear, Reverend?"

"Most of them wear whatever they've got," Colin said. "It'll be fine, Lanie."

"Have we got room to take Daddy some of these cookies I made?"

"Bring all you want. We'll put 'em in the saddlebags."

Lanie quickly filled two sacks full of the oatmeal cookies that her father loved. "I'm ready."

The two moved out on the front porch and then stepped down followed by Aunt Kezia. "Let me have those cookies." Colin lifted the flaps on the worn leather saddlebags mounted over the rear wheel and put them in. "They'll be fine there."

At that instant Lanie looked up to see Cody, Davis, and Maeva coming down the street. Cody broke into a run, then stopped. "I told you not to wear them forked pants. They're a shame and a disgrace!"

"Who died and made you pope?" Maeva said. Her eyes were sparkling, and she moved closer, keeping her gaze fixed on Lanie's outfit. "Those are Davis's clothes."

"I had to wear them, Davis. I'm sorry. I didn't think you'd mind."

"Why, shucks. That's fine with me. I can't get into them anymore," Davis said. "Where you goin'?"

"Your sister tells me she needs to see your dad, Davis. We're all kind of short on money and cars, so I'm taking her there."

"Can three ride on one of those things?" Maeva winked at the preacher. "I wouldn't mind ridin' with you myself."

"You hush, Maeva," Aunt Kezia said.

"Well, all right." Maeva grinned. "But I will say that outfit is mighty eye-catchin'."

Cody looked stunned. Colin Ryan had become an important man in his life, and he was shocked that a preacher would allow such a thing. He swallowed hard, and Colin saw the trouble he was having.

"It's an emergency, Cody," he said, going over to put his hand on the boy's shoulder. "Your dad's not well, and your sister needs to go see him. Try to understand."

"All right, I guess," Cody mumbled. He took one more look at Lanie and shook his head. "Well, all I can say is, it sure is unseemly."

Lanie felt bad about embarrassing Cody. She went over and put her arm around him, hugged him tightly, and whispered in his ear, "I have to go, Cody. You take care of things while I'm gone, all right?"

"Sure, Sis. You tell Dad I miss him."

"Guess we're ready," Colin said. He turned and fished into the saddlebags and pulled out a soft leather helmet with a pair of goggles. "Better put this on," he said cheerfully. "Gonna be windy."

Lanie pulled the helmet on, tucking in her hair and snapping it under her chin. She pulled the goggles down and watched as Colin stepped onto the motorcycle and kicked the starter. The engine broke into a roar, and Colin turned and said, "Get right on. I'll show you where to put your feet." He guided her feet after she straddled the machine.

Maeva came up. "You better hang on," Maeva said loudly. "The best chance you'll ever have to hug a good-lookin' preacher."

Colin merely laughed and waved briefly. He gave the machine a little gas and yelled, "Grab ahold—here we go!"

Lanie was thrown slightly backwards and in a panic she reached out and grabbed him by the shoulders.

"Just put your arms around me. We'll be all right once you get used to it."

Lanie had never been so embarrassed in her life. It seemed wrong somehow to put her arms around a preacher, but as he speeded up, she found she needed to hold on. She hoped he would go out through one of the side streets, maybe down Elm, but instead he turned right down Main Street. They passed over Jeb Stuart Avenue and Stonewall Jackson Boulevard and roared right past the library, the Dew Drop Inn, and the bank. It seemed everybody she knew was standing out watching her. She hoped that no one would recognize her with the helmet on, but as she passed the Dew Drop Inn, Pardue Jessup was coming out. He straightened up, laughed, and hollered, "Hang on, Lanie!"

Does everybody have to see me? she wondered miserably.

Finally they passed the outskirts of town, and as the open country lay before them, Colin yelled over his shoulder, "We're gonna fly now!" Lanie had never experienced such speed! The telephone poles became just a blur. Then Colin said, "Hang on tight! We gotta pass this fella."

With alarm, Lanie looked ahead and saw a lumber truck with a load of pine logs. She expected Colin to slow down, but instead he speeded up and abruptly leaned over to his left. Frantically Lanie grabbed him around the chest and held on, pressing her cheek against his back. She felt the machine tilt and then slowly return upright and lean the other way as Colin guided it back to the right.

That was the pattern for the next twenty minutes. Colin seemed to be running the motorcycle at full speed, and he simply sailed by everything in his path. Once he barely made it back in front of an Oldsmobile, dodging the oncoming truck in the left lane by what seemed like a hair's breadth.

Finally, to her amazement, Lanie discovered that she was enjoying it. Although she was afraid at first, she discovered there was something exhilarating about the speed and the skill with which Colin could weave his way in and out. She felt safe and secure, which was strange considering how fast they were flying along.

She was also aware of something else: She was acutely conscious of pressing herself against the muscular form of Colin Ryan. She tried not to, but whenever the speed increased or they would weave, she had to clutch him firmly. It was embarrassing for her, but it was just the sort of thing Maeva would delight in.

I've got to learn to ride without holding on to him so tight, she thought. But that proved to be impossible.

⌖

Colin pulled in beside a country store, stopping the cycle beside the single gas pump with the glass top. "We need to fill up," he said. "Besides that, I expect you're pretty stiff. We've been going for an hour and a half."

As Lanie stepped off, she was indeed stiff. She moved around stretching her legs, bending over, and found that her arms were cramped from holding onto Colin.

A lean man with a long horse face and a droopy mustache came out. He was wearing a pair of faded Toughnut overalls and a cap that said Burris Mills across the front. "Help ya?" he asked.

"Need to fill up with gas and get a little something to eat. How are you today, brother?"

The lean man grinned. "Doin' finer than frog hair. If I felt any better, I'd have to take shots for it."

Colin suddenly laughed and winked at Lanie. "You must be a believer. Only a Christian can be that happy."

"You're mighty right. I found the Lord twenty-two years ago. Best thing I ever done."

"Where'd you get saved?"

"Well, people ask me from time to time how to get saved. I tell 'em you go down to Grace Landmark Baptist Church, six miles down this road and two miles off to the right back in a grove of pecan trees. You go on Sunday morning. Take the third seat from the back set in about the middle. Listen to the sermon," he said grinning, "and on the second verse of 'I Surrender All' you get up and walk down and fall on your knees at the mourner's bench. You mourn for a while and tell God you're sorry you're a sinner and ask Jesus to save you. That's it."

Colin was laughing and Lanie could not help grinning. "You suppose people have to go through all that?"

"Well, not really. That's the way it happened to me and all I could tell about it. You go on and get you some grub. I'll fill up your machine here."

As the man wound the lever to pump the gas out of the tank up into the pump itself, Lanie went inside followed by Colin. It was a typical small store with one of everything, it seemed, and very rarely more than that. One section was devoted to hardware—screws, nuts, bolts; the groceries were on shelves reaching to the ceiling. There were barrels of pickles and crackers and various calendars decorating the wall. A rangy cinnamon-colored cat lay watching them lazily with enormous golden eyes. Lanie went over and tried to pet him, but he hissed at her.

"Don't pay no attention to Lucifer there," the woman behind the counter called. "He's meaner than the devil. That's why I named him Lucifer."

"Well, I know how to sweeten him up," Colin said. "Give me a can of those sardines." She fished the sardines down, and Colin added, "A box of crackers too."

Colin ordered the lunch, which included sardines, crackers, two big Nehi cream sodas, and a sack full of penny candy, mostly sugared orange slices. Colin opened one of the cans with the key in the top and reached out and got the saucer that was on the floor beside the big tom. He put some of the sardines in, drained some of the juice, and said, "There, Lucifer. See how you like that." The big cat was up instantly and began eating hungrily. As he ate, Colin grinned and ran his hand down the big cat's spine. "I'm afraid he's not much of a Christian at that. He just follows for the sardines."

"You got his number. You folks goin' far?"

"All the way to Cummings," Colin said cheerfully.

"You got folks in there?"

"Yes. We're just gonna make a visit," Colin said smoothly. The lean man came in, and Colin paid for the gas and the food, then they went outside and sat on a bench underneath a Sinclair Oil sign. They ate the crackers and sardines, and Lanie said, "We're going to smell terrible."

"Well, we probably will. I forgot to ask the blessing on this food. I guess I can ask it anyway. Thank you, Lord, for this good food." He turned and said, "How do you like riding a bike?"

"Oh, it's fun." She studied Colin, thinking that most men as fine looking as he was would be swollen with pride, but he didn't seem to think at all about his looks. "What was life like in Africa? Did you ever see a lion?"

"Oh, sure. Lots of them."

"What about the natives there? Are there cannibals?"

"There's some cannibalism. The most interesting natives I ever saw were the Masai. The men are all six feet, some of them up to six six."

"Do they carry spears like we see in the movies?"

"Well, I haven't seen any of the movies, but most of them are handsome people. The women too. You wouldn't like what they eat."

"What do they eat?"

"They have big herds of cattle. When they want to eat, they go out and they milk the cow, catching the milk in a cup. Then they open up a vein on the cow's neck and drain off some blood into it. Then they drink it."

"You're making that up!"

"No, I'm not. They tried me out. Thought a white man couldn't handle it, but I did. As a matter of fact, I've tasted worse stuff here in America."

The two talked for a while, and finally he said, "I've been praying for your dad, but I don't know the particulars. Do you want to tell me about it?"

"It was a terrible thing. There was this man named Duke Biggins who worked for Daddy. He was drunk most of the time, and Daddy went over to fire him. Daddy carried a gun for snakes in the woods. Duke got violent, and in the struggle it went off."

"Well, that would be self-defense."

"It would have been, but Duke's brother, Alvin, and the woman that lives with him, Ethel Crawford, both testified that Daddy brought the gun in and shot him without any warning. They were the only witnesses, so the jury had to find him guilty of manslaughter at least."

Colin was studying the young woman as she spoke. He had heard a great deal about the character of Lanie Freeman, and now he said quietly, "Well, I know you're praying for him to be released. I'll team up with you on that."

"He's such a good man, Pastor." Tears came to Lanie's eyes. "Sometimes I get so tired I just don't think I can make it."

Colin leaned over and took her hand, held it for a moment, then stood up. "God is faithful," he said simply. "We'll pray until he's out of that place. Now let's get going."

When they arrived at the prison, the guard, whose name was Jack Taylor, grinned at Lanie's outfit. "I like that outfit, Miss Freeman. Didn't know you was a biker."

"I didn't have any other way to get here, but my pastor offered to bring me on his motorcycle."

"Never heard of a preacher riding a motorcycle." Taylor grinned.

"We'd like to see Dad."

"Well, you know he's been sick. He's in the infirmary right now. Come along. I'll take you in."

"Do I need a pass or anything?" Colin asked.

"Oh, I'll take care of that. I don't reckon you'll get everybody to bust out, will you, Reverend?"

"No, I won't do that."

Lanie and Colin followed the guard to the building that contained the infirmary, then down a long hall. As soon as they turned in, Lanie saw her father in bed. He turned his head toward them, his eyes widened, and he struggled to sit up. "Muff, where'd you get that outfit?" he asked.

Lanie ran over and put her arms around him and hugged him. "It's Davis's—I had to wear it because we came on Brother Ryan's motorcycle. Daddy, I was so sorry to hear you've been sick. I just had to come."

"Well, I'm glad you did. Who's this with you?"

"This is Reverend Colin Ryan. He's the new pastor of the church."

"Just interim," Colin said. "Holding down the fort until they can get a real preacher. Glad to meet you, Brother Freeman."

Lanie said quickly, "I didn't have any other way to get here, and Brother Ryan brought me."

"You rode a motorcycle all the way from home?" Forrest grinned. "That must have been a different kind of trip."

"Here, Daddy, I brought you two big sacks full of oatmeal cookies with raisins in them. The kind you like."

"Sit down and tell me how everybody is."

Colin said at once, "You two will want some time alone. I'm going to see about visiting some of the other inmates. I'll come back after a while."

As soon as Colin left, Forrest pulled out one of the cookies and bit off of it. As he chewed it, he said, "Never saw a preacher quite like that."

"He's the best preacher you ever heard, Daddy. Of course some don't like him because he doesn't always act like a preacher."

"What does he do?"

"Oh, he goes into awful places and preaches right in the middle of taverns, for one thing. And he doesn't dress like a preacher, for another thing. Only preacher I ever saw that didn't wear a tie on the pulpit."

"Well, I can tell he's a good man. Now, tell me about everything..."

<hr>

Potter Gladden, the warden at Cummings, was talking to Lanie about Colin. "He barged right in here and asked permission to visit with the inmates. I found out he was your pastor and figured it was all right. You know what that sucker did? He got a bunch of the inmates together and preached like there was a thousand people there." Warden Gladden, a short stocky man with a thick neck and intent gray eyes, shook his head as he smiled. "I reckon he's the kind of preacher these fellows need around here. By the way, he told me you needed a place to stay. We've got a cabin here, a little house we use for visitors. You can stay there tonight. I'll find a place for your pastor."

"Thank you, Warden."

"He talked me into having another service tonight. I guess I'll be there. I never knew a motorcycle-ridin' preacher."

Lanie and Colin ate supper with the men. The food was mostly starches but was well cooked. The warden ate with them, and after the meal they went into the large room used for a chapel. The service was crowded. Lanie watched the inmates as they came in, and as Colin preached, she studied their faces more intently. She saw a hunger for God there and prayed for Colin and the men.

After the sermon, Colin gave a simple invitation, and there was almost a stampede to get to the front.

"Are all these men going to be saved?" she whispered to the warden.

"Oh, no," Gladden said. "That's their way of saying they want to get closer to God. Most of them are Christians already. Some of them, though, might find the Lord tonight. That fellow is some preacher!"

Lanie was tired from the exhausting trip and slept like a rock. She got up and spent the morning with her father, and Colin sat with him for some of the time. She could tell that her father liked him a great deal, and she was glad to see that. She was even happier to see that her father seemed well on the road to recovery.

"We're going to have to go, I guess, Daddy. I wish we could stay longer."

"No. You need to make the trip back."

"Is there anything I can bring you or mail to you?" Lanie asked.

"I'm all right."

"You seem a little sad."

"Well, it's nothin' you can do anything about."

"You don't know about that until you ask." Colin smiled. "What is it?"

"Well, you know my regular job here is taking care of Warden Gladden's dogs, the bloodhounds, and his horse. Not really a hard job, but one of the dogs is gonna be put down."

"What's wrong with him?" Colin asked.

"Well, he's sick, and they can't seem to find what it is. He's my favorite too. He's a sweet-tempered dog. You know you think about bloodhounds as vicious, man-eating dogs, but old Booger, he's just as sweet as sugar."

"Booger? What an awful name!"

"It is pretty bad. I didn't name him that."

They were talking about the dog when Warden Gladden came back. "I just wanted to say good-bye to you folks," he said. "You come and visit anytime you want, Preacher."

"We've been talking about Booger," Colin said. "You going to put him down?"

"I can't stand to see an animal suffer. He is a good dog. Best I ever had on the trail."

"I wish we could take him home," Lanie said suddenly. "We've got a fine vet there. He's an Indian named Sixkiller. I bet he could make him well. But we don't have any way to get him there."

"Why, if you want to try it, I can help you with that. We've got an old truck here. You could take him home in that and come back and get your motorcycle."

Forrest said quickly, "I wish you'd do it, Lanie." He looked at Colin and said, "Preacher, I'd be forever grateful if you could help Booger out. He's a fine dog. Finest I've ever seen."

"Why, we'll do it."

"All right then," Gladden said. "I'll have the men fix a bed for Booger in the back of the truck." He left at once, and Colin shook Forrest's hand. "I want you to know there's one fellow that'll be praying for you every day, Brother Forrest, and that'll be me. I'll be back to see you too. Don't worry about Booger. We'll pray him through."

Colin left, and Lanie leaned over and hugged Forrest. She kissed him and whispered, "I hate to leave, as always."

"I'll be fine. Say, that preacher is somethin', isn't he?"

"He is. I wish he was the pastor all the time. Cody thinks he hung the moon."

Lanie left, and as Jack let them out, he said, "You know, for a preacher you ain't a bad fella, Colin Ryan."

"I'm glad you think so," Colin said. "I'll be back to see you, Jack. You watch out for Forrest now."

The two went to the truck and leaned over the back. The big bloodhound was lying flat and his eyes were closed. Lanie whispered, "He doesn't look good, does he?"

Colin was stroking his head. The dog was wrinkled as all bloodhounds are and would have been strong, but he had lost weight. "We'll pray that God'll pull him up and make a strong dog out of him."

"It would make Daddy happy, and me too."

~ CHAPTER 10 ~

Orrin Pierce looked up from the table he shared with Pardue Jessup in the Dew Drop Inn, spotting his friend Nelson Prather. "There's Nellie," he said, a smile touching his lips. "Could we put up with him, you think?"

Orrin Pierce was a distinguished-looking man of thirty with dark hair and striking blue eyes. He was not married, and alcohol had practically ruined his life, but he managed to make a living with a law practice. "Why, sure, Sheriff," he said. "He's a good fellow."

Pardue shook his head. "He's so blasted superstitious. Drives me crazy, but you're right. He's raised up all his younger brothers and sisters after his dad died, and then his mom became an invalid and he took care of her too."

"I wonder why he's never married. He's a nice-looking fellow. Got a good farm, best beef raiser in the county."

"He's pretty shy."

Pardue waved and called, "Come over and join us, Nellie."

Nelson Prather had been about to leave the Dew Drop Inn, for at the noon hour every seat was filled. He stood there, a tall blond man with mild blue eyes and an unpretentious air, then nodded and said, "Don't mind if I do, Sheriff. How are you, Mr. Pierce?"

"I'm fine," Orrin said. "A little bit crowded in here today."

Sister Myrtle Poindexter came over at once. "Howdy, Nellie. What'll you have today?"

"I don't know. What's good?"

Pardue grinned and winked at Pierce. "Better not have any of those burgers."

"What's wrong with the burgers?" Nellie asked.

"Why, they're coon burgers."

"What's wrong with coon burgers?" Sister Myrtle said loudly, her voice carrying throughout the room. "Charlie kills them and I fix burgers out of 'em."

"I don't believe I'd care for any burgers today, Sister Myrtle," Nellie said. "They're such cute things. I don't think I could eat one."

"They'd be better than possum." Pierce grinned. "But they look like big rats."

"What's the special today, Sister Myrtle?"

"Same as it is every Friday. Chicken-fried steak, mashed potatoes, and green beans."

"I'll have the special."

After Sister Myrtle left, Pardue winked at Pierce. Pardue was a big man with rough good looks who not only served as sheriff but operated his own car repair business. "I don't know what's wrong with me," he said, trying to look mournful. "I've been carryin' this rabbit foot now for a week, and nothin' good's happened to me yet."

Instantly Nellie Prather straightened up. "Let me see that rabbit's foot."

He took the rabbit's foot that Pardue held out to him and shook his head. "Why, of course it didn't bring you no luck. It's the front foot of a rabbit."

"What difference does it make?" Pardue asked.

"Well, the only rabbit's foot that's worth a nickel for bringin' luck is the left hind foot of a rabbit killed at the full of the moon by a cross-eyed person."

Pierce covered his mouth with his napkin to keep Nellie from seeing him smiling. It was just the sort of thing that Nellie Prather would say. "Well, they would be hard to come by. Not many cross-eyed people hunt rabbits, I wouldn't think, especially during the full moon."

"That's what makes 'em so good," Nellie said.

"You don't have one, do you, Nellie?" Pardue said. "I'm needin' some luck about this time."

"Don't talk to me about luck," he said sadly. "I'm just about ruined myself."

"What's the matter?" Pierce asked. Nellie, for all of his superstitions, was usually cheerful.

"Well, it started last week. I didn't pay much attention to what I was doin', and I leaned a broom against the bed."

Both men stared at Nellie. "That's bad, is it?" Pardue asked.

"Bad? There ain't nothin' worse! That'll put an evil spell on a bed quicker than you would think. Only thing worse is movin' a broom when you move into a new house."

"I didn't know that," Pierce said.

"Oh, it's terrible! I had a friend of mine that did that, moved a new broom, and a cat—that's bad too—into his new house. Three years later that house burned right to the ground. It just goes to show you."

Sister Myrtle arrived back with Nellie's food and set it down. "You better try one of the coon burgers, Nellie. They're right good."

"Well, they're scavengers. They eat anything they can find," Nellie protested.

"So are catfish," Sister Myrtle snapped, "but you eat them quick enough!"

Nellie bowed his head and asked a blessing, ignoring the other two who were almost finished. He started eating and the voice of Henrietta Green, the telephone operator who was seated at the next table, carried clear. "... and I say it's a shame that a minister of the gospel would act like that."

"Act like what, Henrietta?" Pierce said.

Henrietta replied, "Why, it's what that Baptist preacher's done."

Doc Givens was sitting across the room, but he, like everyone else, could hear Henrietta clearly. "I wish you'd stop talkin' about people in public. It's bad enough when you do it in private."

Henrietta, however, was not to be put off. She turned to Pierce and said, "You haven't heard about what happened. That preacher took Lanie Freeman to Cummings on the back of his motorcycle. She put on pants just like a man and off they went just a roaring."

Doc Givens was glaring at Henrietta. "He was trying to help the girl was all."

"Well, you would take up for him!" Henrietta snipped. "Your partner Doctor Merritt did the same thing. He took that Freeman girl all the way to Oklahoma, just the two of them."

"That was to see about getting her aunt to come and stay with them, Henrietta!" Givens snapped.

"Well, he took her to Cummings too. I tell you it's a shame when a young girl runs around all over the county with men like that."

Alvin Biggins was seated with one of his friends, a small man called Runt. It was Biggins's brother that had been killed and resulted in Forrest Freeman going to the penitentiary.

"He's just like all other preachers. Ain't worth dirt."

Sister Myrtle instantly marched back and looked down. "I don't allow no bad talk and no profanity."

"I didn't use no profanity."

"Well, you was about to. Now you can just leave, Alvin Biggins."

"Aw, Sister Myrtle, let me finish my meal."

"Well, keep your mouth shut then."

Mamie Dorr was seated at one of the tables, and she said, "Now, me, I like that new preacher. I wish he'd stay around." Mamie saw that Pardue Jessup was grinning at her, and she winked at him. "If he stays long enough, even me and you might get converted."

Pardue nodded. "Well, if I ever get any religion, Mamie, it'll be his brand."

As Lanie and Colin pulled up to the house in the truck, the door burst open and everyone came out. Cody was holding Corliss, and immediately he was popping questions. "Where's your motorcycle? How's Daddy? Is he still sick?"

Davis stood back and watched, but he did glance over at the truck. "Why, there's a dog here," he said.

"That's Booger," Colin said. "He was your dad's favorite dog, and he's sick."

Maeva approached and looked at him. "What kind of dog is he?" she asked cautiously. "He doesn't look too good."

"He's a bloodhound," Lanie said.

"You mean they use him to run down escaped prisoners?"

"I guess so, but he's not running anybody down. We're going to take him over to Doctor Sixkiller and see if he can fix him."

"But we don't have any money for that," Davis said.

Colin Ryan grinned, his teeth white against his tanned skin. "Maybe he'll take his fee in preaching."

"Come on in and tell us everything about Daddy," Maeva said.

Lanie picked up Corliss and held her, kissed her on the cheek. "Daddy said to give you a kiss," she said.

"I wish I could give him one," Corliss said.

"Well, we'll pray until that happens. Now come on in. I'll tell you all about him ..."

⊂━⊷

Matthew Sixkiller stood over the dog that was lying quietly on the stainless steel table. He had gone over the dog carefully, and now he turned to Lanie and Colin and said, "I'm going to have to do more tests. But he doesn't look good."

"Could it be heartworm or something like that?" Colin asked.

"Maybe so. After I do the tests I'll be able to tell you some more." He gave Lanie a quizzical look. "You say he came from Cummings Farm?"

"Daddy got real fond of him. They were going to put him down, but the warden said we could bring him home and try to get him well."

Matthew Sixkiller smiled slightly. "Well, I'll do everything I can, Lanie, you know that."

"We don't have any money," she said quickly.

"Don't worry about it."

"I told the Freemans you could take it out in preaching. It might take a year or two to get that much preaching out of me."

Sixkiller grinned. "I've been waiting for a chance to get you in my debt, Pastor. Some of your sermons have been pretty sharp. Almost hurt my feelings. Maybe I can get you to tone 'em down a bit in exchange for healing this dog. What's his name, by the way?"

"His name is Booger."

Sixkiller laughed. "Why don't you name him something dignified like Napoleon or Freddie?"

"No. His name is Booger. Look. He heard me."

The big bloodhound's eyes opened and he tried to lift his head. Lanie put her hand out and said, "It's all right, Booger. You're going to get well . . ."

○══►

Otis Langley looked across the supper table at his wife and said, "I'm going to prayer meeting tonight."

Martha, Roger, and Louise looked at him in surprise. Roger said, "You never go to prayer meetings, Dad."

"Well, I'm going tonight. Somebody's got to take a hand in this business. It's gone too far."

"What are you talking about?" Roger said. "What's gone too far?"

"That preacher, Ryan. He's going to bring disrepute on our church."

"What's he done now?" Roger demanded.

"He took that Freeman girl all the way to Cummings on the motorcycle and they stayed all night. An unmarried man running around with an unmarried woman is not what I expect from my pastor."

Roger shook his head. "I heard all about that. Lanie's father was sick. She didn't have any other way to get there. I think it was pretty nice of Brother Ryan to take her."

Otis looked at him with disapproval. "You've got to learn to show a little discernment, Son."

The argument grew rather sharp, and finally Otis said, "I'm going to bring it to a vote. This is business night. I'm going to get the church to get rid of that preacher."

Roger's face grew red. "Well, I'm sorry to tell you that I've got a vote too, and I'm going to cancel yours out."

"Would you go against your own father?" Otis demanded.

"If he's wrong—and you're wrong about this."

Louise said, "Well, I'm going, and I know how I'm going to vote. That preacher needs someone to cut him down to size."

"Well, I'm going to do all that I can to see that that's done," Otis said. He got up and left the table, with Louise right behind him.

Martha Langley watched as Roger pushed the remains of his pie with his fork, his eyes moody. "Try not to be upset with your dad, Roger," she said quietly. "He's a good man."

"I know he is in lots of ways, Mom, but he's so determined to be *right* all the time. Why is he like that?"

Martha rose and moved around to take the chair beside Roger. He had always been her pride, and it grieved her to see the rift between her son and her husband. "You have to know what a hard time your dad had when he was growing up, Son. He never speaks of it, but his childhood was terrible—and left scars on his soul."

"He never told me anything about that."

"No, he's ashamed of it—though none of it was his fault."

"What happened to him?" Roger asked.

"His father was a beast."

Roger stared at his mother, speechless. "What do you mean?"

"He abused your father from the time he could walk."

"You mean—he beat him?"

"Yes, and did things far worse than that."

"What could be worse than that?"

"He never said a kind word to him, Roger. He put your father down in the cruelest ways you can imagine. He told him he was going to be a failure, that he'd never amount to anything ..."

Roger sat as still as a statue as his mother gave details of Otis's degradation at the hands of his own father. He saw the tears in his mother's eyes and asked, "Did you know my grandfather?"

"Oh, yes, I knew him," Martha said bitterly. "He was such a hypocrite. He'd brag on your father when someone was present that he wanted to impress, then as soon as they left, he'd sneer at Otis and tell him he was making up lies about him."

"I—I never knew any of this, Mom."

"I wanted to tell you a long time ago, but your father won't have it spoken of. All those terrible things that Otis's father did to him hardened your dad. He set out to prove his father was wrong, and he did it by determining never to be wrong. I've tried to help him understand that we all make mistakes, but his hurt is too deep." Martha Langley squeezed Roger's hand and whispered, "I wanted to tell you this so that you could understand why your father is so hard at times. He's afraid he'll fail, just as his own father said he would."

Roger took a deep breath, then said firmly, "Thanks for telling me, Mom. I'll never forget what you've said."

"Try to understand, Son, and don't be angry with him," Martha said. "He hates himself sometimes after he's shown hardness to someone. Nobody knows about that—but me. I've seen him unable to eat for days because he treated someone in an unkind fashion. I've seen tears in his eyes after he behaved badly."

Roger sat for a long time holding his mother's hand, then he leaned forward and kissed her. "I think I see a side of Dad I never knew about—and it'll make it easier for me to understand him." He got up and said, "I'm going to the meeting. I'll sit by Dad and Louise. Even if we don't agree on this, I'll be next to them at least."

"I'll tell you, Dorsey. It's going to be a real showdown at the Baptist church tonight." Henrietta Green had called Dorsey Pender. They each considered it their responsibility to spread information efficiently in Fairhope, so they stayed in close touch to make sure they were always current. Since she listened in on most telephone conversations and Dorsey knew the mail everyone received, not much happened in Fairhope without their knowing about it. Dorsey's one regret was that the people didn't write all their mail on postcards. Of course, he could always ask them what the letter said, but he was continually shocked that some people refused to tell him.

"What's going on, Henrietta?"

"Well, I heard Otis Langley tell Gerald Pink that he's going to vote to get rid of the preacher."

"Is that right! Well, I usually don't go to prayer meeting, but I expect I'd better go tonight."

"I'm going too," Henrietta said. "You suppose they let Presbyterians into the Baptist church?"

"Why, of course they do. Anybody can go. Of course, in a business meeting they sometimes ask the visitors to leave. But you come on anyhow. You can sit with me."

"Mr. Langley's the biggest giver in the church since he moved his membership there. I expect he'll get his way."

"He usually does. I'll see you at church."

⊶

When the Freemans arrived at church, Lanie was surprised at the number of cars in the parking lot. Once inside, she glanced around and saw that the sanctuary was crowded. "What are all these people doing here?"

Davis shook his head. "I don't know, but about half of them don't even belong to our church."

Cody was pleased. "Well, I'm glad to see that people are waking up," he said. "It's about time some of them got to church, and they've come to the right place."

Davis shook his head. "Something's wrong. I'll go find out."

"How are you gonna find out, Davis?" Lanie whispered.

"I will. Just wait here."

Lanie watched as Davis walked over and pulled Sally Delaughter, the sixteen-year-old daughter of the mayor, off to one side. Lanie knew that Sally was absolutely in love with Davis, but then so were many of the high school girls. She watched as the two talked, and finally Davis turned and came back. He said at once, "Old man Langley's gonna try to get rid of the preacher."

"No, he can't do that!" Cody said.

"He's a pretty good politician"—Davis shrugged—"and he's just mean enough to do it too. I wish we had known about all this. We're going to need every vote we can get."

Lanie had a sinking sensation as she took her seat. On Wednesday night there was no choir, and after one hymn Colin stood up. He was wearing a blue shirt with a white collar and a pair of rather worn slacks. "Well, I'm glad to see such a good crowd here. It's always good to see people come out to hear the Word of God. Tonight we're going to continue our study of the heroes of faith in the Old Testament. Tonight our study will be on Moses."

Colin Ryan was an excellent teacher. He had a clear voice, and he always seemed to be excited about his subject. He spoke for a long time about the greatness of Moses, and finally he said, "What I want you to know about Moses is he had to learn to lay aside his natural abilities and talents before he could serve God. You remember that Moses had a rod. It was what he used to herd his sheep with. He was used to it. But God had determined that Moses would use that rod as part of his plan for freeing the Israelites from the Egyptians."

Lanie leaned forward and listened as Ryan spoke of how Moses was commanded by God to do a strange thing. "God said, 'Throw down your rod, Moses,'" Colin said. "And I imagine Moses must have been disturbed. He might have said something like, 'But, Lord, I'm used to it and it's what I use. It's one of my tools.' But God said, 'Throw it down.'

"Do you see what's happening here? Moses had to throw down the rod and put his trust in God, not in the rod itself. He did, and God began to use that rod. Up until this time it was the rod of Moses, but from this time forward it became the rod of God."

Everyone was listening breathlessly as Colin made the application. "Some of you out there may have a great talent. You may have a great singing voice. You may have the gift of teaching or making money. It doesn't matter what it is. What God is asking you to do is throw it down, as he told Moses to throw aside his rod. Before God can use any gift, it must be given to him as a sacrifice. So I'm praying that in this church we all will throw down any natural talent we have, anything that we do well, and let God sanctify it. Then it will not be our voice or our talent or our ability. It will be God working through us as he worked through the rod through Moses."

It was a wonderful teaching, and finally Colin smiled and said, "Now we're going to have a prayer before we have a business meeting. You know sometimes a prayer meeting has everything in it but prayer. It has music. It has fellowship. It has teaching. But tonight we're going to pray. Now, I know all of you have something that you need to bring to God in prayer. I want you to speak out those requests."

As usual several requested prayers for members of their family who were ill or experiencing other hardships. Lanie, however, was shocked to hear Cody's voice out loud. "Preacher, I want us to pray for Booger."

Lanie could sense the shock that ran over the congregation. She caught a glimpse of Otis Langley's face and saw that it was red.

Colin Ryan stepped in. "Some of you may not know about the dog that Miss Freeman and I brought home from Cummings. He's a bloodhound, and he's very sick. He was a favorite of the warden there and also of our brother Forrest Freeman. So we have brought him home and we've taken him to see the good Doctor Sixkiller. Doctor Sixkiller, do you have a report?"

Matthew Sixkiller stood up and shook his head. "I'm sorry to say that I haven't been able to pin the trouble down yet, but he's a very sick animal, and I don't really expect him to live unless there's a miracle."

"Well, we just need a miracle for Booger."

Otis Langley stood up, and his voice was shocked. "I think it's entirely out of place to pray for a dog within our prayer meetings. I insist that we put this nonsense behind us."

Maeva Freeman was never one for church, but suddenly she stood up and faced Otis Langley, her back straight and her eyes dancing with anger. "I expect if God cares about sparrows, he cares for dogs no matter what their name is!"

Otis Langley glared at the young woman, but the pastor spoke quickly, "There was a woman who lived some time ago named Mrs. Alexander. She wrote a beautiful poem. I've always liked it. It goes like this:

The rich man in his castle,
The poor man at his gates,
God made them, high or lowly,
And ordered their estate.
All things bright and beautiful,
All creatures great and small,
All things wise and wonderful,
The Lord God made them all.

"I think God is interested in our world, and many of us have pets that we love, so I don't think it's out of order to pray for this animal. Now, are there other requests?"

The prayer session that followed was unlike anything that had taken place in Fairhope's First Baptist Church. Many spoke their petitions out loud, and almost half of them included Booger in their requests. When the prayers were over, Lanie looked up with tears in her eyes. She saw that Colin was smiling. "I guarantee," the pastor said, "that God has heard your prayers."

Otis Langley said at once, "I want to ask for a meeting for special business."

"Very well," Colin said quietly. "I will ask the chairman of our board of deacons, Brother Pink, to preside."

Gerald Pink reluctantly came forward and said, "What is the nature of this business, Brother Langley?"

"I want to ask the church to vote to bring in Brother Clifford as pastor of the church at once."

A silence fell over the church, and Gerald Pink looked helplessly at Colin, who said, "Take the vote, brother."

But Gerald Pink said quickly, "I'm not sure that this is in order, Brother Langley."

"It's a perfectly normal request," Langley said.

Gerald Pink was a mild-mannered man and usually intimidated by Langley, but something was working in him. "I'm sorry," he said, "you can come to the board of deacons meeting, and we will discuss this matter. But it would be out of order tonight to have such a vote. We've already agreed that Brother Colin Ryan will be our interim pastor. I declare this meeting adjourned."

Cody said loudly, "Well, praise the Lord!" And for once Lanie felt that his exuberance was entirely in order. She turned and hugged Corliss, who asked, "Is Booger going to be all right?"

"Yes," she whispered. "God's going to heal him. You just wait and see!"

✦ CHAPTER 11 ✦

Doctor Matthew Sixkiller stood over the prone body of the big dog, resting his hand lightly on the massive head. Sixkiller, as someone had remarked, looked like one of Sitting Bull's braves who had wiped out Custer at the Little Big Horn. His skin was bronze, his nose aquiline and bent, and his eyes were an obsidian black. At the age of thirty-three, he had the strong body of a young man of twenty, not tall but well built. It had been difficult gaining acceptance in the Arkansas town. Some residents still had prejudice against Indians, although they were not quite sure why.

"What's wrong with him, Doctor Sixkiller?"

Sixkiller looked across the table at Lanie, who was watching him closely. He tried for a moment to think of an answer that would be satisfactory, but finding none he shrugged his trim shoulders. "I just don't know, Lanie. I've given him every test I can think of. There are so many things that can go wrong with animals, and we just don't have all the answers yet."

"Do you think he's going to live?"

"Not unless he turns a corner soon. He's getting worse all the time." He stroked the big dog's head and said, "He's a fine animal too."

"My daddy said he was the best tracker in the world."

"I don't doubt it." He smiled, his teeth white against his coppery skin. "Did you hear Sister Myrtle had her whole church praying for him last night?"

"No, but it sounds like something she would do." Lanie reached into her purse and pulled out a few bills. "Here, Doctor, I want to pay you what I can."

"Not necessary."

"It's all right," Lanie said quickly. "Mamie Dorr put a coffee can in her beauty shop with a sign on it that said Help Save Booger. People have been donating to help pay you."

Sixkiller laughed. "It's a funny thing, Lanie, the way people are. We've got human beings sicker than Booger in this town, and yet nobody's put up a coffee can in a business for them. I guess trying to save a bloodhound is pretty spectacular. So many people sick during these Depression days that it's just become one more thing."

"It's not that people don't care, Doctor," Lanie said quickly.

"I know that. People are naturally drawn to drama. I've often thought that the finest hour of the church's life is when somebody's house burns down. Everybody turns out to help when that happens. We just can't do enough. But if the house doesn't burn down, and people are hurting without showing it, we're not too hard-pressed to find out what's going on."

"You're right, Doctor." Lanie paused and petted Booger's big head for a moment. "I've got to go to town, but I'll come back tonight."

"By the way, how's Annie doing?"

"Not too well. I'm worried about her."

"Well, we'll have the church pray for her too at prayer meeting. I've already started."

Lanie left the vet and climbed into the pickup. As always she held her breath, for it was always a question as to whether the truck would start or not. It wound around slowly, and finally the engine coughed and fired off. When it was running as smoothly as she could expect, she put it in gear and eased out of the driveway. All the way to town she thought about Booger and about what Doctor Sixkiller said. It was rather amazing to her how many people had heard about the big dog. Of course the gossip machine worked better than any other system in Fairhope, thanks to Dorsey Pender and Henrietta Green.

As she approached the city limits, Lanie looked over and saw three men walking along the railroad tracks headed into town. "Boes," short for hoboes, were a familiar sight these days. Most of them were pretty far gone. From time to time, they came into the town, and Lanie fed them whenever she could. It disturbed her to think that not just in Fairhope, Arkansas, but all over the United States homeless men were searching desperately for work. She could not understand the Depression. She could understand an earthquake — that was a natural phenomenon. But it didn't seem like anything had happened to cause this financial catastrophe. Nothing had changed except money was suddenly impossible to come by, and work was a phantom that men traipsed for miles to find and most often failed.

Pulling into town, she stopped in front of Pardue Jessup's auto repair shop. She shut the engine down, and as she did, Pardue came out. He was wearing his sheriff's uniform and grinned broadly at her. "What's up, Lanie?"

"Something's wrong with this old truck. I wish you'd listen to it."

"Old age is what's wrong with it." Pardue shrugged. "Start her up again."

Lanie started the engine. Pardue lifted the hood, and for a time he tinkered underneath it. Finally he came out from under it and said, "Shut it down. It's the carburetor."

Lanie's heart sank. "Will it cost much to fix it?"

"Nah, I can do it with some spare parts I got around here. Come on out and have an RC Cola on the house."

Lanie got out and walked over to the icebox. She opened it and pulled an icy bottle out and pulled the cap off with the opener on the side. "I guess RC Cola is about as good as soft drinks get."

"Oh, I don't know. I like them Nehi strawberry myself."

"Yep, they're good too." She watched while Pardue fixed the carburetor. "Did you know that Mamie put out a coffee can to collect money to help save Booger?"

"No, I didn't hear about that. She's got a good heart though, that woman has."

Pardue was a mystery to much of Fairhope. He was in his late thirties and considered the most eligible bachelor in the county. At six foot two, he was well-built, with black hair and dark eyes. He was admired by the men for his hunting and fishing ability and by the women for his rough good looks and his wit. The gossip mill regularly brought up the subject of why Pardue had not married. Marlene Jenkins sniffed, "There's got to be something wrong with him, a man that don't get married and him in his thirties."

Lanie had often longed to ask Pardue about this, and now would be a good time. "Pardue, can I ask you a question?"

"Let her fly."

"How come you never got married?"

"Why, don't you ever go to the movies?"

"I go every time I can get the money together."

"Well, you ought to know then." Pardue turned. He had a smudge of grease on his right cheek, and his eyes were dancing. "Falling in love is a hard thing, Lanie. What has to happen, a fella has to see a girl for the first time, and suddenly it's like—well, it's like a bolt of lightning hits you. His knees get weak and his hands tremble and he begins to sweat." Pardue suddenly laughed. "It's a whole lot like catchin' the flu, I reckon."

"Oh, that's just the movies."

"You don't believe in romance like that? Why, you was talkin' just last week about how Robert Taylor had seen Barbara Stanwyck and at first look he just got plumb goofy."

Lanie laughed. "You're teasing me, Pardue."

"I guess so." He straightened up and turned his head critically, staring at the carburetor. "That ought to do it, I reckon." He pulled an oily rag off of a nail stuck on the side of the garage and began wiping his hands. "Well, I'll tell you a secret if you promise not to tell."

"I promise."

"Not even Aunt Kezia."

"Not even her. What is it?"

"Well, I always wanted to get me a reading woman."

"You mean like a schoolteacher."

"Could be. That English teacher of yours, Eden Dunsmore. I set out to win her one time, but she's stuck on Dempsey Wilson. I had to give up." Pardue started the truck, checked the running of it, and then stepped outside. "Well, who do you think I ought to marry?"

"I think you ought to marry Cassandra Sue Pruitt."

Pardue laughed. "She's a book woman, all right. You can't get more bookish then being a librarian. But I made a run at her. Took her out one time, but her older sister Leah, she didn't approve of me. I don't have enough education."

"That doesn't make any difference."

"It does to Leah Pruitt. You know her old man was a judge, a big muckety-muck in the legislature. She's waitin' for that kind of fella to come along for Cassandra."

"Well, he better hurry up. Cassandra's twenty-eight. Most women are married and have families by then."

"You know, I think she's lonesome." Pardue suddenly looked down at the ground and continued to wipe his hands automatically. He looked up finally, and there was a sadness in his eyes that Lanie had never seen before. "Well, who ain't," he muttered. He would have said more but at that instant Otis Langley came rushing up. He was huffing from the effort, and his face was red.

"Sheriff, you got to do something about that woman!"

"What woman's that? Some brazen hussy shootin' up the town, Otis?"

"It's not funny," Otis said. He gave Lanie a hard look and waited for her to leave, but she did not. It rather pleased her to see Langley upset. He had upset enough people himself.

"It's that woman they call Butcher Knife Annie."

"Her name is Beulah Ann Toliver, Mr. Langley," Lanie said firmly.

"I don't care what her name is. You have to do something about her."

"What's she done?"

"She's marching back and forth in front of my house with a sign."

"What kind of a sign?"

"It's a sign she made herself. It says Help Save Booger." He turned suddenly and stared at Lanie. "Did you have anything to do with this, Lanie Freeman?"

"No, sir, I didn't even know about it."

"I don't reckon there's a law against carryin' signs around," Pardue said. "You posted lots of signs for your businesses, Otis."

"This is different! That woman is invading my privacy."

"Well, out of my jurisdiction. You'd better get Ed Hathcock. This is a job for the chief of police."

"He's gone to Fort Smith."

Pardue was amused, but he shrugged his heavy shoulders. "Me and Lanie will go over and have a talk with Annie."

"You take care of it, Sheriff!" Langley snapped, then turned around and left abruptly.

"Let's go in this pickup." Pardue got behind the wheel and started the engine.

As they turned out, Lanie said, "Why is Otis Langley so mean?"

"Because he's got money, and he's used to having his own way."

"Not everybody that has money is mean."

"No. That's the truth. Well, one of these days, something's going to come up that money can't fix, and then Mr. Otis Lawrence Langley will come up short."

They drove directly to the Langley home and stopped the truck. When they got out they saw Annie sitting on the curb. Her face was pale. The sign said, "HEp SaVE BOOgER!" Lanie approached her.

"Annie, you're not well. You should be home."

"I'm tired of wallowing around in that bed."

"Come on, Annie. We'll give you a ride back," Pardue said.

Lanie and Pardue argued with Annie, but she was stubborn. Finally they talked her into going home, and twenty minutes later Lanie was tucking Annie in bed. "You stay right here. I've got an errand to run, and I'll be right back to take care of you."

"Don't reckon I'm goin' no place."

When Lanie went out, she said, "We'd better go by and get Doctor Merritt. I'm worried about Annie."

"She kind of reminds me of you. Of course you're a little cleaner than Annie is. She don't take to bathin' much, but she's stubborn like you are. Wants her own way."

"Sheriff, I'm not stubborn."

"Yes, you are. Most young girls would have quit when they had a whole family dumped on 'em. But you didn't. I guess I never told you how much I admire you for that. If you was a few years older, I'd court you myself. You're a book woman."

"You better concentrate on Cassandra."

"Tell you what. Why don't you educate me about books so I can talk to her? All I can talk about is how to gut a fish or somethin' like that. It's not real interesting. And it's not romantic, is it?"

"I'll get you a book and you can read it. Then we'll talk about it and you can bring it up with Cassandra."

"Get one of them Zane Grey books. I like shootin' and cowboys and such."

"No. That won't do. I'll find you just the right thing. Now, I'm going to get Doctor Merritt. Come on. I'll take you back to your garage."

"Annie, I ought to cut a switch to you. What are you doing with that sign?"

"I heered that Langley didn't want to pray for Booger."

Owen Merritt had been examining Annie and now he removed his stethoscope and put it in his black bag. "Doc Sixkiller's taking care of Booger, but I'm gonna have to put you in the hospital."

"Ain't goin'."

Merritt stared at her and tried to think of some way to force the woman to go. "It would be better for you," he said.

Lanie saw the expression on Annie's face. "I'll take care of her, Doctor."

"You've enough to take care of." Owen saw the stubborn looks on both Lanie and Annie's faces, and he knew he was no match for them. "All right, maybe together we can do it. I can stop by and check on her. We'll go by the drugstore and get some medicine, and you can feed her up on chicken soup."

The two left the house, and as they got into Owen's car, he suddenly turned toward her and smiled. "You sure plowed up a snake with that dog Booger. Talk's all over town about it."

"I don't know why people are so nosy."

"Everybody's taking sides. Otis Langley wants to have him put away."

"Daddy says he's the sweetest-tempered dog he ever saw. I hate it when people get upset about things that are none of their business. But Roger told me about his family. They just don't like me."

"Well, it'll pass, Lanie. I hate it on your account. You've got enough on your shoulders. Come along. We'll go by and see what we can find at the drugstore for Annie."

Doctor Givens was sitting in his easy chair, his leg poked straight out in front of him on a hassock. Ever since he had broken his leg, he had been subject to quite a bit of pain, although he never mentioned it. He listened while Owen told him about his cases, and finally he said, "What about Annie?"

"Lanie's taking care of her."

"And what about this Booger thing?" Doctor Givens said. "I'm not a man of prayer, but I'm a dog man. I ain't had a dog now for about a year, but I love the breed. Nothing wrong with praying for a dog that I can see."

"I don't think so either."

Doctor Givens studied his young colleague through half-lidded eyes. He had been doubtful about Owen Merritt making it in a small town. Merritt had been a city doctor, knowing no life except that of Memphis. Givens had told his nurse, "That young whippersnapper won't last six months." He had been wrong about that, however, and now he suddenly wondered about the engagement of Owen Merritt to Louise Langley.

"How're things going with your fiancée? You two have any good fights lately?"

Merritt suddenly grinned. "She's got strong opinions. Hard to change when she gets an idea in her mind."

"That's natural. Louise's always been the prettiest and the smartest and the richest. That's a bad combination. She could always get whatever she wanted one way or another."

"I've told her she should marry a rich man. My dad was a furniture salesman. We never had much."

"You want my advice?"

"Sure. What do you think?"

"Take a stick to her."

Owen Merritt suddenly began to laugh. His eyes studied the older man with fondness. "I guess we can rule out marital counseling as a career for you, Doctor. Well, I've got to get going."

———

Roger had not come home for dinner, and Louise took the evening meal as an opportunity to talk with her dad about her dissatisfaction with what her brother was doing. Martha Langley and Owen Merritt listened to the discussion they'd heard many times. Louise was petulant, which always emphasized the two small lines between her eyebrows that were fairly deeply indented by now. "Roger should be ashamed of himself. He's wasting his life."

"Well, maybe he'll get tired of it. He's working hard," her father said. The incident with Butcher Knife Annie had stuck with him. He was not a cruel man, but he'd forgotten how hard it was to be poor. In his youth he had known, but money had come his way, and with it he had lost something. He glanced over at Owen and said, "How is that woman doing?"

"Annie? Not too well."

"She should be in the hospital. The woman's got no judgment."

Owen Merritt shrugged his shoulders. "She's pretty independent, Mr. Langley. Used to having her own way." He winked at Louise. "Seems pretty common in the women around here."

The family ignored Owen's attempt at humor.

"Well, who's going to take care of Annie? She's all alone, isn't she?" Martha Langley asked.

"Lanie's staying with her some of the time, and I'll be going by every day."

Louise frowned. She started to say something about Lanie Freeman but thought better of it. She had had several arguments with Owen about the time he spent with the Freeman family, especially with Lanie. Now she changed the subject. "Have you thought any more about your practice, Owen?"

"Not really."

"You'd do so well in a big city. If you could practice somewhere like St. Louis or New York—"

"Now wait a minute!" Otis said suddenly. "That would be a mistake. There's going to be a new hospital built in this area—as big as any big city's hospital, state of the art. Big enough to serve the entire county and more. I'm politickin' to get it built right here in Fairhope. If that happens, Owen, you'd be in on the ground floor."

"Well, I'm not much of an administrator, I'm afraid."

"It would be so nice if you could stay here," Martha Langley said.

Owen let the implications of her comment go, and for a while all that was heard was the *chink* of silver against china while the family ate.

"I'm worried about the church," Otis eventually said. "That fellow Ryan isn't the man we need here for a pastor."

"I agree with you, Dad," Louise said. "He's arrogant."

Owen looked at Louise with surprise. "Arrogant? I never thought that about Colin Ryan."

"Well, he is."

"He's different," Owen said. "He grew up in a different culture."

Louise shrugged her shoulders. "I don't like him. He has no idea of dignity."

Merritt lifted his eyebrow. "Well, I guess when you're ministering on the tough streets of Chicago, dignity is pretty hard to come by." He studied the Langleys carefully, and a familiar thought came to him. *Can I please these people? We're so different!* He left that night earlier than he would have ordinarily.

PART THREE

❧ ☙

The Romances

CHAPTER 12

The office of the *Fairhope Sentinel* was relatively calm for a change. The presses were shut down for minor repair, and except for the sound of two voices arguing vociferously from the printing room, all was quiet as Elspeth Patton sat enjoying her sassafras tea. She was a small woman, erect with silver hair and gray eyes, fine looking at the age of sixty-one. Her husband had started the *Sentinel*, and at his death she had taken over as owner and editor. Elspeth enjoyed being a newspaper woman, for she had an active inquiring mind and an independent spirit. Since there was no other newspaper in the county, she did not have to worry about competition.

Suddenly the front door swung open, and Elspeth looked up to see Otis Langley. One look at his face told her that he was unhappy, and she braced herself for whatever he had come to tell her. "Good morning, Otis. How are you?"

Otis said, "I've come to talk to you about the problem with that blasted dog."

"You mean Booger?" Elspeth smiled. "Isn't that a delightful name?"

Otis Langley stared at the woman in disbelief. "I think it's vulgar and almost obscene! I've come down to ask you to write an editorial about it."

"And what do you think the editorial should say?" Elspeth asked, quietly sipping her tea, her eyes fixed on the big man. He was her largest advertiser, for he owned several businesses, but Elspeth Patton was not a woman to be influenced by such a thing.

"This country is going down so fast you can't keep up with it," Otis said. He shook his head in despair. "Half the people in the country are out of work. There are people starving to death, and all we can think about is one sick dog. Doesn't that tell you something about what kind of town we've got?"

"Have you seen the dog?"

"No, I haven't seen the dog," Otis said with irritation. "I don't need to. I understand he's a bloodhound that that oldest Freeman girl brought home from the prison farm. That tells you something about her sense of responsibility."

"Lanie has been pretty responsible, Otis. She took over after her mother died; and then when her father went to prison, she had to assume the burden for the whole household."

It was a touchy situation, for Elspeth knew that Otis Langley had yearned to buy the Freeman homeplace. It was located on the west side of town, where growth would have to come. He had done everything he could to buy the place after Forrest Freeman went to prison, but somehow Lanie had hung on. Otis knew that Elspeth was responsible for getting the mortgage on the place paid off. She had brought the antique dealer to the Freeman place, who offered enough money to pay off the mortgage. Langley never mentioned it to her, but she knew it was a bitter pill for him to swallow—being beaten by a woman!

"I'm depending on you to write an editorial on this thing, Elspeth."

"You may be sure that I will, and I certainly appreciate your bringing this to my attention. Be assured, Otis, the next edition of the *Sentinel* will have a strong editorial on this issue."

"Well, that's fine," Otis said, rather shocked by the ease with which he gained his victory. He won very few arguments with Elspeth Patton, and now he smiled and said, "I'll be looking forward to it."

A sudden impulse swept into Elspeth's mind, and she said, "Otis, don't you get tired of being *against* things?"

Just then the presses started back up and their noisy rumbling filled the building.

"What?" Otis shouted.

Elspeth had known Otis Langley for many years and understood him better than most. She knew his family and was aware that Otis's father had mistreated his son. Knowing his history, Elspeth was always charitable in her thinking of Otis. "Why don't you give a big donation to help the dog, Otis? That would be a generous thing for you to do."

Otis stared at Elspeth with amazement. "Why would I do a thing like that?"

"Because deep under all that hard surface you cultivate so carefully, there's a goodness."

"Why—that's a strange thing for you to say!"

"I remember how generous you were as a child, Otis. You've come a long way and you're very successful. But you fought so hard for success that you seem to have lost something."

"Lost what?"

"Gentleness, kindness, understanding—the things you craved from your father and never got."

"You don't know what you're talking about, woman!" Otis Langley's face was pale and his lips were trembling. He kept this part of his life hidden, but Elspeth had touched him, and he whirled and left the office without another word.

Elspeth shook her head, murmuring, "Poor Otis! You have it in you to be such a good man, but you're chained by those bad memories!" She rolled a sheet of paper into the typewriter before her. She typed rapidly for some time, and then she jerked the paper out, and turning, she yelled as loud as she could, "Stop the presses!" She giggled and leaned back in her chair, looking at the editorial. "I always wanted to yell that, just like in the movies."

The meeting of the Ministerial Alliance of Stone County was held in the Dew Drop Inn on the first Monday morning of each month. They started at ten o'clock, which gave them time to eat breakfast and leave, so Sister Myrtle and her husband Charlie could quickly clean up in time for the lunch crowd.

There was a murmur of talk and some laughter as the members of the alliance waited for Sister Myrtle to bring out the refreshments. Colin Ryan was there, along with Roy Jefferson, the Episcopal priest; Father Robert Quinn, the Catholic priest; Ellison Burke, the pastor of the Methodist church; and Alex Digby, pastor of the Presbyterian church. Madison Jones, the pastor of the black Methodist church, was absent, and Sister Myrtle was in the kitchen. As pastor of the Fire Baptized Pentecostal Church, she was used to being the only woman present.

Roy Jefferson was teasing Ellison Burke about Sherman Teasdale, a man in his eighties who had married a girl only sixteen years of age.

"Didn't you give old Sherm any pastoral counseling before he married Lucille?" Roy asked Ellison, slyly winking across the room at the big form of Father Robert Quinn.

Ellison Burke was a small man, trim and neat in all of his ways. He was the scholar of the group, though he had a keen sense of humor. "Yes," he said, "I did counsel him."

"What did you say?" Father Quinn demanded.

"I told him as tactfully as I could that sex could be dangerous at his age."

"What did he say, Elly?" Alex Digby asked.

Ellis Burke grinned. "He looked straight at me and said, 'Well, Preacher, Lucy will just have to take her chances.'"

A laugh went around the table, and Roy Jefferson sipped his coffee. He was a tall, gangly man without an ounce of excess flesh. He looked, as a matter of fact, much like a piece of farming equipment that was almost as awkward. Still, he was a fine preacher and well liked in the town. He turned to Alex Digby and asked, "How're things at the Presbyterian church, Alex?"

"Fine. Just fine."

"Well," Roy Jefferson put in, "that church is notorious for runnin' preachers off. I can't figure out how you manage to stay so long."

Alex grinned. "Well, I found the secret. I keep the ones who want to run me off away from those who haven't made up their minds yet. If they ever get together, I'm a gone coon."

Sister Myrtle suddenly bustled in bringing saucers balanced on her arm. She put them down in front of the ministers. "There. If you don't like buttermilk pie, you're in the wrong place."

Charlie, Sister Myrtle's husband, came around filling the coffee cups, then went back to the kitchen. Sister Myrtle took her seat and for a time the only sounds in the café were forks digging into the sweet creamy custard and statements of approval about the pie.

They were just finishing up when suddenly Reverend Madison Jones, the black Methodist preacher, came rushing in. He had a newspaper in his hand, and his teeth shone white against his ebony skin. "The *Sentinel* just come out," he said in his booming voice. "Look at this." He held the paper up so that they could see the headlines, which said in extremely large print: PRAY FOR BOOGER.

Quinn slapped the table so hard with his hand that the plates jumped. "Good for Sister Elspeth," he laughed.

Roy Jefferson said with wonder, "That headline's bigger than when war was declared."

Madison passed the newspaper to Alex Digby, then took a seat while Sister Myrtle got him pie and coffee. As she was bringing it, he said, "I asked Miss Elspeth about that, and she told me Mr. Langley told her to write how foolish it was to be carryin' on about a dog. So that's what she done."

"Langley's been frothing about the mouth about that dog for a week," Alex Digby said. "I told him it'd be dangerous to tell Elspeth Patton how to run her newspaper." He looked across the table at Colin. "How are you getting along with Langley? Better than I did, I hope. He was a sorry Presbyterian and probably will be a worse Baptist. Tryin' to run everything."

Colin Ryan was wearing worn jeans, a knit shirt, and a pair of disreputable tennis shoes. "I'm trying to make him happy," he said, "but I don't think it's working. I'm only an interim pastor, and I'll be gone soon. What do you brethren think we should do about the dog?"

Sister Myrtle straightened up, looking for all the world like a lady Pentecostal preacher, with her hair done up in a knot at the back of her head, no jewelry, and sleeves that came down to her wrist. She was a handsome woman who appeared to be opposed to anything that would make this apparent. "I think we ought to get all of our folks together and let God know we want that dog to get healed."

Ellison Burke nodded firmly. "I agree. I've been thinking about it. Why don't we call a special prayer meeting. All the churches coming together to pray, not just for Booger but for God to work a miracle in all of our hearts."

A pleased murmur ran around the table, and for the next fifteen minutes they talked about the meeting, agreeing to have it at the Baptist church. After that the other business was quickly dispensed with, and all of the ministers left except Colin, who took another piece of Sister Myrtle's pie. He grinned and winked at her. "Well, now, you spit in the soup, sister! Mr. Langley won't like this."

Sister Myrtle sniffed. "Well," she said regally, "God likes it!"

⌖

Lanie brought soup over to Annie and also some cat food. The cats welcomed her frantically, as they always did. She heated the soup and sat by as Annie ate it hungrily. "You're looking better, Annie," she said.

"I feel a heap better. I don't reckon I'm gonna go up the flue this time."

"Of course you won't."

The two women sat for a time until they heard footsteps.

"That's probably Doctor Merritt. I asked him to come by," Lanie said. "I'll let him in."

"Weren't no need for that," Annie said.

Lanie ignored her. She opened the door and smiled at Doctor Merritt. "Come in. Annie's looking much better."

"Good." Owen nodded. He went in to where Annie was sitting at the kitchen table and grinned. "Well, I see you're able to sit up and take nourishment."

"Are you going to that prayer meeting I've been hearing about?" Annie demanded without preamble.

"The one about Booger? I sure am."

Annie looked thin and frail. Her eyes were dark and piercing, the liveliest thing about her. She was wearing a tattered housecoat, and she sat watching the two. "Well, I ain't much of a praying woman, but I'd really like to go to that prayer meeting."

"I'm going," Lanie spoke up. "I'll come and tell you about it."

"Sure has got the town stirred up." Owen grinned. "Everyone's talking about it. How is Booger, by the way?"

"I don't know. I'm going over to see him now."

"I'll just go along with you. Maybe Booger needs a second opinion."

The two left after tucking Annie back into bed, and as they drove out to Doctor Sixkiller's office, Owen said, "I think you saved Annie. She looks so much better."

"She's so all alone, Doctor Merritt."

"Why don't you call me Owen?"

"Why, that wouldn't seem right to me."

"I feel like an old man. I'd appreciate it if you would use my first name."

"Well, maybe I will when no one else is around—Owen."

Owen nodded with satisfaction and soon the two were at the clinic. When they went inside they found Doctor Sixkiller concerned. He took them into where Booger was lying down in a cage not moving.

"He doesn't look good," Lanie whispered.

"I've done everything I know how to do," Sixkiller said. He hated to lose hope, but this one had become a real challenge. "He won't eat. He won't drink, and he's getting dehydrated. Sure hope that prayer meeting makes a difference."

Owen asked, "Do you pray for your patients, Matthew?"

"Of course I do. Don't you?"

"Yes, I do. Sometimes I think the prayers help them more than the pills I hand out."

Lanie knelt down and stroked the coat of the big dog. His face was wrinkled, and like all bloodhounds he looked worried. His ears were huge, and she straightened one of them where it had fallen, exposing the pink inner surface of his ear. "You just gotta get well, Booger," she whispered. She patted him again and then got up.

Matthew Sixkiller said, "I'll see you at the prayer meeting."

The two went out, got in Owen's car, and then he said, "I'll drop you off at your place."

"All right, Owen."

Owen had been thinking a great deal about Lanie, and now he asked suddenly, "Are you serious about Roger Langley?"

Lanie turned in the seat and stared at Owen. "I don't know what you mean."

"Well, I mean are you engaged to him?"

"Nothing like that. We just go out sometimes."

"Well, that's good news. I want you to be careful. Marriage is forever—at least I think so."

Lanie was somewhat puzzled by Owen's advice. "Well, I might give you the very same advice about your engagement," she said pertly.

Owen was surprised. "Why? Do you think I'm making a mistake?"

Lanie wanted to blurt out, *Yes, you're making a terrible mistake!* But she said, "You don't seem happy the way an engaged man should."

"Well, I'm busy."

"Too busy to be happy? That's foolishness, Owen."

Owen discovered that he had no way to counter what Lanie suggested. As a matter of fact, he'd been concerned lately over how he and Louise would do when they were married. He did not answer Lanie.

When she got out of the car at her house, she smiled. "I'll see you at the prayer meeting."

"All right," Owen said and drove away.

Lanie watched him go and smiled. "Maybe that'll put a bug in his ear."

Once in a while Aunt Kezia decided to do the cooking, and she refused to let anybody help. This was one of those days. "When I'm cookin', I'm cookin'," she announced. She scurried around the kitchen, a small woman, lean with iron silver hair and snapping black eyes. She called out, "All right, you girls, come and put it on the table."

Lanie and Maeva entered quickly, and Maeva said, "What did you cook?"

"Get it on the table. My business is to cook it. Your business is to serve it and eat it."

Lanie laughed and winked at Maeva. "I bet it'll be good."

"If I cook it, it's good. Now let's get it on the table so we can lay our ears back and fly right at it."

The food was put on the table, and Aunt Kezia bowed her head and gave a short lively prayer of thanks. She looked up and said, "Now. There's plenty of it."

Davis was closest to the big pot on the table. It was the main dish. When he lifted the lid and looked down, a puzzled look came into his face. "What is this, Aunt Kezia?"

"It's Presbyterian Pig Tail Perlow."

"It's what?" Davis exclaimed.

"You heard me. It's Presbyterian Pig Tail Perlow. Start dippin' it out, Davis."

Davis scooped into the pot with a large spoon. "It's pig tails!" he exclaimed.

"I'm not eatin' any pig tails!" Maeva exclaimed.

"You're gonna be hungry then."

Lanie was staring at her aunt and then suddenly picked up her plate. "Give me some of that Pig Tail Perlow," she said. "Where'd you get all these pig tails?" she asked.

"I went down to the slaughter house and traded Dave Garver a bunch of sassafras roots for pig tails. Lots of folks ain't got sense enough to know they're good to eat."

Lanie picked up one of the pig tails and tried it. "Why, this is good! How do you cook it?"

"Well, you salt and pepper the tails and fry 'em down until they're good and brown. Then you put in some onions. When the onions are brown, you add enough water to cover it and you simmer it until the tails get all nice and tender and juicy. You add rice and bring it to a boil and you cook it until it's good. The only thing I like better is hog head cheese."

Despite Maeva's proclamation she would not eat pig tails, she found that they were delicious.

Cody ate rapidly, and finally he leaned back and said, "What's for dessert, Aunt Kezia?"

"I made us all a Pleasin' Pappy Cake."

"Pleasin' Pappy Cake. Why do you call it that?" Maeva demanded.

"Well, that's what it always does. My ma made it for my pa, and it pleased him so good that's what we've always called it."

Pleasin' Pappy Cake was simply a white cake, but so light and fluffy that it seemed to melt in your mouth. While they were eating the cake, Cody said, "What do you like to eat best in all the world, Aunt Kezia?"

"Buffalo tongue."

"Buffalo tongue! That sounds awful!" Lanie exclaimed.

"The best part of a buffalo except for maybe the innards."

"Don't talk about that," Maeva whined.

Cody said, "I been thinkin' about goin' to tell the Indians about Jesus when I get a little older."

"You don't have to go west to find heathens," Aunt Kezia announced firmly. "There's plenty of them right here in Fairhope."

Davis grinned at his aunt. "You're right about that. Are you goin' to the prayer meeting about Booger?"

"Certain I am."

"Well, I'm goin' too," Cody said, "and I might have a word to say."

Lanie at once grew apprehensive. "You be quiet at that meeting."

Cody stared at her. "Well, if I was an old Episcopalian, I would. Ain't nobody gets to say anything in their meetings, but us Baptists got our rights. We can say all we want to, and I might just do it!"

❦

The Baptist church was packed with people, and many of them were visitors. As Colin got onto the pulpit to call the meeting to order, he recognized Presbyterians, Methodists, Pentecostals, and even a few Catholics. He said at once, "We're meeting in the Baptist church, but I don't think this is a Baptist meeting." A quiet came over the congregation, and Colin said, "I'm going to ask all the pastors to come and say a word."

One by one the pastors got up and spoke briefly. All of them seemed to be pleased that the ecumenical gathering was going on.

Finally, after the last minister had spoken, Colin said, "I love dogs, and Booger is a fine one. Forrest Freeman thinks a lot of him. You know, God uses some odd things to get the kingdom on track. And I think we're here to pray for a lot more than a sick dog. I think God wants to use his people in this town in a mighty way, and I'd like to see this meeting as the beginning of a revival, a movement in the Spirit of God. We're going to pray for Booger, but we're going to pray more for ourselves, and I need it more than anyone in this building!"

"What I'd like to do," he continued, "before we begin to call on God, is to praise the Lord. We have some mighty fine singers in this church, and I'm sure that the other churches in this area have the same. Brother Madison Jones"—he paused to look up in the balcony where the black congregation had gathered—"has a magnificent singing voice. Reverend Jones, lead us in some songs of praise and worship."

Madison Jones had a powerful voice. Without preamble he began to sing the hymn that all of them knew:

Holy, Holy, Holy, Lord God Almighty!
Early in the morning our song shall rise to Thee.
Holy, Holy, Holy, merciful and mighty
God in Three Persons, blessed Trinity.

The robust voice of Reverend Jones was joined by sopranos, altos, tenors, and the deep voices. It seemed that the best singers of all the churches were there, and the auditorium was filled with a glorious sound.

As Lanie sang, tears came to her eyes. She always loved to praise the Lord, and she loved songs like this one that did exactly that. She put her own problems out of her mind and concentrated on the holiness of God.

Others in the auditorium were doing the same. Latecomers arrived, and as the singing continued, some people began to come without invitation to the front. They fell on their knees and began to pray. Others turned around and knelt right at their seats. Some held their hands high in the air.

Lanie was caught up in a way that she rarely was. She was suddenly conscious that this went on for over an hour and no one left. Finally Lanie looked over to see Doctor Matthew Sixkiller coming in. He was smiling, and there was a spring in his step as he moved to the pulpit. He mounted the rostrum and suddenly said, "I hate to interrupt worship like this, but I think you all need to know something."

A silence fell over the congregation, and Matthew Sixkiller lifted up his hand in a motion of victory. "Two miracles have taken place in Fairhope. One is ..." He hesitated and then turned to face Lanie. Their eyes met, and he said, "Booger came out of that coma he's been in. About a half an hour ago he suddenly got up and began to whine and bark. I fed him, and he drank about a gallon of water, and as far as I can see, whatever was wrong with him is over."

"Well, hallelujah and praise the Lord!" Cody yelled out, and others joined him.

"The second miracle," Sixkiller said, "is what's happening here tonight. I see people from every church and every denomination all together with one purpose, and that's what God's kingdom and Christians should be."

Owen Merritt had been listening to this and felt moved in a way he rarely did. He quietly left the meeting and went to the home of the Langleys, who had refused to attend the prayer meeting. Louise was waiting for him, and when he told her what had happened, she said, "Well, I think it's disgraceful to get everybody together to pray for a dog."

"Is that all you see in this, Louise?" Owen said quietly. "You know, the first time I ever saw you, I thought you were one of the most beautiful women I'd ever seen. But there's something missing in you. Where is your heart?"

Louise stared at him and her mouth opened, but she could think of nothing to say. She was angry, and for some reason her irritation fixated on Colin Ryan. "It's that preacher—Ryan! He stirred all this up!"

"No. I don't think so, Louise." He paused and looked at the floor. Then sadly he met her eyes again. "Good night."

Louise Langley was not accustomed to having men walk out on her. She stared at the door that closed behind Owen, and suddenly her shoulders began to shake. "What's wrong with him? What's wrong with everyone?" she cried and ran to her room.

☞ CHAPTER 13 ☜

September brought cool breezes to north Arkansas, and Lanie leaned on the windowsill drinking them in. The house was quiet for a change since Davis, Maeva, and Cody had started the school year just three days earlier. Aunt Kezia and Corliss were both napping, so Lanie had the time to herself.

Outside, red birds were gathering the scraps and seeds that Lanie always put out for them. Not for the first time she wondered, *Why are the males always more brightly colored than the females?* She watched as one of the males picked up a seed, hopped over, and put it in the mouth of the female who sat there patiently waiting. It was a scene she had noted before, and it gave her a special fondness for the species. "That's a good husband," she murmured aloud, smiling. A large blue jay descended, scaring the red birds, who flew away rapidly. The big jay strutted for a while and began pecking at the food. "You're nothing but a bully," Lanie said indignantly.

She leaned forward, putting her chin on her hand, and weariness seemed to creep up on her. She had worked hard the day before putting up jam and jelly. The kitchen was still hot even though summer was fading, and the thought of the rows of mason jars lined up on the shelves didn't give her any excitement. She was too tired for that. "I wish," she said, "some day we could just go in the store and get store-bought food instead of doing it all ourselves."

The instant the thought crossed Lanie's mind she felt ashamed. She thought of how the lean years of the Depression had driven so many people into bankruptcy, and men now roamed the country looking for work. "I'm sorry, Lord," she whispered aloud, "I don't mean to complain. I'm grateful for all that you've given us."

A scratching at the bedroom door caught her attention, and with a sigh she got up knowing well that it was Cap'n Brown. Crossing the room, she opened the door and then stood staring down at the cat. He had brought her a gift, and with disgust Lanie said, "Well, you've done it again, Cap'n Brown. Give me that mouse."

It was not a mouse, she saw, as she removed the victim from Cap'n Brown's powerful jaws. It was a tiny shrew no more than half the size of a mouse. She had seen them often enough and had read in a book somewhere that they were one of the most voracious eaters in the animal world. This one seemed tame enough, however, and for a moment she stroked his silky fur wondering at the smoothness and the texture of it. Then she said, "You get in here and stay until I come back." Shoving Cap'n Brown in the room, she shut the door to keep him confined, went outside, and walked for twenty yards into where the tall grass began. She leaned down, let the shrew go, and watched him scurry away.

As she turned, she suddenly bumped into a solid object and nearly fell over it. "Booger!" she exclaimed. "You ought not to sneak up that way."

The big bloodhound had recovered completely from his illness. Some of the people in the countryside were calling him the "Resurrection Dog," because it seemed that God had brought him back from certain death. His coat was brown and sleek, his eyes were warm and lively, and the wrinkles in his jowls were deep. He opened his mouth and gave a low moaning sound, for he hardly ever barked. Her father had told her that the hardest thing about training a bloodhound to pursue someone was to teach them not to bark, so the escapee would not know how close they were. Booger did "talk" a lot, however. He moaned and made chuckling noises in his throat, and now he extended his huge paw to Lanie, asking for attention.

"You act like you're love-starved, Booger," she said, running her hand over his broad forehead. She reached out and grabbed the loose jowls and smiled. "You got too much face is what you got." She laughed as Booger shoved himself against her, nearly upsetting her. "I don't have time to fool with you now. After supper I may take you out for a walk." She shoved her way past the big dog, went back upstairs, and when she went inside, she saw that Cap'n Brown had climbed into the bed and was already asleep. She stroked his fur and listened to his purr. "I wish I didn't have any more worries than you did," she murmured as she often did.

Moving over to the chest, she opened the bottom drawer and took out a tablet, a pen, and several pencils. Sitting at the table beside the window to catch the breeze, she began to think. She had been reading in Scripture lately about the beginnings of the ministry of Jesus and was trying to find a subject for a poem. Now as she sat there, she unconsciously prayed, "Lord, help me to write a poem that would please you."

For some time she sat there, the silence broken only by the buzzing of a big fly that had flown in through the open window. She picked up a swatter and annihilated him without breaking her thought. *I'll bet the disciples were surprised when Jesus called them. You take Matthew, for instance. He was a tax collector, and the Jews didn't like tax collectors. There was Peter and his brother, Andrew, James, and John, all of them just fishermen. I'll bet they nearly fell out of the boat when Jesus said, "Come and follow me, and I'll make you fishers of men."*

A thought came to her then, and as always, she knew it would turn out to be a poem. *I'll bet the people who followed Jesus around when he first started expected he'd get influential men to be his disciples—bankers and lawyers and priests in the synagogue maybe.* The thought intrigued her, and as she sat there, the thoughts and words and lines seemed to arrange themselves in her head. Her brother Davis had asked her once, "How do you think of these poems?" and she couldn't answer him. If she thought on a subject long enough, it just came to be. The most difficult part was over when she had decided what to write about, and now she thought about the early disciples and what people must have said when they saw such a poor, uneducated group being called out, one by one, by Jesus. She picked up a sharpened pencil and put a verse of Scripture across the top of the page.

"And he ordained twelve, that they should be with him, and that he might send them forth to preach" (Mark 3:14).

While she was writing, Lanie went into a world of her own and time ceased to exist for her. At times the pencil seemed to move of its own accord. At other times, however, the words and thoughts were evasive, and she struggled with them.

When she finally finished, the poem filled several pages, but many lines were crossed out. Now she made a copy on a clean sheet of paper. When it was done, she blew on it and read it aloud in a whisper.

Disciples

Oh, Sarah, look, there's the carpenter —
You know, the one from Galilee who's out
To save us all.
Better if he'd kept to mending chairs!
We get a bumper crop of backwoods prophets
Here who've "heard the call" to lift us out of sin.
Out of this rocky ground that won't grow corn
Messiahs spring each year like bitterweed.
This Jesus is the latest, but he'll soon find
Men aren't as easy to repair as chairs!
Look at them — his disciples there.
If this rabbi hopes to change the world
He'd better learn to watch his company.
That big redheaded one? Nothing but
A fisherman. He's loud enough to preach;
Tough enough, they say, to punch a head.
He won't save souls with noisy talk or fists!
Give him a month — glad enough he'll be

To get back to his nets again.
Men aren't caught as easily as fish.
You see those two? That's James and John.
What tempers they both have!
Smash an oar to splinters in a rage
Just because of a missed fish or two.
No wonder they're called the Sons of Thunder!
Look right there — I'd heard the carpenter
Had called a tax collector named Matthew;
Well, won't that make the rabbi popular
With all the Jews who hate the name of Rome!
Let's go, Sarah, this depresses me.
A foolishness, to call such men
From useful work — for what? They'll fail
Like all the others.
What's that? Why, yes, he is the one
Exception in the crowd — see how fine he looks,
Just as a preacher should — and glad enough
That crowd should be to have a businessman
Like Judas there to keep an eye on things!

What she had written pleased her, and she put it into a large file envelope that she had bought at Kress Ten Cent Store. She looked at some of the other poems she had written about the life of Jesus and wondered if anyone would ever see them. She rather thought not, for she didn't know anyone who had published any poems. But at least she enjoyed doing it. Now it was time to go down and do some chores, but she felt refreshed after working on her poetry.

❦

The family bowed their heads while Aunt Kezia asked the blessing. One never knew how she would go about this activity. Sometimes she would pray for every individual thing on the table, "Lord, bless the beans and bless the taters ..." clear on down to mentioning the salt and pepper. At other times she was very brief.

"Lord, bless the vittles. In Jesus' name. Amen."

Cody stared at his aunt indignantly. "That wasn't no fit prayer, Aunt Kezia."

Aunt Kezia stared at him, her dark eyes snapping. "What do you mean it wasn't a fit prayer! I thanked God for the food, didn't I?"

"Well, you didn't say enough."

"You think a prayer's measured by how long it is?" Aunt Kezia shot back. "God knows all of our hearts."

"Well, sometimes you pray for everything on the table," Cody argued.

"Cody, let Aunt Kezia alone," Lanie said.

Cody was still under the impression that as the spiritual head of the Freeman family, he was called upon to point out the shortcomings of each family member. He pointed his fork at Aunt Kezia and said, "You talk enough when you're fussin' at me, I guess you can spare a few more words to thank the good Lord for the food."

"Oh, shut up, Cody!" Maeva said. She was dipping purple hull peas out of a large dish onto her plate and gave him a disgusted look. "You got so holy you wouldn't eat an egg laid on Sunday. You give me a pain in the rear!"

"Did you hear what she said?" Cody yelped. "She cussed."

"I didn't cuss. Tell me one cuss word I said."

"You said 'rear.'"

"That's not cussin'." Maeva grinned, winking at Davis. "You don't know cussin' when you hear it. You ought to go down sometime when the men are playin' horseshoes at the park. Then you'll hear some *real* cussin'."

The argument went on, Cody aligned against the unbelievers, seeing himself as the apostle. The dinner of fried hominy, fried ham, hoecakes, and purple hull peas had all come from their own garden and from the hog that they had killed last fall, except for the store-bought cornmeal for the hoecakes.

Davis opened a jar of hot peppers and fished out several that had turned brilliant crimson. He tossed them on the top of his purple hull peas and Lanie exclaimed, "You're gonna burn out all your taste buds, Davis!"

"Well, I haven't done it yet. It makes things taste better. Here. Try some."

"Not me," Lanie said. "They burn my tongue."

The talk went around the table until finally Cody said, "What's for dessert?"

"Fresh persimmons. I got 'em from old man Miller down the road." She went over to the icebox, opened it, and took out a bowl of fruit. "There. All plump and sweet as can be. The possums are gonna miss these."

"I'd rather have pie," Cody said.

"Why, Cody," Aunt Kezia said, "I expect you to bust out in a thanksgiving prayer for those persimmons. After the sermon you gave me, I think you ought to."

Cody struggled to find an answer and said, "Well, I'm just more grateful for some things than others."

"You're not going to get the best of him, Aunt Kezia. He'd argue with a stump."

Davis looked out the window and said, "I reckon you and me better cut some more wood, Cody." He shook his head. "You know, if a fellow knew how cold the winter was going to be, he'd know how much wood to cut. Last year I didn't cut enough. Had to go out in the freezin' weather and cut some. The summer before last we had twice too much. It's a shame we don't know what the weather's going to be."

"Well, you can know if you want to," Aunt Kezia snapped. "Why didn't you tell me you wanted to know?"

Everyone looked at Aunt Kezia. She was always springing rather startling information on them. Davis turned his head to one side. "All right. I'm askin'. What's the winter going to be like? Cold or warm?"

Aunt Kezia picked up one of the fresh persimmons and said, "You got the answer right in there, boy. Don't they teach you nothin' at this school you're going to?"

"Well, they don't teach me how a piece of fruit can be a weather prophet." Davis winked at Lanie.

With a sigh of disgust, Aunt Kezia picked up a knife and sliced through the persimmon. With the tip of it she fished out one of the seeds.

Picking it up with her forefinger and thumb, she held it up. "Why, the answer's right in there. Inside every seed you'll find one of three things. Either you'll find somethin' that looks like a knife or somethin' that looks like a spoon or somethin' that looks like a fork."

Lanie was fascinated by her aunt. "I didn't know that, Aunt Kezia."

"Of course you didn't. You don't listen. Young folks don't ever listen to older people."

"Well, what do the things mean, the fork, the spoon, and the knife?" Cody demanded.

"A knife means it's going to be so cold it'll cut right through you. If you see a spoon in there, you'll get some snow, enough to use a shovel with. And if it's a fork, why, it'll be plum warm weather all winter."

Aunt Kezia took the paring knife, slit the seed, and peered down into it. "Better get lots of wood, Davis," she announced. "Look at that."

Davis took the seed and blinked. "Why, I'll be dipped!" he exclaimed. "It *does* look like a knife." He passed the seed on until everyone had looked at it, but Cody, as usual, argued. "How would a seed know when it's going to be warm or cold?"

"The same way crickets can tell what the temperature is."

Maeva stared at her aunt with disbelief. "What do you mean? Bugs can't tell temperatures."

"That's all you know."

"How do they do it?" Davis asked, fascinated by his aunt's knowledge.

"Well, they just know. God made 'em to know. You count the number of chirps during a quarter of a minute and then you add forty." Aunt Kezia looked around at the shock on the faces of the children. "I guess you young 'uns don't even know you can tell how hard a winter's going to be by how thick a caterpillar's fur is—or how thick the hull is on an acorn."

She got up and shook her head. "What do they teach these young 'uns in school these days?"

Davis suddenly laughed. "Well, I guess I'd better cut more wood that I'd planned on. That means we're going to need more winter clothes too."

The mention of winter clothes brought a troubled frown to Lanie's face. *Where's the money coming from to buy more clothes?* She got up and began to collect the dishes and said little as she tried to figure out a way to provide for the winter.

⌐━⊷

Lanie was sitting on the floor playing with blocks with Corliss when Cody said, "Somebody's coming." He had the sharpest hearing of anyone in the family and got to his feet. "Who could be comin' to see us tonight?"

Lanie got to her feet quickly. "I'll see who it is." She went to the door, opened it, and smiled to see Roger standing there. He had a bundle of some kind in his hand and a grin on his face. "Hello, Lanie. I brought you a birthday present."

"It's not my birthday."

"Well, it will be some day."

"Come on in, Roger."

Roger stepped inside. The cool air had brightened his cheeks, and he looked handsome as he stood there before her. "Here," he said.

"Happy birthday." The others had all come in and Roger greeted them, snatching Corliss up and planting a kiss on her cheek.

"Why, it's a ham!" Lanie exclaimed with surprise.

"A big one too!" Davis exclaimed. "That hog must have weighed eight hundred pounds."

"You shouldn't have done it," Lanie said.

"Yes, he should," Aunt Kezia said. "Davis, don't just stand there. Take that ham into the kitchen and slice some chunks off of it for breakfast in the morning. Maybe a few for tonight. I didn't get enough supper."

Davis took the ham from Lanie, disappeared, and Lanie said, "Come on into the living room, Roger."

Maeva at once grabbed Roger's arm and held it tight against her side. "It was so nice of you to come by and see me, Roger, and to bring me that ham."

"Why, it was for Lanie!" Cody protested.

"No. It was really for me. Roger's struck on me. He just pretends to come see Lanie."

Roger laughed out loud. "You're a caution, Maeva Freeman."

"Won't do you any good to come moonin' around Lanie. She's stuck on Doctor Owen Merritt," Maeva said.

"Maeva, you hush your mouth!" Lanie said furiously. She could feel her face flushing and knew that her embarrassment was obvious to all of them.

Roger laughed and sat down on the couch. At once Maeva sat down on one side of him and Cody on the other. "Tell us about that ham," Maeva said, still holding his arm.

"Well, it was like this. I was over at Parkin surveying today, and I ran out of water. It's pretty thirsty work. So I went to this house to ask for a drink and this pretty young lady came to the door. I asked for a drink of water, and she asked me inside and gave me lemonade. To tell the truth," he said with a straight face, "I hate to mention it, but she just fell in love with me. I could tell."

Maeva's eyes were dancing. "Did you kiss her?"

"No, I didn't. And when she tried to make up to me, I made every excuse I could to get out of there. She forced the ham on me as a token of her devotion."

"Roger Langley, you are a story!" Lanie said, her eyes dancing.

"I guess I am. Jake Perkins just killed one of his hogs, and I done some work for him, didn't charge him for it, so he made me take it. I thought you all could use some fresh ham."

Cody said, "I been wantin' to talk to you, Roger. You've been to college. I've got an idea for a business. Maybe you and me could go in it together."

"A business? What kind of business, Cody?"

"Well, we could sell people edible pets."

Everyone stared at Cody, and Maeva exclaimed, "You've lost your mind! What do you mean an edible pet? Pets aren't edible."

"Not when they're little. You take a little rabbit and how they're cute and fuzzy. Lots of people give their kids little rabbits for Easter. Then the things get big and just troublesome. So my idea is to sell people cute little things when they're little, and when they grow up people can eat them. You know especially around Easter—rabbits and those little colored chicks—they dye 'em and who wants a red or a blue chicken runnin' around the house? So just play with 'em until they grow up and then eat 'em."

"Cody Freeman, you have the weirdest ideas of any human being I ever saw!" Roger laughed as did the others. "Did it occur to you that the kids would get attached to a rabbit and would have a fit?"

"Well, that'll just have to happen. You know I like the little pigs sometimes, but by the time they get to be killin' size, I've kind of fallen out of love with 'em and don't mind a bit when hog killin' comes."

"Cody, you got fifty ideas an hour with gusts up to seventy-five or eighty. One of these days you're gonna get a good one," Roger said.

Davis came back from the kitchen and said, "How about if we have some pickin' and singin'?"

"Sounds good to me. I can't pick but I'll sing a little bit."

A scramble began for the youngsters to get their instruments. All of them played an instrument, most of them more than one. This time Maeva played the guitar, Lanie the dulcimer, Davis the fiddle, and Cody the mandolin. Corliss Jeanne insisted on playing with the autoharp, although she could not play it yet. The songs they played at first were country songs such as "I'm Thinking Tonight of My Blue Eyes," "Lonesome Valley," and "Keep on the Sunny Side."

"Hey, Davis, do one of Jimmy Rogers's songs."

Davis said, "Which one?"

" 'Waitin' for a Train.' "

Without preamble Davis started singing, and the others picked up to follow him. A young singer named Jimmy Rogers had become popular, and Davis could imitate him perfectly, even down to the yodel that was Rogers's trademark.

The singing went on for quite a while when finally Roger said, "Well, I've got to go. Up in the mornin' to go to work. Hey, there's a medicine show comin' to Cedar Grove, and there'll be a dance. I heard the Carter family was going to be there and a young fellow named Roy Acuff. They say he can sing as good as Jimmy Rogers."

"Bet he can't!" Davis exclaimed, for Rogers was his hero.

"What about it, Lanie? We'd have a good time."

"I don't know if I should go or not," she said. "There's always drinking and fighting at those things."

Maeva suddenly laughed. "You better go. I'm goin' with Jesse Cottrel. He's a lady-killer, you know." She suddenly nudged Lanie in the ribs with her elbow. "You better go just to watch out I don't get in trouble."

"You see!" Roger said. "You'll have to go now."

Lanie suddenly smiled. "All right. I'll go, but we'll have to come home early."

CHAPTER 14

Louise greeted Owen, and said at once, "Come into the parlor."

"Sorry I'm late. Got a call to go out. Turned out to be an appendectomy. Pretty close call." He took off his coat, handed it to her, and followed her into the drawing room.

"Sit down, Owen. Something has come up."

"What is it?" Owen said quickly. "No trouble, I hope."

Louise studied Owen Merritt's face. She had great plans for Owen, more than he knew. He was content to be a doctor in a small town. Her father had bigger plans in the event that a regional hospital was built in Fairhope, but even that was not enough for Louise. The dream of her life was to live in either New York or Chicago or Los Angeles, some big city where a great deal was happening. She loved concerts, the opera, and classical music of all kinds, but Owen did not seem open to the city, so she rarely mentioned her dream to him.

"I've decided we ought to set a wedding date, Owen," she said and studied his face. He seemed surprised, and she said quickly, "I'd like to get married in December. Sometime in the first part of the month."

"December? That's less than three months away. You wouldn't want to wait until June?"

"Oh, no. That's just an old superstition. This will give us plenty of time to get ready."

Owen suddenly grinned. "I'm ready now. Why don't we just go down to the parson's house and get married up and leave on a honeymoon."

"Oh, Owen, don't be foolish. We can't do that. My family would be shocked."

"I suppose so." He sat still for a minute and said, "It'll take a little doing, Louise. I'll have to find a house."

"Oh, Daddy will take care of that." Louise shrugged her shoulders. "He's already said he would either buy us a house or rent us a very nice place."

"I don't think I'd care to do that," Owen said carefully.

"Why not?"

"I suppose I'm just old-fashioned, but I'd rather handle it myself."

"Why, that's foolish! It would be so easy. You're busy with your practice. You don't have time to pick out a house. I'd planned all along to take Daddy's offer, and then we could think about building one later."

"I'd rather not," Owen said, and something in the way he said it made Louise understand at once that she could pursue this no further. Usually Owen Merritt was an easygoing man, giving in to her whims with a smile. From time to time, however, he would reveal a stubbornness that lay under his easy exterior. She saw it now and quickly changed the subject.

"Well, we can talk about a house later. By December we'll have a regular pastor to perform the ceremony."

"You don't think Colin will be here?"

"Oh, certainly not. He's just an interim. The church will have called a regular pastor by that time."

"Maybe not," Owen said. "Sometimes a pastor has to give notice to a church just like anybody else."

"I don't want Colin Ryan performing the ceremony."

Owen leaned back and studied Louise. "You don't like Colin. You never have. I don't understand it. I think he's a fine preacher."

"Well, there are all kinds of preachers," Louise said firmly. "On the streets of Chicago dealing with rough people I'm sure he's the best, but in a small town like this a pastor has to have tact, and Colin

Ryan doesn't have any of that. He doesn't even know how to dress like a preacher."

"I never even thought about that. What does it matter what he wears?"

"I think he's vain. He's good-looking, and half the women in the church are in love with him," she sniffed with disdain. "He encourages it."

Owen was silent for a moment, then shrugged. "I guess we just won't see eye-to-eye on this, and there's no point arguing. You're probably right. He'll be gone by the time December comes."

"I'll have the announcement put in the paper this week." She leaned over, pulled him close, and kissed him. "It's going to be wonderful being married to you, Owen."

Owen held her tightly. He was always taken somewhat aback by the passion that Louise showed once in a while. Occasionally she would reveal that there was a desire in her as there was in him. "You'll make a good wife," he said huskily and kissed her again.

⌒⊷

"Hey, Lanie, come out here."

Lanie had finished her chores for the morning and was sitting in the kitchen when she heard Davis call out. She went outside and said, "What is it?"

"You see this?"

"It's a coat. Whose is it?"

"It belongs to Bascom," he said. Bascom was the son of Reverend Madison Jones, pastor of the black church. "He came by here earlier this morning while I was choppin' wood. He helped me for a while and took off his coat, then he left."

"Well, he'll remember where he left it."

"He won't have to. I'm gonna find him."

"Do you know where he went?"

"No. I'm gonna find him though." He turned and said, "Booger—come here. Come here, boy!" When the big bloodhound came loping up, Davis grinned. "We're gonna find out if these bloodhounds can really track people."

"You're gonna let Booger track Bascom?"

"Sure am. Here, boy, smell this coat." Booger, evidently, knew the drill. He began to sniff the coat eagerly, and Davis cried, "Get him, Booger!" The hound turned at once and began sniffing the ground. "Look at him. He's huntin' for the trail!" Davis cried.

Cody came out and said, "What are you doing?"

"We're gonna let Booger track Bascom. That's what bloodhounds do."

Cody was at once involved, and within a few moments Booger barked sharply one time and then turned toward the north.

"He's headin' for the river," Cody cried. "Come on. Let's follow him."

Lanie laughed and said, "You boys go play with that dog. I've got work to do."

The two boys took off after Booger, who kept his head low. He stopped from time to time and moved around in circles, but confidently continued.

They crossed two open fields, followed a path through some heavy woods, and then Davis cried, "Look. There's the river!" Singing River held Fairhope in one arm, as a poet might have put it. "I bet he's gone fishin'."

Indeed, that was the case. They reached the bank, and Booger went down one bank and then turned and traced the other one. He made a soft sound but never once did he bark.

"I thought they were supposed to holler loud when they trailed people," Cody panted as they chased after the dog.

"They train 'em not to do that so the one that's escapin' won't know they're at 'em." They turned a bend, and Davis hollered, "Hey, Bascom!"

Bascom Jones was standing by the bank holding a cane pole. He turned and his teeth shone whitely against his dark skin. "Hey, Davis. Hi, Cody. What you fellas doin'?"

"We tracked you, Bascom."

"What you mean you tracked me?"

"You left your coat at our house this morning, and Booger here found you. He followed your scent."

"Well, ain't that a caution now." Bascom grinned. He reached over and rubbed the big dog's head. "That sure is handy, ain't it?"

"I know what we could do," Cody said. "We can find people with him."

"Find what kind of people?" Davis asked.

"Well, people lose kids and some of 'em lose grown people. When somebody gets lost, we can take Booger and track 'em down."

"That's about as foolish as most of your notions. How many people you hear about gettin' lost?"

"Leroy Hopson got lost."

"He was back in two hours, and he wasn't lost. He just run off to play."

"Well," Cody said, "if it ever comes up, we can charge a bunch of money."

Bascom grinned and winked at Davis. "That brother of yours, he's gonna be rich some day. Anybody with as many schemes as he's got bound to run onto one that will trot!"

⊚═⊷

The dance was held in an old schoolhouse. The desks had been taken out, and now the sound of fiddles and guitars filled it. It was a rather large building, but it was crowded now. The band was at one end, and to their right and left were tables where people could buy drinks. Liquor was not supposed to be served, so the drinks were mostly RC Colas.

Lanie and Maeva had both been dancing, and then the star of the show began to sing. Roy Acuff had a powerful voice, and he played a fiddle better than anyone Lanie or Maeva had ever heard—except for their daddy, they both said loyally.

"That's some fiddle player," Roger said with admiration. The song was "The Wabash Cannonball," and Acuff performed it in a lively fashion. He was a small man, trim and neat, and when he finished the song, he put the bow on his chin and balanced it there for quite a while, then announced that the band was taking a short break.

"Come on, Maeva. Let's you and me go outside and get a breath of fresh air." Jesse pulled on Maeva's arm.

"No, you don't, Jesse," Lanie said at once. "I know what you're goin' outside for." Jesse was a tall, dark young man with handsome features and a poor reputation. "You're going out to take a drink is what you were going out to do. Either that or take advantage of my sister."

Maeva laughed. "Lanie's trying to be a sheriff's deputy," she said. "You better be careful, Jesse."

Jesse grinned ruefully. "Well, let's go have an RC then."

Roger left Lanie talking to a friend and walked over to speak with Roy Acuff. He introduced himself and said, "If your throat gets dry, Mr. Acuff, there's a couple of girls you ought to hear. The best singers you ever heard."

"Your lady friends, both of 'em?" Acuff grinned.

"Well, I'm tryin' to make one of them fit that description. The other one's her sister. There's four a them kids, and they all sing and play just about everything."

"Where are they?" Acuff asked. Roger pointed Lanie out in the crowd and Acuff said, "A nice-lookin' lady. You think they'd sing for the folks?"

"Well, Maeva will. I don't know about Lanie. She's pretty shy."

Roger went back and claimed Lanie. "Next dance is mine," he said, but then he heard Acuff's voice rising over the noise of the crowd.

"Well, ladies and gentlemen, we've got a treat for you tonight. We have a couple of young ladies who I hear sing almost as good as they look. Want you to give them a hand now and encourage the Freeman girls to honor us with a selection."

Lanie turned and said, "You did that, Roger."

"I did. Now go on and sing."

Lanie was reluctant, but Maeva was eager. She grabbed Lanie's arm and said, "Come on. Here's our chance."

Acuff grinned broadly as the two girls came forward. "Ain't they somethin', folks? Pretty as a speckled pup under a wagon! What are you girls gonna sing? We'll try to stay up with you."

"We're going to sing one of yours, Mr. Acuff. 'The Great Speckled Bird,' if you don't mind." Maeva grinned.

"I don't mind a bit. You girls start in, and we'll find the key. Some of my boys read music, but it don't hurt their pickin' none."

Lanie and Maeva both had perfect pitch, so they started off together, and at once Roy Acuff and the rest of the musicians broke right in behind them. They both had strong voices, but Maeva was by far the better singer. They filled the building with the song, and when it was over Roy Acuff was the first one to break out into applause. "That was prime! That was prime! That was prime!" he exclaimed. "How about another one?"

"Just you this time, Maeva," Lanie said. She refused to argue, and Maeva turned at once and said, "Mr. Acuff, do you know 'I'm Thinkin' Tonight of My Blue Eyes'?"

Acuff laughed. "Honey, I know it well. Come on, boys, let's play it sweet for the lady."

This song was entirely different from the other songs. It was a plaintive song, and Maeva made it even more so. Her voice was clear and sweet, and as loud as anyone's in the country. She sang it as if her heart were breaking, the sad lyrics made even sadder by her expressions and by the poignancy of her voice.

When she finished, the crowd broke into wild applause.

"We'll never get her down from there," Roger whispered. "She's stagestruck."

Indeed, Maeva was persuaded to sing three more songs, one with Roy Acuff himself.

Finally the singing was over, and Roy Acuff came down to speak to Lanie. "Thank you, girls, for singin' with me. You got beautiful voices."

"Oh, that's Maeva mostly," Lanie said. "She can make anybody sound good."

Roy Acuff pulled a card out of his pocket. "If you girls ever want to hit the road and go into show business, there's my address. I won't be there probably, but it'll catch up with me."

They left at once, and as soon as they were in Jesse's car, Maeva said, "Let's do it, Lanie."

"Do what?"

"Go on the road. Sing with Roy Acuff. We could become stars."

"Didn't you look around you tonight, Maeva? Didn't you see the drinking? There were two fights, and you could just tell by lookin' at some of those dancers they had bad things on their mind. Don't even think about it!"

⌖

"Well, that was quite a night," Roger said. The two were sitting out on the front porch. They had gotten home at ten o'clock, and Maeva had gone right in to tell the others about her triumph. Roger had asked Lanie to sit down with him, and they watched the silver moon.

Lanie said, "I wish I hadn't gone—or I wish Maeva hadn't gone."

"That wasn't the first time she's been to a dance."

"No. But it's the first time, as far as I know, that she ever got an invitation to be a paid singer. I hope she'll forget it."

"I hope so too, but you know Maeva better than anybody."

The two sat there for a time talking about the dance. Finally Roger said rather abruptly, "You know what, Lanie?"

"What?"

"You're the sweetest, prettiest girl I ever saw."

"Maeva's a lot prettier than I am."

"Not to my notion. I just been thinkin' that it's one thing for me to go around having feelings about you, but not fair if I don't tell you about them."

Lanie suddenly felt strange. "What do you mean, feelings?"

"Why, don't you know? I think I'm falling in love with you."

"Roger, that's impossible."

"Why is it impossible? Am I so hard to take?"

"No, not you. You don't know what a crush I had on you in high school." Lanie laughed. "Of course every girl there did. You were the best looking and always the smartest."

"Not as smart as you. Not as good-looking either." Roger grinned. He reached out, took her hand, and suddenly lifted it to his lips and kissed it. Lanie was stricken speechless. He said, "What I want to know is how you feel about me."

At that instant Lanie actually had no idea of how she felt about Roger Langley. True enough, she had been dazzled by him in high school. He was a star athlete, fine looking, and had everything, but that was when they were kids. Now he was a full-grown man, and she admired the way that he was making his own way. But for all this, she did not know how she felt about him. "I don't know, Roger. I can't say."

He was silent for a moment, and Lanie suddenly realized she had hurt his feelings. "You're—you're the finest young man I know, Roger."

The words stirred something in Roger. He was a lonely young man. He was cut off, to some degree, from his family, who disagreed violently with his ambitions to make his own way. He had many friends, but something in Lanie Freeman drew him. He knew she was not a young woman given to idle caresses as some were, but a recklessness seized him. He reached out, pulled her to him, and when she did not draw back, he lowered his lips and kissed her. Suddenly the heat of something rash and timeless came to him. She had the power to stir him, and he held her tightly, savoring the softness of her lips. Then she pulled away and at once he released her.

"You—shouldn't have done that, Roger."

Roger was shaken, but he only said, "What should I do—shake hands with you? It was just a kiss, Lanie."

"I know."

A thought came to Roger at that moment, and before he thought it out he blurted the words. "You still have a crush on Owen Merritt, don't you?"

"Roger! He's engaged to your sister!"

Those were not the words Roger wanted to hear. He wanted to hear her say she felt nothing for Owen Merritt. He and Merritt had one brief brush here on this very porch, and he had seen that Owen, despite his disavowals, felt something for Lanie. He hoped it was just the admiration of a good man for a determined young woman who could perform well under difficult circumstances. But now he was more troubled about what Lanie felt for him. He got to his feet and said, "I guess I'll say good night, Lanie. Thanks for going to the dance with me."

Lanie rose too. "It was fun, wasn't it?"

"Will we do it again sometime then?"

"Of course. Good night."

Roger left and as he stepped down off the porch, an owl sailed over his head. Roger heard nothing but saw the shadow on the ground. Quickly he looked up and saw the hunter, silent as the grave, move across the yard and to an open field. He saw the owl suddenly double up and fall to the earth. He heard a faint squeal and then silence. It gave him a bad feeling, and he hurried away.

~≈ Chapter 15 ≈~

"Davis, I wish you wouldn't go to Fort Smith for that ball game." Davis looked up from his place at the table where he was finishing the last of the meal Lanie had fixed for him. It was a Saturday, the other children were out playing, and Aunt Kezia was taking her daily nap. Davis shook his head and said, "I've got to go, Sister. They'll pay me ten dollars, and we need it for winter clothes." He tried to smile and said, "Get the Monkey Ward catalog out and pick some winter coats for Cody and Maeva."

"What about you?"

"I can wear Dad's old coat."

Lanie sat down across from her brother and gave him a fond look. "You're as tall as he is now."

"Not as wide though."

Lanie reached over and took Davis's hand. "That bunch of ball-players are not good people for you to be around. Most of them drink and even worse."

"I don't have to be a part of that. All I have to do is play ball." He hesitated and then shoved his plate back. "I've been thinkin' that I ought to quit school. I'm not learning anything. Can't read. But I can get a job somehow and help with the expenses."

It was an old argument, and Lanie at once shook her head. "You can't do that, Davis. Daddy wouldn't like it, and you know how strict Mama would have been about any of her children dropping out of school."

"But I can't stay up with the others. I feel like an idiot."

"I know it's hard, and I don't know why you can't read, but somehow God's going to help you. I just know it."

The two sat there bonded together by the burden of keeping a household going. Lanie had taken over as a surrogate mother, and Davis, being the oldest son, was forced to become the closest thing to a father the family had. The two of them had been drawn closer together by their responsibilities, and now Davis suddenly got up and walked around the table. Leaning over, he hugged Lanie and said, "You're a winner, Sis. Don't worry about me now. I'll be all right."

"I'll wait up for you, Davis, and I'll have a surprise. Something you really like." She hugged him, then watched as he picked up his canvas bag and his bat. "Don't they furnish bats for you at these games?" she asked.

"Oh, they got some, but this is my lucky bat." He grinned. "Got lots of hits left in it yet." Davis winked at her and left the house.

Lanie watched him go and felt a sudden pull at her heart. Her brother was so mature and capable—she didn't know how she would have handled this family without him. She admired his strength and his cleverness, which made it even more difficult for her to understand his inability to read. It had become the prayer of her heart, ever since his deficiency had shown itself, that one day God would touch him. Now she prayed that God would keep him safe on his journey to Fort Smith.

The game was anything but a pitcher's duel! The score at the bottom of the ninth, with the Mountaineers up, was ten-ten, and now with two outs, Davis dug in and waited for the pitch. The game had been hard fought, with runners slashing into the basemen and a fight turning into a bench-clearing brawl.

The pitcher for the Lions was a huge redheaded man of twenty-five. He had come in to relieve the starter, and now he grinned at

Davis and jeered. "Well, they got the nursery in. Why ain't you home with your mama, sonny?"

Davis had learned to ignore the talk of the players on other teams. He simply stood there in the batter's box taking a few practice swings and then went into a crouch. He had an odd way of hitting the ball, stooping down almost to a sitting position with the bat held way back over his shoulders. When he decided to swing, his whole body uncoiled and seemed to explode as it made contact with the ball. Many years later, Davis would learn that Stan Musial, the star for the St. Louis Cardinals, had exactly the same kind of batting stance.

The redheaded pitcher, whom everyone called Bubba, took his windup and threw the ball—straight at Davis's head. Davis had the best reactions of any man in the Mountaineers and pulled his head back, nearly falling to escape the pitch.

"Cut that out, Bubba," the Mountaineers manager said, "or we'll bean you when you come up."

Bubba simply grinned and took the ball back from the catcher. "I missed you that time, baby, but I'll get you this time."

Davis had developed the art of reading pitchers, and the thought flashed through his mind, *He threw at me that time, and he's threatening to throw at me again. That means he won't. He'll throw a strike right over the plate expecting me to dodge back to keep from getting hit.*

He set himself, and sure enough, when the pitch came, it was a fastball right down the middle. Davis unwound, and when he heard the crack of the bat, he knew by the sound that it was gone. Tossing the bat down, he smiled at Bubba and said, "There's your ball game, Bubba." He trotted around the bases ignoring the sullen glances of the Lions, and when he got back across home plate, Tal Bonner, the manager of the Mountaineers, was grinning.

Bonner was a short fireplug of a man with two missing teeth in the front, which made his words hard to understand. "That's good, Davis. Give you a five-dollar bonus for that."

"Thanks, Mr. Bonner."

"You be ready to play next week. It'll be the last game of the season. We'll be playing the Seals over at Marion."

"All right, Mr. Bonner. I'll be there."

The team had permission to use the high school facilities, so they showered. Afterward Bonner said, "We're gonna celebrate, boys. The drinks are on me."

Davis's heart sank, for he knew what that meant. The team would find a bar or a gin mill somewhere and get drunk, everyone except the driver. He had no desire to participate, so he approached the manager and said, "Mr. Bonner, I think I'll get on home. My sister will be worried about me."

"Well, you deserve a little relaxation."

"No. I better get on."

"Well, you can't walk the whole way."

"No, but there's a train that goes right through Fort Smith and stops outside my house about eight o'clock for water. You can see it every day. I'll find an empty boxcar."

Bonner argued, but Davis was adamant. He left the high school and began walking, taking the fifteen dollars out every once in a while to look at it. It was more money than most men would earn in two weeks. A dollar a day wasn't a bad pay for the time. A warm glow came to him as he thought of how it would feel to lay it down before Lanie and say, "There, Sis. There's the winter coats for the young 'uns."

⊷⊶⊷

By the time Davis got to the train yards, he saw that his timing was just about right. Darkness was beginning to fall, and he would not be easily seen by any of the crew. He moved quietly and waited until the engine gave a blast that reverberated throughout the air, and then quickly ran. He had studied trains, as all boys did, planning one day to hop a freight and do as the hoboes did, but he never had. Now he spotted a boxcar with the door cracked about a foot, and running quickly, he shoved it further open even as the train began to move. It was an easy task for him to haul himself up, and as he sprawled on the floor, he heard the familiar clicking of the cars as the engine pulled them over the tracks. He got to his feet and moved over to the door and watched as the outskirts of Fort Smith flashed by. The train picked up speed, but he did not sit down for a time. It was an adventure, and there was not much of that in Davis's life.

A small noise suddenly caught his attention, and Davis was startled. He turned and squinted his eyes. It was gloomy in the boxcar, almost pitch dark, and he took a few steps toward the back of the car. "Who's that?" he said.

"Just me."

Davis moved back and was cautious. He knew some pretty rough men rode the rods, as it was called, and he said, "What are you doing here?"

"Same thing you are. Gettin' a free ride."

Davis was nervous, for though the voice was not rough, one could never tell. "What's your name?" he said.

"Cass."

"Where you goin'?"

"Headed south."

"Well, you're not headed south on this train. It's headed east."

"Don't matter."

Davis hesitated, then shrugged. "I'm only going as far as Fairhope. Then I'm jumpin' out. The train takes on water there." He got no answer and then decided that his unseen companion was no danger. He sat down and watched the scenery go by. The moon was bright so he could see the fields and especially the forest. The train route was circuitous, for the track had been laid through the valleys rather than crossing the tops of the mountains. He had always thought the mountains were the prettiest part of the world, and to him the Singing River was the prettiest river, although it was practically the only one he had ever seen.

Davis sat there growing sleepy by the *clickety-clack, clickety-clack, clickety-clack* of the wheels passing over the tracks, and finally he felt the train slowing down. "This is Chesterville," he said. "Train always stops here to pick up freight."

"Will they load this car?"

"I don't think so. Usually there's a baggage car. They put mail and packages and stuff like that in there."

The train ground to a stop. They heard the engine release a blast of steam, and then there was silence for a time. But suddenly there was a sound of running feet, and without warning the door was shoved open. Davis moved back as three men clambered on. They were obviously hoboes. He could see that much from the light of the moon, and he could smell the raw alcohol as they piled into the car. The biggest one saw Davis and came to his feet at once. He put his hand in his pocket and said, "What you up to, bo?"

"Just ridin' to Fairhope."

"You got anything to eat?"

"No."

"How about money?"

"I'm keepin' what's mine." Davis held the bat in a cocked position, and the hobo suddenly laughed. "You're a tough kid. Ah, keep your money." He turned to the other two and said, "Watch out for this one. He's tough."

"He don't look tough to me, Rufe." The speaker was a short man.

Rufe immediately responded, "Watch out for him, Shorty. You and Tad don't know bad guys when you see 'em."

The third member, Tad, was a tall, skinny man. He said nothing but stared at Davis.

"You think you can whip all three of us?"

"Try me and find out," Davis said. His adrenaline was pumping, and as the train began to pick up speed, he measured the distance. If he had to, he could jump for it, and he didn't figure these three would follow him.

The big man called Rufe laughed harshly, but he suddenly turned and squinted. "Who's that back there? You got a friend here, tough guy?"

"No. Just another rider."

Suddenly the big man pulled a flashlight out of his pocket. He threw the beam back, and Davis, for the first time, saw the figure in the corner at the back of the car. He was wearing the usual garb of a tramp, oversized rough-looking clothes and a soft cap pulled down over his face. "Hey, bud, you got anything to eat?"

"No. I ain't got nothin'."

"What you got in that bundle?" Tad said. The tall man moved quickly and reached out and grabbed the bundle. The passenger stood up and held to it. "Leave me alone!"

"Leave me alone," Tad mocked. "Hey, Rufe, I think he's got some grub in here."

"Well, take it away from him. You know the rules of the road, bo. You've got to share what you've got."

Tad reached out and grabbed the bundle, but the rider struggled and Tad swung and struck him in the head. The blow knocked the soft cap off, and Davis was shocked to see the long blond hair of a woman as it fell about the hobo's shoulders.

"Well, look at this," Rufe said with a coarse laugh. "We got a lady friend here."

Shorty went over to join Tad. "Look at this. Ain't she a pretty thing."

"Leave me alone!"

Now that Davis knew this was a woman, he wondered why he had not heard it in the voice before. He watched as Rufe went over and the three stood there in a semicircle.

Rufe was laughing. "Don't be afraid of us. We're real friendly, ain't we, fellas?"

"Yeah, real friendly," Shorty said.

There was danger in the situation. Davis had a sudden thought of what it would be like if Maeva or Lanie were trapped in a boxcar with three men like this. He watched them close in, and Rufe reached out and touched the girl's hair. "What's your name, sweetie?"

When the girl did not answer, Rufe reached out and took her arm. "Come on. Be friendly. We ain't gonna hurt you."

"Leave me alone." The girl pulled back, or tried to, but the big man's hand still held her fast. The other two reached out and began to paw her, and the girl cried out, begging, "Please don't hurt me."

The girl's voice went right to something deep inside of Davis Freeman. He knew that the three were rough, and they probably carried knives if not a gun between them, but he had to do something. Reaching down, he picked up the bat. He stepped forward and said, "You fellows leave that girl alone."

Instantly all three turned to face him, and Rufe laughed. "Well, we got a hero here. Just like in the movies. You must have been watchin' too many of them moon pictures, boy."

"Leave her alone," Davis said. He managed to keep his voice steady, and he held the bat loosely in his hand.

Shorty snarled, "He's just a kid! I'll take care of him." He came forward, a bulky shape, and suddenly there was a knife in his hand. He was laughing softly as if something pleased him, and as he passed by the door, Davis saw the glint of the blade. Without hesitation he stepped forward and swung the bat. He struck as hard as he could but did not strike for the head. The bat hit solid flesh and drove Shorty to one side. The bat had struck him on his left arm, and Davis thought he heard the crack of a bone.

"Hey, he hit Shorty!" Rufe said. "Come on, Tad, get him!"

The two were old hands at this, and as they approached, they separated, attacking him from two sides. Davis knew they both had knives, and there was no hope unless he struck quickly. Turning his back on one, he took a crack at the biggest man. Rufe jumped back, the bat merely grazing his shoulder. He let out a yelp, and at the same time the one called Tad was on Davis. He felt the blade of the knife as it grazed his side, ripping through his clothes, but he was able to swing the bat backhandedly. Fortunately it caught the tall man in the head and he fell with a low moan.

Davis's back was to the big man. As he turned, he saw that Rufe had drawn a knife and was on him. There was no time to draw back the bat, but at that instant the girl threw herself between the two. Davis saw the knife make a wild slash and heard the girl cry out. But he had time to swing the bat, and this time he caught the big man right in the torso.

"Ow, you broke my ribs!"

Davis picked up the knife the big man had dropped. He folded it and stuck it in his pocket. "Get off this train," he said.

"We can't jump off—it's movin'," Shorty gasped.

"Then I'll beat your brains out. Take your choice." He jumped toward Shorty and lifted the bat, and the short man with a single cry turned and leaped out the door.

"You two blow out of here!"

Tad stared at him, but the bat was a lethal weapon, and with a curse he turned and left.

Rufe was holding his side. "You're a pretty tough kid after all. If you didn't have that bat, I'd show you something."

Davis stepped forward and said, "I'll make mush out of your head if you don't jump off the train, Rufe."

"You'd do it too, wouldn't you?"

"Just try me!"

With a crude laugh, Rufe looked at the girl, who had backed up against the wall. "You got a real hero here, sweetie. You better hang on to him." He turned, went to the door of the car, and leaped off.

Davis found that he was shaking. Now that it was over, he was having a reaction.

"Are you all right?" he asked in a voice not quite steady.

He got no answer, and putting the bat down he went over, but his foot struck the flashlight that Rufe had dropped. He picked it up and turned it on the girl. She was small and seemed to be no older than he. "Are you all right?" he repeated.

"He—he—cut me."

"Let me see."

With the flashlight he saw that she had a cut across her back and her shoulder.

"You're bleeding bad," he said. "We've got to stop that. Sit down."

Without a word the girl sat down and Davis said, "Have you got any kind of clothes I can use to make a bandage?"

"In the—bundle."

Quickly he pulled the bundle open and grabbed the first garment he saw. It was a shirt. He went back and said, "Here. Turn around." She turned and tried to untuck her shirt, but she was shaking. Davis said, "We've got to get something on that to stop the bleeding." He pulled up her shirt and his heart lurched as he saw the gap across her back. "That's got to be sewn up," he said. "You need to see a doctor." He tore the shirt up, made bandages, and was able to use the sleeves as ties to hold it in place. He tried to think. "We'll be in Fairhope pretty soon. I can get you to a doctor there. I know a good one. You'll be all right. He'll get you fixed up."

The girl said nothing. She was sitting on the floor, and suddenly she began leaning to one side.

"Hey, don't faint on me, Cass!"

But the girl slumped, and Davis reached out and caught her. He put his arm around her, avoiding the wound as best he could, and held her as the train sped toward Fairhope.

✑ CHAPTER 16 ✑

"It's closing time, Lanie."

Startled, Lanie looked up from the newspaper she was reading to find the librarian, Cassandra Sue Pruitt, looking over her shoulder. She was a woman of medium height with auburn hair and blue eyes and had been a great friend to Lanie.

"I'm sorry, Cassandra. I didn't realize it was so late."

"Reading the newspapers?"

"Yes. There's not very much good news. They're having a riot in London. It seems the Depression's not just in this country but there too."

"I know. It feels like the whole world is in the grip of some terrible catastrophe."

"Look. It says here that Major James Doolittle set a record for coast-to-coast travel. He flew from California to New York in eleven hours, sixteen minutes. Isn't that something?"

"It really is. Just think how long it would have taken back in the days before the automobile or the trains to cross this country. Months and months, I suppose." Cassandra suddenly said, "Wait right here. There's something I've been wanting to show you, Lanie."

Lanie carefully folded the newspaper and put it back on the rack, and Cassandra came to stand beside her. "Look at this," she said. "I clipped it out of the paper for you."

Lanie took the paper the librarian held out. "'National poetry contest,'" she read aloud. "'First prize five hundred dollars.' Why are you showing this to me?" she said.

"Because they've got a category there for young people. Anyone under eighteen can enter."

Lanie blinked with surprise. "You don't mean I should enter it, do you?"

"I surely do. I haven't seen much of your poetry, but I know it's good."

"Why, I wouldn't stand a chance, Cassandra."

"You might. All it costs is a postage stamp. You can gamble three cents, can't you?"

Lanie laughed. "I'm not even sure about that."

"Well, take it with you; there's a list of rules and an application. You have to be sponsored by a teacher or a librarian, and that's me." She reached out and hugged Lanie and said, "You fly right at it."

"All right. I'll think about it, but I doubt if I'll be risking three cents."

Leaving the library, Lanie wandered home. It was still light, but the days were getting shorter now that fall was just around the corner. She walked down Robert E. Lee Avenue to Walnut, took a shortcut through a vacant lot, and spoke to people she knew who lived in the houses set back off Walnut Street. The homeplace was set in a block fronting Jefferson Davis Avenue on the east. She thought again how nice it was to have a place that was both in town and out of town. The five acres was big enough to keep a cow and some pigs, and being just outside the city limits there were no problems with zoning. The house was an old two-story frame painted white, with a porch running on three sides.

Going inside, she went about the business of fixing supper, but her mind was on Davis all the time. She worried about him getting home safely from Fort Smith, and thinking of him naturally led to more worry about his reading problem. After supper she worked on a dress that she was making for Corliss and for a time played checkers with Cody. Cody was a terrible player. Whenever he made a jump he liked to slam his man down with such violence that it jarred most of the checkers out of their places. When he got beat, he groaned and pulled at his hair and declared that it was all luck.

Finally the household went to bed, and Lanie sat up waiting for Davis. She read a brand new book she had checked out of the library, *The Good Earth*, by a woman called Pearl Buck. She was intrigued by the novel, which dealt with a family struggling to live through hard times in China. *I guess*, she thought, *there's no easy place to live. China's just as hard as America.*

She finished the book and was almost dozing off when Aunt Kezia came in.

"Are you still up, Lanie?"

"Yes. I'm waiting up for Davis."

"I couldn't sleep a wink, as usual," Aunt Kezia said with a loud yawn. "You're worried about Davis getting back from his game?"

"Yes, a little. But Aunt Kezia, I just can't seem to stop thinking about why he can't learn to read. He's so smart in some things. Science and math, anything with numbers. Nobody knows what's wrong with him."

"Well, it won't help you to worry about it. I decided a long time ago to give up worrying." Aunt Kezia plunked herself down on the couch beside Lanie. She was wearing a flannel nightgown made of the most hideous purple material anyone had ever seen. Cody declared it hurt his eyes just to look at her, but Aunt Kezia treasured it.

"What do you mean you decided to stop worrying? You can't just decide things like that."

Aunt Kezia looked like a bright bird as she perched there. "Why, you can decide whatever you want to. Didn't you know that?"

"Well, how did you decide to stop worrying?"

"It happened when my second husband Calvin Butterworth was sheriff in Kansas. He got word that a tough character—Long Dave Matheny—was mad at him and was comin' to shoot it out with him."

Lanie's eyes opened wide.

"Now he was a sight paradin' up and down! Wore his hair long. It was yellow. He had eyes like I never seen before. They was dead eyes. Looked like there was nothin' behind 'em, and he was mean too. Just as soon kill a fellow as look at him."

"Why was he mad at your husband?"

"'Cause he got drunk, and Mr. Butterworth had to arrest him and lock him up. So the word got around that he was gonna come and shoot him next time he came to town. He was in town and everybody was skeered to death. I didn't sleep a wink for four days. Mr. Butterworth kept tellin' me Matheny was just a big blowhard, but I knowed that wasn't so. He was a vile person."

"Well, what happened?"

"What happened was after I worried myself sick, Matheny came into town. He went into a saloon and boasted about how he was going to shoot my husband. He sat down in a card game, and a feller come in the back door, crept up behind him, and shot him dead."

"How awful."

"Well, when I heard about it, I saw how foolish I'd been. God knew all the time that that man wasn't gonna shoot my husband. I wasted all my time worryin' about it. So now I just don't do it anymore. If I'm gonna worry about anything, it's about somethin' that's happenin' right now, like the beans gonna burn on the back burner. Somethin' I can fix. I ain't gonna worry about some problem that might never come around."

Lanie laughed, her eyes sparkling. "I think I'll adopt your system."

"I been meanin' to talk to you, Lanie. Have you got your cap set for that Roger fella?"

Instantly Lanie grew defensive. "Oh, I don't know. How does a girl know she likes a man? I mean, enough to think about marrying him. How did *you* know?" she demanded of Aunt Kezia.

"Well, twice I didn't know." Aunt Kezia's eyes grew dim as memories stirred her. She rubbed her hands together and finally shook her head. "I married my first husband because I was in a hard place and I wanted to get out of it. I married my last husband because I was stupid. I thought I had to have somebody to take care of me. But I married Calvin Butterworth because the Lord told me to."

"That's wonderful that God pointed out the man for you to marry."

"Mr. Butterworth didn't think so at first. I was foolish enough to tell some folks I was gonna marry him and I hadn't even met him. So one day I was comin' out of a store, and there he was big as life. My, he was handsome! It fluttered me so much I spilled all my groceries. He helped me pick 'em up, and he was laughin' at me. Well, his eyes was. He had laughin' eyes, that man did."

"What did he say?" Lanie asked. Although she had heard the story, she loved to hear Aunt Kezia tell it.

"He said, 'I hear you tellin' it around that you and me is gonna get married.'"

"What did you say?"

"I couldn't say nothin', Lanie, not a word. He just laughed at me and said, 'Well, I'll be around about supper time tonight. If we're gonna get married, I expect we need to get to know each other better.' So he come around and he took me out, and a week later he proposed. Two weeks after that we got married up. Happiest time of my life. Maybe you better wait until the Lord tells you. Some of these jelly beans that hang around young girls ain't fit to be kilt."

Lanie held up her hand. "Listen. There comes Davis."

Both women got up and went toward the door. Lanie opened the door and froze. Davis stood there half supporting what appeared to be a young man in baggy clothes and a soft cap. She could see by the porch light that the young fellow was bleeding.

Davis gasped, "Lanie, this is Cass. Hurt pretty bad."

Lanie at once said, "Well, bring him in."

Davis entered the door and his face was pale and his eyes were filled with worry. "He ain't a boy. Her name is Cass Johnson."

"Well, don't give us her biography," Aunt Kezia said. "Bring her in here and let's have a look at that wound."

Davis half carried the young woman in, and Lanie put an old quilt over the couch. "Put her right here, Davis."

Davis helped Cass down, put her feet up, and then said, "I got to go get the doctor."

"I'll do that, Davis. You stay here."

"She just about saved my life, Lanie," he said. He pulled the hat off the young woman and the golden blond hair tumbled out. Her face was white as paper, and Davis said in a shaky voice, "Hurry with that doctor. She's lost lots of blood."

❦

Lanie slammed the brakes on the pickup, cut the engine, and jumped out. Running around the vehicle, she dashed up the front steps of Doctor Givens's house and banged on the door. It was close to midnight, but she did not care. She banged incessantly until finally a light came on and a voice said through the door, "Who is it? What do you want?"

"It's Lanie Freeman. I've got to see Doctor Merritt." The door opened, and Matilda Satterfield, Doctor Givens's housekeeper, stood there clutching her robe about her. "What's the matter?" she demanded.

"There's been an accident. Don't have time to explain it. I've got to see Doctor Merritt."

Even as she spoke, she saw Owen coming down the stairs. He was pulling on a robe and Lanie cried out, "Doctor Merritt, Davis brought a young woman home. She's been hurt pretty bad. You've got to come."

Merritt said instantly, "All right. I'll get dressed. Give me five minutes."

❦

On their way back Lanie explained as best she could the circumstances. When she finished, Owen asked, "So you don't know how it happened?"

"Must have happened on the way home from the ball game."

"She probably ought to be in the hospital."

"I was afraid to take that much time."

Merritt pulled up in front of the house and jumped out. He hurried in, followed by Lanie, and found that everybody in the house was up.

"How is she?" Owen demanded of Aunt Kezia.

"She's hurt pretty bad, Merritt."

Everyone started to crowd back into the living room, but Lanie said, "No one goes in there. You all go to bed." It took some doing, but finally all except Davis were shooed out of the living room. By that time Lanie saw that the girl was sitting up, and Owen turned and said, "This has to be stitched."

"Can I help you, Doctor Merritt?" Lanie said.

"Yes, you can. Get some hot water boiling to sterilize the instruments."

Lanie quickly went to the kitchen, and when she got back with the water, the young woman was on her face on the couch. Davis was standing back watching without saying a word. Lanie watched as Owen carefully stitched the flesh back together. It was very quiet in the room, and Cass did not make a sound, although it must have been very painful. Finally Owen put the bandage on, saying, "No way to hold this on except to make kind of a harness." He held the bandage in place by strips that crossed the girl's chest and over her shoulder. "You're going to be all right, Cass. How'd this happen?"

The girl just shook her head. She had lost a great deal of blood, and it was Davis who told the story.

He ended up by saying, "I think that fellow would have killed me if she hadn't jumped in. She saved my life."

"What happened to those three?" Owen asked.

"We made 'em jump out. I hope they didn't get hurt bad. I guess they could have been killed."

"You did the right thing, Davis," Owen said. "I'm proud of you." He stood looking down at the girl who had dozed off. "You think you could keep her tonight, Lanie? We'll see about the hospital tomorrow."

"Of course. We'll fix her a place and take care of her."

"I'll stop early in the morning and see how she makes it through the night. But there shouldn't be any trouble. If she wakes up, get her to drink as much water as she can, and she needs to eat too."

Owen left, and Aunt Kezia stood looking down at the young woman. "Well, we got another mouth to feed."

Lanie went over and said, "I'm proud of you, Davis, taking up for a young woman like that."

Aunt Kezia nodded and said, "So am I. It's just the kind of thing Mr. Butterworth would have done."

⤙ CHAPTER 17 ⤚

C ass was disoriented as she began to wake up. She slowly opened her eyes and startled in fear, for everything was strange, but the sudden movement caused a stab of pain to shoot down her back and high up on her shoulder and arm. She groaned and closed her eyes. She could tell she was lying facedown on some sort of a sofa. Images came flooding back, but she could make sense of very little that had happened except for the doctor stitching her up like a rag doll.

Opening her eyes again, she saw that she was in a large room with wallpaper figured in small daisies. The window was open, and she could hear the sounds of crickets singing outside. Turning her head carefully, another shock ran over her as she encountered the gaze of a small girl watching her with intent dark blue eyes. The girl was standing so that her face was not twelve inches away from that of Cass. She waited for the little girl to speak, and when she did not, Cass said, "What are you doing?"

"I'm watchin' you." The young girl had a round face with translucent skin and a solemn expression.

"Why are you watching me?"

"Wanted to see if you were going to die."

The words struck Cass, and she did not know whether to laugh or be afraid. Was she really that bad off? "I never seen anybody die. Did you?" the girl said.

"No, I didn't."

"Lanie said you wouldn't die, but she doesn't know everything. My name is Corliss Jeanne Freeman, and I'm three years old. What's your name?"

"My name is Cass."

"How old are you?"

"I'm sixteen."

"Where do you come from?"

Cass stared at the child, but before she could answer, a young woman came through the door. Cass remembered her vaguely as she spoke. "Corliss, stop pestering her."

"I wasn't pestering. I just wanted to find out who she was."

Cass looked at Lanie. The pain was bad and it made it difficult to speak. "She's only three years old?"

Lanie smiled. "Yes. She just started talking all at once like a grown person. How do you feel?"

Cass did not answer for a moment. She was studying the young woman carefully. "Who are you?"

"I'm Lanie Freeman. This is our house. I live here with my brothers and sisters."

"Don't you have a mama or a daddy?"

"Our aunt lives with us. Our mother's gone to be with the Lord, and Daddy's not here."

"Where is he?"

"He's in prison," Corliss piped up. "He shot a man, but it wasn't his fault, and God's going to get him out some day."

"My name's Lanie and your name is Cass, Davis tells me. Can you let me take a look at that bandage?"

Cass nodded and laid her head back down. She felt Lanie's hands lifting her shirt and adjusting her bandages. "Doctor Merritt will be here pretty soon, and he can change this dressing. Can you eat something?"

"Guess so."

"I'll go fix you something. Doctor Merritt said you need to drink as much as you can." She poured some water out of a pitcher and the girl rolled over. "Can you sit up?"

Cass did not answer. The pain coursed through her as she tried to pull herself upright. She took the glass and drank thirstily, then handed it back. "Where is this place?"

"Fairhope."

"I mean what state?"

Lanie gave her a look of surprise. "Fairhope, Arkansas. Where were you headed when all this happened?"

"Headed south." The answer came grudgingly, and then she said, "What happened to my things?"

"Don't worry about it, Cass. Davis brought your things with you. I don't know how he carried you and your bag and his bat, but he did. See. There's your things over there on that chest."

Cass relaxed then and lay there as Lanie left. She insisted on taking Corliss with her, telling Cass that the child would drive her crazy with questions.

As soon as the two were gone, Cass sat up, reaching back over her shoulder. She could not reach the cut place, but it hurt when she moved. She looked up quickly as a young man came through and she recognized Davis. He looked worried and came over and said, "Are you all right, Cass?"

"I'm okay."

"Doctor Merritt will be here pretty soon. He did a good job of sewing you up. Must have hurt like everything." When she did not answer, Davis said, "Is there anybody we need to get in touch with? Your folks might be worried about you."

"No. There's nobody."

Davis was taken aback by the brevity of the answer. Everybody he knew had somebody, and he studied the young woman's face. She had hair as blond as any he had ever seen, and her eyes were a light blue or gray. He could not tell which. They were large eyes, deep set and wide spaced, and her face was an oval shape. She looked thin, and he said, "I'm glad we made it back. It was pretty iffy there for a while."

"Why'd you take up for me?"

Davis could not think for a moment, for the answer to him was obvious. "Why, you needed help." He noticed that her accent was odd. It was not an Arkansas accent, and he was familiar with other accents such as Oklahoma, Tennessee, and Missouri. He said quickly, "I'm sorry you got hurt trying to help me. It's a good thing you did. Those fellows were pretty rough."

"I'm glad you brought my things back."

Davis shrugged his shoulders. "I wish I could have done a little better looking out for you."

At that point Lanie came in, followed by Cody, Maeva, Aunt Kezia, and Corliss.

"I brought you some broth that Aunt Kezia made. Let me introduce you to the family. You may not remember them from last night. This is our Aunt Kezia. This is my brother Cody, my sister Maeva, and, of course, you already met Corliss."

"I hear you saved Davis's life," Maeva said moving closer. "That was pretty neat."

"Well, he was taking up for me."

"Where you from?" Cody asked. "You talk funny."

"Cody, you hush!" Lanie said. "That's not polite."

As always Cody was surprised when he was rebuked for his manners. "Well, I just wanted to know. We're from Arkansas. You're not from here, huh?"

"No. Not from here."

"Don't be so nosy, Cody," Maeva said. "You'll have to excuse him, Cass. He doesn't have many manners."

"I got *perfect* manners," Cody said indignantly.

"All right. That's enough talk. All of you can get out of here now. I want Cass to eat and rest before the doctor comes." As they left the room, Lanie and Cass could hear Cody speaking loudly. "I'll bet she's from the north. Probably from Massachusetts."

"You'll have to forgive Cody. He's very nosy and so is Corliss."

She put the bowl of soup down and said, "Do you think you can manage this?"

"I can eat it." Cass took the soup and carefully began to eat it. It had big chunks of chicken in it, and Lanie smiled. "That's Aunt Kezia's recipe. She's really a fine cook."

Cass ate hurriedly and seemed half starved. When she finished the bowl, Lanie said, "I'll go get you some more."

She went back to the kitchen, but when she returned the girl was asleep. Her blond hair was spread out on the pillow, and there was a look of troubled innocence on her face. Lanie stood over her for a moment, then turned and left the room.

"She looks plumb wore out," Aunt Kezia said as Lanie went back into the kitchen. "I'll be glad when Merritt gets here. I want to give that girl some of Doctor Luthor's Phosphorus Water."

"Don't you be dosing that girl, Aunt Kezia. You let Owen do the doctoring."

Aunt Kezia sniffed. "If you wasn't in love with him, you wouldn't have so much confidence in him. You don't know as much about doctors as I do."

"I am not in love with Owen Merritt, and if you say one more word, I'm not going to take you to that awful movie you want to see!"

Aunt Kezia opened her mouth to argue, but she saw a certain look on Lanie's face she had learned to recognize. She longed to challenge her, but she said, "Well, you're gettin' uppity, Lanie, I'm sorry to tell you. And the Bible says uppityness goes before a fall."

"It doesn't say that. Now, you behave yourself."

⌐✦⌐

The Dew Drop Inn was packed, as it usually was on Wednesday at noon. It was the day Charlie Poindexter made his specialty—calf liver and bacon. Charlie cut the liver into slices, fried it in bacon, then put the liver in the dish and the bacon on top. He served it up with gravy made in a pan with boiling water, parsnip, onion, and lemon. The only trouble with the specialty was that the two vegetables were inevitably greens and black-eyed peas. He also made cold-water corn-bread, which somehow tasted better than the regular kind. He would never reveal his secret for the cornbread, but Pardue Jessup thought he put brandy or beer in it. "Tastes too good not to have a little bait of alcohol," Pardue had joked. And Charlie had not disagreed with him.

As usual, Pardue and Orrin Pierce were sitting together, and they were both pleased when Nelson Prather came in and joined them. They all three ordered the special and were eating when Pierce noticed the necklace Nellie was wearing. "What's that you got around your neck, Nellie?"

Nellie reached up and touched the nut that was hanging by a piece of string. "Why, this here's to keep the fever off."

"What is that—a pecan?"

"Just the shell of it, but it's what's inside that counts," Nellie said. He fingered the pecan and held it up cautiously. Nellie was one of the best-looking men in the county but never failed to live up to his reputation as the most superstitious man that ever drew breath. Now he nodded firmly, "There's a spider in there."

"A spider! What for?"

"Why, Orrin, everybody knows that spiders is good luck espe-cially if you wear one in a nutshell around your neck. It keeps fevers off. I been wearing one off an' on since I was six years old and I ain't never had a fever. Don't you see? You fellows ought to get one. As a matter of fact, I'd be glad to make you one, if you like."

Both Orrin and Pardue tried to keep their smiles from showing, for Nellie was a sensitive man. He lived alone now after having raised his brother and sister and caring for his mother until she died. Most of the young women in the county had tried to entice Nellie into mar-riage, for he had a fine farm and was known to be one of the kindest, best-natured men in all Stone County.

Sister Myrtle came by at that time with a pitcher of iced tea to freshen up their drinks. She stopped and looked down at Nellie Prather and without preamble and with her usual piercing, thunderous voice said, "Nellie Prather, you ought to be ashamed of yourself."

Startled, Nellie looked up. "About what, Sister Myrtle?"

"Because you're robbin' some young woman."

"Why, I never robbed a woman in my life nor anybody else."

"You're robbin' 'em of a husband. Why in the world don't you get married? How old are you anyhow?"

"I'm thirty."

"Then you're late."

Nelson fingered the nut containing the deceased spider and did not seem to be aware that every customer in the Dew Drop Inn was listening to his answer and smiling behind their hands. Everyone liked Nellie, though they all teased him about his superstitions.

"Well, I been thinkin' about that a lot lately, Sister Myrtle, and I thought I had a handle on it. But my uncle Seedy—you remember him, Sister Myrtle?"

"I remember him. What about him?"

"Well, my uncle Seedy told me how to go about findin' out who to marry."

"I'd like to know that myself," Pardue said, winking at Orrin Pierce. "How does it work?"

"Well, you do it this a way," Nellie said, serious as a judge. "You get out a bunch of socks before you go to bed at night and you name each one of them socks, don't you see, after a lady you know, and then you put 'em under your pillow. Then the important part is you don't get into bed like usual. You get into bed over the footboard backwards. You gotta be careful to do it right. It's kind of hard to do. But it's the only thing that works. You get in from the side that's no good at all."

"Oh, I wouldn't think so," Pierce said. "Then what?"

"Well, if you do it right, the lady you dream about that night, it'll be one of them you named a sock after. And that'll be the one you marry."

"Have you tried it?" Pardue demanded.

"Yeah, I did."

"Well, how come you didn't marry?"

"Well, the one I named, she ran off with a paint salesman before I had a chance to ask her. So I guess I done somethin' wrong."

Myrtle exclaimed, "That's the most foolish thing I ever heard of! You wanna get married, I'll help ya. I know all the young women, and I can tell you which ones you don't want to hitch up with."

Myrtle started going over a list of young women in the county that would qualify as a wife for Nellie Prather, but at that moment Owen Merritt came in. She turned and exclaimed, "And speaking of marriage, why, it's the soon-to-be groom, Doc Merritt! Louise Langley finally twisted your arm into setting a date, eh, Doc?"

Owen made a face. "Sister Myrtle, did you ever stop and think that some people might not want their business announced at the top of your lungs at the Dew Drop Inn?"

"If they got nothin' to be ashamed of, it don't matter none. Besides, your engagement was announced in the *Sentinel*! Not like it's a secret."

Owen shook his head. "Fine, Myrtle, talk about my engagement all you want."

"I will, Doc, and I'll be lookin' for some details soon." Myrtle switched gears quickly and demanded, "How's that girl Davis brought home from the ball game?"

"You really are something, Myrtle," Owen replied.

"How is she? What's her name? Where's she from?"

"There's such a thing as doctor-patient confidentiality."

Owen was peppered with questions, and finally Orrin Pierce said, "Sit down here, Owen, and have the special. Give him room, folks. He's gonna be stingy with that story."

Owen sat down and lowered his voice saying, "The girl and Davis were assaulted by three hoboes, but I don't guess there's anything to do about 'em."

"Just give me their names. I'll lock 'em up."

"Don't know, but I'll tell you this much. Davis threw 'em all off the car. Used his baseball bat on the three of them."

"He did? Well, I do admire his spunk."

Owen sat there eating his meal listening to the other two tease Nellie about his superstitions, but finally when Nelson and Pardue left, Owen leaned forward and said to Orrin Pierce, "You remember I told you my brother Dave was going to try to find Thelma Mays?"

"The one that's supposed to be a witness to the shooting of Duke Biggins?"

"That's the one. Well, Dave found her."

Orrin leaned over, his face intent. "Did he get anything out of her?"

"No. She won't talk. I think she's afraid she'll get drawn into the shooting somehow or other. Dave's going to keep after her. She's a low-down woman. I think she might be out to make some money on this."

"That wouldn't do for a witness."

"You think we ought to tell Lanie?"

"I think so," Orrin said. "At least it'll give 'em a little hope. Lord knows they don't have much of that right now."

"Well, I've got to go by and visit Cass, the girl Davis brought home."

"I know you couldn't tell everybody, but how is she doing?"

"She'll be all right. Got a bad cut. The thing is she won't talk about herself. Don't know where she's from. Just kind of a female hobo."

"She look pretty tough?"

"No. On the contrary. She'd be a real pretty girl if she gained a little weight, but she's troubled. I can tell that much."

"Well, let me know if I can do anything. Does she need help?"

"I thought about putting her in the hospital, but Lanie's willing to keep her, so I guess that would be best for a while."

"Let me know then, and let me know about how your brother comes out with Thelma."

Davis had brought some iced tea to Cass. He put it down on the table and saw her starting to get up. "Here. Let me help you." He reached out and took her arm, but she struck out at him, hitting him across the chest. "Don't you manhandle me!" she said. Davis was shocked to see the fierce anger in her eyes.

"Why, I was just—"

"I know what you were *just* doing. You keep your hands off me, you hear?"

Davis stood shocked by the sudden burst of anger. He could not even think for a moment how to speak to her. He turned without a word and left, meeting Lanie in the hall along with Doctor Merritt.

"How is she, Davis?"

"Mean as a snake," Davis said. "I was gonna help her sit up and she hit me." There was hurt in the boy's eyes.

Lanie said, "She's obviously had a hard time, Davis. Don't hold it against her." Davis shook his head and walked away. "He's so sensitive, Owen. Just like a woman almost."

"Well, let's see what the spitfire's doing."

"Don't you pick on her now," Lanie warned.

"I won't."

The two went in, and Merritt was indeed gentle with the girl. He changed the bandage and then said, "Don't see why you can't get up and move around a little bit more. You'll get stiff if you lie there."

"Thanks."

The single word of gratitude was grudging, but Merritt said cheerfully, "That's all right. You don't want to do too much. They treating you all right here?"

Cass shot a glance at Lanie and nodded.

Lanie took all this in, and when she went outside with Owen, she said, "Something's wrong with her."

"Yes, there is. She's healing fine physically, but she's mad at the world. You can see it in her eyes."

The two discussed Cass for a moment, and finally Owen said, "I can probably get her into the hospital."

"Oh, don't do that, Owen. She can stay with us."

Lanie walked out to the car with him, and he stood there looking across the field. "You know, I'd like to just forget about doctoring and go fishing over at Singing River. How about it?"

"What, me go fishing with you?"

"Sure," he said recklessly. "Nobody's dying."

"I couldn't do that, Owen."

"Why not?"

"Because. It wouldn't be right."

Owen looked befuddled for a minute and said, "I keep forgetting you're a grown-up young woman now. It was easier when you were just a little girl."

Suddenly Lanie asked a question that had been on her mind, but she had been afraid to ask. "Are you happy, Owen?"

"Happy? About what?"

"Why, about getting married, of course. It's coming up quickly now."

The question seemed to trouble Owen Merritt, for he snapped back at once, "Well, of course I'm happy. Why wouldn't I be?"

Lanie studied his face. She had always thought him to be a handsome man, but now there seemed to be something troubling him. "You don't seem happy."

"Well, shucks, Lanie. A man can't go around grinning like an idiot and singing love songs all the time, can he?" He shook his head. "Good-bye. I'll come back to see how Cass is doing later."

Lanie watched as he got in the car and drove away, squealing the tires as he went.

"I don't know what he's so mad about. " Suddenly Lanie squared her shoulders and said angrily, "Lanie Freeman, you've got to stop thinking about Owen Merritt."

Part Four

—◦⊃·‹ ·›⊂◦—

The Transformation

~ CHAPTER 18 ~

U sually from her seat in the choir, Lanie got a good view of the back of the minister's head, but seldom did she see his face. She was used to it and didn't mind, but the coming of Colin Ryan changed everything. Ryan was as unorthodox in his pulpit mannerisms as he was in his dress. He ignored the pulpit and with a Bible in his left hand he would move from one side of the rostrum to the other, often turning around to face the choir. On occasion he would even step off the rostrum and move up and down the aisle, confusing many of the members who were accustomed to a preacher as firmly fixed behind the pulpit as if his shoes were nailed to the floor.

Lanie liked to sit in the choir, for even if she could not see the preacher's face, she could see the congregation. She knew exactly who would go to sleep during the sermon, and could read various reactions to the preacher's words. It had been especially interesting since Colin Ryan had come, for his preaching was revolutionary, and during every message the expressions in the congregation ranged from disapproval to delight, depending on how the sermon struck the individuals.

After the choir had sung their special, an arrangement of "I Come to the Garden," everyone settled down for the sermon. Usually preachers edged into their topics carefully, laying a foundation and background for their message, but Lanie was not too shocked when Brother Ryan rose up and swung his Bible around in a circle, pointing first to the congregation, then to the choir, and without preamble began to read Scripture.

"In the twenty-first chapter of Luke we find these words: 'And he looked up, and saw the rich men casting their gifts into the treasury. And he saw also a certain poor widow casting in thither two mites. And he said, Of a truth I say unto you, that this poor widow hath cast in more than they all: for all these have of their abundance cast in unto the offerings of God: but she of her penury hath cast in all the living that she had.'"

Excitement brightened the face of Ryan as he began to speak, and something about his attitude and his posture and the tone of his voice warned Lanie that something was coming that the Baptist church in Fairhope, Arkansas, was not accustomed to.

"I doubt seriously that there is anyone in this congregation who has ever done what this poor woman did. The Bible said she had what would amount to a few cents in our money, but it was all she had. Instead of saving something for tomorrow, she put everything she had into the offering. And the Lord Jesus commended her for it."

Lanie looked over the congregation and her eyes fell on Louise Langley. She watched Louise every Sunday morning, and as she expected, the young woman was sitting bolt upright, her lips drawn together in a tight line. She made no secret of her dislike for Colin Ryan, and now she was sitting there waiting to see what she could criticize.

"I think the Lord God put this incident in the Bible as a challenge to see if there would be one individual or a church or even a denomination that would love Him enough to put their last two pence, their last penny into His service. This morning I'm going to find out if we're one of those rare churches who trust God enough to do this."

Opening his Bible, he said, "I want to read you one more Scripture and then give you a challenge. This one verse I'm going to read was written by the wisest man who ever lived on the face of the earth, Solomon, the son of David. In the book of Proverbs, chapter nineteen, verse seventeen, the Scripture says, 'He that hath pity upon the poor lendeth unto the LORD; and that which he hath given will he pay him again.'"

Closing his Bible, Colin began to walk from one side of the rostrum to the other. He turned often to the choir, and once his eyes met Lanie's, and she gave him an encouraging smile. He winked at her, then continued to speak. "I'm not going to preach a sermon this morning. The two Scriptures I've read are plain. I've never heard of anyone challenging the interpretation of these two. Number one, Jesus commended the woman who gave all that she had. Then in Proverbs the Lord says that anyone who gives to the poor is not really giving to the poor at all. He is giving to the Lord. And He says that whatever we give to the poor, God will give it back to us again."

Colin suddenly became very serious. "It's one thing to come and sit in a comfortable pew, and it's another thing to throw ourselves into the battle against the works of the devil. I'm going to ask this church this morning if you are willing to do what that widow did. I'm going to ask you—will you trust God? Will you lend God some money and wait until He pays you back?"

Lanie could see the resistance building up on many of the faces in the congregation. Louise Langley especially was waiting, as if to pounce on whatever point Colin Ryan was about to make. Colin stopped abruptly and said, "This church has almost six thousand dollars in a building fund." He looked around and swept the auditorium with an eloquent gesture. "We don't need a new building."

A rustle went over the congregation, and several feathers were ruffled by this proclamation. Lanie knew that many had been pushing for a new building, one that would equal the size of the Presbyterian church built three years ago. She saw the opposition as plainly as if it were written on a page.

"We are in this beautiful building sitting on comfortable pews. None of us are starving, and in the wintertime we're warm, but there are many in this country who are out in the cold and who don't have food enough to eat. There are those in our own community who are destitute and desperate for help. Some members of this church have lost their jobs and don't know how they're going to pay their rent."

Ryan stopped and looked up for a moment as if he expected to hear a voice from heaven. It did not come, but when he looked over the congregation, his eyes darting here and there, he said, "I'm going to challenge this church to take the money in that building fund and do a wonderful and glorious thing. I'm going to ask you to lend that money to God by spending it on those who need food and shelter and medical care. I'm going to ask you to put your faith and trust in the Word of God. Do you really believe the Bible? I know this is not the Baptist way. But I'm going to ask how many of you would be willing to take this money that's sitting in a bank doing no good to anybody and spend it on the family of God who have such desperate needs. How many of you would be willing to do that? Raise your hand."

Lanie raised her hand instantly, and as her gaze swept the congregation, she saw that the vote would be close. As she expected, none of the Langleys lifted their hands, and to her surprise suddenly Louise Langley stood up. Her face was red, and her voice was as hard as chilled steel. "Reverend Ryan, may I say a word?"

"Certainly, Miss Langley."

"You are an interim pastor. You'll be gone from here soon. The rest of us will be here, and we have to think of the future. No one would object to helping the poor, but to take the entire building fund would be improvident, and I'm going to ask you to withdraw your challenge."

"I'm sorry, Miss Langley, I can't do that. I believe the Lord has put this on my heart, and I'm asking the church to make a decision." He turned and said, "Brother Pink, I'm going to step aside and ask you to lead the church in whatever direction you think is right."

Gerald Pink looked as if he had been suddenly shot. He owned the only drugstore in Fairhope and was a devoted Christian, but he was not a particularly quick thinker. He needed time to think things over, and now he rose from his place in the choir and stuttered, "Well—I don't know—it seems to me that we need to move carefully." Several amens, especially from the Langleys, could be heard. "I will put this matter off until Wednesday night. We will have a special business meeting to consider this one item of business."

"I think that's very wise, Deacon Pink," Ryan said. "And now let's all stand and sing 'Amazing Grace,' and as we sing it, I hope this amazing grace of God that we sing about will fill our hearts."

Lanie rose with the others, and she could tell that even in the singing of the hymn a division had come. Those who favored spending the building fund money sang loud and looked happy. Those who did not, for the most part, did not sing at all. They simply stood there waiting, and after the benediction was pronounced by Gerald Pink, they turned and left. Lanie saw that Louise Langley gave Colin Ryan a look that was almost frightening before she walked out, her head high in the air.

❧

The town of Fairhope rarely got excited, but the news of the meeting at the Baptist church on Wednesday night had carried itself everywhere. Cody loved it! He made it his business to go to as many of the church members as he could, informing them in no uncertain terms that their duty was to vote, as he put it, to "spend that old building fund money on something that is worthwhile."

At the height of his excitement, while he was out rounding up votes for a welfare committee, Cody stopped Mrs. Butterworth, whose husband owned the Rialto Theater. "Hallelujah!" Cody greeted her. "You gonna vote for or against the building fund?"

"What are you talking about?" Mrs. Butterworth said. She did not know Cody by name, and now she stared at him with consternation. "Are you talking about that business at the Baptist church?"

"That's right. I want you to vote right."

"I'm not a member of the First Baptist Church."

"Oh," Cody said with disappointment. "Well, here's something for you anyhow." He tore out a page of the Bible he carried and handed it to her.

"What's this?" Mrs. Butterworth exclaimed.

"Read it. It'll do you good." Cody dodged around Mrs. Butterworth and left her reading the page in the Bible. Her face grew red as she studied it, and she said, "I'm going to see about this."

She turned at once and started for the First Baptist Church, determined to have it out with the preacher she had heard so much about. She found him out in front of the church raking leaves.

"Reverend Ryan, may I have a word with you?"

"Why, certainly. Mrs. Butterworth, isn't it?" Colin said, smiling. He put the rake aside and said, "Will you come into my office?"

"No. I just want to tell you that you're going to have to control your church members."

"I'm not sure I can promise that. I can't even control myself. What's the trouble?"

"Look at what one of your members, a young boy, gave me." She described Cody, and Colin said, "Yes. That's Cody Freeman. What's he done?"

"He gave me this. Look what it says." She whispered as she read the words, "It says here, 'A bundle of myrrh is my wellbeloved unto me; he shall lie all night betwixt my breasts.'"

Mrs. Butterworth thrust the page at Colin, saying, "It's a disgrace passing out this sort of thing."

"Well, it's from the Song of Solomon in the Old Testament, Mrs. Butterworth."

"It should be read in private."

Colin tried to keep from smiling. "It's a very beautiful book in the Bible. It's a love song. It preaches the love between God and His people as between a husband and a wife, between two lovers."

He knew he was fighting a losing cause, and finally Mrs. Butterworth said, "Well, if that's the sort of thing you Baptists do, I'm glad I'm not a member of your church!"

Colin Ryan watched as Mrs. Butterworth sailed away and shook his head. "Poor woman. She's missing a lot." He turned his thought to the business meeting that would take place at seven o'clock and began to pray, "Lord, I have no idea how the church is going to vote. I just ask that You get glory out of this situation."

⊂══⊀⊱

The Baptist church was filled for the business meeting. It was not the first time, for the Baptists had stirred up the town on more than one occasion. As Colin looked over the congregation, he smiled, seeing that there were more non-Baptists than Baptists. He asked Gerald Pink to take over, as was proper, and he sat there as Pink got up and began to approach the subject as if it were a stick of dynamite.

"Folks, you know why we're all here. Our interim pastor has suggested we take the money in our building fund and use it to help people in need. Do I hear a motion that this be done?"

"I move that we use the money in the building fund to help the needy."

Lanie was shocked, for she had never spoken at a business meeting. The words seemed to pop out of her, and she flushed and sat down, but she saw that Colin Ryan was smiling at her warmly and even gave her a quick conspiratorial wink.

"Do I hear a second?"

"I ain't no Baptist, but I second the motion anyhow," Sister Myrtle Poindexter said loudly.

"I'm afraid it has to be a second by someone who's a member of the church."

"I second the motion." Doctor Owen Merritt's voice rose over the congregation, and Lanie saw that Louise gave him a quick look and whispered in his ear. *She's dressing him down, I reckon*, Lanie thought, and it gave her a perverse pleasure.

In Baptist churches, once a motion is made and seconded, any member of the church is free to speak. Other denominations have some degree of freedom, but in an independent Baptist church, a twelve-year-old who has just been baptized into the fellowship has a vote and the right to speak exactly as has the oldest member, no matter if he is a deacon. Lanie had always enjoyed the fact that the Baptist church was a democracy, although at times in critical situations the meetings did get a little bit rowdy. Now, for the next half hour, the battle raged.

Lanie sat back and listened, and she could have prophesied who would be for the motion and who would be against it.

Finally the vote was taken, and it carried only by a slender majority of six votes. In a democracy, however, that was enough.

"The motion is carried," Gerald Pink said, and then stood there waiting helplessly as if he didn't know what to do next.

Louise Langley rose at once. "I move that we elect a responsible member of the church to distribute the funds alongside the pastor."

"I second the motion," Otis Langley said loudly.

The motion was carried, and Gerald Pink said, "Nominations are now in order."

Colin Ryan had said nothing during all this. Now he stood to his feet and said, "I'm not a member of this church, only the interim pastor, but I would like to ask the church to nominate and elect Miss Louise Langley."

Lanie saw that Colin Ryan's words shocked Louise severely. She stood there, and her jaw actually dropped open. She did not move. Deoin Jinks said loudly, "I move that Miss Louise Langley be appointed by acclamation of the church."

"Second the motion," several people said. And the vote was unanimous.

For a moment there was silence in the church. So much had happened that it was as if a bomb had gone off, and now people were trying to find out who had been wounded.

Discussion began to determine exactly how to go about implementing the welfare project. Various members brought up names of families in the community who were in need of assistance right away, and it was decided that Colin and Louise would begin by immediately providing food, clothing, and money to those in the most dire straits. The two were granted access to the building fund, provided they kept an accurate accounting of how each dollar was used.

Lanie watched as Gerald Pink announced the benediction. Lanie saw Colin go to Louise, and she was close enough to hear him say, "I'm sure the welfare committee will be well led. Shall we meet tomorrow to begin our work?"

"I'll be at your office at eight o'clock," Louise said. Her voice was cold, and she turned and walked away without another word.

Orrin Pierce was not a member of any church but had come for the meeting. He had heard Louise speak coldly to Colin, and now he came and whispered, "I think you're going to have your hands full with that one, Preacher."

"She'll be all right," Colin said cheerfully. "You'll see."

❧

The next day after the meeting, Lanie went out to the cemetery as she often did to tend to her mother's grave. She carried her notebook with her, thinking she might write. It was a quiet place, of course, and she had gotten some fine thoughts there.

After she had tended her mother's grave, she sat down, and when she lifted her eyes she noticed a tombstone that was almost hidden behind grass over at the edge of the cemetery. The cemetery was joined to a wood, and the men of the various churches came periodically to clean it out. She moved over to the stone, wondering that she had never noticed it before. She leaned down and saw the words. The carving was worn and faded. She made out the letters by running her fingers over them. "C. S. A. Christopher Scott. Company B Sixth Battalion. The Army of the Stonewall Brigade."

A strange feeling came over her as she thought about the man. This was the grave of a soldier who had fought in the Civil War. The grave was not tended, and as she thought about the man, trying to picture him, she wondered what kind of a life he had led and whether he had gone to meet God with joy, or if he was lost.

She looked down and saw that there were some more words that were almost covered. Just the tops of the letters were visible. She began to dig and uncovered a poem that someone had carved low on the stone. It was hard to read, but she finally was able to decipher it all:

Warm summer sun shine kindly here.
Warm southern wind blow softly here.
Green sod above lie light, lie light.
Good night, dear heart,
Good night,
Good night.

Tears came to Lanie Freeman's eyes. Someone had loved this man enough to write a few beautiful lines. They had been almost destroyed by time and weather, but they were still there. She whispered, "I wish I could write something beautiful like that."

A thought came to her. A poem began to take shape in her mind, and quickly she grabbed her pencil and began scribbling. She wrote rapidly for a time, then slower, and the sun moved across the sky until finally an hour had passed, and she looked down at what she had written.

Confederate's Epitaph — Fairhope Cemetery
From where he lies, Chris Scott
Can see the Levi plant.
Over his grassy plot
Shadows fall aslant;
Twisted and grotesque
From a radio tower,
In patterns arabesque
They cross his final bower.
Once he heard at Shiloh
The loud artillery grumble —
Now the alien echo
Of city traffic's rumble.

He hears sometimes the hymns
From the small church just south
On Main. They fall like dim
Caresses on his mouth.
So many times I've read
The epitaph with lichen's blot
Above the Rebel's head:
C.S.A. CHRISTOPHER SCOTT
But could not know the man.
So strangely still he kept
I could not cross the span
Nor stir the sleep he slept.
Until by chance I read
The tombstone's buried hidden face.
What someone once had said
Was furred with moss, like lace;
With fingertips I brushed
The deep-grooved secret lines —
Deep, O deep, the quiet hush
When I read his love's design:
"Warm summer sun shine kindly here.
Warm southern wind blow softly here.
Green sod above lie light, lie light.
Good night, dear heart,
Good night,
Good night."

She studied the words and knew this was the poem that she would send to enter the contest. She put her hand on the tombstone and ran it over, brushing the secret lines that had been lost for so many years, and murmured, "Good night, dear heart. Good night ..."

⟿ CHAPTER 19 ⟾

For some perverse reason Louise Langley had donned her most expensive and ornate outfit for her meeting with Colin Ryan. He himself would be dressed like a tramp, she thought as she slipped into her dress. It was a silk, flat-crepe frock with rippling flares and tiny pleats. She admired it in the full-length mirror, turning to notice the gay little bows and the neckline, remembering how her father had rebuked her for spending so much on a dress. She always had been able to get what she wanted from him, and she smiled as she thought of it. It was turning cold outside, the last of September, and going to her closet, she chose to wear her newest coat. It was all wool, extra warm, and the collar was genuine silver fox. The coat had cost a hundred and fifty dollars, and she had kept it a secret from her father.

Her hat was a genuine Adrienne Ames made out of soft wool with silver fox trim. She put it on, turned it down in the front, up in the back, and put a jaunty soft crease in the crown. Spinning around she studied herself and then said aloud, "That preacher may go dressed like a hobo, but I'm going to dress like a lady!"

Leaving the house, she drove to the church and found Colin Ryan sitting on the steps. As she expected, he wore a pair of cotton slacks, a blue dress shirt open at the neck, and a worn leather jacket. He wore no cap, and his black hair glistened in the morning sun.

"Ready to go?"

"Before we leave," Louise said clearly, "I want it understood that I will keep the record for every penny we spend. I brought a notebook and I'll be the accountant."

"That's fine. Suppose we go by and pick up some supplies. I've got a pretty good idea of what we ought to buy for today."

"Very well." Despite herself Louise was struck by the good looks of Colin Ryan. She usually tried not to notice his chiseled features, tan skin, and deep-set electric blue eyes. She had heard some of the young women in church sigh over the cleft in his chin, which they thought was adorable. She, however, did not sigh but said viciously, "All right. Let's go."

"Can we use your car? I don't have one, you know."

"That's why I brought it," Louise said sharply. "Now let's go."

The two went at once to the center of town, where Colin loaded the car down with groceries. He also stopped at the clothing store and picked out some winter clothes. Louise followed along taking receipts and keeping a running list of expenses. Colin was spending money like it was water, and she clamped her lips tightly together, reserving her opinion for later.

"I guess that's it," Ryan said. "You want me to drive?"

"I'll drive. You direct me."

⊫⟶

The drive proved to be longer than Louise had anticipated. They left the city limits and went to the very edge of town, and Colin pointed at a shack that sat by itself. "We'll stop there first. That's the Taylor place. Just pull up there. Mrs. Taylor's washing, I see."

Louise pulled up slowly and got out. A woman was stirring clothes with a stick. The fire crackled under a black pot, and the woman's hands, she noticed, were red and rough. Her face was lined, and she wore clothes that seemed insubstantial for such weather. A faded red sweater was so short the sleeves came halfway up to her elbows.

"Well, how are you, Sister Ada?"

"I'm fine, Pastor."

"I'd like for you to meet Miss Louise Langley. You've probably seen Louise in church."

"I suppose so," Ada said. The woman was thin, and her face was drawn together in the perpetual sign of one who has to struggle just to stay alive. She had no chance to say more, for two small children came running out of the shack, one carrying an infant. They were all dirty with runny noses, but Colin swept them up. "How you doin', Ailene?"

A girl no more than three grinned at him and said hello shyly.

"And, Dooley, how's that young brother of yours?"

Dooley, no more than six or seven, handed the baby to Colin. Louise watched as he cuddled the infant in his arms. "Well, how are you doin', big fellow? Is that cold any better, Sister Ada?"

"Yes. That medicine you brought helped a lot, Pastor." She hesitated, then said, "Will you come in?"

"Of course we will. We'll visit for a little while." Colin kept the baby in his arms, and when Louise followed him inside, she was shocked at the poverty that met her eyes. It was what was called a shotgun house with one room in front that served as living room and bedroom, and the second room through the door was the kitchen, dining room, and general workroom. There was, she saw, no bathroom, and no sign of running water.

Louise had never been this close to abject poverty. She stood there helplessly watching as Colin laughed and kept the baby in his arms while he was ruffling Dooley's hair and pinching Ailene's cheek. She did not know what to do with herself and was acutely aware that she was embarrassingly overdressed.

Finally Colin said, "The church has started a new program, Sister Ada. It's kind of a pre-Christmas thing, so we brought some things out for you. Here. You hold this young man, Miss Louise, while I go get the things."

The baby was thrust into Louise's arms, and she had no choice. She held onto it awkwardly, and when Colin left the room, she looked down and said, "He's a beautiful baby."

"Yes. I reckon he is. My husband thinks he looks like him."

"Is your husband at work?"

"No, ma'am, he went to St. Louis to try to find work. I'm hopin' he finds it soon."

Louise had no answer for that. The destitution of the family appalled her, and she could only stand there helplessly until Colin came back burdened down with two huge sacks. He put them down, fished inside, and came out with a sack of candy. "Hey," he said, winking at the two older children, "I bet I could eat more candy than you can."

"Bet you can't!" Dooley said. Colin gave the two children candy, popped a lollipop in his own mouth, and shoved one at Louise, who rejected it.

For the next twenty minutes Louise stood there while Colin saw to it that the winter coats fit and that the shoes he had bought were right.

She wondered how in the world he knew all the sizes. Ada Taylor stood there, and Louise saw that tears were filling her eyes. She could hardly speak when she whispered, "I don't know how to thank you, Pastor."

"Oh, it's not me. You'll have to thank Miss Louise here. I'm just a fly-by-night preacher. She's chairman of the committee that takes care of all this."

The woman turned and said, "I thank you kindly, Miss Langley."

"You're so welcome." Louise could hardly get the words out. She stood there while Colin shook Ada Taylor's hand, and then they left.

"Well, that's one," Colin said as they got into the car. "She's a fine woman. Her husband's a good man too. Doesn't have any skills, so they've had a rough time of it."

"Are—are there many like that in our town?"

"Too many," Colin said, "so let's get started on the rest."

~⊨⊷~

By three o'clock Louise Langley was as tired as she could ever remember. They had visited nine families and returned to the stores twice to replenish their supplies.

Colin was as cheerful and energetic as ever, but as they came out of the last house, he said, "Let's call it a day. You're tired."

Louise was not sure why she was so exhausted. She gamely said, "Why, I can go on."

"No. We've made a good beginning." They were seated in the car, and he faced her curiously. "So what do you think about the welfare program, Louise?"

She was shocked at the use of her first name. "I —" She started to say she thought it was a good thing, but pride suddenly rose up in her. She could not admit that she had been wrong. "It's very nice, but you can go overboard on these things."

Colin Ryan stared at the young woman. "Do you really think so?"

"Yes. I'll total these up, and you can check my figures tomorrow."

Ryan laughed. "Never could keep books, but I'll be ready to go again tomorrow. Maybe we can visit some folks in need that you know."

"Perhaps," Louise said, but suddenly she realized that she didn't know anyone in that condition. And somehow the thought humbled her. "All right," she said. She took him back to the church and let him out with a mere, "Good day."

The rest of the day was troublesome to her. Her father asked her how it had gone, and she was short with him. That night when she went to bed, she was restless for a long time, and when she finally did go to sleep, she had a terrible dream. She dreamed that she was poor and had no money, and her clothes were torn and ragged. She woke up frightened to death and found that her hands were trembling. It was almost impossible to go back to sleep, but finally she did, although it was not a sound rest.

<hr />

Cass had been up and around more than usual and found that, although her back and arm were still sore, she was getting better. The food had been so much more than she was used to, but not once had she said a thank you to anyone. She was sharp when Lanie tried to find out more about how to help her. Corliss followed Cass around and had witnessed the rudeness of the girl toward her sister.

One day Cass suddenly turned on Corliss and said, "What are you staring at?"

"Why are you so mean?"

The direct question from the child startled Cass. "I don't know."

"You don't have to be mean."

"You'd be mean too, if you—"

Suddenly Aunt Kezia, who had been sitting across the room reading a *True Romance*, looked up and said, "Child's right. You don't have to be mean."

"I don't need any sermons from you!"

Aunt Kezia got up and came over to stand before Cass. "I don't like to eavesdrop," she said, "but when Davis was trying to read his lesson last night, you found out he can't read good and you called him stupid."

Cass dropped her eyes, unable to meet those of Aunt Kezia. "I was surprised. That was all."

"Maybe you're surprised, but you're also cruel. I don't know what you've been through, child, but I know there ain't no excuse for meanness. Lanie and these kids have done their best to make you feel at home. Davis plunged in to help you when nobody else was there. What you need is a good larrupin', and I expect you'll get it one day. The only way I can think of for you not to get it is to give your heart to Jesus."

"Don't talk to me about religion!"

Aunt Kezia looked up at the girl, who was taller than she. "What have you got against Jesus?"

Cass bit her lip. "I'm not gonna talk about it," she said. Turning around, she walked off.

Aunt Kezia called after her, "You're gonna have to settle this Jesus question sooner or later." She watched the girl disappear, slamming the door behind her. "That girl's headed for a fall," she said, then went back to her *True Romance*.

⟿ CHAPTER 20 ⟾

As he often did on Thursday nights, Owen ate dinner with the Langleys. Martha put out a wonderful meal as usual, but Owen was unimpressed, since he knew they had a cook, Julie, who did nothing else. He said nothing about the welfare work until after he and Louise were alone in the parlor. She put on a new record called "Life Is Just a Bowl of Cherries." *It's ironic*, Owen thought, *to think of life as something as nice as a bowl of cherries when the Depression is tearing the life out of the country.*

He turned to Louise. "You look worn out."

"I am tired."

"I've been hearing about the welfare work you're doing. How's it going?"

Louise started to answer and then suddenly realized that his simple question had no uncomplicated answer. She had been going out every day with Colin Ryan, and she had seen more poor people and more hard things in the past week than she had seen in her life. Finally she said, "It's going fine."

"I was talking to the treasurer of the church, Deoin Jinks. He told me a rather marvelous thing."

"What's that?"

"He said checks have been coming in, three very large ones, and that the money that's come in has almost equaled the money that you and the committee have spent so far. I think that's a miracle."

Louise knew about this, but she said, "Well, it's just a coincidence."

"I don't think so," Owen said. "I think God is keeping His word. Makes me feel good."

"It's just a coincidence," she repeated.

Owen turned to her. "Have you changed your opinion of Colin?"

"In a way I guess I have. I'll have to say this for him—for all his crazy ways, he stays busy. I've never seen anybody with as much energy."

"I think he knows everybody in town. I don't know how he does it."

"He does have a heart for poor people. I found that out."

Owen laughed suddenly. "He's pretty popular too. Marilyn Simms is out to marry him."

"How do you know that?"

"Well, she was foolish enough to tell Henrietta Green, and, of course, that's like putting it on the front page of the *Sentinel*."

"She's a foolish girl."

"I suppose so, but she's got good taste." Owen suddenly reached over and took Louise's hand. "Maybe I ought to be jealous, your running around with a good-looking fellow like that."

"Don't be ridiculous," Louise snapped. She got to her feet and began to pace rapidly. "I can't believe he's as good as he makes out."

"I think he is, Louise."

"Just wait," she said. "He'll do something that'll show you what he really is."

"Why do you dislike him so?"

Louise could not answer. She knew deep in her heart she disliked Colin Ryan because he had a simplicity about his life that she lacked. There was a goodness in him, and she had learned over the past week it was not something he did for show. Preachers that were trying to rise didn't spend their time with poor people. They went after the big fish. And they didn't spend all their money on welfare. They built enormous churches. She shook her head and said, "I just don't trust him, Owen. He'll show what he is one day."

⌖

"We've got to go quite a long way this time. It's almost all the way over to Pine Ridge."

It was getting late in the afternoon, and it had been a busy day. Louise was driving the car over the rutted road. They had left the main highway, and she said, "How much farther is it?"

"About two or three more miles. It's rough going. It turns into a logging road when you get to the end of this one. This is the good part."

The Oldsmobile dropped a wheel into a pothole that jarred Louise's teeth. She was thinking about her conversation with Owen last night. She glanced over at Colin, who was sitting loosely in the seat beside her. He seemed perfectly relaxed, as always, and she wondered again if he was the real thing.

He directed her, "Right up there." He studied the road for a moment. "Maybe we better walk the rest of the way. The rain's made the road pretty sticky."

They got out of the car, divided the load between them, and made their way to the house. The family was named Logan, and were in even worse shape than most they had visited. They were appreciative for the gifts, and seemed to enjoy the company even more. Louise was a little bit more comfortable, and she certainly had dressed more conservatively than on their first trip. As they left the cabin, she said, "How do you meet all these people?"

"Oh, I just keep my ears to the ground. People talk. I heard Dempsey Wilson talk about this family back here, so I looked them up. You're doing a good job," he added.

Louise did not answer. She could not understand why she was upset with Colin Ryan, and she was tired of thinking about it.

The ground was muddy, and she moved around a log to keep from stepping in a deep puddle. Her shoe went down deep and came off when she pulled her foot out. She bent over to pick it up and as she did, she suddenly heard a sharp whirling sound. She lifted her eyes and not three feet away was the most enormous rattlesnake she had ever seen! He was curled and had lifted his head in the striking position.

Louise Langley had been terrified of snakes all her life, and this was a monster. She'd heard of the speed of a striking rattlesnake but could not seem to move.

Suddenly she was thrown violently to one side as Colin struck her in a full body blow. As she slammed to the ground she was aware that the snake had moved also, and terror raced through her, but she felt no bite. She rolled over in the mud and raised herself up and saw that Colin was getting up slowly. He said, "Come on. Get away from that snake."

Scrambling to her feet, Louise found at first she could not breathe, and then she was hyperventilating.

Approaching the car, she said, "I've always been terrified of snakes."

"I don't like them myself. We'll have to get back into town in a hurry."

"What's wrong?" she asked.

Colin pulled his pants leg up and she saw two red marks on his calf. "He got me," he said. "I wouldn't waste any time." He got in the car, and Louise scrambled in. She started the engine, turned the car around, and asked, "Are you all right, Colin?" It was the first time she had ever used his first name.

"I don't think so," he said. He laid his head back on the seat and said, "Better hurry."

Louise gunned the car and slung the mud out as the car lurched forward. She sped toward town, ignoring potholes and skidding around corners. Terror came to her and she caught a glance of his face, a pale white, as he lay back. Then the thought came to her, *He took that bite for me!*

⊸ CHAPTER 21 ⊷

Otis Langley rushed in through the front doors of the hospital and demanded of the receptionist, "Marlene, where is my daughter?"

Marlene Stanley, a tall stately woman with silver hair, pointed up. "Second floor. She's up there with the preacher."

"What happened?" Otis demanded. "I just got a call."

"It wasn't Louise. It's that preacher. He's got bitten by a snake."

Langley whirled and ran to the stairs, skipping the elevator. He took the stairs two at a time, and when he stepped out into the hall, he saw Louise standing at the window at the far end. "Louise, what in the world happened?"

Louise stared at her father. She was pale and could not seem to answer. Finally she whispered, "He—he jumped in between me and that awful snake. It bit him instead of me."

"You look terrible. Come home, Louise. You need to go to bed."

"No. I've got to stay here."

Otis blinked and tried to think of something to do. Finally he said, "Can you tell me more about what happened?" He stood there and listened as Louise got the story out. She spoke in broken sentences and her voice was hushed. He could see that she was in a state of shock and was just about to insist that she come home when Owen came out of the room.

Louise ran to him and said, "Owen, how is he?"

Owen shook his head. "There's not a lot we can do for snakebites. This must have been a big one."

"It was—monstrous." Louise swallowed hard and then asked almost timidly, "Is he—is he going to be all right, Owen?"

"I don't want to be too optimistic. A lot of people have died from snakebites, but Colin's got a lot going for him. He's led a healthy life. He's a strong man, and I'm not going to give up on him."

"Can I see him?"

Owen hesitated. "He won't know you. He's in a coma. Happens sometimes with these bites. Not very pretty."

"I don't care. I want to see him."

"Don't be foolish, Louise!" Otis said sharply. "You can't help him here."

"You go home, Daddy," Louise said, and without another word turned and walked toward the room.

Owen said, "I've never seen her this stubborn."

"She's in a state of shock. You need to make her go home," Langley demanded.

"You're her father. If you can't force her, I doubt if I could. Why don't you go home. I'll bring Louise home pretty soon."

"All right. I'll go home. Her mother will be worried."

Louise had stepped inside the door and took a startled breath. Colin Ryan was lying flat on his back. His face was red as if he had a fever. His limbs were twitching, and she was shocked to see that his right leg was swollen to almost twice its normal size. She could barely stand to look at him.

She heard the door close and turned to see Owen. "He looks pretty bad, doesn't he?"

"It's awful. His leg."

"That often happens with snakebites."

The two stood there silently for a time, and finally Owen said gently, "There's nothing you can do, Louise. You might as well go home. Your mother will be worried."

"Daddy will tell her I'm all right. Can I stay here for a while?"

"Of course," Owen said gently. He moved across the room, drew a chair up, and said, "Here. I'll come back from time to time to check on him, and I've got the nurses all on notice to call if there's any change." He hesitated and studied her. He had never seen her like this before, and there was something pathetic about her expression. He had always known her as a self-confident, strong young woman, able to handle anything. Her good looks and her riches had always provided a shelter, a shield. Now she was different somehow, vulnerable, and he put his hand on her shoulder. "God's able to do all things, Louise. We'll pray for Colin."

After Owen left the room Louise suddenly began to tremble. She had kept herself stiffly in motion ever since the incident had occurred. Now, however, in the quietness of the room, staring at the young man who had thrown himself into harm's way for her, she suddenly felt a weakness. Without warning tears rolled down her cheeks. She leaned forward and buried her face in her hands and began to weep.

❧

Lanie was ironing as she and Aunt Kezia talked of the plight of Colin Ryan. Both of them were concerned, for they had a fondness for the young minister. Now she put the iron down and stared at Aunt Kezia. "I'm ashamed of myself, Aunt Kezia."

"Ashamed of what?"

"Why, I've been sitting around here worrying about how we're going to make ends meet, and there's our preacher in bed with a snakebite and maybe won't live."

"You worry too much. I've talked to you about that before."

"The taxes on this place will be due in a few weeks, and we don't have the money. I wanted to mail a letter to Daddy yesterday and didn't have three cents for a stamp."

"Oh, posh! I've got three cents."

"No. I can't be living off of you. It's just such a struggle. Of course we've got a place to live, a garden, chickens, and a cow, so we make out better than a lot. But it's hard. And yet, at least we're all healthy, right?"

Lanie and Aunt Kezia continued to discuss the struggle to exist, and neither woman noticed that Cass had come to the door. She stopped abruptly and listened to Lanie, and then with an odd expression on her face turned and disappeared, tiptoeing away.

No sooner had she left than Maeva, Cody, and Corliss came in. Maeva said, "Come on, Aunt Kezia. We're gonna be late for the movie."

"Where'd you get the money for movies?" Lanie demanded.

Aunt Kezia waved her hand. "Me, of course. It's only one time, and it's forty cents. We can take the popcorn we popped last night and eat that."

"They're gonna be good today," Cody said eagerly. "*Buck Jones* and *The Cisco Kid*."

"Yep, and Charlie Chaplin in *City Lights*," Aunt Kezia nodded. "I'd rather see *Dracula*, but that ain't on no more."

"Isn't Cass going with you?" Lanie asked.

"No." Maeva shrugged. "She ain't feelin' good today. She was sick this morning. Said she had some kind of stomachache."

"I didn't know that. I'll see how she's doing later."

The moviegoers left, and Lanie gave a sigh of relief. She valued her quiet time, and putting the ironing away she went upstairs and did what she often did to uncoil and relax. Taking out her folders that contained her writings, she began to work on a poem. She had been reading in Scripture about the woman who had touched the hem of Jesus' robe and was healed instantly. She had decided to call the poem "The Touch," and for the next hour she worked silently. As always, time flew by as she changed words, rearranged sentences, found just the right word that seemed to click. She tried to put herself in the mind of that dying woman who so desperately needed a touch from the Healer. Finally she was satisfied, made a fresh copy, and read it aloud just to see how it sounded:

The Touch

"And a certain woman … when she had heard of Jesus, came in
the press behind, and touched his garment. For she said, If I may
touch but his clothes, I shall be whole." (Mark 5:25 – 28)

Come, Jacob, see the breakfast I have made —
Hot bread and honey cakes, ripe figs, and thick
Warm milk with rice plumped thick with juicy raisins.
O Husband, so many days I've watched you cook
While I lay sick, more your patient than your wife;
So now, to rise and fix a simple meal
For you — almost it seems I am a bride
A second time so strong and young I feel!
Was it but yesterday I woke
So drained and weak you had to hold my cup?
Now see how easily this heavy jug
I toss — O do not scold me — not today!
Since I touched his robe my whitened blood
Has flushed to scarlet (see the pulsing throb?)
Overflowing my heart and quickened like
Spring freshlets fed by drenching harvest showers.
Not so when yesterday I dragged myself
Through crowded streets holding to the walls,
And would have fallen, but so packed the street
Like close-set grain, we held each other up.
Then he came — the air so noisy grew
My voice was drowned like a cricket's chirp.
How did I ever have the strength to push
Myself between those bruising bodies, to reach
My sticklike arm until the tendons stretched
Like tensioned wire?
I know but this: I touched his robe
More lightly than this breeze brushes my hair,
Just so — then muted all the clamorous noise;

A sudden force broke forth, the throbbing blood
Beat through my veins and drummed so loudly that
I almost failed to hear his voice:
"Daughter, thy faith hath made thee whole."
So strong the pounding of my blood I did
Not see him go, but in a silent street
I found myself alone.
But Jacob,
How can we really be alone when God
Walks down our streets —
And lets himself be touched?

Satisfied with her effort, she put the work back in the folder, concealed it in the bottom drawer of her chest, and started out of the room. She went down to the room that Cass shared with Maeva and knocked on the door. When there was no answer, she called softly, "Cass, are you awake?" Still no answer, so she opened the door. She saw instantly that the room was empty and the bed was made up. A small square of paper was on the bed, and she went to it at once. She picked it up and alarm ran through her as she read:

You're not able to take care of me. Thanks for all you've done.
Cass.

At once Lanie ran down the stairs and sailed out the back door. Davis had planned on hunting with Gerald Ramsey later in the afternoon instead of going to the movie. She cried out, "Davis, Cass is gone!"

Davis had raised the maul that was used for splitting wood, and he stared at her. "What do you mean, gone?"

"She wrote a note. She said we can't afford to keep her."

Davis took the note and stared at it. "How long has she been gone, do you think?"

"She was there when the kids went to the movie. That's about an hour or an hour and a half ago." Lanie's mind worked quickly. "I've got to go get Sheriff Jessup. He'll have to help us look."

"That'll take too long. She's real weak. She couldn't have gone far." Suddenly Davis's eyes lit on Booger, who was sitting a few feet away staring at the two as they spoke. "Booger can find her!" he exclaimed. "Go up and get something she's worn."

"She took all of her things," Lanie said. Then she cried out, "I know. She's been wearing a dress of mine. That would have her scent on it." She dashed into the house and was back in a moment.

Davis took the dress and said, "Come here, Booger." The big dog came over wagging his tail furiously. "Smell this." Booger sniffed eagerly, and finally when Davis said, "Find her, boy," he put his nose to the ground and began running in tight circles. Cass, of course, had been out in the yard before, so her trail was crisscrossed, but finally Booger turned out of the yard and headed north. "He's found her track," Davis said. "You wait here, Lanie."

"No! I'm going with you."

The two followed the big dog, who moved with incredible speed. He kept his nose to the ground and didn't turn to the right or the left.

"I think he's headed toward the railroad. She might have gone there to catch a train out," Davis said.

"Well, there's not a train for another three hours, so she'll still be there."

<hr />

Cass had made it to the water tank and now was sitting in the shade. She had thrown up on the way, and her head was whirling. She was so dizzy she could hardly keep her head up. Sitting there, she tried to think about what she would do, but apart from getting on a freight and getting away from Fairhope, she had no plan.

From far away came voices and the sound of footsteps, but she paid no heed. She had never felt worse in her life. Besides being physically ill, she was in a deep state of despair. She was accustomed to hard times, but the cumulative effect now seemed to press down upon her like a dark cloud. She sat there despondent, wishing she was dead. She bowed her head and closed her eyes, overcome with weakness and vertigo, and went off into a half doze.

Suddenly her head jerked. She heard her name being called. Looking to her right, she saw the big bloodhound Booger galloping toward her with his ears flapping. Behind him, coming at a run, were Lanie and Davis. She tried to get up, but before she could make it Davis was next to her on one side and Lanie on the other.

"You can't do this, Cass," Davis said. He put his hand on her shoulder. "Come on. You've got to go back home."

"I don't have any home."

"Yes, you do. Your home is with us," Lanie said. "You're in no condition to go anywhere. We're going to take care of you."

Cass could barely speak, but she summoned up all her strength and said, "You can't afford to keep a stranger. I heard you and Aunt Kezia talking about how hard things are."

Davis Freeman was not an eloquent young man. He was much better with a bat on the ball field or fixing something mechanical than making fine speeches. But there kneeling beside the girl whose face was ashen pale and whose baggy clothes concealed the first signs of young womanhood, he managed to say something that was absolutely right.

"You're not a stranger, Cass. You're family. God has put you to be with us for now."

"That's right," Lanie said. "Now get up. You're going home where we can take care of you."

Tears came to Cass's eyes, and she wiped them away as the two helped her up. She tried to think of something to say, but her mind was in a whirl. As they headed back toward the Freeman house, she surrendered herself to the two. The big dog Booger kept close at hand, often nudging Davis with his nose, and was rewarded by a pat on his head. Cass finally managed to say, "Nobody's ever been so good to me." That was all she had the strength for, and she concentrated on making it back to the house.

✦ CHAPTER 22 ✦

"Martha and I are worried sick about Louise, Owen. Ever since that preacher got snakebit she's been here at the hospital except for a few hours when she comes home to sleep."

Otis Langley was a man who was in charge of most situations. He was able to handle things, as a rule, but this time he had not been able to control his daughter, which troubled him considerably. He squeezed his hands together in a nervous fashion and said, "I've never seen her act like this, Owen."

"Well, she's never had anything like this come up in her life," Owen explained.

"It was an accident, but it's almost as if she feels responsible."

More than once Owen noted that Louise had drawn close to Colin, but he put it down to the rather traumatic experience and her gratitude for Colin's help.

"The way I understand it," Owen said, "that snake would have gotten her if it hadn't been for Colin. He jumped in between them, and it got him instead of her. When someone saves your life at the risk of their own, it's bound to have some effect."

"I suppose you're right, but—"

"If I were you, I'd let her show all the concern she wants to."

"But it's been three days. How is that preacher anyway?"

"He's recovering. He's going to be all right. The leg's gone down, but that snake must have been a doozy. Colin got a big dose of poison. As I've told you before, there's not a lot we can do about the snakebite.

It mostly depends on the constitution of the one who was bitten." Owen put his hand on Otis's shoulder. "You ought to be proud of Louise," he said quietly. "I know that I am."

"She's not behaving logically."

"Well, some things aren't very logical. Sometimes our lives get to be too organized, I think."

"What do you mean by that?" Otis demanded.

"Well, did you ever read *Robinson Crusoe*?"

"Yes, I did. A long time ago."

"I think that fellow got too caught up with neatness and efficiency. Everything had to be just so. The big change in his life came when he found a footprint. That meant he had a fellow human being to respond to. That's the way we are sometimes. We get caught up with our business or with our hobbies, until suddenly we notice a footprint. We become aware of another human being, and we know we're responsible for them somehow or other. I think that's what happened to Louise, and I don't think it's a bad thing at all."

Otis stared at the young man in front of him wondering, not for the first time, what he was like. This was the man that Louise was going to marry, and the desire of Otis Langley's heart was that his children would make good marriages. He said finally, "I wish you'd make her go home."

"I couldn't do that, Otis. Like I said, I've never admired Louise so much as I do over the way she's caring for Colin Ryan."

⟐

The blackness turned to a milky whiteness, and the voices that had seemed far off became clearer. He could hear a whirring sound and feel the coolness of a breeze blowing on his face.

Opening his eyes, Colin first saw the fan that was trained to blow on him. He lay there, his mind reaching out, as he tried to think where he was. The room was white, and there was only a bedside table, except when he looked over to the right, he saw a chair. It took him a long moment to recognize that a woman was in it. His thinking processes were moving slowly, and after a few moments he realized, *Why, I'm in a hospital, and that's Louise Langley.*

And then the memories came rushing back. The instant when the snake's fangs had sunk into his calf, the trip to the hospital, and the descent into a blackened bottomless pit interrupted, at times, by fiery waves of pain and nausea.

Looking down, he saw that his leg was enormous. It felt tight and looked like a sausage. "Well, aren't you a pretty sight," he murmured.

The sound of his voice stirred the stillness of the room, and Louise, who had been dozing, sprang to her feet at once. She came over to look down at him. Her face was pale, and for some reason her lips were trembling. "Hello, Sister Louise," he whispered. "This is a pretty mess, isn't it?"

Louise reached out and put her hand on his arm. "You're awake," she said in an unsteady voice. "How do you feel?"

"I feel like I've been dragged through a knothole." He looked down at the leg and said, "That snake should have bit me in both legs, then I'd have a matched set."

"Don't—don't talk like that," Louise said.

"It all seems kind of like a bad dream. I can only remember parts of it."

"You remember the snake biting you."

"I thought he was going to get you," Colin said slowly. "He was a big one, wasn't he?"

"If you hadn't jumped between us, he would have bitten me."

Colin's mind was clearing up now, and he shrugged his shoulders and stretched. Looking at her, he grinned slightly. "Well, women don't have a good history with snakes. I think it all started with Eve."

Louise could not help smiling. "I don't see how you can joke. It's been terrible."

"You know, you look worse than I've ever seen you," Colin said. "How long have I been here?"

"Three days."

"Three days! I can't afford to lose three days. There's too much to do."

"You're not going to do anything for a while," Louise said firmly, "but rest."

Colin Ryan laughed softly. "You are the bossiest woman I've ever seen. If I were any kind of a man, I would get up and walk out of here and go my own way."

Louise put her hand on his chest. "I wouldn't let you." She tried to think of some way to thank him for what he had done, and finally she swallowed and said, "If it hadn't been for you, that snake would have bitten me. Owen talked to me about it. He said that being smaller, the poison would have worked more damage on me than on you. He said I probably would have died if the snake had gotten me."

Colin Ryan studied the face of the young woman. She had, he knew, a tremendous self-sufficiency, and she would always be on guard. Her pride could sweep her violently, but that pride had somehow been broken, and he saw this in her eyes and in her posture. "Well, when's somebody coming to give me the medal?"

"What medal?"

"The medal for saving your life. Maybe there'll be a check to go with it."

Louise found herself with a lightness of spirit that buoyed her up. "You're impossible," she said. "You almost died, and you lie there joking."

"Well, if I saved your life, you owe me a favor."

"A favor? What do you want?"

"I want to be sure that the church keeps on lending money to God."

"You mean the welfare program," Louise said. "You want me to keep it going."

"Yes. I think it's been a great thing for the church."

"I'll do that, Colin." Calling him by his first name felt natural. As she looked down on him, she was considering his request. She knew that if she were in his position, she would not have been thinking of poor people but of her own misfortune. *Something's been left out of me that's in this young man*, she thought. And as she stood over him, she was determined to somehow find out what that element was and how she might appropriate some of it.

⟝⟜

As Owen entered the room, he saw that Louise seemed much better. The drained expression that had manifested itself in her features during the first three days of Colin Ryan's sickness was gone, and she was smiling. He turned to study Colin, who was sitting upright in bed. "How's my patient today?"

"Well, I'm a little bit lopsided. One leg's bigger than the other. Is it going to be that way forever, Doctor?"

"Come on, Reverend, it's gone down considerably." Owen went over and studied the leg and said, "I think we can put you in a wheelchair."

"I'd like to go home."

"Well, you can't." Owen suddenly laughed. "Now, if you were married and had a wife to take care of you, that would work out fine."

"Well, I don't suppose it would be very romantic to marry a woman just to take care of me. But I would almost be willing to do it."

Louise had been standing back, and now she asked, "Are you really so unhappy here, Colin?"

"I don't like hospitals."

Louise said impulsively, "You could come and stay with us until you're well."

Both Merritt and Ryan gave her a look of surprise. "I don't know why you're so shocked about that," Louise said, her face reddening. "We've got a huge house and a spare bedroom."

"Well, your father might have some objections," Colin said. "He hasn't been leading the cheering section for me since I've come to town."

"I know you two have had your differences, but you wouldn't even have to see him. Julie's a good cook, and we could bring you your meals just as they do here. If you'd like to come," she said rather stiffly, "it would be all right with me."

"Well, it sounds a little ungracious to say this, but I'd stay anywhere to get out of this hospital. Doctor, you think your fiancée is capable of taking care of a snakebit preacher?"

"I think she'll do a fine job." He turned to Louise and smiled. "I'm surprised. I didn't think you had it in you."

Louise suddenly laughed but seemed embarrassed. "I'm surprised at myself." She looked at Colin and said, "Don't worry. It'll just be for a few days."

"Maybe I'll have a relapse." Colin winked at Merritt. "You'll have me on your hands for a year or so."

Louise said, "I'd better go tell my parents."

She left the room, and Colin grinned broadly. "You're quite a fellow, Owen Merritt. Most fiancés would be a little bit jealous."

"Well, I'm not."

"Something's wrong then. To put your fiancée within range of a good-looking, charming, witty fellow like me. Most men would find that a little bit not to their taste."

"I think Louise can handle you. I'll go arrange for your release."

⌖

"I have something to tell you that may be a shock," Louise said quickly. She had called her parents together in the parlor and was staring at them with a certain stubbornness in her eyes.

"What is it, Louise?" Martha asked. "Is something wrong?"

"I'll bet it's that preacher. Has he had a relapse?"

"No. But it's about him I have to talk to you." Louise had practiced her speech on the way home, and now she said it quickly and with energy. "Brother Ryan is sick of that hospital. Owen says he doesn't have to stay there, but that he has to have some care for a few days. I invited him to stay with us. He can stay in our guest room and won't be any trouble."

Martha was surprised indeed. "I thought you didn't like the man, Louise."

"He saved me from that snake, Mother." She hesitated and then said, "I've had bad dreams about that. It was an awful-looking thing, and he saw it and jumped right between me and that snake. I don't think I would do that for anybody. I couldn't!"

Otis tried to think of a reason why this would not work, but he saw the stubbornness in his daughter's eyes. He couldn't help smiling as he recognized where she had gotten that quality. "Well, I suppose it will only be for a few days."

"Of course, Daddy, and I'll see that he doesn't bother you." She turned and began calling for Elsie, the maid. Her parents stood there listening as she gave orders to have the guest room cleaned.

"Where does she get that willful stubbornness from, Martha?"

Martha Langley turned to her husband and smiled. "Not from me, dear," she said sweetly, then turned away.

❦

The rain had begun early in the morning and was still falling when Louise came into the guest room where Colin was staying. He was dressed and seated in the chair, and she said with surprise, "I thought you'd stay in bed today."

"No. I'm sick of bed. What's for breakfast?"

"Just what you ordered. Ham, eggs, and biscuits."

Colin took the tray and balanced it on his knees. "You know, I could get used to treatment like this." It was his second day visiting with the Langleys, and he had slept like a log and was feeling much better. "Actually, I might feel strong enough to go to church."

"You're not going to church," Louise said firmly. "Brother Pink got a substitute preacher."

"Who did he get?"

"I forgot his name. It doesn't matter. You're not going."

Colin turned his head to one side and studied her. "You know, you sound an awful lot like a domineering woman."

"I am a domineering woman. Don't tell me you haven't noticed."

"Oh, I like domineering women myself. It saves me from having to make decisions of my own." He looked down at the food and without closing his eyes said, "Well, Lord, I'm thankful for this food. Amen."

"You call that a blessing?"

"I don't pray eloquently when I'm hungry." He took a mouthful of eggs and said, "Tell Julie the eggs are just right. Did you notice she put some bell pepper in them and some hot sauce?"

"That's the way to ruin good eggs." Louise smiled. "I tried them and it tasted horrible."

"I've got a favor to ask. You haven't done anything for me in the last ten minutes."

"What is it, Colin?" She suddenly said, "I shouldn't be calling you Colin. It should be Brother Colin or Brother Ryan."

"I like Colin. I'm just sort of an imitation preacher anyhow. Just a fill-in until the real man gets here. As long as we're in private, let's just call each other by our names, okay?"

"All right," Louise said. "What's the favor?"

"I was talking with Pardue on the phone trying to get him to go to church. He wouldn't come, but he told me that the Freemans' truck had broken down. He's got it in his shop working on it. They were gonna walk to church, but it's pouring out there. Would you mind going by and getting them, taking them to church this morning?" He watched her cautiously.

Louise hesitated for a moment then said, "Of course I'll do that. Any other requests?"

"Don't run off too quick. I may want another helping of these eggs."

"I've got to go or I'll be late. After church I'll come back and tell you how much better the preacher's sermon was than yours."

"Take notes, will you. I'll use the material and improve on it."

∘══✦═

"I love that new dress, Maeva," Lanie said. "It's the prettiest one you've ever had."

"You're a right natural seamstress, you are," Aunt Kezia said. "When you gonna make me a dress?"

The family had gathered to go to church. Deoin Jinks from across the street had come over with a message from Brother Ryan that someone would come to pick them up.

"Did you ask Cass to go to church?" Lanie spoke to Davis.

"She said she didn't feel like it. She really needs to see Doctor Owen. She's been sick for a week now. I'm worried about her."

"I'll tell him at church. Maybe he'll come by," Lanie said.

Cody said, "Well, we're a little bit early, so I have an announcement to make."

Everyone turned to look at Cody, not knowing what to expect. "What is it this time, Cody? You gonna give us another sermon?" Davis grinned.

"No, but I'm here to announce that our financial worries are over." He looked around in triumph as everyone stared at him. "I found out a way to make lots of money. I want to show you what it is. Stay right here."

He dashed out of the house, and Corliss went over to watch through the window. "He's going to the barn where he works on things," she announced.

"Another one of his inventions, I guess." Maeva shrugged. "Some day he's going to invent one that's really useful."

The rain was still pouring down, and Cody was wet as he came inside. "I have to change shirts," he said, "but I couldn't wait until after church to show you this."

He put an object down on the table and said, "Well, there she is. What do you think?"

Everyone crowded around and stared at the object. It was about fourteen inches high and made of black walnut. Cody was an excellent woodworker, and the wood gleamed. On the bottom of it was a round flat pan of some kind. Lanie said, "What is it?"

"What is it! Why, I was looking at a Monkey Ward Catalog and I seen one of these things. I put on my thinkin' cap and I invented one."

"Well, whatever it is, the wood sure is nice," Davis said.

Cody said in a disgusted tone, "Why, it's one of them mixin' machines, don't you see?"

"A mixer?" Lanie said. "Where are the blades?"

"Right here." Cody whipped one out of his pocket. He shoved it up where it caught somehow and said, "There. Look. It tilts back. Let me get a big bowl. Come on into the kitchen. I'm going to try it out."

At that instant there was a knock at the door. "We'll have to do it later, Cody," Lanie said. "Our ride's here." She went to the door and opened it and saw Louise Langley standing there.

"Hello, Lanie," Louise said. "Brother Ryan said your truck was in the shop. He asked me to take you to church."

"Why, how thoughtful of you, Louise. Come in. We're almost ready."

Louise stepped inside. Lanie said, "Come on into the kitchen. Cody was about to show us his new invention."

Louise followed Lanie into the kitchen, and Lanie said, "Look. Louise came to take us to church."

"Well, that's right neighborly of you, Miss Louise," Davis said with a smile.

Cody said, "You're just in time to see my new invention."

"You invent things?" Louise said.

"He does, and none of them ever work," Maeva said. "Let's go to church."

"Wait a minute. It won't take but a few seconds. I want to show you how it all works. You can see too, Miss Louise. It's a mixer."

"Oh, yes. We have one of those."

Cody said, "How much did it cost?"

"That's none of your business," Lanie said.

Louise suddenly laughed. "I have no idea. I suppose around ten or fifteen dollars."

"Well, my mixer only cost twenty-five cents. That's what the beater blade cost. The rest of it I made up out of stuff I found. Here. Let me show you how it works." He grabbed a big bowl from the cabinet and said, "Lanie, put some stuff in here like you mix up for a cake, whatever it is. Flour and chocolate and butter and stuff like that. We'll actually make us a cake."

"We don't have time for this."

"Sure we do," Cody insisted. "I just want you to see a genius at work."

"Go ahead," Louise said. "I came a little bit early. I'd like to see this invention work."

"All right," Lanie said. Quickly she added the various ingredients to the big bowl, including eggs, chocolate, flour, and oil. "Here," she said. "What next?"

"Why, you just put the bowl right here. It's what's called a Lazy Susan. That means it just rolls around while the stuff is mixing. You see the top tilts back so that the beater's out. And you see this? This is the switch. You turn it on here." He turned it on, and the beater began to whir.

"Well, the thing works," Davis said. "I'm shocked."

"Oh, I've tried that part out before. I just didn't have the ingredients to make nothin'. Everybody ready? Gather around close so you can see."

Everybody got as close to the table as they could, and Cody said with a triumphant voice, "Here we go—!"

What happened then was so quick that nobody could actually see it. Lanie did see Cody lower the blade into the dish containing the ingredients—but then it was like a bomb going off. The ingredients of the dish simply disappeared when the blade hit it. There was a universal gasp as the mixture flew out of the bowl—and onto everybody else.

"My dress!" Maeva screamed. "Look at my dress!"

Lanie saw that the front of Maeva's dress was spattered with the dark brown mixture—as was her face. It looked like she had brown freckles. Maeva reached up and touched her hair. "My hair! You got this mess in my hair!" she cried. "You monster!"

Everyone was looking around, and Davis, who was spotted as much as the others, said, "Look. It's all over the ceiling and the walls. What did you do, you idiot?"

Cody's face was speckled and dotted, and his hair in front was one solid mass of cake mix. His white shirt was spotted, and he opened his mouth but could not frame the words.

Aunt Kezia was licking her finger. "Mmm. Not bad, Cody."

Suddenly Lanie remembered Louise. She whirled quickly and saw that the beautiful clothes Louise wore were as spotted as everyone else's. Her face and hat were also spotted, and her eyes were wide open with shock. Lanie was totally humiliated. "What have you done? This is awful." She knew that Louise Langley would never let them forget this.

Suddenly Louise began to giggle. She touched her face and said, "If I look as bad as the rest of you, I'd hate to see myself in the mirror."

"I'm so sorry, Louise," Lanie whispered. "He's—he's just terrible."

Davis marched over and looked at the machine. He reached out and said, "Where did you get the motor for this crazy thing, Cody."

"Why, off of an old washing machine—it ran fine."

Davis suddenly began to laugh. "A mixer runs around eight or nine hundred revolutions per minute. You know how many revolutions a minute a washing machine motor makes, Cody?"

"No. I don't have no idea."

"Three thousand one hundred and twenty-five."

Suddenly Aunt Kezia began to laugh. "Well, we're gonna be quite a sight if we go to church looking like this."

Louise said quickly, "I think we're going to have to regroup. Why don't I go home and we'll all get cleaned up, and I'll come later and take you to the night service."

"That's so sweet of you, Louise. I'm surprised you'd ever speak to us again," Lanie said.

Louise looked over at Cody and said, "It must be interesting living with you, young man. Let me know the next time you have an invention to demonstrate. I'll arrange to be somewhere else." She laughed again, touched her face, and smeared the chocolate. "I think I'll just step in to see our pastor and show him what sort of reception I got."

She was still laughing as she left, and Maeva stared after her. "What's got into her? She's always despised us. How come she's so nice?"

Cody stood there with his speckled face looking at his invention. He looked up then and pronounced his version of what had happened to Louise Langley.

"Well, it's pretty clear to me what happened." He nodded confidently. "That snake scared the meanness out of her. Maybe," he said, "we ought to put a snake on her dad and it'd do the same for him."

"That makes about as much sense as your stupid invention," Maeva said. "You've ruined my dress." She turned and fled from the room.

Corliss came over to Cody and reached up and took his hand. Turning her speckled face up, she said, "That was fun, Cody. Let's put somethin' else in there and do it again!"

⊷ CHAPTER 23 ⊶

Lanie pulled on a sweater, for the room was cold, then she sat down, opening her journal, and began to write:

November the second, 1931. The papers have all been filled with how Al Capone has finally gone to prison. They say he murdered a great many people, but they couldn't catch him, and now they've sent him to jail for income tax evasion. What really troubles me is that people treat him like a hero. One of the stories said that thousands of people lined up just to see him as he was carried out of the courthouse. Why would people admire a man like that? I think it's awful.

It's been almost a month now since Brother Ryan was bit by that awful snake, and praise the Lord, he's completely recovered. I think that experience affected Louise more than it did Brother Ryan. She's changed so much! She's thrown herself completely into the welfare program, and she and Brother Ryan run all over the place trying to help people who need it.

It's a great work, but wouldn't you know it, there's already gossip floating around about how it's not right for an unmarried preacher to be escorting a young woman around so much. I don't think you could please everybody, but I'm happy that Louise has had a change of heart. I can see it in her face from where I sit in the choir. She seems to have a joy now that she never had before. I do notice that she's different toward Brother Ryan.

she keeps her eyes fixed on him when he's preaching, like he was Moses. Nothing wrong with that, I suppose, but I think —

A knock at the door interrupted Lanie, and she closed the journal quickly and called out, "Come on in."

Davis came in and said, "Are you busy?"

"No. What is it?"

"I been thinkin' about Cass. I don't like what's happening to her."

"Sit down, Davis." Lanie waited until Davis sat down on the bed, and she noticed how his face was drawn with worry. He was a serious teenager, far more so than Cody or Maeva, and was the one that Lanie could talk to about her problems. "I know she's having a hard time. She's trying to help around the house, but her heart's not in it."

"She seems so hopeless, Lanie. It's like her whole world has stopped."

"She's had a hard life. You can tell that."

"I've tried to get her to go to church, but she just won't go. I don't know why."

The two sat there talking for some time, and Lanie's heart went out to Davis. He was a gentle young man far more concerned with the problems of others than most boys his age. Finally he got up and sighed. "Well, I wish you'd try to talk to her, Lanie."

"I will. And you talk to her too. Between the two of us, we'll see her come around."

❦

The snow was falling as Owen Merritt walked along the street toward the church. The flakes were small and hard, and they bit at his face, as he was not wearing a hat. It was late afternoon now, and already the sky was darkening. Merritt lifted his eyes and saw Louise coming out of the church. He hurried forward and said, "Louise!" When she turned, he smiled and said, "I came to get you."

"What for?"

"I wanted to talk to you."

"Oh, Owen, I can't right now. Colin and I've got three more families to see today."

"We were supposed to go out and have dinner tonight."

"I don't think we'll be back in time. Let's postpone it."

Owen wanted to remind her that they had postponed several engagements, but he refrained. "I've got some good news then. I was going to buy you a good supper and tell you while you were eating, but I guess it'll have to be here."

"Good news? What is it, Owen?"

"I found us a house."

"A house? What do you mean?"

"I mean we've been talking about where we're going to live after we're married, and I found just the place for us." Owen waited for her to light up, but she did not. She only looked harried.

"Can't we talk about this later, Owen?"

"Sure. I just thought you'd want to know. But I want to warn you, it's not a fine place. Just a little two-bedroom house. The little white one off of Gaines Street across from the Millers. It's been vacant quite a while now and will need a lot of fixing up. But I talked to Mr. Oz who owns it. We can get it cheap. It'll be fun moving in and fixing it up."

"Well, that's nice, Owen."

Owen was disappointed in Louise's response. He had worked hard to find a house that would fit within their budget. He was finally excited about it, and now Louise's attitude dampened his spirit. He said, "Well, we can look at it later if you like."

"Hello, Owen." Colin came out with his arms loaded, carrying a big box. "Looks like we're going to get some weather."

"I guess so."

"Colin, we'd better hurry if we're going to make all of our stops." Louise seemed anxious to leave.

"All right. This is the last box. You want to come with us, Owen?"

"No. I've got another house call to make." He hesitated, then said, "I can't tell you how happy I am that your welfare program has worked out."

"It's been a miracle," Louise said, her face brightening. "It was just as Colin said. The more we give, the more keeps coming in. I don't think I could ever doubt God again."

Colin looked at her fondly, then winked at Owen. "She's gonna be the preacher around here if I don't watch out."

Owen smiled and nodded. "Well, I'll see you tomorrow, Louise, for dinner if you can get free."

"Oh, I'm sure I can." Louise smiled, then turned and said, "We'd better get going, Colin."

◦═══◦

Louise was holding the baby, who looked up at her with owlish eyes. "He's such a beautiful child," Louise said. The two had come to the home of the Williamsons and had delivered the groceries. It was in the poorest section of town, and the Williamsons were in desperate need. Louise had grown accustomed, more than she would have dreamed, to the hard face of poverty. Now she touched the baby's chin and laughed when he suddenly smiled at her toothlessly. "You're a charmer, you are."

Colin winked at Mrs. Williamson. "You better watch out. She's liable to be one of those fairies that steal babies."

"Don't be silly, Colin," Louise said.

"Well, we have to leave. Sister Williamson, you let us know if there's anything else."

Mrs. Williamson was a small woman. Between three children and a husband who was often ill, she was worn down. But her eyes were bright, and there was spirit in her voice as she said, "Thank you so much, Pastor, and you, Miss Langley. I don't know what we would have done without you."

The two left, and as they came down the porch steps, Colin looked up and said, "I've never seen it snow this hard. Look. The flakes are almost as big as quarters."

"I love the snow."

"I love it when it's falling, and I love it the morning after," Colin said. He took her arm and led her down the walk and toward the car. "What I hate is getting around in the slush and trying to get a car started."

Colin opened the door, helped Louise in, and then started the engine. "The first car my folks ever had was a Model T. You remember those?"

"Yes. We had one," Louise said.

"You had to crank the thing. My father broke his arm with that. That crank spun around and snapped it like it was a dry stick. He let me do the cranking from then on." He grinned and started the engine. "Self-starting engines. Now that's progress."

The snow was coming so thickly that it was almost impossible to see more than a few feet ahead. Colin drove very slowly. Leaning forward, he peered through the windshield that was cleared only momentarily of the snow. He was listening as Louise spoke of the visits that they had made that day. She began talking about other people that were on their list. Colin turned to look at her, and when he looked back he suddenly saw a form on the highway directly in front of them. Desperately he twisted the wheel, and the car skidded sideways then turned completely around and dropped the rear wheel off into the ditch with a resounding racket.

"What was that, Colin?"

Colin stared out the side window. "It was a deer, but I thought at first it might be a person." The car was tilted over toward the passenger's side. Colin gunned the engine, but the wheel spun. "This is not good," he said. He got out, walked around the car, came back, and got in. "No way we can get out of this ditch without help," he said. "I better start walking. There's a house about three or four miles down the road."

"I'll go with you."

"No. Look at those shoes. You'd freeze your feet."

"Then let's just sit here. Somebody will come along pretty soon. They can take us into town. We can have Pardue send somebody to pull the car in tomorrow."

"All right. I guess that's the best thing." Colin sat there and remarked, "Do you ever notice how quiet snow is? It seems to muffle everything."

"It is quiet, isn't it?" She turned to face him and could barely make out his features. "You don't worry about things much, do you, Colin?"

"I try not to."

"What are you going to do?"

"You mean now? We're going to wait for a car."

"I mean after you leave Fairhope."

"Don't know." Colin shrugged. "Don't have to know. God knows and that's enough."

Louise was silent for a time and then shook her head. "I never took God into my confidence. I mean, whenever I wanted to do something, I just did it."

"That's what most people do."

The two sat there talking, and despite the unpleasantness of the situation, Louise was not worried. This amazed her, for ordinarily the old Louise would have been worried sick right about now.

The cold, however, began to bite at both of them, and seeing Louise shiver, Colin said, "I've got to go for help. We could be here all night."

"You're not strong enough for that. Not after that awful time with the snakebite."

"Why, I'm fit as a fiddle. They might have a tractor they could pull us out with, or maybe some mules."

"I don't want you to go."

"Well," Colin said, "we'll wait another half hour. Then if someone doesn't come, I'll have to go. Here. What are we thinking of.

We've got some blankets we were going to give away." He leaned over and pulled a blanket out of the backseat. "Just one left. Here. Put it around you."

He undid the blanket and put it around her, but she said, "You get under here too. You're freezing just like I am."

Colin hesitated, then laughed. "All right. You know what this reminds me of?" he said as he arranged the blanket. He was sitting close to her now, and it seemed a natural thing to put his arm around her shoulder. "It reminds me of bundling back in the old Puritan days."

"Bundling? What was that?"

"It was a custom the Puritans had. When a young man was courting a young woman, he'd stay all night, and they'd sleep together in the same bed with just a board between them. Sometimes not even that."

"Sounds dangerous."

"I don't think it's a custom that needs to be revived."

Louise was getting warmer. The blanket helped, and Colin was sitting very close to her with his arm around her. She sat there amazed that she could be contented, and finally she said, "I've never told you how sorry I am for the way I treated you when you first came to town."

"I've been treated lots worse than that."

"Well, I'm sorry, and I want you to forgive me."

Colin turned. Her features were clear in the moonlight. She had large expressive eyes, and the perfume that she wore was faint but distinct. "Well, I don't think I've told you how much I've admired the way you've changed and how happy I've been for you."

"Changed?"

"You're a different woman. I've always thought you were beautiful on the outside, but now since I got bit by that snake and you took care of me, and with the work we've done on the welfare project, I see something beautiful on the inside as well."

A warmth came to Louise Langley then. "Nobody's ever said anything like that to me before. It makes me feel—very good."

Louise had learned during her time with Colin Ryan that he was actually a very lonely young man. He stayed busy enough, but there were times when she would see in him a hunger for something more than his work. She watched him now and realized that she did not admire any man as much as she admired this one. She whispered, "It's been wonderful working with you."

At that moment she was also aware of the strong attraction this man had for her. A shock ran along her nerves as the thought came, *Why, I want him to kiss me and to put his arms around me.*

Then as if he had read her thoughts, he pulled her close and without stopping to consider, she lifted her face. His lips were firm on hers, and she knew as he held her that she had a power over him, and the thought pleased her. She was aware of the urgency of his need, for it made a turbulent eddy around them both. She knew, somehow, she should be afraid, but it was only a strange sort of breathless anticipation she felt. The pressure of his wants held her there, and for the first time in her life she was aware that the potential to stir a man was in her in a way she had never known.

Colin lifted his head and said huskily, "I shouldn't have done that."

"I ... I guess we're entitled to one mistake."

Both of them were aware at that moment that they were on the edge of the mystery that exists between men and women. It was that moment when neither knew where they were going, and now Louise felt a sense of possessiveness. She reached up and touched his cheek. "I feel safe with you, Colin."

Colin Ryan suddenly straightened up and cleared his throat. His voice wasn't steady as he said, "I've got to go get help, Louise. We can't stay here all night."

Louise smiled, for she knew his motives. He did not trust himself with her, and she understood that. "I didn't think preachers did things like this."

"I don't. That is, I never have. But I'm human like everyone else." He started to leave and had thrown the blanket back, but then he turned to face her. "Louise, are you in love with Owen?"

Confusion suddenly filled Louise. "I ... I thought I was."

"It's something to think about. You need to know." He opened the door and said, "I'm going to get help." He shut the door and left.

The windows were covered with snow, and Louise could not see him. She pulled the covers around her, tucked her feet up under herself, and in the silence of the car she reviewed her decision to marry Owen. She went over it in her mind, and she suddenly realized that she had always expected to marry a "comfortable" man, and that's what Owen was. Comfortable—and a doctor. He fit all her preconceived notions of the perfect husband.

Suddenly she thought, *I've never been stirred by Owen as I have been by Colin.* And as she sat there in the silence, she knew she would have a hard time getting away from the memory of their caress.

PART FIVE

The Thanksgiving

⇥ CHAPTER 24 ⇤

Aunt Kezia was firm about choosing the time to kill the hog they had been fattening up. "If you kill a hog in the new moon and slice it and put it in a pan," she said, "you can't fry the grease out of it hardly. You don't want to kill it on the new moon. We got to wait for the full moon." Lanie considered this to be superstition but agreed to wait until later in November, and now as the whole family was gathered together, she thought rebelliously, *I'd rather do anything in the world than kill and dress a hog.* Still, it had to be done, for there was no money to buy the meat at the grocery store.

Cass joined the family, but she was pale, and now as Davis approached the hog, she asked Maeva, "What's he going to do?"

"Why, he's going to kill that hog, of course."

No sooner had she said this than Davis lifted his rifle and shot the hog in the back of the head. He reached down at once, pulled out his sheath knife, and cut the jugular vein.

Cass turned deathly pale and muttered, "I can't stand to look at this."

Lanie looked up and said, "If the rest of us can stand it, Cass, I guess you can too."

"No. It's going to make me sick." Cass turned and walked blindly away, her head bent and her hand over her mouth.

"It wouldn't hurt you to do a little work," Lanie called out as the girl walked away. Ordinarily she would not have thought of speaking this roughly to anyone, but Lanie, who hated every step in the process, was not herself. She had become fond of the hog, named her Suzy, and was angry that there was no alternative to killing her. In addition Lanie was frustrated with Cass's constant listlessness and lack of gratitude, and now she uncharacteristically allowed her fury to fly. "You come back here, Cass!" she called.

Davis turned to go after her, and Lanie said, "Davis, you come back here. We've got to get this hog dressed."

Davis hesitated and then said, "You get the water scalding hot. Somebody needs to tell Cass it's okay."

Turning without another word, Davis ran off and Lanie said, "All right. Let's get the water boiling. We've got to get this hide scraped." The process was complicated enough and a nasty business. The hair had to be scraped with a dull knife until all the hair was off the hide. All except Corliss gathered around to pour the scalding water and scrape.

Cody hated the job as bad as anybody else. "I don't see why we just can't eat bologna all the time," he muttered.

"You'd be the first one to complain if you didn't get your bacon and ham and pork chops," Lanie said. "Now hush and get to work."

"I sure hope there ain't no hogs to be killed in heaven," Cody said.

"Why, you ninny, of course there won't be any hogs to kill in heaven!" Maeva said crossly. She was wearing her oldest dress and dumped more scalding water that splattered on her. "There's no death in heaven."

"I know that, but I always figured it meant humans wouldn't die. What are we going to eat in heaven? I always figured it would be about like here."

"Will there be ice cream in heaven?" Corliss asked, edging in closer toward Cody.

"Well, of course there'll be ice cream in heaven. What kind of a place would it be without ice cream?"

Maeva was irritated with Cody. "Show me one place in the Bible where it says there'll be ice cream in heaven."

Cody did not like to lose arguments, and he immediately changed the subject. "Let's get this here hog butchered as quick as we can. One of these days," he added, "I'm going to invent a machine that'll butcher hogs. Just march one in with the hair all on them and out the other end comes sausage and hams all tied up neat. Won't that be something?"

❧

"I'm sorry Lanie's so sharp, Cass," Davis said. He caught up with Cass, who had walked into the woods and now sat down on a rotting log. Her face was pale, and her lower lip was trembling. Davis sat down beside her. He wanted to put his arm around her to pat her shoulder, but he had discovered that she hated to be touched. "It's just Lanie hates killing hogs, and I guess everybody else does too."

Cass sat there looking as miserable as a young woman could. Davis glanced at her occasionally as he tried to make things right. It was hard to remember that this was the same young woman he had met in a box car. She wore one of Maeva's old dresses, which was too small for her, and the sunlight set its rich shining on her light hair. He noticed that her lips were pleasantly firm, and her eyes were well-shaped, but now they seemed to be filled with misery. They were shadowed and obscure and reserved, made that way by some past that she refused to speak of. There was a silence about her, and Davis felt a sudden gust of compassion go through him. He could not help but notice that she was round and mature, and once or twice he had seen her laugh and knew that there was humor in her that she did not often allow to be seen. Now as he studied her, he saw that there was an undertow in her spirit, something that was pulling her down. Thinking it must be the hog killing and the sharpness of Lanie's words, he said, "Don't be mad at Lanie. She's got a hard row to hoe. We'd all be in foster homes now, separated, if it weren't for her."

Cass suddenly shook her head, and her lips were pulled together into a line. She looked at the ground for a time and then she whispered, "I'm leaving here, Davis."

Davis blinked with surprise. "Why, you can't do that, Cass. We don't have much here, but you've got a place to sleep and there'll always be food. You can—"

"I can't stay here anymore."

"We all want you to stay."

Suddenly Cass turned and looked full at Davis. Her lips trembled, and her voice was unsteady as she said, "You won't want me here when you find out—"

Davis waited for her to finish, but she said no more and turned her head away. He had seen the tears in her eyes, and more than ever he wanted to help her. "Why would you want to leave here?"

The silence was broken by the voices of the others as they worked on the hog. From far off they could hear Beau barking at some hapless squirrel that he had run up a tree. The weather was cold, and the sounds carried sharply. Davis reached out and touched Cass's shoulder. "What's wrong, Cass?" he said. "Why would you want to leave here?"

"You'll hate me when you find out that ..." She hesitated again. "That I'm going to have a baby."

Davis dropped his hand immediately. The shock of her words ran through his nerves. He was a fairly innocent young man, although he knew such things happened to young girls. He had heard about it, but somehow he never imagined that this could happen to anyone he knew. He felt tied to her in some peculiar way that he could not understand or explain to anyone. He tried desperately to find some way to answer her, and finally he said, "Well, I'm sorry. You should have told us before."

"I couldn't. I'm too ashamed."

Davis felt completely beyond his depths. "Cass, you got to talk to Lanie about this."

"Oh, I can't do that. She'll hate me. Everybody will."

"Lanie never hated anybody in her life. You go on to the house now. I'll get Lanie off to one side and tell her, and then you two can talk. It'll be all right."

"No. It won't be all right. Not ever." Cass got up and walked away without a backward look.

Davis watched her go and then his shoulders sagged. Turning back, he walked back toward the others.

Lanie said, "Come on. We've got this critter scalded. Now let's hang him up."

"Okay."

Davis worked automatically. Once the hide was scraped and the hamstring was exposed on both hind legs, a stick sharpened on both ends was slipped behind the exposed tendon. This was used to pull the hog up to hang upside down from a log that was set in forked supports.

Davis was the best at what came next. He made a long incision on the underside and across the chin, taking care not to cut the intestinal membrane. Cody was there to shove a tub under, and when Davis made the second incision, the worst part for most of them happened, when the intestines dropped from the cavity and were caught in the tub. The work went on silently except for the complaints from Maeva, and finally the fat was cut off while the white carcass was still hanging. It was thrown into a fat pot to be rendered into lard and cracklins.

Davis then took an ax and chopped all the way down both sides of the backbone, and from this point it was a matter of cutting up the meat. "All right. That's done. Now we got to cure this meat and smoke it," Lanie said, her lips tight. "Let's hurry up. I'm glad this only happens once a year."

"I sure am glad there won't be any hog killing in heaven," Cody muttered, and they all hurried to finish.

⌐═◦←

It was almost dark by the time the curing and the smoking process had started. As they went back toward the house, Davis said, "Lanie, I've got to tell you something."

"What is it, Davis? I'm tired."

"It's Cass. She's — she's going to have a baby."

Lanie suddenly stopped dead still. "What?"

"That's right. She told me earlier today. That's why she's been sick, I guess."

Lanie remembered the sicknesses and upset stomachs, and suddenly it all made sense. "What else did she tell you about it?"

"She said she was going to leave here. I told her I'd tell you and you'd talk to her." Davis suddenly broke out in a desperate voice. "You've got to help her, Lanie. We all do. She doesn't have any place to go. If she did, she'd have gone there. Will you talk to her?"

Lanie paused, thinking. She turned resolutely to Davis. "Of course I will. I'll get cleaned up, and then we'll both go."

❦

Davis and Lanie were sitting across from Cass. The girl's head was down, and tears were running down her cheek. "It's going to be all right. Don't cry, Cass."

Lanie had been gentle with the girl. She saw the terrible fear in Cass's eyes and tried to imagine if she herself were in such a condition. Now she said, "What about the father, Cass?"

Cass simply shook her head. "No," she murmured. "I can't go back there."

Resolving to carry this further when the girl was more open to talk, Lanie said quickly, "Well, we're going to see Doctor Merritt tomorrow. We need to find out more about how to take care of you."

Cass looked up and said, "I wish I were dead." Her voice was toneless, and her cheeks were stained with tears.

"No, you don't," Davis said quickly. "Everything is going to work out. You'll see."

"Not for me," Cass said tightly. "Nothing ever works out for me." She turned away from the two of them.

❦

"Well, Cass, you're going to have a baby. No question about that." Owen Merritt studied the young woman that he had just examined. He had become interested in her when he had first treated the wound in her back and arm, and now compassion for her rose within him. "You're strong and healthy and shouldn't have any trouble."

Cass suddenly turned to face him and straightened up. "You've got to help me with this."

"Help you? Why, of course I will."

"No. I mean—" Cass suddenly flushed. "I don't want to have this baby. You've got to help me get rid of it."

Instantly Owen said firmly, "I can't do that, Cass. I don't think it's right."

"But I can't have a baby. I can't take care of one. Please help me."

"It's out of the question. You have lots of help, Cass. I'll help you. The Freemans will help you. And there'll be others too."

"If you don't help me, I'll find someone who will," Cass said, stubbornly lifting her chin.

"That's a good way to kill yourself. These granny women have murdered a lot of young women. It's just wrong, Cass."

That was the end of the interview as far as Cass was concerned.

But Owen was worried. As soon as he could, he took Lanie aside to speak with her privately. "You've got to watch her. She'll go off and get an abortion."

"She wouldn't know where to go."

"I hope not," Owen said grimly. "She's going to need a lot of love and a lot of acceptance. I don't know how you can do it with all that's on your shoulders, but I'll help all I can, Lanie." He put his hand on her shoulder, and when she turned to face him, he managed a smile. "We can do it, don't you think?"

"If you say so, Owen."

"I think we're going to have to tell the rest of your family. They'll need to help too."

"I'm going to see Daddy day after tomorrow. I'll tell them before I go. That way they can keep an eye on her."

"Tell your dad I'm still praying for him. I'm still believing God's going to get him out of that prison."

"I'll tell him, Owen." Lanie hesitated, then said, "I — I need to ask you something. I'm worried about something."

Instantly Owen lifted his head and studied the young woman. He could see that she was troubled and asked gently, "Tell me about it, Lanie. Are you sick?"

"No, not really. But I — I've been having a dream, Owen, and it scares me."

"A bad dream, like a nightmare?"

"Oh, no, not really. Actually it's a *good* dream, in a way."

"Have you had this dream many times?"

"Yes! Over and over, and always the same."

"Can you tell me about it?"

"I dream about Mama, about when she was alive and taking care of all of us. And I dream about Daddy too ..." With considerable hesitation, Lanie spoke of the dream that had come so often. Finally she took a deep breath and said, "It scares me, Owen. It's like ... like when I go to sleep, I always go back to those times. Like I'm somehow ungrateful for all the blessings we *do* have, like I'm always wanting *more*. And I can't accept that Mama is gone forever, and Daddy is gone ... who knows how long. What does it all mean? Am I a bad person? Or am I just going crazy?"

"Of course not!" Owen said quickly. "You're just dreaming of a good part of your life, a simple time when you weren't responsible for the rest of your family. You shouldn't let this dream trouble you."

"But — why do I dream it over and over?" Lanie whispered. She lifted her eyes to his and Owen saw the trouble there.

"I think all of us dream," Owen said slowly. "Most of us day-dream — think of good times and a life without problems. You dream at night of the same things."

"Do you dream of a life that's better than the one you have now?"

Owen didn't answer for a moment and seemed to be searching for an answer. In all truth, he *did* find himself longing for a life that was—*different*. He didn't dwell on these thoughts, but even as he felt Lanie's eyes on him, he became aware that a strange discontent troubled him. It had come before, but he'd shoved the thoughts aside, and he knew he could not really speak of them to Lanie.

"Why, I guess I sometimes think of a life that's a little easier, but that's normal. Now I don't want you to worry about this, Lanie. Can you promise me that?" He reached over and took her hand, adding, "You've had to bear a heavy burden, but God's given you courage, and I admire you more than I've ever admired anyone."

Warmth flooded Lanie, and she felt her face glowing. "What a nice thing to say!" she exclaimed. She was aware of the strength of his hand, and of the admiration in his eyes. "I guess it's not right to worry about good dreams."

"God sometimes uses dreams. Maybe He gives you this one as a promise that everything is going to be fine."

Lanie stood up and smiled. "Thank you, Owen. I promise not to worry about my dream. Thanks for listening to me."

⌐━◦━

"Well now, if this isn't a meal fit for a king!"

Forrest Freeman was seated at a table across from Lanie. He did not live in the units with the other prisoners but was a trustee assigned to take care of Warden Gladden's horses and dogs. The warden also liked to raise his own meat, so Forrest took care of feeding the hogs and the chickens.

Along with his job, Forrest had a room over the garage with a bath and a tiny kitchen—or at least a stove and a sink.

"Look at this Thanksgiving dinner!" he exclaimed and pulled a leg off of the hen.

"Well, I didn't cook a turkey. I'm gonna have to do that for everybody else."

"This is fine, Muff. There's not many folks that have a Thanksgiving dinner this good."

Lanie had brought a fat hen and a big pan of cornbread dressing. Her father didn't like cranberry sauce with the dressing as most people did, but he loved grape jelly, so she had brought a jar of that. She had also brought English peas and rolls. She had made two pies, one pecan and one pumpkin, and knew that he would feast on them after she left.

"Now tell me about everything," Forrest said as he ate hungrily. He listened, stopping to inquire once about Booger, and was pleased to hear that the big dog was as healthy as he could be.

Finally, after a piece of pumpkin and a piece of pecan pie, he leaned back and picked up the coffee cup. "If I ate any more, I'd bust," he said. He added, "You know, I like this meal, but I love the poems you send me. They're downright beautiful, Daughter."

"Thank you, Daddy."

"You ever send any of them off to a magazine?"

"No. I never have. I sent one poem off to a contest, but I'll never win it."

"You don't know about that."

Lanie was anxious to change the subject. "You remember the girl that Davis brought home?"

"The one named Cass? Sure I remember. How is she?"

"Not good." Lanie went ahead to explain the situation, and Forrest shook his head.

"Poor girl," he said. "We'll have to pray that God will give her a love for that baby she's carrying."

"I'm praying for her all the time. I wish I brought you better news, Daddy."

"Well, let's see. How about Owen and Louise? They got hitched yet?"

"No. Not yet."

Seeing something in Lanie's face, Forrest leaned forward. "What's wrong?"

"Well, Louise has changed, Daddy. She was always so selfish and really mean. But something happened to her. It had something to do with Brother Ryan getting snakebit and almost dying." She hesitated then said, "She's spending an awful lot of time with Brother Ryan. The two of them are involved in a program to help people that need it. Food and clothing and fuel. There's a lot of gossip going around about them. It's not fair to Owen."

Forrest knew his daughter well. He could read her as easily as he read the printed page of a book. He knew how sensitive she was, and he had been aware from the beginning that she had a special feeling for Owen Merritt. "You still feel something for Owen, Daughter?"

"Why, no, not really."

Forrest did not argue because he saw that Lanie did not want to talk about it. He did not mention Owen again, but when she got ready to leave, he put his arms around her, and his last words to her before she left were, "God's got big plans for you, Muff. You wait and see."

❦ CHAPTER 25 ❦

Cody Freeman looked over the table burdened down with food and bowed his head to ask the blessing. Praying over the Thanksgiving meal had always been his father's responsibility, but Cody felt that the mantle had fallen upon him and that he was now the spiritual head of the family. His voice assumed an unctuous tone as he began the blessing.

"Lord, we thank you for the turkey that lies before us. We thank you for the drumsticks, for the dark meat, and for the breast and the white meat. Lord, we are especially grateful for the cornbread dressing, and I know, Lord, that there's probably not enough sage in it because Lanie doesn't make it as good as Mama did, but forgive her for that, I pray. We're thankful for the celery we couldn't afford, but since we always had celery when Mama and Daddy were here, we felt, Lord, that it would be appropriate to spend the extra money for that. This was Lanie's idea, as you probably know, but forgive her for being a spendthrift in this particular instance."

Maeva looked up indignantly ready to protest, but she met Lanie's eyes. Lanie's mouth formed the word, *No*, and she clamped her lips together and shook her head angrily.

"And now, Lord, we're grateful for the rolls, which I must admit in all honesty that Maeva makes better than even Mama did, and I'm glad that there's one thing that she can cook better than Mama."

Roger Langley had joined the Freemans for Thanksgiving, giving vent to his rebellious streak and his need for a break from his family.

Now he was doing his best to keep from laughing out loud. He opened his eyes and saw that Davis was grinning broadly, and winked at him. Davis returned the wink, and they both listened as Cody proceeded to bless everything on the table. Finally, when he had touched on every item—including the salt and pepper—he said, "And, Lord, we thank you for these knives and the forks and the spoons—"

Suddenly Maeva's voice rose up, drowning Cody out. "While my brother finishes his prayer, the rest of us are going to eat," she said. "Amen."

A laugh went around the table, and Cody opened his eyes and said indignantly, "I wasn't through with the blessing yet, Maeva!"

"You go right ahead and bless. I'm eating."

"That was a beautiful prayer, Cody," Lanie said quickly. "I'll bet there's not another one more thorough spoken anywhere in this country. Now, Davis, you start carving that turkey while the rest of us load up on the trimmings."

The trimmings were distributed, Roger taking an enormous dollop of potatoes, hollowing out a space with his spoon and forming a volcano of sorts, and filling the cavity with giblet gravy. His plate was soon crowded, but he found room for both white meat and dark meat.

The dining room was noisy, except for Cass. She said little and appeared to pick at her food. Davis said, "You know, Mama and Daddy always went around the table on Thanksgiving, and everybody had to tell something they were thankful for. So I'll be first. I'm thankful that I've got a family better than any in the world."

Maeva, who was sitting next to Davis, piped up with her mouth full of turkey, "Well, I'm mighty grateful for the new shoes that I finally saved up enough money to buy. I can't wait to go dancing in them."

Cody said, "There are a lot of things I'm thankful for. First of all—"

"Just *one* thing, Cody," Maeva said. "That's the way Daddy always did it."

"Well, one thing then. I'm grateful for all of the money my inventions are going to make."

"They haven't made anything yet," Maeva said spitefully.

"Are you forgetting how much we made on the toilet seats?" Cody asked.

"Well, that didn't last long," Maeva retorted.

"Are you working on a perpetual motion machine?" Roger grinned.

"I been working on that for quite a while. It's slow, but I'm going to get there."

"What are you grateful for, sweetheart?" Lanie smiled at Corliss.

"I'm grateful for that nothing got in and ate our new chickens," Corliss said.

"Amen. That's a good prayer," Lanie said. "And I'm grateful for Cass here. That she's with us today."

Cass looked up and everyone saw that her face was pale.

"You have to tell something you're thankful for, Cass." Corliss nodded earnestly. "That's the way we do on Thanksgiving."

Cass swallowed hard and said, "I'm grateful." She suddenly stopped and tears came to her eyes. "I'm grateful to be here with people that care about me."

"Well, you got that right," Roger said, warmly smiling at the girl. "This is a loving bunch if I ever saw one."

"What about you, Aunt Kezia?"

Aunt Kezia had a mouthful of turkey, but that didn't stop her. Waving a giant drumstick, she declared, "Why, I'm downright tickled my eyes are good and I still got the use a these here limbs. Gave me a chance to come here and whip you sorry young'uns into shape." Her eyes twinkled as she stifled a grin.

They all laughed, and soon conversation resumed.

Cass had almost nothing to say during dinner. She was a shy young woman and still uncomfortable with the boisterous Freemans. Even so, she had been trying over the last few days to be helpful around the house. She was not from a farm, and her efforts to milk had been ludicrous, but at least she was trying.

After the meal was over they all helped to clean up. Then they went into the parlor where the instruments were produced, and soon the house was filled with music. Even as they played, however, Lanie's attention was focused on Cass. The girl took a chair as far back as she could with her back against the wall, and the longer the music went on and the happier it got, the more sober and even sad she seemed. Finally, after one of the songs, Corliss went over to Cass and said, "Don't cry, Cass. That was a happy song."

"I can't help it, Corliss."

Everyone stared at Cass, and Lanie put her dulcimer down and went over to sit beside her. "This is Thanksgiving, the day that we give thanks to God for all of our blessings. And you bless us just by being here."

Cass looked around and then said in an unsteady voice, "I didn't know there were people like you in all the world."

"What about your family?" Davis asked quietly.

"They weren't like you. All I had was a daddy and a stepmama. She had four kids, and I was the only one my daddy had. My mama died when I was six. It wasn't—it wasn't a happy place."

The group was silent. Lanie held her breath, for this was the first time Cass had said anything about her past. She hoped the girl would tell more, and she was not disappointed. "I know all of you are wondering about me and it's only fair, since you've been so good, to tell you what happened. I was put out to work when I was thirteen. I worked in a place that put medicine in bottles. That's all I did all day long, fill up tiny bottles and put a cap on it. It was awful hard and long hours and not much money. I was miserable at home and they took all the money I made, and then—" She choked and tears gathered in her eyes.

"Here. Take this," Lanie said, fishing a handkerchief out of her pocket.

Cass took the handkerchief and wiped her eyes and said, "You all know I'm going to have a baby. I know you're wondering why the baby's daddy's not here. He'll never be here. He was just a year older than I was, and he was poor too. He was good to me and—well, we done wrong. We was going to get married, but he—he died. He got killed in an accident in the steel mill. When my family learned about the baby, they put me out. I didn't have anywhere to go so I started to come south where it would be warm in the winter."

Lanie glanced around the circle and saw that everyone was listening breathlessly. She reached over and took Cass's hand. "We're your family now, Cass, and we'll be a family to your baby too."

Suddenly Cass began to weep. "I want to keep my baby."

"We're going to pray right now for that baby. Everybody come pray for Cass and for her baby." Everyone in the room came close to Cass, putting their hands on her. They all began to pray. Cody, this time mercifully, was silent, and it was Davis who finally said, "Lord, we thank you for this child that's to be born. Whether it's a boy or a girl, put your hands upon this baby. Let Cass know that not only do we love her, but you love her, and let her be filled with happiness."

Aunt Kezia, who had said almost nothing, now reached over and took the girl in her arms. "Your baby is going to have lots of brothers and sisters," she said, "and one grandma. That's me!"

⌐━⌐

"That was a wonderful thing, Lanie," Roger said. It was dusk now, and the two of them were out walking toward the river. Roger had asked her to go, and Lanie had slipped away with him.

Now as they reached the banks of the Singing River, Lanie looked down. "I think that's the most beautiful river in the world," she said. "It's not the biggest but it sings."

Roger reached out and took her hand. "It does sing, doesn't it?" The two stood looking down into the dark waters of the river. It was not a large river as rivers go, not like the Mississippi or the Missouri, but the waters were clear, and it did make a sibilant musical sound over the stones at their feet.

Roger suddenly pulled Lanie toward him and said without preamble, "Lanie, I told you once before, and now I'm sure of it—I'm in love with you."

Lanie could not help knowing that Roger had developed an affection for her, but she was unprepared for the intensity in his next words. "I love you and I want you to marry me."

A thousand things seemed to flash through Lanie's mind at that moment, but she knew her answer instantly. "Roger, it wouldn't be right to even think of such a thing. You've got to get through college, and I've got my family to care for. Besides that," she added with some hesitation, "your family wouldn't ever accept me."

"I'm not asking you to marry my family. I'm asking you to marry me."

Lanie was aware of the warmth of his hands as he held hers and tried to think, but her thoughts were jumbled up. "I can't give you an answer, Roger. I'm not sure that you're the one God wants me to marry."

"But can we be engaged then? We can be secretly engaged. No one will have to know it."

"Why, Roger, that wouldn't be fair to you. Next year you'll be going off to college. You'll meet lots of girls there. You have to be free to make your choice."

"You're my choice, Lanie," he said.

"I can't think of marriage, Roger," Lanie said. "Not for a long time."

Roger suddenly pulled her forward and put his arms around her. He was gentle, and when he kissed her, she was aware of his tenderness. She put her hand up on his cheek. "You're the finest young man I've ever known, but I can't promise to marry you."

Roger did not argue. He smiled and shook his head. "I'm a stubborn fellow, Lanie. I'm going to get through college in three years, then I'm going to go to work, marry you, and take care of you."

Lanie knew that such a thing bordered on the impossible, but she felt a warmth and a fondness for this young man. He was so far above her in every way. He came from a fine family that had money, and she came from a family that was poor with a father in prison. She looked down at the river as it purled around her feet and said, "The river does sing, doesn't it?"

❦

When Roger walked into the front door, he heard his name called, and from his father's voice he knew he was in trouble.

"Roger, come in here. We've got to talk to you."

Roger walked down the hall and turned into the larger of the two parlors. His father and mother were there waiting for him, Louise sitting off to the side pretending to read.

"Where have you been, Roger? We expected you here for Thanksgiving dinner."

"Why, Dad, I told you I was having Thanksgiving dinner with the Freemans."

"I thought I told you not to do that."

"Well, Dad, you did tell me, but I'd already agreed to go. I thought I made that clear."

"You've lost your mind over that girl and over those Freemans. You prefer them over your own family. I told you that wasn't right."

Roger hated these confrontations with his father. More than once he had determined to move out of the house, but he loved his mother and his sisters and yes, he loved his father too, so he had toughed it out. "Let's not argue about this, Dad. On Christmas I'll be here for dinner. I promise."

"That's not good enough. I'm disappointed in you, Roger. You're not being a good son."

Roger turned pale. "I'm sorry you feel that way, Dad."

"Well, I do feel that way," Otis Langley said, and his voice was hard. He was a man who had risen in the world through relentless struggle and always being tougher than his competitors, but unfortunately he had not learned that what worked in business did not necessarily work in other relationships. Finally he said, "You've managed to spoil Thanksgiving for your whole family. I hope you're satisfied."

"I'm sorry, Dad. I'm sorry, Mother," Roger said. He turned and walked out of the room, keeping a tight hold on his temper.

As soon as he left the room, Martha shook her head. "You were too hard on him."

Louise had remained silent, but now she said, "Mother's right. Roger's a fine boy. You don't agree with him, but I'm proud of him."

Otis, who was stung by Roger's refusal to bow to his will, turned to her. "I don't think you're one to be talking. I spoiled everyone — Roger, Helen, *and* you. My son won't obey me, one daughter's about to flunk out of school, and the other's making a spectacle of herself by running all over the countryside with that preacher."

Louise gasped as if he had struck her. "Daddy, there's absolutely nothing wrong with my working with Colin."

She turned and stalked out of the room. Martha said, "I wish you hadn't done that, Otis."

Indeed, Otis himself wished he had not behaved as he had. He was often like this, acting impulsively and regretting it later. But he refused to back down. "You're to blame for all three of those kids. Especially Louise, the way she's carrying on with the reverend."

"Why, how can you say that, Otis?"

"You should have told her to stop going around with that man. It's unseemly for a woman, and what can Owen be thinking of? He's letting another man spend more time with his fiancée than he does."

"He trusts Louise, and I do too. And I think you should," Martha said. She turned and walked away, and Otis Langley stood alone, angry and unhappy.

⚬═⚬

The dawn had barely begun to touch the east when Roger stepped out of the house. He was carrying his rifle and bundled up against the cold. Terribly hurt by his father's words, he had decided to take the day off and go to the mountains. He didn't care about hunting so much, but he did want to get away and be alone. His father's words seemed to burn into him, and he turned toward the hills that lay to the north of Fairhope. He usually hunted in the hills to the west, but they were low hills, and he had the desire suddenly for height.

As he walked along, he went over in his mind what his father had said and questioned whether he had done the right thing. He wanted to honor his father, but there was no understanding in Otis Langley. Roger wanted to be treated as an adult. His father had never appreciated that.

He walked quickly and easily and realized that the long hours he had spent on the survey team had strengthened him. He had always been strong and active and a good athlete, but the past few months he had walked miles every day. Now he broke into a trot, anxious to put Fairhope and his family and the words of his father behind him.

From the flat land of the valley to the low-lying hills, the earth followed a gentle incline, then rose more steeply to the sharp breaking ridge that reached upward. Mount Benton was the highest spot in the county, and it lay before him, ghostlike in the clouds. The cold bit into him, and the sting of tiny fragments of sleet stung his face, but there was an exultation in him as he climbed into the silence and solitude of the mountains. The trees still had traces of the last snow clinging to the tops, and as he went higher, from time to time the pull of gravity would cause a clump of snow to turn loose and drop to the earth.

Finally he turned to look back, and he could see what seemed to be his whole world laid out before him. Fairhope lay in the distance, but he could see the smoke rising from the chimneys. Over to the west the ridges broke the flatness of the plain.

On and on he climbed until finally he was scrambling up, having to use his hands. He reached a point where he had to cut around. Something had shaken the rocks loose, and there was only a narrow defile that went around a sharp rising bluff. Roger had to struggle to hang on to his rifle and at the same time keep from slipping. He looked down to his right, and there far below, it seemed, was the forest where the first-growth pines covered the earth. On the slope there were smaller spindly bushes, and Roger moved more carefully.

Finally he reached a point where the path was less than a foot wide. He looked at it and wondered if he could find an easier way. The land sloped beneath him at a very steep angle. He leaned out to see if the path widened and then decided to go back. As he turned, his foot caught on a rise in the rock and threw him off balance. He made a wild grab at a small sapling. Dropping his rifle, he caught the tree but both feet slipped and he fell, pulling the sapling out by the roots.

The world seemed to go round, and as Roger tumbled down the slope, the length of his body crashed into small saplings and brush. When he hit a larger tree that struck him in the side and flipped him over, he suddenly somersaulted. Grabbing to find a purchase, he found nothing, but his hands were scraped by the rocks. He shot out over a small precipice, fell seven or eight feet, and slammed down on his shoulders, knocking his breath out. His mind was working, but his body was rendered helpless by the force of the fall. He ended his slide by crashing through some small trees, and then his foot caught between two saplings, and he cried out as a searing pain shot through his leg.

He lay motionless, his eyes shut, fighting against the waves of pain that went through his body. He knew his leg was broken, and as he freed it, he looked up and saw the height from which he had fallen. Despair seized him.

The enormity of his plight came to Roger as he lay there. He had no gun with which to fire a shot to draw any hunters that might be near. He couldn't walk. He had told no one where he was going. No one knew where he was, no one at all.

The earth beneath him was damp, and he found he was lying in a small puddle of icy water. The trees above partially protected him, but the whistling winds brought fine particles of sleet to sting his face.

The wind had an ominous note to Roger, and he lay there in pain and fear knowing that he could not get himself out of this trouble.

❦ CHAPTER 26 ❦

Martha Langley picked up the phone and said, "Hello." At once she heard Ralph Mixson's voice. Mixson was Roger's boss on the surveying crew. "Hey, is this Mrs. Langley?"

"Yes, it is."

"Ralph Mixson here, Mrs. Langley."

"Oh, yes. What can I do for you?"

"I'm wondering if Roger is there?"

"Why, no. I assumed he was at work."

"No. He didn't come in this morning. Not like Roger. I thought maybe he was sick."

"Well, just a minute. Let me go check his room."

Laying the phone down on the table, Martha went to Roger's room, looked in, and saw that the bed was not messed up. She stopped Elsie, the maid, and said, "Did you make up Roger's bed this morning?"

"No, ma'am. Yesterday morning."

"Have you seen Roger?"

"Why, no, ma'am. I ain't seen him in two days now."

A troubled frown creased Martha Langley's brow and she went back to the phone. "Ralph, Roger's not here."

"Well, we'll go out on the job without him. If you find him, tell him to come on out. We need him today."

"I'll tell him, Ralph."

Martha pressed the cradle down and then dialed the number of Otis's office.

He answered on the fourth ring. "What is it, Martha? Don't have much time this morning."

"Have you seen Roger today?"

"No. Why would I?"

"Well, he's not here, he's not at work, and he didn't sleep here last night. I'm worried about him."

"Oh, he's probably out with some of his friends."

"Roger's very responsible, Otis. You know that."

"Well, make a few calls, and I'll have Grace do the same thing here. He's all right."

Martha laid the phone down and then picked up a book of phone numbers. She dialed the first one and said, "Hello, Harry, have you seen Roger this morning?"

"Well, hello, Louise," Lanie said. "Come on in."

"No. I can't stay, Lanie. I'm looking for Roger. Is he here?"

"Roger? Why no," Lanie said. "I haven't seen Roger for — oh, for a couple of days. Since Thanksgiving."

"And he didn't call you or come by yesterday or this morning?"

"No. What is it, Louise?"

"He and Dad had a disagreement on Thanksgiving, and he disappeared, and we haven't seen him since. I'm sure he's fine, but, well, we're worried about him."

"You don't think he moved out, do you?"

"No." Louise shook her head. "His clothes are there, toothbrush, everything. But he's gone. He didn't go to work, and we've been calling his friends. I'm going down to talk with Dad. We're going to talk to Pardue about putting a notice on the police radio."

"Why, I hope it's nothing serious, but I'll get word to you if I see him."

"Thank you, Lanie."

"Look, Pardue, I don't know how you go about these things, but we've got to get the police to be on the lookout for Roger."

Pardue Jessup was wearing his sheriff's uniform instead of his mechanic's uniform. He had been sitting in his chair when Otis Langley came in and told him that Roger was missing.

"Well, it's easy enough to do, but most of the time missing people aren't really missing. They're just out of place."

"That's what I told Martha, but she insists that something's wrong. I've checked around the house, and it looks like his rifle and hunting clothes are gone, but no tenting gear. He's never gone off overnight before without his tent — or without telling us."

Pardue gave Otis Langley a careful glance. The man seemed worried, and Pardue asked in a casual tone, "Has Roger been upset about anything lately?"

Otis reddened and said, "Well, to tell the truth, he and I had a disagreement on Thanksgiving. It was just a little thing, but he may have gotten his feathers ruffled."

Pardue chewed his lower lip thoughtfully. "Well, he often goes hunting over on Blue Ridge, but it does seem like he would have returned by now. I'll alert the state police. We'll get it on the radio so all the police stations in the area will get a description. You go on home now. I'll call you if I get anything."

❦

Colin got the news about Roger's disappearance from Louise. She had come to the church and he assumed that she was ready to go out on missions to those who needed help. But she had said at once, "Colin, have you seen Roger?"

"Roger? No. Should I have?"

"I was hoping you did," Louise said. She fumbled nervously with her purse. "He and Dad had a big fight on Thanksgiving, and he hasn't been seen since. Not like Roger to be this thoughtless. He's got Mom and Dad worried sick — and me too."

"Have you gone to the police?"

"Yes. Dad went to Sheriff Jessup, and it's on all the police radio channels. Pardue says we ought to put it on the regular radio station, maybe as far away as Fort Smith, with a description." Louise suddenly bit her lower lip. "I'm scared, Colin."

"Oh, come now. It's not that bad. Roger's able to take care of himself."

"Daddy's getting some of the men that work for him to start searching."

"You mean in town?"

"I doubt he's in town. Somebody would have seen him. But Pardue says that sometimes he goes hunting over at Blue Ridge. They're going over that way."

Colin nodded briefly. "I'll tell you what. I'll get ahold of all the preachers in town. We'll join in the search."

"Colin, what if something's happened to him?"

Colin saw that Louise was terrified. He had been very careful not to touch her since that moment in the car, but now he reached forward and she fell against him with a slight sob. He held her gently, patted her back, and said, "We'll get all the people to search the rest of the day, and then tomorrow instead of having church we'll have all the men out. We'll comb this whole county. We'll find him. Don't worry."

⊂━⊷

Sunday morning at ten o'clock the church was filled but not with the usual congregation. Lanie looked over the auditorium and saw that the crowd was mostly older people and those very young, and most of them were women. She sat there quietly with her arm around Corliss, and after a time she saw Otis Langley come in with his family. "You wait right here, honey," she said to Corliss. "I'll be right back."

Rising from the pew, she made her way to Otis and said at once, "I'm awfully sorry, Mr. and Mrs. Langley, but Roger will be all right. I'm sure of it."

Otis Langley looked different. It appeared to Lanie that he was broken, something she never thought she'd see. He was trying to keep a rough exterior, but Martha Langley's eyes were filled with fear, and Louise was little better off. Lanie said, "I'm sure that God will help the men to find him."

A shadow crossed Otis's face as he remembered how he had treated the Freemans. He had been terribly angry when Lanie had beaten Roger for a scholarship award when they were in high school. He also remembered how he had tried by means not too gentle to get the homeplace away from them. He bowed his head for a moment, and when he looked up, his voice was unsteady. "I haven't — I haven't been generous to you, Lanie, and I haven't been fair to Roger. But if God gives me another chance, I promise him and I promise you here and now I'll do better."

"There's nothing more we can do," Louise said. "The men are searching along the Blue Ridge, but it's such a big area. And we're not even sure he's there."

"I wish I could do something," Otis murmured. "Anything. But I just don't know what."

At that moment Lanie stood absolutely still. She had heard from her English teacher that there was such a thing as an *epiphany*, a sudden idea or concept that just leaped into the mind, and Lanie had often wished that she could have such a thing happen to her.

And it did happen!

Without any doubt, she knew what to do. She turned and ran over to where Maeva was with Corliss. "Take care of Corliss," she said, and then started out.

"Where are you going?" Maeva called out.

"I had an epiphany."

Corliss watched her older sister leave the church. "What's an epiphany?"

"I don't know," Maeva replied, "but trust Lanie to have one of them if such a thing is possible!"

CHAPTER 27

Dashing into the house, Lanie took the stairs two at a time. After quickly changing her clothes, she rushed into Davis's room, looked around wildly, and then saw a box over by the wardrobe where he kept his clothes. Tearing it open, she nodded with satisfaction. "They're here," she whispered as she grabbed some shirts and then turned and ran down the steps.

The clothes had belonged to Roger, who had outgrown them and had passed them along to Davis. She could only hope they had not been washed.

She ran outside and called, "Booger — Booger, come here!"

At once the big bloodhound came loping up, his eyes bright. "Come on, Booger. You got a job to do," she said. She opened the door to the truck, and Booger jumped in beside her. Beau whined and wanted to go, but Lanie said, "No. You can't go this time, Beau."

She drove faster than usual until she got to the Langley house. Piling out of the truck, she ran around, opened the door, and Booger came out. Opening the box, she pulled out the shirts and turned and bent over. "Here, Booger. Smell these. You've got to find Roger."

Booger sniffed and snorted and finally without being told, he put his nose to the ground and began running in small circles. He had not gone far when he suddenly said, "Woof!" Lanie knew he had been trained not to bark on the trail, but the way he started out she knew he had found the scent. Of course Roger's scent would not be hard to find around the house, and Booger might be on an old trail, but she prayed that he would find the right one.

Booger took off directly down the street, then turned and headed north on Jefferson Davis Avenue. There was a purposefulness in the big dog, and Lanie wondered for a moment if she should have gotten someone to go with them. *What if I find him and he's hurt? I won't have any way to bring him back.*

But Booger was in pursuit and there was no stopping him. The big dog had soon passed the last of the houses in Fairhope and was on a little-used country road headed toward the mountains to the north. Lanie was panting, trying to keep up with Booger, and had to call him back once or twice.

They had just passed through a large cotton field with the stalks bare and reaching up to the sky as if in prayer when Lanie looked up and saw a car coming. She felt a gladness, for she recognized it as Owen's car. She waved frantically, and Owen stopped and rolled the window down. "What are you doing out here, Lanie?"

"Booger's tracking Roger. He's on his trail. Will you come with me?"

"Sure. Why don't you drive the car and I'll follow Booger on foot."

Lanie was out of breath and said, "All right." Owen got out and took off toward where Booger was fast disappearing. Lanie got behind the wheel and kept behind Owen a safe distance.

She was praying all the time and knew with certainty that God was going to work another miracle in Fairhope.

⌁

"I don't think we can take the car any farther," Owen said. They had turned off the main road onto an old logging road. It was barely wider than the car and full of deep ruts. Fortunately the ground was frozen so they hadn't gotten stuck, but now they had apparently run out of room.

"We'll follow him anyway and leave the car here," Lanie said.

"All right. Be rough going. I better take my bag." He reached into the back of the car, grabbed his black bag, and nodded. "Come on. Let's see if we can keep up with that hound."

The two crashed through the brush, and through an even older logging trail. It must have been at least twenty-five years old. The trees were big enough to impede their progress, but finally they got to the foot of the mountain. "It'll be easier going here. Booger's going right up the side of the mountain. The trees aren't so thick," Owen said.

For the next half hour the two followed Booger, always climbing upward. Finally the trail grew narrow, and Owen said cautiously, "I don't know if we can follow this trail."

"Look. Booger's found something," Lanie cried.

The two edged forward on the narrow ledge. Lanie had never liked heights, and now as she looked down, it made her dizzy, so she turned her face to the wall.

"What is it, Booger?" Owen said. When he got there, he bent over and cried out, "Look. It's a rifle."

"Let me see." Lanie took the rifle and nodded. "It's Roger's! It's got his initials carved in the stock."

"He wouldn't have dropped it here," Owen said. "Where is he, boy?"

There was little room to maneuver, and Booger was whining. He refused to go any farther, and suddenly Lanie looked down. "Owen, I bet he fell off and slid down this slope."

"I hope not," Owen said. He stared down and said, "That has to be what happened."

"We can't go down that slope."

"No. We'll have to go back and find a better way. Look." He turned and pointed upward. "You see those two points there? Kind of like small volcanoes?"

"Yes. What about them?"

"When we get down there, that'll be our point of location. Right down from those points is where we want to be. Come on."

The two made their way back down, and when they got to the lower land, they skirted the heavy timber. Booger was running to and fro and moaning slightly. Owen called out, "There are the peaks. Can you make it?"

"Yes. I can make it," Lanie panted and struggled on, trying to catch her breath.

⊂══✦⊸

Roger was shaking with the cold. His lips were dry and chapped, and the pain in his leg was constant. He lay there only half conscious and tried to slip back into a dream he had had. He could not remember much about the dream except he had been warm and felt safe.

He moved his leg and cried out involuntarily. He thought about calling for help, which he did a few times, but his voice had sounded tiny and fragile in the midst of the heavy woods.

Time ceased to exist, and he had no idea how long he had been there. He thought he could remember two nights, terrible nights, during which he shook with fear and cold and cried out in pain.

Finally he felt himself slipping back into the dream—only this time the dream was different. In the other dream he had heard nothing. He had simply been warm, but now he heard something. He listened carefully and whispered, "It's a dog. It's a dog whining."

And then suddenly a shadow crossed his face, and he felt something warm. Opening his eyes he saw a huge dog. He tried to speak, but his lips were numb.

Out of the blue there were voices. He couldn't call out, but somehow people were there and they were talking.

"Roger! Roger, are you all right?"

Roger tried to focus his eyes. A face came into focus, and he managed to croak, "Lanie, is it you?"

"Yes. You're going to be all right." Her voice was like an angel's, and he thought he must still be dreaming.

"Where are you hurt?"

Roger turned his head and saw Owen Merritt. *The doctor!* "My leg," he whispered.

He felt Owen moving the leg slightly and he could not keep from crying out.

"Well, it's broken. Here. Take a big swallow of this." Owen fished a bottle out of his bag, then lifted Roger's head up while he held the bottle to his lips. "Take two swallows," he said. "You're going to need it."

The drink was bitter, but Roger gulped it down. He turned his eyes to Lanie and stammered, "How'd you find me?"

"It was Booger."

"Good old Booger!"

"But it was more than that," Lanie said. She had knelt down and was holding Roger's head in her lap now. "I was at church talking to your father, and the Lord spoke to my heart and told me to use Booger to find you."

Roger listened, but already the strong narcotic was beginning to work. He felt himself slipping away, but he reached up and when Lanie took his hand, he said, "Well—you'll have to marry me now. You saved my life and you owe it to me." He tried to smile, but the world slipped away.

Owen was crouched beside Roger. He listened to the last words, and he said, "You going to marry Roger?"

"He doesn't know what he's saying, Owen."

"Well, I don't want to leave him out here while we go back to town and get help. I gave him enough to knock him out. We'll have to get him to the car and take him to the hospital."

In the end Owen simply carried Roger's limp body over his shoulders. By the time they got the young man into the backseat of the car, Owen was gasping for breath. "I'm not in training for this kind of thing," he said.

"We'll have to take Booger with us."

"Sure. Get in, Booger."

Booger scrambled into the front seat while Lanie in the backseat held Roger's head in her lap. "It was a miracle, Owen."

"Well, yes, it was." He started the car, turned it, and gunned the engine as they sped back toward Fairhope.

❊ CHAPTER 28 ❊

The rescue of Roger Langley was the big news in Fairhope. The story of how Lanie Freeman and Doctor Owen Merritt had used the bloodhound with the abysmal name of Booger to find the young man was featured in the *Fairhope Sentinel*. The reporting stressed how Booger, the miracle dog who'd been saved by the town's prayers, had now saved the life of one of Fairhope's citizens.

Both the *Arkansas Gazette* and the *Arkansas Democrat* in Little Rock had sent reporters. Pictures of Booger and Roger as well as Lanie and Owen were in a Sunday feature in the *Gazette* and a special editorial in the *Democrat*.

The Chamber of Commerce had struck a medal for Booger with Hero engraved on one side and the date of the event on the other. The medal was now attached to Booger's collar, and everybody in Stone County was familiar with the big dog's heroics.

Roger had recovered in the hospital. His father had scarcely left his side, and finally Martha had to practically drag him home.

By the time a week had passed and the congregation was gathering in the Baptist church, most of the talk was still about Roger's narrow escape from death.

Lanie was seated in the choir, and her neighbor, Isabelle, pressed her repeatedly to tell the story of Roger's rescue.

"Not now," Lanie whispered. "I'll tell you later."

"Look. There comes the family now."

Lanie quickly turned to see all of the Langleys coming in. Their younger daughter, Helen, had returned early for the Christmas holiday, and now she and Louise followed their father and mother. Otis was pushing a wheelchair with a grinning Roger in the seat. His eye caught Lanie's, and he waved cheerfully and winked at her.

The Langleys always sat in the third row from the front on the left-hand side of the church. There were no name plates or reservations in the Baptist church, but most people had staked out a territory. Once Gerald Pink had even approached a stranger who had innocently taken Gerald's seat and asked him to move. The man had said, "I'll move, all right. I'll move right out of this church."

But there was no confrontation today. As they entered, there was applause, and Otis Langley looked around with shock and surprise written on his face. The family moved into the pew with Otis on the end and Roger in his wheelchair in the aisle.

Colin got up and went down the aisle at once to shake hands with Roger, and then with Otis, who said, "Would you mind if I say a few words, Pastor?"

"Not at all. This is your church and these are your people." Colin smiled.

Otis Langley got to his feet and turned around so that he could face the congregation. The room grew quiet, and Otis seemed to have trouble putting his words together. Finally he said in a rather subdued voice, "I want to thank everyone for your support during this trying time for my family." He hesitated and then cleared his throat. "I—I never really thought of the church as a family. I suppose I thought of it more as a social club such as the Elks, but I was wrong about that. My family's been overwhelmed by the many expressions of concern and love that have come our way from all of you." He hesitated, and then suddenly his voice grew firm. "We're not Catholics here so we don't go to a priest to confess, but I have something to confess, and I think it's fitting that I confess it to the whole church."

Every sound in the building was muted then. Every eye was fixed on Otis Langley, and he spread his hands out and said, "I want to confess that I have not been the father I should have been to Roger. I put undue pressure on him, and I refused to let him make decisions that were rightfully his to make. Most of you know that I am a driving sort of fellow, used to throwing myself into things, thinking I can solve any problem if I fight it hard enough. But there are times in a father's life when he needs to step back and give his children room. I should have recognized that but I didn't. So, Roger, I want to ask you to forgive me and to help me be a better dad."

Roger reached up, grabbed his father's hand, and pulled him down. He hugged him fiercely and said, "You bet, Dad. I'll be going back to college, and we'll go back to your original plan."

Langley stood up and had difficulty speaking. "While I'm confessing, I could mention that I have not shown the right spirit toward many of you here." He turned, his eyes fixing on the Freeman family and then on Lanie in the choir. "I want to ask the Freeman family to forgive me. I took advantage of them at a time when they needed help and love and support. So I ask each one of you to forgive me."

None of the Freemans seemed to know what to say—except Cody. He stood up at once and said, "Well, sure we forgive you, Mr. Langley. You was pretty much of a pain in the rear, but we all get that way sometimes, don't we?"

Snickers and muffled laughter went around the church. Langley could not help but smile. "That's a very gracious thing for you to say, Cody."

"Of course you ought to give some credit to Booger."

"I am thankful in my heart for Booger. I'm sorry that I wasn't one of you good people who prayed for him and paid for his treatment when he was ill, because without Booger my son wouldn't be here today."

Langley sat down abruptly and bowed his head as if unable to face anybody's eyes. His wife, Martha, put her arm around him and hugged him, whispering fiercely, "You did fine, Otis, just fine!"

Owen dropped in for breakfast at the Dew Drop Inn the next day. Much of the conversation consisted in teasing him about his marriage, now that it was only a couple of weeks away. There was something comical that he could not understand about a man getting married. Total strangers would come up and make suggestive remarks, and even now Pardue was ribbing him. "Enjoy your freedom, man. Soon you'll be chained up just like the rest of them married fellows."

"I hope you marry a woman that'll keep you on a short rope, Pardue." Owen shook his head.

"Oh, all the women do that," Pardue said. He started to elaborate on his theory when he said, "Whoops, I'll tell you more about this marriage stuff later, but here comes your fiancée."

Owen turned with surprise and saw Louise coming toward him. He got up and could tell that she was troubled. "Owen, I have to talk to you."

"Well, sure. You want to sit down?"

"No. Not here."

Owen turned to Pardue and said, "You can have the rest of my eggs, Sheriff."

He followed Louise out of the café, and she walked over to the car. She didn't get in, however, but turned to him, and he asked at once, "What's wrong?"

"Owen," Louise said. She seemed to be short of breath. Her face was pale, and her hands were unsteady as she gripped them together. "I don't know any tactful or any nice way to say this."

"To say what, Louise?"

Owen had no idea what to expect. It was obvious that he and Louise had been drifting apart, although he had found himself more enamored of her since she'd been working on the welfare committee. She seemed to have changed, and he'd decided to let go of any lingering doubts about marrying her.

"Owen, it would be a mistake if you and I got married."

Owen stared at her, unable to speak for a moment. He had come to the idea of marriage slowly, and now he felt as if he had been walking across a bridge that had collapsed beneath him. All of his future plans seemed to lie about him in a wreckage. "Why would you say that, Louise?"

"It's very simple, Owen," Louise said. "I've been thinking about it and praying about it, and I don't mind telling you I've been crying about it. I don't love you like a woman should love the man she's going to marry. And I don't think you love me as much as you think."

A tiny alarm suddenly went off in Owen Merritt's head. He hesitated, thought about what he wanted to say, and then asked simply, "Is there someone else you care for, Louise?"

"I don't know, Owen. You're a fine man. There's none finer, but I just don't feel comfortable—" Suddenly she broke off and shook her head. "Everything I say sounds foolish and ridiculous, but you'll never know how hard it was for me to say this."

"I can imagine."

"I hate to be wrong. You know that. But better to have a little embarrassment now than to have a marriage that isn't what I'd like it to be."

"Are you sure about this, Louise?" Owen asked gently.

"Yes." She looked up at Owen. "You hate me now, I suppose."

"Why, Louise, that's foolish. I care for you. Maybe not as much as I should. This comes as quite a shock." He took her hand, held it for a moment. "I don't want this to be a burden to you. I don't have very many friends, and I'd like for you to be one of those no matter what happens."

Tears came to Louise Langley's eyes. "That's like you, Owen," she whispered. "It's so much like you!"

"So," Owen said, squeezing her hand and dropping it. He tried to adopt a light air. "How does one go about announcing a broken engagement?"

"That's easy," Louise said. She was trying to get control of herself and looking for the right remark. "We'll just let Henrietta Green or Dorsey Pender know."

"Let's tell both of them. That way Henrietta can take care of telling folks on the phone. Dorsey goes to every house in town to deliver the mail. Maybe we should have him pass out fliers."

They both laughed awkwardly, and then Louise asked rather timidly, "Are you—all right, Owen?"

"I don't know. I think so. I've never been dumped by a prospective bride."

"I'm sorry, Owen."

"I know you are, Louise. So am I." The two stood for a moment, then Louise turned and walked away. As she did, both of them knew they were saying good-bye to the life that they had planned. But somehow neither of them felt a very deep grief.

The news of the breakup between Doctor Owen Merritt and Louise Langley was not announced in the *Sentinel*, but it may as well have been. Martha Langley called the church to cancel the date for the wedding, and Henrietta Green, who happened to be listening, at once put two and two together and came up with four. She called her best friend, Alice Haynes, and said, "Alice, you mustn't tell a soul, but Louise Langley has broken her engagement with Doctor Merritt. It's true, as sure as I sit here. But you mustn't tell a soul. Promise me."

Of course that promise meant nothing and by nightfall, with the help of the telephone and Dorsey Pender, just about everyone in town had heard the news. By the time Dorsey got home in the darkness, he said wearily to his wife, "Well, it's been a hard day, but I managed to get the word out about the doctor and Louise Langley."

After a week and a half, news of the breakup between Owen and Louise had become stale. Lanie had not seen either of them, but there had been enough talk to keep her informed. She confided her own thoughts to her journal:

> *Owen and Louise broke up. I suppose I should be grieving for them, but somehow I can't. I never thought they belonged together.*

Lanie had wanted to write much more, but the thought came to her, *What if I put down how I really feel about Owen and I die and somebody finds this journal? That would be embarrassing to me even if I were dead.*

Lanie had refused to talk much about the matter. She was spending a great deal of time these days with Cass. They were talking about the baby late one Thursday, and Cass was apprehensive. "Lanie, I don't have anything. I don't even have any diapers."

"Don't you worry about that, Cass." Lanie smiled. "I'm going to give you a shower and there'll be other showers. The people of Fairhope will make sure we have everything we need. It's going to be wonderful, Cass. I love babies. What about a name?"

"If it's a girl," Cass said with a shy smile, "I'm going to name her Belle, because that's your middle name. And if it's a boy I'll name him Lee, because that's Davis's middle name."

"Those are both good names. There's a book with baby names in it—"

A knock at the door interrupted the two, and when Lanie got up, she found Dorsey Pender. "Well, you're getting important, Lanie. I got a registered letter for you all the way from Chicago."

"A registered letter? What's that?"

"Why, it means that you have to sign for it saying that you've received it. Here. You sign right here."

Wondering what this could mean, Lanie signed the slip that Dorsey handed to her and then took the envelope. "I don't know what this could be."

"Well, just go on and open it up, then we'll know."

Lanie did not choose to do this. She simply said, "Thank you, Dorsey," and started to step inside.

"Well, I hope it's good news, but registered letters usually ain't." Without a break he said, "Too bad about Doctor Owen, ain't it? He's grievin' his heart out over Louise. I been afraid he might do harm to himself. Has he talked to you about it?"

"No, he hasn't."

"Well, I knew it was going to happen. I've got a feeling about things like that, Lanie. They weren't meant for each other."

"I suppose not. Excuse me, Dorsey." Stepping inside, she quickly shut the door and then stared at the letter. Maeva had come in from the kitchen, followed by Cody. "What's that?"

"It's a letter. A registered letter."

Davis was on the floor playing with Corliss. "Well, open it," he said and got up to come over to stand beside her.

Lanie did have a slight fear. Ever since there had been an attempt to break up the family and put them in foster homes, she had been apprehensive about official letters. She looked at the return address, but it meant nothing to her. Slowly she said, "Well, let's see what it is." Carefully she opened the envelope and took out a single sheet of paper. Her eyes fell on the first word. "'Congratulations,'" it says. "It must be good news."

"Maybe not." Davis grinned. "They may want to sell you a car or something."

But Lanie was reading down, and the second line seemed to leap out at her. It was very brief, and she was aware that the others were staring at her.

"Well, what is it, Sister?" Cody demanded.

"I won second place in the National Poetry Contest," she whispered, her face pale. "Look. Here's a check for three hundred dollars."

"Three hundred dollars!" Cody yelped. "Why, we're rich!"

There was a celebration then! They all danced around Lanie hugging her, and even Cass joined in. When they finally quieted down, Cody said, "Well, I always knew you'd be a rich and famous writer."

"You never told me that." Lanie smiled.

"Well, I didn't think you needed to be told. Now let's see what we're going to do with the money. I'll tell you what I want. I want to buy a new fishing rod."

"Wait a minute. That's not your money. That's Lanie's money!" Davis protested.

"No, Cody's right. This money will come just in time to pay off the taxes on the house, but I want every one of us to get something that we can keep forever and remember."

"Well, I can remember that fishing pole and keep it forever." Cody nodded assertively.

"All right. You will have it. What about you, Davis?"

She went around, and everyone mentioned something they might like to have, but when she got to Cass, she put her arm around the girl and said, "Now. What would you like, Cass?"

Cass's eyes were shining. "You mean it, Lanie? I can get something?"

"Of your very own."

"I'd like my baby to have a cradle."

"Why, of course. Absolutely."

Maeva waited until the others had left, then she came over and put her arm around Lanie. "I want lots of makeup so I can look like a scarlet woman."

"Don't talk that way."

"Just teasing." Maeva gave Lanie an arch look. "Well, now that Louise has dumped Owen, there's your chance. You can get him if you play your cards right."

"Maeva, hush that talk."

Maeva laughed. "I know you too well. If you want any tips, you can always count on me."

Lanie stood there holding the check with a contented feeling that the taxes would be paid. It also gave her pleasure to give gifts, something she had not been able to do much of. She went to her room and sat there for a long time staring at the check, then she got on her knees and thanked God for His faithfulness.

The wind had died down, but the winter had been sharp in Stone County. Lanie had come down to the Singing River and brought her pencil and her tablets with her. She seated herself on a log, and for a time she watched the river and listened to the noise of its passage. It did make a melodious sound.

Finally she opened the tablet and began to write. She worked on the poem until her hands grew numb, but she finally finished it and read it with satisfaction.

Suddenly she heard her name called, and she turned quickly to see Owen walking toward her. She closed the tablet, and he said, "Lanie, I've been looking for you."

"Hello, Owen. What are you doing way out here?"

"I got lonesome."

"I'm glad you came," she said.

"Well, I wanted to congratulate you on winning the prize in that contest."

"It was only second place."

"Only second place!" Owen cried. "Why, that's great. It was a national contest. The first thing you sent off, I'd guess."

"Yes, it was."

"Then let's have no more *only* second place. I'm so proud of you!"

Lanie knew she had to say something about Louise, but could not think of a way to put it. Finally she said, "I was so sorry to hear about you and—"

She could not finish, and Owen laughed shortly. He ran his hand over his hair and said, "Well, I'm no longer an engaged man. Everybody's heard about it, I suppose."

"I'm sorry."

"I've been thinking about it. I've spent a lot of time alone lately. There's a play by a Frenchman about a man called Candide. This man believes that everything that happens to a person is really good, no matter how bad it seems. When he breaks his leg, he thinks that's exactly the way it should have been. A family gets a terrible disease, and he says it's meant to be. His nose rots off, and he's thankful for that. I remember he said he was thankful because now he'd be so ugly no woman would have him, and that's good because he would never leave a widow or orphans."

"What a terrible play!"

"It's pretty awful."

"Do you feel like that, Owen, that this is good?"

Owen dropped his eyes and seemed to study the ground for a moment. "I didn't at first, but Louise said something that I've thought about a lot."

"What was that?"

"She said she didn't care for me as a woman should care for the man she's going to marry. So I think she's right about that."

Lanie's heart suddenly went out to Owen Merritt. "I'm so sorry to see you hurt, Owen."

Owen suddenly smiled. "You'd be sorry for Judas or Attila the Hun."

"I—I have a present for you—well, kind of a present."

"What is it?"

Lanie opened the tablet and said, "It's just a little thing I wrote thinking about you." She took the page out and handed it to him. He looked down and read it aloud:

To Doctor Owen Merritt
He brings hope to those who have only fear.
Day after day he is the knight who fights
The dragons of sickness and death.
His armor is not burnished steel,
He wears instead a pale cotton gown.
No lance or sword he bears;
His weapons are compassion and love.
And how is he paid, this man who gives so much?
Not in coin but in gratitude from thankful hearts.

Let those who will admire the knights of old,
I will keep my admiration for the man in white.

When Owen finished the poem, he looked up and took a deep breath and studied the face of the young woman in front of him. He'd thought of her as a child when he had first met her, but now she was a woman. He studied her wide and clean-edged lips and the fair smoothness of her skin, the gleaming of her hair, and then he said, "That's the best thing anyone has ever given me. You're good for a man, Lanie." He suddenly reached out and took her free hand and held it.

At that moment something passed between the two. It touched them both, and they stood unable to move. There was a mystery about it all somehow, and Lanie felt at that moment that if he took her in his arms and kissed her, she would not resist.

"Lanie, I want you to know—"

Whatever it was that Owen Merritt wanted Lanie Freeman to know was shoved aside, for Owen was struck in the back by a heavy weight. He was thrown off balance, tripped over a branch, and fell headlong. He turned around to face Booger, who had reared up on him. Booger at once put both feet on Owen's chest and began licking his face.

Owen grabbed the dog and held him away. "Booger," he said as he struggled to his feet, "you sure know how to break up a tender scene."

Lanie was disappointed. She had wanted to hear what Owen was going to say, and now the moment seemed to be broken. Owen petted the huge dog, and when he turned to face her, she saw the honesty and the truth in his eyes, and knew that this man had something that no other man had, at least for her. She reached up and put her hand on his cheek. "Please don't feel bad, Owen."

Owen put his hand over hers and held it firmly there. "As long as you're around to pick me up, Lanie Freeman, I'll be fine."

The two stood there and Booger looked up expectantly. He was often puzzled by the things that his people did, and now he watched them, waiting to see what would happen next. He was disappointed when they simply turned and moved away from the river. They were holding hands, and when he shoved his way between them, they both laughed.

GILBERT MORRIS

Bestselling Christy Award-Winning Author

The
MIRACLE

⊱ SINGING RIVER SERIES ⊰

ZONDERVAN

Read an Excerpt from Gilbert Morris's Next Novel—*The Miracle*

Chapter 1

A grinding cold had settled down over Stone County and most of northern Arkansas. As Lanie Freeman hurried to slip into her dress, she noted the frost on the windowpanes and shivered. Her upstairs bedroom had a small wood-burning fireplace, but she only used it when she stayed up late reading or writing. Her dress was made of gray lightweight wool with long sleeves, a high neckline, and a fringe of black lace around the edges. Even so, it did not provide enough warmth against the early morning chill.

Moving over to the mirror above her dresser, she studied herself with a critical eye. A faint memory brushed the edges of her mind, pulling the corners of her lips into a smile. The memory brought back a day when she had cried because she was so skinny. One of the boys at school had called her rake handle, and she had flown at him in a rage. Only Davis had been able to pull her off of the boy.

"Well, I'm not skinny any more." The young woman who gazed back at her from the mirror, on this last day of December 1931, certainly was no rake handle! As Lanie considered the lissome curves clearly outlined by the dress, she remembered an entry she had made in her journal when she was much younger.

Moving to the pine chest of drawers against the wall, she opened the bottom drawer and pulled out one of many notebooks concealed beneath her folded clothing. She opened the book and, ignoring her shivers, read the entry dated April the twelfth, 1929:

I had to kill Lucille today and it broke my heart. I hated to do it, but I had to admit she was delicious. I fried her for supper, and we ate all of her. Mama only ate a little bit of the breast and some of the gravy. I'll be glad when the baby comes and mama's strong again, and I'll be glad if I ever fatten up a little bit.

Lanie felt a keen sense of pain as she remembered her mother who had, at the time, only a short time left on earth. She was carrying Corliss and would give her life to bring the baby girl into the world.

She leafed through the journal, sometimes smiling as her words brought touching memories, sometimes frowning as her words brought with them pangs of sorrow. When she came to an entry where a letter marked the place, she smoothed back the page and read her words again, just as she had many times before.

They're going to put us in a foster home if something don't happen. But I've heard about my daddy's aunt who's in a nursing home in Oklahoma. We're going to go try to get her to come and live with us so the government won't break our family up.

Lanie next opened the letter, which was from her Aunt Kezia to her father.

Forrest, my husband has died and the fool spent all his money on a hussy from Muskogee. I'd have shot him if I had caught him and her, too. He didn't leave a cent, and I'm living in a room in a rundown boarding house full of idiots! Got a little money, but when that plays out, they'll put me in some kind of old folks home. Bah! I'll shoot myself before I put up with that.

A wave of affection for Aunt Kezia filled Lanie. For all her many years, the old woman had brought safety to the Freeman household. With Lanie's mother dead and her father in prison, the state had almost broken up the family, but Aunt Kezia had provided a safe haven for them all. She was indeed difficult to live with at times, but Lanie loved her.

She thumbed through the pages and stopped abruptly at the entry marked July the fourth, 1931. That had been the last Fourth of July, and the memory of it was etched clearly on her memory. As she read her words, her cheeks turned warm.

> *At the fair today I was standing at the Ferris wheel afraid to get in it because they always scare me. Suddenly Owen was there, and he teased me into getting on the Ferris wheel with him. We got in and I hung on but, as always, I was scared. He put his arm around me, and when the car started rocking I just threw myself against him and hung on as if I was a little girl and he was my daddy.*
>
> *But it wasn't like that. As I was pressed against him, I knew he was aware I wasn't the little girl he always thinks of when he thinks of Lanie Freeman. And I knew he wasn't the father figure either. I could have let go but I didn't want to. I just held onto him and pretended I was frightened. I know it was wrong, but it'll never come to anything else. He's engaged to Louise now, and I've had to put that dream away.*

For a long moment Lanie stood in the center of the room staring down at the words. She had written things in this journal she would never share with anyone else. The thought drew her to her writing table. Still shivering against the cold, she pulled on a sweater and rubbed her hands together to warm her fingers. Then she opened the notebook, picked up a pen, and began to write:

> *December the thirtieth, 1931. Owen is not married to Louise Langley. That's the biggest thing in my life right now. She broke their engagement, and when I heard of it my heart nearly jumped out of my chest.*
>
> *Roger wants me to marry him but I can't. I've got too many problems. I've got to handle all of these things.*
>
> *1. Davis can't read.*
> *2. My sister Maeva has a wild streak that's liable to bust out at any time.*

3. *Daddy's in prison and may not be out for a long time.*

4. *I want to be a writer but there's no way I ever can be.*

5. *The Depression is getting worse, and I don't see how we can pay the bills.*

6. *I've got Cass to think of. Davis brought her home and she's going to have a baby, and I've got to help her somehow or other.*

She held her pen poised over the journal for a moment, and then she added one note:

In a few hours it's going to be a brand new year. I'm going to trust God for every one of these problems.

Firmly she blotted the ink, closed the notebook, and put it back in the lower drawer of the chest. Then she rose and left the room, her head high.

As she started down the hall toward the stairs, she stopped by the room that Maeva shared with Cass. She opened the door and saw her sister propped up in bed, wearing a heavy mackinaw coat to keep off the cold. She was reading a copy of *True Romance* magazine, and looking up, she grinned. "You ought to read some of these stories, Lanie."

"Never mind those stories. Get out of bed. It's time to go to church."

"I'm not going to church this morning. It's too cold."

"You've got to go to church. You know that, so let's not argue about it."

"You can't make me go. I'm bigger than you are."

Indeed, it was true that Maeva, at sixteen and one year younger than Lanie, was larger. She was also stronger and more athletic. She stared at the girl and tried to think of a way to convince her. "You know," she finally said, "I can't make you go, but if daddy were here, you'd go, wouldn't you?"

Maeva bit her lower lip, threw the magazine on the floor, and came out from under the covers. "All right. I'll go to church." She glared at Lanie. "I'm telling you. You need to read a few love stories. All you ever think about is money!"

The words hurt for Lanie knew some of what she said was true. Maeva was convinced that all her sister thought about was money—which was *not* true. Of course she had to think about money. Somebody had to pay the bills, and considering the desperate times of the Depression, it was a tight squeeze. Almost everybody in Fairhope, in Stone County—in the whole country for that matter—was enduring hardship.

As she turned and went down the stairs, Lanie thought of Maeva's charge that she had no romance. *I've got as much romance in my heart as you have, Maeva. I just don't fly a flag about it.* The angry thought bounced around in her, but she put it aside firmly as she went into the kitchen. The warmth from the wood-burning cook stove greeted her, and she saw at a glance they were all there: Aunt Kezia, Davis, Cody, Corliss, and Cass, the newest member of the household. Cass was wearing an old dress of hers and a coat that had belonged to her mother. The girl had been in pitiful shape when Davis had found her riding in a box car. He had brought her home, not knowing what else to do, and when it was discovered she was only sixteen years old and going to have a baby, by common consent they had agreed to keep her.

"Well, is everybody ready to go to church?"

"Not yet," Cody said. He was a wide-eyed young man of fifteen with red hair and green eyes much like his father's. He was short and stocky with a head as packed with ideas as an egg is packed with a yolk. The fact that most of these concepts never got off the ground never seemed to trouble Cody. His eyes were gleaming.

Davis, his older brother, said, "We got a new invention, Lanie." Davis was tall, lanky and had auburn hair and blue eyes. He looked a great deal like his father and was a good athlete like him too. "We don't know what it is yet. He won't tell us."

"We don't have time for that, Cody," Lanie said. "We've got to get to church."

Aunt Kezia grinned. She never wore old ladies clothes but, instead, wore whatever suited her. The dress she had on today was a bright red and white, fit for summer, and over it she had on a coat with a fur neckpiece that was rather bare in spots. She was ninety one now, but her mind was as sharp as ever. "What is it this time, Cody? Is it a perpetual motion machine?"

"Nah. I'm working on that, but I ain't quite got it yet. Here it is."

Lanie moved closer to see the invention. It was a strange-looking device, but Cody was expert at creating strange-looking things. It had a steel rod in the middle and blades of some sort that seemed to circle around it.

"What is it, Cody?'

"Why, can't you see? It's a potato peeler. Here, lem'me me show you how it works. Give me a potato, Lanie."

Maeva pulled a potato out of the bin and tossed it to him. "I bet ya a nickel it won't work."

"You ain't got a nickel." Cody grinned. "Besides, you already owe me a nickel." He plunked the potato down, impaling it on the upright pole, and then reached for a wheel that was on one side. "You watch this now. No more sitting around with a knife trying to get that skin off of there and picking out them little eyes. Cody Freeman's never-fail, sure-fire, always on the spot, potato peeler is going to make us rich!"

"Let's see the silly thing work," Aunt Kezia said. "I peeled enough infernal potatoes that it'd be a good thing if you could put a stop to that."

"Watch out. Here we go." Cody turned the wheel, and the blade slashed and circled the potato. It was all over in a few seconds, and then Davis began to laugh. "Look at that. You peeled that potato all right."

Lanie couldn't help but smile. The blades had not just peeled the skin off; it had removed all the potato except a stubby round shape no more than an inch thick.

Maeva snorted. "I told you that dumb thing wouldn't work. Now you owe me a nickel."

"No I don't. You wouldn't bet." They all waited to see how Cody would defend his failure, for he never admitted defeat. Since he had been converted recently and baptized in the Singing River, he considered himself the spiritual head of the Freeman dynasty. "It's gonna work. It just needs a few adjustments."

"We got to do something about this lack of confidence you got, Cody." Davis grinned.

"You just wait." Cody nodded firmly. "I got another invention. It's going to work, too."

"What is it?" Lanie asked.

"It's a chicken plucking invention."

"Oh, that'll never work." Maeva shook her head and scowled. "You probably want to pluck 'em while they're still alive."

"We can argue about that some other day," Lanie said, "but right now we've got to get to church. So let's go."

She picked up Corliss who had been watching the doings of the grown ups. At the age of three she was the pet of all the Freemans. She was her mother all over again and all they had on earth left of her. She would have been spoiled rotten, but she was the sweetest tempered, smartest child any of them had ever seen. "Going to church," she said with a bright smile.

"Yes. Going to church." Lanie kissed her on the cheek and said, "If everybody in the world were as sweet as you, it'd be a good world."

They piled into the ancient Ford pickup, the girls in the front, and Davis and Cody in the back. The engine turned over slowly and burst into a cacophonous roar. "I'm sure glad Pardue put a self-starter on this thing," Lanie said to Aunt Kezia.

Kezia was bundled up to the eyes. "I wish there wasn't nothing but horses. You didn't have to crank them. Just get on and go."

Since Aunt Kezia had grown up in the world where the horse was king, the girls could not argue. Lanie moved the Ford away from the curb. As she drove down the street, she waved at the neighbors who waved back. In a town like Fairhope almost everyone went to church. The Catholics had already been, most of them going to an early mass, but the Presbyterians, the Methodists, the Baptists, and the Pentecostals were making their way to their respective churches.

When she got to the Baptist Church, Lanie had to park a block away. Everyone got out, and they walked toward the church joining others from their congregations. Reverend Colin Ryan was there to greet them. He was the interim pastor of the Fairhope Baptist Church, and many said with his black hair and dark blue eyes he was too good looking to be a preacher. He came forward to meet them. "Well, here's my favorite folks."

Lanie smiled. "You say that to everyone."

"Well, I guess they're all my favorites. How you doing, Cody? Still preaching the word?"

"Every chance I get, Brother Colin." Ever since Cody's conversion he had stuck as close as possible to the pastor. Colin Ryan rode a motorcycle, rarely wore a tie, and broke most of the conventions that Baptists usually expected their pastor's to follow. Those who didn't like his ways comforted themselves by saying, "He'll soon be gone from here."

"Better get in. It's crowded this morning." He smiled, showing his cleft chin to its fullest.

Lanie went inside and deposited Corliss in the nursery where she at once began playing with blocks spelling words out with them. She had already learned her letters, which mystified all the other Freemans.

As she left the auditorium, Lanie encountered Louise Langley, which gave her more than a moment's worth of discomfort. The history of the Langleys and the Freemans had not been congenial. Otis Langley, the patriarch of the clan, had been furious when Lanie won an academic prize he felt it should go to his son Roger. Then later, when Louise had been engaged to Doctor Owen Merritt, the whole family had been, more or less, jealous of the attention Owen paid to the Freemans—especially to Lanie.

Now, however, Louise was smiling. "Hello, Lanie, it's good to see you. What a pretty dress."

"Hello, Louise. It's cold out today."

"Yes." There was a moment's silence, and Lanie wondered whether she should say something about the broken engagement. Finally she said, "I ... was surprised to hear about your breaking your engagement to Doctor Merritt."

Louise's face changed momentarily, but then she smiled. "It was a hard thing to do, but it was the right thing to do."

"I haven't seen Owen lately."

"No. He's keeping to himself. I suppose he's hurt by my decision not to marry, but he'll thank me for it some day." Lanie noticed there was no sign of regret on Louise's face.

"I must get to back to the choir room," she said. "We're singing a special today so we need extra practice."

Leaving Louise, she went to the choir room where the practice was being led by the choir director, Dempsey Wilson. Wilson was the high school football coach and was almost as attractive as Colin Ryan. Lanie was amused at how the women in the choir could not keep their eyes off him. He was single, and those who had no ambitions for him themselves had daughters they wanted to promote.

Loreen Parks leaned forward and said, "Why don't you set your cap for Dempsey? He likes you. I can tell."

"Oh, hush! Dempsey likes everyone."

As soon as the choir filed into the loft, Lanie's heart warmed, for she saw that Colin Ryan had gone over and squatted down beside Cass who was sitting at the end of the row toward the back of the sanctuary. The young girl's face was usually tight with tension, but something Colin said amused her, and she was smiling. It struck Lanie that she was indeed an attractive girl, but a girl with lots of troubles.

She watched the little drama of the church, which was what it seemed from her place in the choir loft. *Why, this church is like a cosmos, a little world of its own—or maybe like one of the old English sailing ships. It has a captain—that's the pastor—and the deacons are the officers. Everyone has to do their job at the church, just like sailors on a ship....*

Lanie rebuked herself for her wandering thoughts, but it *was* a good place to observe what was happening. She noticed, for example, that Louise Langley did not seem particularly distraught about her broken engagement. Her gaze was firmly fixed on Colin, and Lanie remembered that Aunt Kezia had once observed, "That woman can't keep her eyes off the preacher. She's looking at him like he's a piece of caramel cake!"

Finally the song service began, and when the choir special was over, Colin came around and stood before the choir, his back to the congregation. "That was what music in heaven must sound like." He smiled, showing off the cleft in his chin. "Thank you, choir." He had a way of showing gratitude that made people feel good, and as he turned and began to preach, Lanie's gaze went back to Louise, who still watched Colin intently.

She's not grieving over Owen, that's for sure!

There was satisfaction in this for Lanie, and she settled back with a little secret smile.